WOLFSBANE

BY ANDREA CREMER

Nightshade
Wolfsbane

Coming Soon
Bloodrose

WOLFSBANE

ANDREA CREMER

www.atombooks.net

ATOM

First published in the United States in 2011 by Philomel Books, an imprint of
the Penguin Group (USA) Inc.
First published in Great Britain in 2011 by Atom

A CIP catalogue record for this book
is available from the British Library.

ISBN 978-1-907410-30-7

Printed and bound in Great Britain by
Clays Ltd, St Ives plc

Papers used by Atom are from well-managed forests
and other responsible sources.

MIX
Paper from
responsible sources
FSC® C104740

Atom
An imprint of
Little, Brown Book Group
100 Victoria Embankment
London EC4Y 0DY

An Hachette UK Company
www.hachette.co.uk

www.atombooks.net

For Will, for always

Force and fraud are in war the two cardinal virtues.

Thomas Hobbes, *Leviathan*

PURGATORY

PART I

I was exhausted; with the two of us uncertain of our way,
we halted on a plateau lonelier than desert paths.

Dante, *Purgatorio*

ONE

I COULDN'T SHUT OUT the screams. Darkness surrounded me. A terrible weight pressed into my chest, making me struggle for each breath as I lay drowning in my own blood. I sat up with a gasp, blinking into the shadows.

The screaming had stopped. The room became still, flooded with silence. I took a couple of painful swallows, trying to moisten my parched mouth. It took me a moment to realize that the screams had been my own, each cry clawing my throat until it was raw. I brought my hands up to my chest. My fingers moved along the surface of my shirt. The fabric was smooth, with no sign of rips or tears from the crossbow bolts. I couldn't see well in the dim light, but I could tell this shirt wasn't mine, or rather, wasn't Shay's borrowed sweater—the one I'd been wearing the night everything changed.

A blur of images rushed through my head. A blanket of snow. A dark forest. The pounding of drums. Howls calling me to the union.

The union. My blood grew cold. I'd run from my own destiny.

I'd run from Ren. The thought of the Bane alpha made my chest tighten, but when I dropped my face into my hands, another figure replaced him. A boy on his knees, blindfolded and bound, alone in the forest.

Shay.

I could hear his voice, feel the brush of his hands on my cheek as I'd slipped in and out of consciousness. What had happened? He'd left me alone in the dark for so long. . . . I was still alone. But where?

My eyes adjusted to the low light of the room. The cloudy skies filtered sunlight through tall leaded windows stretching the length of the opposite wall, tingeing pale shadows with a rose-hued gleam as I scanned the room for an exit, finding a tall oak door to the right of the bed. Ten, maybe fifteen feet from where I sat.

I managed to slow my breathing, but my heart was still pounding. Swinging my legs over the edge of the bed, I tentatively put weight on my feet. I had no trouble standing and felt each muscle spring back to life, coiled and taut, ready for anything.

I'd be able to fight, and kill, if I had to.

The sound of booted footsteps reached my ears. The knob turned and the door swung inward to reveal a man I'd seen only once before. He had thick hair, deep brown like the color of black coffee. The contours of his face were cut at strong, chiseled angles, slightly worn with lines and covered with the shadow of several days of unshaven, salt-and-pepper stubble—neglected but still appealing.

I'd last seen his face seconds before he coldcocked me with the pommel of his sword. My canines sharpened as a growl rumbled deep in my chest.

He opened his mouth to speak, but I shifted into a wolf, crouching low, snarling at him. I kept my fangs in plain view, a steady growl rolling out of my throat. I had two options: tear him to pieces or bolt past him. I was guessing I had only a few seconds to pick one.

His hand went to his waist, pushing back his long leather duster to rest on the hilt of a long, curving saber.

A fight it is.

My muscles quivered as I hunched down, angling for his throat.

"Wait." He moved his hand off the hilt, lifting his palms in an attempt to pacify me.

I froze, stunned by the gesture and a little irked at his presumption. I wouldn't be calmed that easily. After a quick snap of my fangs, I risked a glance toward the hall at his back.

"You don't want to do that," he said, stepping into my line of sight.

I answered with a growl.

And you don't want to find out what I'm capable of when I'm cornered.

"I understand the impulse," he continued, folding his arms over his chest, the sword in its scabbard. "You might get past me. Then you'll run into a security detail at the end of the hall. And if you get past them—which I think you probably could, given that you're an alpha—you'll hit a larger group of guards at any of the exits."

"Given that you're an alpha." How does he know who I am?

Still growling, I backed off, throwing a glance over my shoulder at the tall windows. I could easily smash through them. It would hurt, but as long as it wasn't too high a drop, I'd survive.

"Not an option," he said, glancing at the windows.

What is this guy? A mind reader?

"That's at least a fifty-foot drop onto solid marble." He took a step forward. I backed up again. "And no one here wants to see you get hurt."

The growl died in my throat.

His voice dropped low and he spoke slowly. "If you'd shift back into human form, we could talk."

I gnashed my teeth, frustrated, sidling along the floor. But we both knew I was feeling less sure of myself by the minute.

"If you try to run," he continued, "we'll be forced to kill you."

He'd said it so calmly that it took a moment for me to process the words.

I let out a sharp bark of protest that turned to dark laughter as I shifted into human form.

"I thought no one here wanted to hurt me."

One corner of his mouth crinkled. "We don't. Calla, I'm Monroe."

He took a step forward.

"Stay where you are," I said, flashing my canines.

He didn't come any closer.

"You haven't tried to kill me yet," I replied, still scanning the room for anything that would give me a tactical advantage. "But that doesn't mean I can trust you. If I see that steel hanging from your belt move an inch, you lose an arm."

He nodded.

Questions pounded in my skull, making my head ache. The sensation of breathlessness threatened to overwhelm me again. I couldn't afford to panic. I also couldn't afford to show any weakness.

Memories stirred deep within me, swirling beneath my skin and raising gooseflesh along my arms. Cries of pain echoed in my head. I shivered, seeing wraiths ooze around me like nebulous shadows while succubi screamed overhead. My blood went icy.

"Monroe! The boy is over here!"

"Where is Shay?"

I choked on his name, terror welling up in my throat as I waited for Monroe's response.

Snatches from the past flitted through my mind, a blur of images that wouldn't stay in focus. I struggled with the memories, trying to catch them and hold them in place so that I could make sense of what had happened, how I'd gotten here. I remembered racing through narrow halls, realizing we'd been cornered, and finding our way into the library at Rowan Estate. Shay's uncle, Bosque Mar, eroding my outrage with doubts about what was happening to us.

Shay's fingers clutched my hand so tightly it hurt. "Tell me who you really are."

"I'm your uncle," Bosque said calmly, walking toward us. "Your own flesh and blood."

"Who are the Keepers?" Shay asked.

"Others like me, who want only to protect you. To help you," Bosque replied. "Shay, you are not like other children. You have untapped abilities that you cannot begin to imagine. I can show you who you truly are. Teach you to use the power you have."

"If you're so invested in helping Shay, why was he the sacrifice at my union?" I pushed Shay behind me, shielding him from Bosque.

Bosque shook his head. "Another tragic misunderstanding. A test, Calla, of your loyalty to our noble cause. I thought we offered you the best of educations, but perhaps you aren't familiar with Abraham's trial with his son Isaac? Isn't the sacrifice of one you love the ultimate gauge of your faith? Do you really believe we wanted Shay to die at your hands? We've asked you to be his protector."

I began to shake. "You're lying."

"Am I?" Bosque smiled, and it almost looked kind. "After all you've been through, have you no trust in your masters? You would never have been made to harm Shay—another kill would have been provided in his place at the last moment. I understand such a test may seem too terrible to be fair, too much to ask of you and Renier. Perhaps you are too young to have faced such a trial."

I balled my hands into fists so Monroe wouldn't see them shaking. I could hear the screams of succubi and incubi, hear the hissing chimeras and the shuffling gait of those horrible, desiccated creatures that had crawled out of the portraits lining Rowan Estate's walls.

"Where is he?" I asked again, grinding my teeth. "I swear if you don't tell me—"

"He's in our care," Monroe said calmly.

There was that half smirk again. I couldn't puzzle out this man's reserved but confident demeanor.

I wasn't sure what "care" meant in this case. Keeping my fangs bared, I edged across the room, waiting for Monroe to make a move.

Even as I watched him, blurry images of the past wavered before my eyes like watercolors.

Cold metal encircling my arms. The click of locks and the sudden absence of weight from my wrists. The warmth of a gentle touch rubbing away the icy chill on my skin.

"Why isn't she awake yet?" Shay asked. "You promised she wouldn't be hurt."

"She'll be fine," Monroe said. "The enchantment from the bolts acts like a heavy sedative; it will take some time to wear off."

I tried to speak, to move, but my eyelids were so heavy, the darkness of slumber pulling me beneath its surface again.

"If we can reach an agreement, I'll take you to him," Monroe continued.

"An agreement?" I was right about not wanting to show weakness. If I was making any sort of deal with a Searcher, it had to be on my terms.

"Yes," he said, risking a step toward me. When I didn't protest, he began to smile. He wasn't being deceptive—I didn't catch the scent of fear—but his smile was chased away by something else. Pain?

"We need you, Calla."

My confusion buzzed more loudly, forcing me to shake it off like a pesky swarm of flies. I had to appear confident, not distracted by his strange behavior.

"Who exactly is 'we'? And what do you need me for?"

My anger had dissolved, but I concentrated on keeping my canines razor sharp. I didn't want Monroe to forget for one minute who he was dealing with. I was still an alpha—I needed to remember that as much as he needed to see it. That strength was the only thing I had going for me right now.

"My people," he said, vaguely gesturing behind him toward whatever lay beyond the door. "The Searchers."

"You're their leader?" I frowned.

He looked strong but grizzled—like someone who never got as much sleep as he really needed.

"I'm *a* leader," he said. "I head up the Haldis team; we run operations out of the Denver outpost."

"Let's talk about your friends in Denver."

Somewhere in the recesses of my mind, Lumine, my mistress, smiled and a Searcher screamed.

I crossed my arms over my chest so I wouldn't shudder. "Okay."

"But it's not just my team that needs your help," he continued, turning suddenly to pace in front of the door. "We all do. Everything has changed; we don't have any time to waste."

He ran his hands through his dark hair as he spoke. I considered bolting—he was clearly distracted—but something about his manner mesmerized me, enough so that I didn't know if escape was what I really wanted anymore.

"You might be our only chance. I don't think the Scion can do this alone. You might be the final part of the equation. The tipping point."

"The tipping point of what?"

"This war. You can end it."

War. The word set my blood boiling. I was glad for it; the heat coursing through my veins made me feel stronger. This war was the one I'd been raised to fight.

"We need you to join us, Calla."

I could barely hear him. I was trapped in a red fog—thoughts of the violence that consumed so much of my life filled my being.

The Witches' War.

I'd served the Keepers in their battles against the Searchers since I could cut flesh with my teeth. I'd hunted for them. I'd killed for them.

My eyes focused on Monroe. I'd killed *his* people. How could he possibly want me to join them?

As if sensing my wariness, he froze in place. He didn't speak but clasped his hands behind his back, watching me, waiting for me to speak.

I swallowed, forcing steadiness into my voice. "You want me to fight for you."

"Not just you," he said. I could tell he was fighting to control his words as well. He seemed desperate to flood the air between us with his thoughts. "But you're the key. You're an alpha, a leader. That's what we need. It's what we've always needed."

"I don't understand."

His eyes were so bright as he spoke I didn't know whether to be afraid or fascinated. "The Guardians, Calla. Your pack. We need you to bring them over to us. To fight with us."

It felt like the floor had dropped out beneath me and I was falling. I wanted to believe what he was saying, because wasn't this the very thing I'd hoped for?

A way to free my pack.

Yes. Yes, it was. Even now my heart was racing with the thought of returning to Vail, of finding my packmates. Of getting back to Ren. I could take them all away from the Keepers. To something else. Something better.

But the Searchers were my enemies . . . I could only tread carefully if I made a pact with them. I decided to play up my reluctance.

"I don't know if that's possible. . . ."

"But it is!" Monroe lurched forward as if to grab my hands, a mad glint in his eyes.

I leapt back, shifting into wolf form, and snapped at his fingers.

"I'm sorry." He shook his head. "There's so much you don't know."

I shifted back. His face was etched with deep lines. Haunted, full of secrets.

"No sudden moves, Monroe." I took slow steps toward him, extending my hand, warding off another approach. "I'm interested, but I'm not convinced that you know what you're asking of me."

"I do." He looked away, almost flinching at his own words. "I'm asking you to risk everything."

"And why would I do that?" I asked.

I already knew the answer. I'd risked everything to save Shay. And I'd do it again in a heartbeat if it meant I could get back to my packmates. If I could save them.

He stepped back and extended his arm, clearing my path to the open door.

"Freedom."

TWO

THE DOOR LED INTO A WIDE, well-lit hall and I swallowed a gasp. The walls were hewn from gleaming marble, its surfaces reflecting a glimmering veil of sunlight that spilled through glass.

Where am I?

The startling beauty of my surroundings distracted me enough that I failed to notice that Monroe and I weren't the only ones in the hall.

"Heads up." A distinctly sullen voice made me jump.

I turned, barely maintaining my human form, bristling with anger at being caught off guard. I almost shifted again when I saw the speaker.

Ethan. I'd met him twice and both times we'd been fighting. First at the library and then at Rowan Estate. My lips curled back so I could flash my fangs. Looking at him, I clenched my fist in front of my chest. His crossbow bolts had almost killed me before Monroe knocked me out. Ethan stared back at me, nose still slightly crooked from when Shay had broken it. Instead of marring his hardened good looks, it had the effect of making him seem that much more danger-ous. My muscles quaked as I watched him. The slightest twitch of his fingers in the direction of the dagger sheathed at his waist was all it took.

I shifted as I leapt, my cry of outrage turning into a howl, mind a frenzy when I barreled into him.

Stupid. Stupid. Stupid. Two kind words from Monroe and I'd walked right into an ambush.

Ethan's fingers twisted in the fur at my chest, shoving me away so my fangs snapped just short of his throat. He spewed curses as he writhed beneath me. I wrenched free of his grasp, but before I could tear into his unprotected flesh, someone else slammed into my back.

Arms and legs wrapped around my torso, clinging tightly, refusing to let go. I snarled and bucked, twisting my head around as I tried to free myself of this new assailant. I couldn't get a good look at the attacker nor could I manage to sink my teeth into the arm locked around my chest. A deep masculine whoop and the sound of laughter only fueled my rage. I crow-hopped and whirled in a circle, desperate to throw him off.

The laughter was coming from Ethan, who'd jumped to his feet and was watching me struggling with a satisfied smirk on his face.

"Ride 'em, cowboy! Only eight seconds, Connor, and you're golden," he said. "You've already made it to five."

"Stop this!" Monroe loomed up between me and Ethan. "Calla, I gave you my word. You aren't in danger here. Connor, get off her."

I thrashed as the rumble of Connor's laughter rippled through my back. "But Monroe, this is almost a new record for me."

"Welcome to Wolf Rodeo." Ethan was laughing so hard he'd bent over, hands resting on his knees so he wouldn't fall.

"I said stop." Nothing in Monroe's voice was amused.

I was so startled when Connor slid off me that I continued to buck and nearly tumbled over.

"Whoa there, sleeping beauty." I whipped around to find Connor grinning at me. I had no trouble remembering him: the other Searcher who'd ambushed Shay and me at the library. And he'd been at Rowan

Estate as well, scooping up Shay—unconscious and a wolf—and whisking him away from Bosque's onslaught of wraiths, succubi, and incubi. I shuddered, both at the memory of the horde and at the sick dread I still felt at not knowing what had happened to Shay.

Unlike Ethan, whose gaze had made me certain he wanted to stick a knife in my gut as much as I wanted to sink my teeth into his throat, Connor was working hard not to laugh. With that expression he looked boyishly appealing, even a little innocent, but I recalled too well the way he could wield swords. Two swords, curving sabers like Monroe's, were sheathed at his waist at this very moment. I snarled at him, backing slowly away from the three Searchers.

"Not a morning person, are we?" Connor smiled. "I promise we'll get you some breakfast, wolfie. You just can't eat Ethan. Deal?"

"Calla." Monroe was walking toward me, shaking his head. "We aren't your enemies. Please give me a chance."

I met his dark eyes, which had locked on me, intense and a little fearful. Pulling my gaze off Monroe, I glanced at Ethan and Connor. They'd taken flanking positions behind Monroe, but neither had drawn a weapon. Conflicting impulses paralyzed me. All my instincts were screaming to attack, but the Searchers had only acted defensively. And they weren't trying to hurt me now.

Still uneasy, I shifted forms.

"I like her better this way, don't you?" Connor murmured with a sideways glance at Ethan, who only grunted.

"What are they doing here?" I pointed at the other two men but spoke to Monroe. "I thought you said I'd be safe with you."

"They're members of my team," Monroe answered. "And you'll be working closely with them. You can trust them just as you can trust me."

Now it was my turn to laugh. "No way. These two have tried to kill me more than once."

"No more fighting now that we're on the same team," Connor said. "Scout's honor."

"Like you were ever a Boy Scout." Ethan's smile was there and gone in less than a second. "Besides, she just tried to tear my throat out!"

"Ethan." Monroe spared him a stern glance.

But Ethan's hostility offered me more reassurance than Monroe's promises or Connor's jibes; at least Ethan's threats made sense. These were Searchers and I was a Guardian. What could we offer each other besides bloodshed?

"Calla," Monroe said. "Our worlds are changing faster than you can imagine. Forget what you think you know about us. We can help each other. We all want the same things."

I didn't respond, wondering what exactly he thought I wanted.

"Will you come with us?" he asked. "Will you hear what I have to say?"

Pulling my eyes off him, I looked up and down the curving hall. Nothing was familiar. If I ran, I wouldn't know where I was going. At least I could keep an eye out for an escape route while I was following Monroe around.

"Fine," I said.

"Fantastic!" Connor laughed. "No more fighting! I guess that means we're bosom buddies now? Very nice."

With that he looked pointedly at my chest.

"She's a wolf," Ethan snapped. "That's twisted."

"Not at the moment," Connor said, not moving his gaze and taking a few steps closer. As he drew near, I caught the scent of cedar and violet tinged with the aroma of coffee. The mixture was familiar—one I'd been close to before. I snarled and jumped back, shaking away the new cloud of memories forming in my mind.

"Are you sure she's an alpha?" Connor asked, tucking me against his chest when I stirred. "She doesn't look that tough."

"You have a selective memory, moron," Ethan snapped. "Just because she's a pretty blonde now doesn't mean the wolf is gone."

"Silver lining, man." Connor laughed. "Gotta live in the moment. And in this moment there is one fine-looking girl in my arms."

"Stop talking about her like I'm not here!" Shay yelled.

"Oh, horrors, I've angered the Great One," Connor said. "Will I ever gain his forgiveness?"

"Don't push the boy, Connor," Monroe said. "We're nearly at the rendezvous point."

"Sorry, boy." Connor smirked.

"That's it." Shay snarled and I heard the scuffle of feet.

"Whoa!" Ethan's body loomed in front of me. "Can't let you do it, kid."

"That's enough," Monroe said. "There's the portal. Just go."

I tried to move again, squinting to see more of my surroundings. The air seemed to sparkle; cold gave way to warmth. Connor's arms tightened around me as I slipped into unconsciousness again.

Staring at Connor's puckish smile, I knew I'd seen it before—even if the memory was fuzzy. He returned my gaze, eyes sparkling with mischief. I balled my fist, gauging whether I'd get the most satisfaction out of hitting him in the gut—or just a bit lower. If he wanted to avoid a fight, he'd need to bite his tongue around me.

But Monroe got there first. "Back off, Connor. She could use a little adjustment before she has to deal with your sense of humor."

"Sir, yes, sir!" Connor stood at attention, but he was laughing.

I was back to being confused. Ethan grunted, still eyeing me warily, but he didn't make a move. Apparently they weren't looking for a fight. Having encountered these men only when I was trying to kill them, I couldn't make heads or tails of their strange, casual banter. Who were these people?

"Anika's expecting us in Tactical," Monroe said, not quite masking his own laugh with a clearing of his throat. He turned away and headed down the hall. "Let's go."

I practically had to trot to keep up with him. I still wasn't comfortable with Connor and Ethan at my back. It took a lot of willpower to keep from looking over my shoulder at them, if only to bare my teeth in warning.

The farther we walked, the more confused I became. The hallway curved constantly; we passed many doors, but no corners or turns. Whatever this place was, it seemed to be circular, all of it flooded with sunlight, brightening every minute as morning blossomed into day. I had to blink against the light, which glittered in the air. Even the walls were sparkling. Tiny veins of multi-hued crystals ran through the marble floors and walls, slicing through the surfaces in rivers of color that joined with sunbeams to fill the space with ghostly rainbows. The hypnotic patterns of light held my focus, so when Monroe came to an abrupt stop, I just avoided smacking into him.

We'd reached a point where the curving hallway was interrupted by a broad open chamber with new paths that led off to our right and left. The path on our left, which headed into what must have been the center of the building, wasn't a hall but glass doors that opened onto a bridge of the same marble. My eyes followed the carved stone walkway and I lost my breath at what I saw. The walls dropped away to reveal an immense courtyard below. It must have been fifty, maybe sixty feet to the ground.

Looks like Monroe was telling the truth about the windows.

The courtyard was filled with . . . glass houses and gardens? They looked like gardens, but there weren't any growing plants. Then again, it was almost winter. Or was it? How long had I been here?

I looked up and saw that unlike the hallway we'd followed to this point, the courtyard opened up to the sky itself. On the other side of the glass doors, thin flakes of snow drifted lazily to the dark earth below.

A hand touched my shoulder and I jumped.

"Business first." Monroe was smiling. "I promise you'll have a tour later."

"Right," I said, following him down the hall to our right. A blush bit into my cheeks, and I hoped I hadn't looked too dumbstruck when I'd been ogling the building.

This new hall was much wider than the one we'd come from, and unlike the first hall it was straight. There were doors on my right and left and two solid wooden ones directly ahead of us. When we reached them, I gasped. Carved in each tall surface was the alchemical symbol for earth—the same triangle that had marked Haldis Cavern on the pages of *The War of All Against All*.

"She's done her homework," Connor said. "Silas will be thrilled."

Monroe and Ethan ignored him and I bit my lip, trying to remember that I needed to keep my reactions hidden. But all such thoughts fled when Monroe pushed open the doors. We walked into a great room with a single table in the center. It was round and massive, like something that had been lifted out of King Arthur's court. The walls were lined with books—old and leather bound, like those we'd hunted through at Rowan Estate. The similarity was enough to set my teeth on edge.

Out of the corner of my eye I saw two people standing near a set of bookshelves, talking quietly as they looked over the titles on the spines. And one of the two people was someone I knew. And loved.

Shay's head tilted as he listened to the girl with him. She looked about my age and had large liquid brown eyes half veiled by wisps of mahogany hair that had escaped from the thick knot caught with a metal clasp at the back of her neck. The girl was the first Searcher I'd seen who wasn't armed to the teeth, though, like the others, she was dressed in fierce apparel: heavily worn leather pants, thick-heeled boots, and a close-cut tunic of undyed linen. Clothes just like those I was now wearing. Slung low on her hips was a wide belt, from which two strange, slender metal spikes hung. I couldn't puzzle out what they were. About two feet long, they looked like skinny, bright silver railroad ties that tapered to needle-sharp points. In one hand she held a sheaf of folded papers, which she tapped rhythmically against her thigh.

I bristled when I saw her other hand resting on Shay's arm. Jealousy's bite startled me, and its teeth sank in deeply. I didn't want any other girl touching him. He was mine.

Shay lifted his head as if he'd heard my thoughts. But when he turned, I realized that he'd recognized my scent. The thought made my skin hum and I found myself running to meet him, casting the dark-haired girl a menacing look as I pushed past her.

"Calla!" Shay said, reaching for me. "Are you all right?"

My heart was beating too fast and I could barely catch my breath. I'd been afraid I might not see him again. That neither of us would live through this ordeal.

I started to nod just as my legs gave out, but Shay was there. His arms caught my waist as I collapsed. I clung to him, knowing that he was as strong as I was now. I could crush him in my grip without fear that I might hurt him. Shay tightened his arms around me and I pressed closer. One of his hands came up and cradled my head against his chest, his lips brushing the crown of my hair.

Shay. Shay. I took a deep breath. His scent, the scent of spring, warm and hopeful as the sunlight that filled this place, poured through me.

Burying my fingers in his hair, I pulled his face to mine. I could taste his surprise, sweet and bright, when I kissed him. The sweetness turned to warmth, then heat as his mouth trailed over my cheek.

"Calla," he whispered, catching my earlobe in his teeth—a wolfish gesture that made me nuzzle his neck affectionately. *Mine. He is mine.*

"It was killing me that I couldn't be with you," he said, pulling back so he could look at me. "God, it's good to see you."

Connor whistled, and the girl's curious gaze sparkled with mischief. Despite my relief at Shay's presence, I silently cursed the momentary lapse in caution. I should know better. This wasn't a private reunion. Our every move was being observed. I'd missed Shay, every ounce of my being ached with wanting to touch him from the moment I laid eyes on him, but I didn't need the Searchers to know that. I forced steadiness into my muscles, wriggling out of his embrace.

"I'm fine, Shay," I said, trying to ignore the wrench of loss I felt now that he wasn't holding me. "For the most part. A little confused."

"That's why we're here," Monroe said, coming toward us. "Shay, I trust you're well."

"I'm better now," he said, not taking his eyes off me. My toes curled as he ignored my attempt to distance myself and pulled me back into an embrace.

"I'm pleased that Calla has made a full recovery too," Monroe said. "It would have been tragic if we'd lost her."

I barked out a harsh laugh. "Lost me? I seem to remember being shot by him." Ethan didn't flinch when I threw an accusing glare his way before looking back at Monroe. "And that you knocked me out."

He nodded, offering an apologetic smile. "We needed to know more about who you were before we knew if you could be an ally."

I cast him a suspicious glance.

"And we did everything in our power to ensure that you recovered swiftly."

This time it was Shay who snorted. "Yeah, like I have any reason to trust your healers."

I turned in his arms to look at him. "Healers?"

My memories of the time between the battle at Rowan Estate and waking here were jumbled at best, terrifying at worst. It was obvious something had healed me, but I didn't remember when my wounds had been treated.

"I don't know what they did to you." He shot an angry look at Monroe, who shrugged.

"The bolts kept her under for a long time," Monroe said. "That's what they're designed to do. Our healers made sure all the toxins were removed from her blood. There shouldn't be any lingering effects."

I howled, struggling across the floor to his side. Each step was agony. The crossbow bolts still protruded from my chest. The blood in my lungs was slowly drowning me.

When I reached him, I shifted forms, buried my hands in his fur, and shook his shoulders.

"Shay! Shay!" Even as I clung to him, I could feel strength ebbing from my limbs.

"Enchanted bolts; hope you're enjoying the ride." Ethan's gravel-rough voice drew my eyes to the side. He had the crossbow trained on me once more. "Are you the one who turned him?"

My chest was on fire, my vision blurred. I nodded and slumped to the floor, rolling alongside Shay.

My fingers flew to my chest again, which had tightened at the memory, at the thought of bolts piercing my flesh. Kept me under?

"How long?" I whispered.

"What?" Shay had put his hand over mine, curling my fingers in his own.

"How long was I out?" I asked. "How long since we left Vail?"

"About a week," he said.

A week. In some ways it didn't sound like much time at all. But when I thought of what could have happened to my pack in a week, what could have happened to them in a matter of hours once my flight from the union had been discovered, it sounded like an eternity.

And Ren. What had they done to him? He'd lied so we could escape the pursuing Bane pack, and there was no way the Keepers hadn't discovered that treachery.

I trembled and Shay tightened his grip on me, but in my mind I was in the arms of someone else.

Ren's voice seemed to come from right behind me.

"I don't know how to believe you. Any of this. What else is there? This is who we are."

"That doesn't make it right. You know I wouldn't abandon my pack unless I had to," I said quietly. *"Unless it was the only way to help them."*

His eyes met mine, strained and uncertain.

"We don't have much time," I said. *"How did you get ahead of the others?"*

He glanced in the direction from which we'd come. "There was an uproar when they found Flynn's body, but I caught your scent and took off. The rest of them were still regrouping. My father's pack. The elder Banes."

He tensed and cold flooded my limbs.

"What about the Nightshades?" I asked.

"They're being held for questioning."

"What happened in Vail?" I had to pull away from Shay, needing to get my bearings.

No one answered me, and I fought off a chill like the one I'd felt the night of our escape.

Right now I couldn't afford to be consumed by the fear of what might or might not have befallen my packmates. Unwavering strength and steel resolve were my best—no, my only—shots at helping them.

"What about the fight? How did you find us? Did you kill Bosque Mar?"

Connor laughed. "Kill Bosque Mar. No one can kill that thing."

"Thing?" Shay's eyebrows went up. "What do you mean, thing?"

"No one can kill Bosque Mar yet," Monroe said, looking at Shay before speaking to me. "We're still trying to determine what's happening in Vail."

"Do you know anything?"

"Watch your tone, wolfie," Ethan said, adjusting the crossbow slung over his shoulder. "If it weren't for us, you'd have bled out in that library."

"You were the reason I was bleeding out in the library!" I lunged forward, remaining human but grabbing Ethan by the jacket and slamming him onto the tabletop. Leaning down, I made sure he was looking straight at my fangs. "Don't ever tell me to watch my tone; you have no idea who you're dealing with."

"Calla!" Monroe was at my side, pulling me off Ethan. "Please, this isn't necessary."

Ethan jumped up. "The hell? You'd better curb your dog, Monroe."

I smirked. "And you'd better learn not to call me a dog."

The girl who'd been in the room with Shay when we first arrived began to laugh. "Nice."

"Go to hell, Ariadne." Ethan was still livid.

"Language." Ariadne clucked her tongue.

"We need Calla," Monroe said, unflinching despite Ethan's glare. "This isn't negotiable."

"There's that, and she's right," Connor added, eyeing me warily but with an admiring grin. "You did shoot a bunch of bolts into her."

"This is bullshit," Ethan said. "First negotiating with this kid and now the wolf. We're better than this."

"The kid is the Scion." Monroe held Ethan in a steady gaze. "And an alpha wolf could be the key to winning this war."

Ethan snorted. "The Scion hasn't done anything for us, and no way are wolves winning this war. This is our fight and they are on the other side!"

"I'm sure things will be different now that Calla has joined us."
Monroe raised an eyebrow at Shay, expectant.

Shay shoved his hands in his pockets. "Yeah, I guess."

"That's not good enough, Shay." A shadow of irritation flitted
across Monroe's face.

"What is he talking about?" I asked.

Shay stopped glaring at Monroe long enough to look at me. "I
wouldn't tell them anything about Vail or what we'd found in the
library until you were here. Healthy, safe."

"Oh." Somehow I managed not to blush, but I felt a flash of heat
deep in my body.

Ethan's fists were clenched and he began to pace near Monroe. "I
don't care if he is the Scion. He's practically a baby to our world. He
needs to follow orders, not try to set terms."

"I can leave anytime you'd like," Shay snarled. "If I've overstayed
my welcome."

"There's the door." Ethan gestured to it.

"That's enough! This is the way things are, Ethan," Monroe said.
"From now on. Is that clear?"

Ethan stared at him silently, then finally turned and walked to
the opposite side of the room.

"Well, then," Ariadne said. "Since I'm guessing we can't actually
talk about Vail until Anika joins us, maybe we should take care of
introductions."

She moved forward fluidly, smiling as if the tension of the room
didn't exist.

Monroe frowned at her. "Introductions?"

"Of course," she said. "You seem to have forgotten this is my big
debut. With all the excitement about Shay here, no one cares. But I've
been ordered to report to you, Monroe." She slapped the sheaves of
paper against his chest. "I trust you're satisfied with my completion

of the Academy training. I'm ready for my assignment with the Haldis team."

He sighed when he took the documents. "Yes, Ariadne. Congratulations on completing your examinations. We couldn't be more proud to have you on board."

She offered him the imitation of a smile.

"It's just Adne now," she grumbled. "The whole name is such a mouthful."

"If you insist. You've completed your training at an astonishing speed, and you did receive the highest commendations from your trainers," Monroe said. "You can have your pick of assignments."

"I know," she said, eyes narrowing.

"You don't have to work with Haldis."

"I know." Her teeth were clenched. "It's done, okay? You're stuck with me."

"You know that's not what I meant," Monroe began, but she shook her head.

"Drop it."

She brushed the fringe of dark hair from her eyes, turning a genuine smile on Connor. "Are you happy to see me? You've been at the outpost for what—three months now?"

"Try six," he said. "And you've clearly forgotten all about me. I saw the way you were hitting on our Scion when we walked in. Quite the little coquette, aren't we?"

"I wasn't flirting," she said, but I thought I caught a blush chase across her cheeks when she glanced sidelong at Shay. "You know perfectly well where I was and why I had to be here," she said. "I didn't abandon you."

I dug my nails into my palms when Shay looked at me guiltily. Who was this girl?

"A man knows when he's been jilted." Connor put a fist over his heart.

"Is that what you're calling yourself these days?" she asked with a wry smile. "A man? I was thinking stooge . . . or maybe poser."

"Nope," Connor said. "I think we'll stick with man. Would you like to see the proof?"

"I'd be grateful if you said no, Ariadne." Monroe grimaced, but I could see him hiding a smile behind the irritated expression he'd put on.

The secret smile faded when she snapped, "I know better than to ask whether you missed me."

"Well, I'm elated to see you," Connor said quickly as Monroe grimaced, crossing the space between them. He bent down and kissed her on the cheek. "Tess and Isaac are always out. Ethan's too grumpy to be any fun. And not half as nice to look at as you."

I looked at the new girl again. She was pretty . . . too pretty. Had she been flirting with Shay while I was unconscious?

"He's kidding," she said, throwing a glance at Shay while turning her back on Connor.

"No, I'm not," Connor said. "No offense, Ethan."

"I'm devastated," Ethan said flatly.

Ariadne faced me with a smirk. "And this is the wolf girl? Shay talks about you all the time."

I smiled at her. Even if she had been flirting with him, Shay's thoughts had still been focused on me. Good. That was how I wanted it.

"This is Ariadne," Shay said. "She's been showing me the ropes around here."

"Call me Adne," she said.

"My name is Calla," I replied, straightening to take advantage of the inch I had on her. Even if Shay wasn't interested, I still wanted to make sure this girl knew how things stood between us.

Her own eyes glimmered with mirth. "So I've heard. A Guardian named Calla . . . like the flower. That's a nice touch."

I couldn't stop the groan that welled up from my throat. "Uh-huh. Like the flower." This was exactly the impression I didn't want to make.

"That's just fantastic," she murmured, a smile ghosted across her mouth. "Well, it's great to meet you, Lily. At least if you really are on our side."

THREE

LILY.

I could hear Ren laughing.

Will you ever stop calling me that?

Never.

My knees threatened to buckle while I stared at her. "Why did you call me that?"

The instinct to shift was overwhelming. The room felt like it was closing in on me.

Run, Calla. Run to your pack. You don't belong here.

Shay must have sensed my anxiety because he grasped both my arms, forcing me to look at him.

"Calla? Hey, take a breath. She didn't mean any harm." I realized he thought it was anger at Ariadne that had made me want to change. But that wasn't the problem.

"Yeah, he's right. Sorry if it annoyed you." She shrugged, the gleam in her eyes brightening, as if she had *wanted* me to attack her. "It just came to mind. It fits and it's hilarious."

I could barely hear her because of the roaring in my ears. It was like being sucked back into a dream. No, not a dream, a nightmare. Feelings that I'd been able to bury while I'd been alone surfaced, flooding my chest.

Her amused expression faded. "Something wrong?"

I shook my head, tongue-tied and wishing the floor would open up and swallow me. I could hear Ren whispering the nickname in my ear. Couldn't Shay and I have a reunion for more than five minutes without being reminded of the one person who could drive us apart?

Shay answered her, his own teeth clenched. "It's just that some-one else used to call her that."

Someone else. Now I wasn't just hearing Ren's teasing whisper. I could see his face and remember the way he'd pulled me against him the night I'd run from Vail. From the ceremony where I should have become his mate. He'd kissed me, pleaded with me to stay. Where was he now? He'd lied to help us escape. I didn't want to think about the price he'd paid for that lie.

Vail. Home. My heart hammered against my rib cage, making it difficult to breathe. *Why am I here?* I dug my nails into my palms, struggling not to turn on the Searchers and fly at them as the wolf snarled within me, desperate to fight, desperate to be with my pack.

Adne's eyes moved from Shay's twitching jaw to my face, assessing.

"Ah," she said quietly, not trying to hide the smile that slid over her lips. "Someone else. I see."

An uncomfortable silence filled the room. Connor finally cracked his knuckles and looked meaningfully at Monroe.

"So are we going to get out of prison duty?" he asked. "Not that it wasn't thrilling, especially compared to the mortal combat you usually send us into."

"Do you ever shut up?" Shay snapped. A guilty flush crept along the back of my neck. I knew that Shay's mood was much more about me than Connor's jokes. Even if the jokes were getting a little irritating.

"Manners, manners," Connor said. "Since you're the Chosen One, you need to make a good impression. Too bad they don't teach etiquette here. You know—which fork for salad. Calligraphy. The stylish way to disembowel an opponent."

For a second I thought Shay would take a swing at Connor.

"That's enough, Connor." Monroe's calm words carried a flint edge. "Let's sit tight until Anika arrives."

"She's arrived." A woman came striding through the door. She was dressed like the other Searchers, but an iron medallion in the shape of a compass rose hung from her neck. Her hair, caught in a ring of braids at the crown of her head, was like corn silk.

She was accompanied by another woman whose appearance brought only one word to mind: fierce. Her jet black hair was cropped close to her head, and a tattoo of intricate lace-like patterns wrapped around the caramel skin of her neck. The belt around her waist was filled with knives, their bright hilts catching the sunlight and throwing back flashes like deadly warning beacons.

"Lydia!" Connor bolted across the room, catching the tattooed warrior woman in a bear hug.

"Nice to see you too, Connor." Her laugh was low and husky. "How's Tess?"

"Still fighting with Isaac." He grinned. "And missing you of course."

She returned his smile. "If all goes well, I'll get to see her in a few hours."

Connor put his hands on her shoulders. "Tonight won't be much of a reunion."

"I'll take what I can get," she said.

Ethan approached the pair. He caught Lydia's elbow, turning her. "You're all dressed up."

Lydia and Ethan locked forearms in what struck me as some sort of ritual greeting.

"I heard we had special guests," she said, looking around the room. Her eyes settled on me and she inclined her chin. I had a hard time not stepping back in surprise. The gesture had clearly been one of . . . respect. Two questions chased each other through my mind: *Who do these people think I am? What do they want from me?*

Lydia gave a stiff bow to Monroe. "We good to go?"

Monroe looked from her to me. "We haven't quite gotten there yet."

The austere-faced, blond woman smiled at both of them. "That's fine. It means we won't have to backtrack."

She beckoned to me. "Calla, it's an honor to meet you. My name is Anika."

"Thank you." I took her extended hand, not surprised by the strength of her grasp. Everything about this woman, from the rich contralto of her voice to her regal bearing, bespoke authority. "Though I'm not sure about the honor part."

She laughed. "You saved the Scion and that means you might have saved us."

Shay had come to stand beside me. "You haven't told me what it even means that I'm the Scion yet. Adne's been babysitting me ever since we got here."

"It's not babysitting," Adne protested. "I haven't had to spank you once, which is a shame."

Shay's eyes went wide. He glanced at me, shaking his head, but it didn't stop my blood from boiling.

"Adne!" Monroe gave her a stern look.

I half expected Connor to high-five her for taking a line right out of his usual repertoire, but he looked even more upset than Monroe. I took in the girl's slight frame and began calculating the time it would take to rip her arms from their sockets. *Definitely less than ten seconds. Maybe less than five.*

"Lighten up," she snapped, but then glanced nervously at Anika. "Sorry, Anika."

"Apology accepted." A smile played across Anika's mouth, briefly transforming her. "It will take time to teach you who you are, Shay. I'm certain it's frustrating to wait, and for that I'm sorry. But your role lies a little further down the road. What Calla's place will be in all this is the more pressing question."

"My place?" I asked, managing to tear my eyes off Adne, who I'd expected would go back to teasing Shay. But she was watching Connor with a smirk on her face.

"I'm the Arrow," Anika said. "So at the moment I give the orders around here."

"Huh?" I frowned.

She touched the iron compass rose that hung from her neck before pointing to Monroe. "The Arrow directs the Guides of each division. You've already met the Guide for our Haldis division."

"What is the Haldis division?" I asked, thinking of the earth symbol on the door.

"We'll explain everything in due time," she said. "I promise. But there's an urgent matter at hand that requires our immediate attention. We need your help, if you'll give it."

"How can I help?" Suspicion crept back into my voice. No matter how many times they asked me to trust them, I kept waiting for the Searchers to spring some sort of trap.

She smiled, but it was a joyless expression. "We need you to go back to Vail."

I hoped I'd managed to keep my expression neutral. *Go back to Vail.* That was what I wanted, wasn't it? Then why did it feel like my skin had turned to stone?

"You've got to be kidding." Shay stepped forward, half shielding me from Anika's piercing gaze. "They'll kill her the minute she sets foot back there."

I shot a stern look at Shay. He wasn't wrong, but I'd been born to fight. My initial shock at Anika's words had dissolved, leaving my canines sharp in my mouth. *I'm an alpha, Shay, not a pup. You'd better not forget that.*

"Not back into her life," Anika said. "Now that you're here—you, the Scion—the war will rage without ceasing. The Keepers will come at us with everything they have. We need to gain the advantage."

"How will sending her back to Vail give you any advantage?" Shay asked.

"We want to try something." Monroe put his hand on Shay's shoulder, pulling him back. "Something that worked a long time ago. An alliance."

An alliance. The Harrowing. The first Guardian revolt. It was all falling into place.

"Oh," I said, feeling both a surge of hope and a skittering fear beneath my skin. War. *The Searchers are going to war and I'm their first volley.* My shoulders tightened at the thought of battle, powerful, ready.

"Wait a second." Shay shrugged Monroe's hand off. "You mean an alliance with the Guardians?"

"It's happened in the past, and made a huge difference in our ability to resist the Keepers."

Shay shook his head. "That's not how I read it. I know about the Harrowing. You're lucky the Guardians aren't extinct."

Stop trying to protect me. He ignored my warning growl, keeping his eyes on Monroe.

"The Harrowing ended badly," Monroe said. "But for a time it was a successful endeavor. This time such an alliance could be the difference between winning and losing."

"And there's one vital piece we have that didn't exist at the time of the Harrowing," Anika said.

"And what's that?" Shay asked.

"You," she said.

Now it was Shay's turn to say, "Oh."

I watched him, wondering if he'd learned anything more about his own role in the mystery we'd unraveled in Vail. Anika had called him vital—the difference between why the Harrowing had failed and why the Searchers thought they could win this war now. I hoped she was right, considering what saving Shay had already cost me.

"Why?" Ren hissed. "What about him is worth risking your own life?"

"He's the Scion," I whispered. "He might be the only one who can save us. All of us. What if our lives belonged only to us? What if we didn't serve the Keepers?"

I remembered the words passing from my lips, but there had been another question. One that I hadn't dared voice to Ren. Not when my life and Shay's were on the line.

What if I could choose my own fate?

My body quaked at the flash of memories. I loved Shay. From the first moment he'd touched me, he'd wakened parts of myself I hadn't known were slumbering. Our secrets, stolen moments, forbidden kisses, what we'd both risked for each other—all of it had led to the choice that brought me here.

I turned from the path of my destiny because I couldn't let him die. But that wasn't the only reason I'd fled Vail. The world I'd known had crumbled around me. An alpha protects her pack. Leads them. I'd abandoned them, but only because I'd believed it was the only way I could save them.

Jumping on Shay's distraction, I seized the moment to stake my own claim in this fight. Despite my wariness of the Searchers, I needed their help. This might be the chance to get my packmates away from the Keepers.

"Yes," I said. "I'll do it."

"Calla," Shay began.

"No," I said, silencing him with a glare and flash of my teeth. "They're right. An alliance is what I want. What my pack would want."

"Good," Anika said.

I thought I heard Ethan grumbling as he stalked back to the corner where he'd been sulking before Lydia and Anika arrived.

"We could use some logistical information before we move forward," Monroe said.

"I'll tell you what I know," I said. "I'm not sure how much it will help with planning an attack."

"Anything will help," he said.

Good.

"But let's start close to home. We lost two Searchers in late autumn. Do you know what happened to them?"

Not good. I managed not to cringe. This wasn't going to help with forging a new alliance.

"I do."

One question and they'll probably kill me if I answer it truthfully.

"Calla, wait." Shay stepped closer to me, a warning note in his voice. I was certain his mind had jumped to the same dire place mine had.

I shook my head. "If they want an alliance, they need to know who they're making it with." *And if they want revenge, so be it.* I glanced around the room. The doors were closed. Solid, but not solid enough to withstand a Guardian crashing through them at full speed. *I can make it if I have to run.*

"But—" Shay's fingers wrapped around my wrist.

I ignored him. "They're both dead."

Adne looked at the floor. Anika and Lydia sighed, but Connor scratched the shadow of whiskers on his jaw.

"That's not exactly new information, Monroe."

"We knew about Kyle," Monroe said quietly. "He was among the Fallen. But we needed confirmation on Stuart. No one is counted as lost without a firsthand account of his or her death."

The hairs on the back of my neck stood up. "Firsthand?"

"Yes," Anika said. "That's our protocol."

I wondered what they would do when they found out exactly how firsthand my view of the other Searcher's death had been.

"Hang on a sec." Shay was frowning. "What are the Fallen? I read that name in *The War of All Against All*. Are those the things that climbed out of my uncle's gross paintings?"

As much as I didn't want to, I shuddered the moment Shay mentioned the creatures that had pursued us through the cavernous halls of Rowan Estate. The way they'd shuffled, moaned—how empty their eyes had been.

"Yes, but we don't have time to get into that now." Monroe gave him a stern glance before turning back to me. "Now about Stuart, if you know anything . . ."

I nodded and tried to ignore how breathless I felt.

"What happened to our operatives, Calla?" Anika asked. "We need to know how they were taken. Our sources in Vail don't have any information."

"Sources?" I frowned.

The look on Monroe's face squashed the question the moment I'd asked it.

"Just answer."

Alarm sparked in Shay's eyes. "I really think we need to put this in some kind of context."

I pulled my wrist free of his grasp, ready to bolt or attack. "They already have the context, Shay. I'm a Guardian. They know what that means."

"Aw, shit," Connor muttered. He and Lydia exchanged a glance and they both began to inch toward Ethan, whose head had taken a deceptively innocent tilt as he watched me.

Adne looked at Connor sharply. "What?"

He shook his head to silence her, keeping his eyes on me.

I swallowed hard. "I was with Shay outside Efron Bane's club when your men came after us."

"Go on." Monroe's jaw tightened.

"It was my job to protect Shay. I killed one of the men on sight."

"Stuart," Lydia murmured. She and Connor stood alongside Ethan like two sentinels.

"Are we done talking now?" Ethan's voice was quiet.

"Keep your head," Anika said. "Winning the war is what matters. Wars make casualties."

"Her kind make the casualties," Ethan snapped.

"Look at her, Ethan. She's just a girl," Monroe said. "Remember what we've talked about. The Guardians aren't what they seem. She may be able to help us bring them over to our side."

The gentleness of his words startled me. I wasn't too keen on his calling me "just a girl," but I was glad enough that revenge wasn't what Monroe was after. Unfortunately his perspective wasn't shared by everyone in the room.

Ethan's face contorted, twisting with outrage. In the next moment his crossbow was off his shoulder and aimed at me.

"Stand down, Ethan!" Anika shouted.

Connor wrenched the weapon from his hands. "Maybe you should leave."

"I don't think so," Ethan replied without looking at Connor. "What happened to Kyle?"

"Other Guardians showed up," I said, watching Shay step in front of me, almost blocking my view of Ethan. "They said the Keepers wanted him alive."

Ethan nodded, the veins in his neck throbbing. "And?"

"They brought him to Efron Bane for questioning," I said. I had to close my eyes, abruptly awash in the horror of that night—the way Efron had leered at me, how my skin had crawled at his touch. The sickening sensations gave way to rising anger. *Let's see him try that again—this time I won't sit still and take it.*

"Were you there?"

"Yes." It felt like I was back in that office, hearing the Searcher's screams while Ren gripped my hand. I shuddered.

"Did you do the questioning?" He looked calm. Too calm.

"No."

"Then who did?"

"Ethan, this has gone far enough," Monroe interrupted. "You know what happened to Kyle. We saw him at Rowan Estate. It's over; let it go."

Ethan glared at Monroe. "I have the right to know what happened to my brother!"

Brother? Ethan's hateful glances, his constant sullenness—all of it made sense. Twinges of sympathy pinched my chest. I cleared my throat, which was suddenly thick as Ansel's face flashed in my mind. "I'm sorry you lost your brother. I have a brother; if anything happened to him . . ." *What was happening to my brother? And to Bryn, who is as close to me as a sister could be?*

He turned wild eyes on me. "So tell me—"

"Wraiths," I said quickly. "They always use wraiths to interrogate prisoners."

"Wraiths?" His voice was strangled now. "They gave him to wraiths?"

His eyes closed for a moment, then his hand went to his waist. I saw the flash of steel as he drew a dagger from his belt. My body tensed, ready to shift in the next moment.

"And you were there," he hissed. "He's Fallen, and you were there. You soulless bitch, you could have stopped it!"

When his eyes opened, they blazed with grief-filled rage. He took a step toward me, the dagger held low. I was about to lunge at him when Monroe stepped between us. In the same moment Shay dropped to the floor—a golden brown wolf hunched defensively just in front of me. He bared sharp fangs at Ethan, snarling.

Ethan's smile dissolved and he paled even more.

"And you're the one who made the Scion into a monster. I'll flay you myself and wear your skin for a coat."

Shay tensed, his ears flattening as Ethan lunged.

"No!" Anika shouted.

Monroe's arm shot out, catching Ethan around the waist.

"Lydia, Connor, get him out of here!" he shouted as he restrained the furiously struggling man. "We'll deal with this later."

Spittle and a string of curses flew from Ethan's mouth. The two Searchers rushed to aid their leader. With considerable effort they dragged the shrieking, sobbing man from the room. I could still hear his agonized cries as they disappeared from sight.

Monroe shook his head, grief etching his face. He glanced at Shay, who still crouched low, his eyes fixed on the doorway.

"Do you mind?" Monroe sighed.

"Shay, shift back," I murmured. "Now." And then a young man stood next to us again, though his eyes remained wary.

"If anyone hurts her, you'll be sorry," Shay said to Monroe.

"She won't be harmed."

Their conversation, taking place as if I wasn't there, left me uneasy. I could understand, and even appreciate, Shay's desire to protect me, but I was a warrior. I didn't need protecting. A burr of resentment settled beneath my skin.

"An incident like that won't happen again," Monroe said. "I assure you."

"I'm sorry about what happened," I said suddenly, no longer willing to be voiceless while my fate was being discussed. "I know it probably doesn't mean anything to you."

I looked at the empty doorway through which Ethan had been dragged. "Or him."

"It means something, if it's sincere." Monroe said, regarding my troubled expression with thoughtful eyes. "It will take some time before he trusts you. If he ever will."

"This isn't going to work." Shay paced back and forth, fists clenched at his sides. "How can we get anywhere if one of you is always trying to kill her?"

He had a good point. I wouldn't be helping my pack anytime soon if I had to worry about vengeful Searchers shoving daggers into my back.

"Ethan may be grief-stricken and angry, but he still follows my orders," Anika said. "No one will harm Calla while she's under my protection."

I pivoted to face her, arching an eyebrow. "Under *your* protection?"

Maybe Shay was right. This alliance could never work. Alphas didn't need protection. The Searchers didn't understand my world or me. But was there any way I could save Ansel, Bryn, and the others on my own?

Anika offered me a wry smile. "I'm afraid that is your lot, Guardian. At least until you manage to convince the others of your loyalties."

"My loyalty is to my pack," I responded automatically, and then winced. *The pack I left behind.* I thought of Ethan's crazed sorrow, wondering if I would have responded any differently had our situations been reversed. Would I have any room in my heart for forgiveness? I might not have killed Kyle myself, but he was dead because I'd done my job. I couldn't blame Ethan for focusing his rage on me.

I don't have any other choice; this alliance has to work.

Shay folded my hands in his own. The warmth of his touch pulled me from my dark thoughts. I met his eyes and remembered why I'd been willing to leave Vail. My earlier resentment draining away, I threaded my fingers through his and ran my thumb over his wrist. He smiled and my pulse stuttered.

"We're going to help them, Cal," he said quietly. "I'm back now, and that's what we'll do. We'll help Ansel, all of the pack."

I nodded, though the smile I wanted to give him in return wouldn't appear. The lines around Monroe's eyes tightened as he glanced at our entwined fingers. Self-conscious, I shook Shay's hand off, wondering if all the Searchers despised the notion that their precious Scion could love a Guardian. My chest tightened when a nagging worry flitted through my mind. If they did, would it change how Shay felt about me?

"That's what we all hope for," Anika said. "But we need to know a bit more before we can make the next move. How long have you been planning to rebel against the Keepers?"

How long had I been planning to what?

"Uh . . . I—" Words tangled with my tongue. I hadn't planned anything. Every decision I'd made had been about saving Shay. Choices made in the space of a breath. And it had been utter chaos.

"She was being forced to marry someone," Shay said, revulsion edging each of his words. "At age seventeen . . . can you believe that?"

Monroe nodded, opening his mouth to respond. But I felt like I'd been punched in the gut. *Why does it always have to come back to me and Ren? Doesn't Shay realize the sacrifice Ren made by letting me go?*

"That is not what—" I bit off the words, realizing that I didn't want to air my relationship issues in public.

"I know it's not all," Shay said. I saw his sharp canines flash as he spoke. "But it's important. That ceremony, having to be with *him,* it was insane."

"How can you talk about him that way?" I snapped. "Ren tried to help us. He lied for us and the Keepers will know it. They could kill him!"

No, it was worse than that. And the awful truth of it was what fueled my rage. I lowered my lashes and spoke to the floor. "They *will* kill him."

I didn't bother to hide my grief when I looked at Shay again, unblinking though my eyes had filled with tears.

Shay's face paled; the veins in his neck were throbbing, but it was Monroe who reacted to the sound of Ren's name.

"Ren?" His eyes widened. I could tell he was fighting to keep his tone neutral. "Do you mean Renier Laroche?"

"You know who he is?" I asked, startled.

Monroe turned his face away. "I know of him," he said, his voice rough.

Anika was watching Monroe carefully. "That's an interesting development. It could be vital, don't you think?"

Monroe didn't meet her eyes, but he nodded.

"Tell us more about this ceremony," Anika said. "It would help us to understand exactly what we're walking into in Vail."

"Calla and Ren were supposed to form a new pack this spring," Shay said, still glaring at me. "Another set of Guardians to protect Haldis Cavern." His jaw clenched. "One of the Keepers' arranged unions."

I glared back at him, biting my tongue. Hadn't I run from the union, leaving Ren behind, risking everything to help Shay escape? What else did I have to prove to him?

"We're familiar with that practice." Monroe met my gaze. "You were running away from him?"

"No, not from him," I said. Shay's hands formed fists and though it was petty, I felt a pinch of satisfaction. "The Keepers were going to make us kill Shay as part of the union. I found him tied up in the woods. I had to run to save him."

Shay wasn't looking at me anymore, and the ripple of smugness faded to guilt. It didn't help that Adne had taken his hand, leaning in to whisper to him. *Great, now I'm a slutty bitch and she gets to be the good friend. Nice work, Calla.*

"The sacrifice," Monroe said. "We knew that was going to happen at Samhain, but we didn't know where. We tracked the Scion's location to Rowan Estate."

"Lucky for us," I said, shuddering at what might have happened if the Searchers hadn't appeared that night.

"Were the Guardians tracking you?" Monroe asked.

I nodded. "They sent the Banes after us."

"An entire pack?" Anika frowned. "How did you elude them?"

Shay sighed, as if he were conceding a major point. "Ren helped us get away. He caught up with us in the woods, and he let us go, kept the rest of the pack off us."

"He helped you?" Monroe's eyes found me; the dark glint of his gaze remained utterly unreadable.

"Yes." My response was barely a whisper. I was finding it hard to breathe. Each moment I relived from that night was like a stone placed on my chest, piling up one after the other to suffocate me.

Adne continued to watch us.

"That's good to know," Monroe said.

"Yes, it is." A smile appeared on Anika's lips and vanished just as quickly. "That bodes very well for our plans."

Connor reappeared in the doorway. "What'd I miss?" His eyes flicked to Adne and Shay's twined fingers, and he grimaced. "Let me guess, the Scion proposed to you."

"She knows Renier Laroche," Adne said, grinning at his sour expression and keeping her hand clasped in Shay's. "They both do."

Shay grimaced and twisted his fingers free of hers, looking at me sideways. I smiled at him, and his expression softened.

Connor whistled, his irritation giving way to surprise. "Isn't that interesting."

The two of them exchanged a knowing glance. *Why do the Searchers all know about Ren?*

"For the moment that's not our concern," Monroe said curtly. "Where's Ethan now?"

"I sent him to work point for the Reapers," Connor replied. "I think the outpost is a safe enough distance."

"He's just come off patrol." Monroe frowned. "He's not due to go back out until tonight."

Connor shrugged. "Lydia thought it was a good idea too. Ethan needs something to keep his mind occupied. Besides, you know he's our best sniper."

Monroe made a low, affirmative sound, leveling a serious gaze at Shay. "I understand why you were about to attack Ethan, but you'd best avoid shifting into your wolf form while you're among us unless we're out in the field, fighting. There are a lot of itchy trigger fingers around here that belong to soldiers trained to shoot Guardians first and ask questions later."

"I'll keep that in mind," Shay muttered.

"Thank you," Anika replied. "Calla, before you left, had any of your packmates expressed discontent with their lot? If Ren was willing to take that risk for you, it would follow that others might come to our aid—with your leadership, of course."

Would they? I thought about Mason and Nev. About Sabine. Life under the Keepers was brutal for them. They'd jump at a chance to leave, wouldn't they?

And Ansel. He wanted the freedom to choose a life with Bryn. But that wasn't the only thing convincing me that my brother would join us without a second thought.

I would never betray the Keepers. Unless you asked me to . . . alpha.

And it wasn't just Ansel. By keeping my first encounter with Shay a secret, Bryn had risked her safety. She was just as loyal as my brother.

"Yes," I said. "They'll join us."

"Your parents?" she asked. "It would be all the more helpful if the elder Nightshades would come over to our side."

"Maybe—" My heart jumped beneath my rib cage, leaving me breathless. My father and mother were alphas, my alphas. I'd always submitted to their will. What would they think of their own daughter trying to lead them? Guardians weren't big on shifting hierarchies.

"What about the Banes?" Shay asked. "Don't you want all the wolves?"

"Some of the younger Banes, maybe," Monroe said. "But the elders won't join us."

"How do you know that?" Shay asked.

"We have some history with the packs," Anika said lightly. "Emile Laroche would never seek an alliance with us."

History.

"You mean they won't join you because the Banes that would have revolted are already dead," I said. "They died the last time you tried for an alliance. When Ren's mother died."

Monroe drew a sharp breath. "How do you know about that?"

"We found the Keepers' records of the Guardian packs," Shay said. "We know that Corrine Laroche was executed for planning a revolt with Searchers."

"But all I'd ever been told about her was that she was killed in a Searcher ambush at the Bane compound when Ren was only a year old," I added. "Until the night you attacked Rowan Estate, we were the only ones who knew otherwise."

Silence swept over the Searchers, all their faces paling as they exchanged troubled glances.

"No wonder the Guardians serve so loyally," Anika murmured.

"The Keepers have twisted your minds about the way lives around you have been broken."

A trembling began in my shoulders, traveling down my back. "That's what Ren believed, but the night we ran, I told him the truth."

They all stared at me.

"You told him?" Shay hissed. "You didn't say anything about that!"

"It's the reason he let us go," I whispered, unable to return his gaze. Part of the reason. I kept my second thought hidden, remembering again the desperation in Ren's face. The way he'd kissed me. And he was somehow caught up in this. The Searchers weren't telling us everything.

Monroe suddenly turned on his heel, walking swiftly away. "If you'll excuse me."

"Monroe!" Anika called, but he was already out of the door.

"I'll go after him," Connor said.

Adne was shaking her head. "It's always the same."

What just happened? I glanced at Shay, but he seemed just as confused as I was.

"Maybe he shouldn't be part of this mission," Anika said.

"You think he'd ever let it happen without him?" Adne laughed, but it was a bitter sound. "He's waited years for another shot at this. He's waited my whole life."

Anika's mouth flattened. "Show a little respect for your father, child. You don't understand how much he lost."

"Your father?" Shay asked. He looked at her in a way not unlike how he'd just looked at me, like he'd been betrayed.

The sudden bite of jealousy was sharp as teeth snapping at the back of my neck. How close had they gotten while I was recovering?

Adne cringed, blushing as if she'd revealed a terrible secret. "Yeah. Monroe is my father."

"You never told me that," he said. "Why didn't you say anything?"

"It's not that important." She turned away, crimson painting her cheeks.

I frowned. "Why do you always call him Monroe?" I'd deferred to my own father as Nightshade alpha, but I still called him Dad.

"Because I don't want special treatment," she said. "And because it drives him crazy."

"Respect, Ariadne," Anika said. "It matters more than you think."

"I'll try," Adne said, but it looked to me like she was trying not to roll her eyes.

Anika clasped her hands at her waist. "Despite this unfortunate little disruption, what you've said confirms our hopes about the Guardians. We'll execute the mission accordingly."

"When?" I asked. "When am I going to find my packmates?"

Anika smiled. "Now."

FOUR

NOW? BUT THAT MEANT ... Could they really be planning an attack on the Keepers this soon? The thought of returning home frightened me as much as it compelled me. I wanted to get back to my pack as soon as possible, but was I ready to fight side by side with Searchers? I didn't trust these people. My captors. They wanted an alliance, but they had yet to tell me anything else.

"Excellent," Lydia said, re-entering the room. "I would have been so disappointed if I'd sharpened my daggers for nothing."

A ripple of tension slid through my body. Lydia's appearance was ferocious enough that it was a struggle for me not to shift when she was nearby. The scent of her clothes, the gleam of steel at her waist— she was everything I'd been trained to kill.

"Right now?" Shay strode across the room. The air around him was buzzing and I worried he was about to shift forms again. Apparently we were both on edge among the Searchers. "Are you insane?"

"Shay." Anika spoke calmly, but her tone wasn't unlike a sword sliding out of its scabbard. Smooth and deadly. "You are important here, more than I could possibly convey to you. But I am still in charge, and you will follow my orders."

"I barely know who you are," Shay snarled. "Why would I take any orders from you?"

I swore under my breath. He was about to change. Lydia seemed to sense it too. Her hands shot to the bright hilts at her waist. I snarled. The moment those weapons appeared, I'd shift too. I did a quick scan of the room. We were evenly matched—not good.

"Time-out, kiddo," she said. "Take a breath. Or several."

I knew Shay wouldn't listen to any of them. His wolf instincts were taking over, and they were threatening something he considered his territory . . . me. He was acting like I was his mate. His alpha counterpart. And that meant I was the only one who could intervene. Though my instincts were shrieking for blood, I fought them off. It wasn't worth the risk.

"Shay, wait," I said, grasping his arm. His pulse was racing; I could feel each staccato beat beneath my fingertips matching my own. "It's okay."

"How is it okay?" He was still on the brink of shifting, but at least his focus was on me now.

"Because I want to go," I said. "I need to go."

As I spoke the words, their truth settled deep in my bones. No matter how little I knew about the Searchers, my pack was worth risking everything. I had to go back for them. I needed a fight. I was desperate for one. If that meant I had to fight with the Searchers at my side, I could find a way to make it work. At least I hoped I could.

Shay watched me, uneasy, but he was listening. I was taken aback by how deeply the wolf had marked him. The way he reacted to me was the way one alpha took counsel from another. That partnership made strong, unwavering leaders. If his mind was working on those terms now, I knew how to sway him.

"The pack, Shay," I whispered. "Think of our pack."

My skin prickled at calling the Haldis wolves "our" pack—Shay's and mine instead of Ren's and mine. But it worked.

"Do you really think this could save them?" he asked, and I saw his anger begin to fade.

"It's our only shot." I showed him my sharp canines. He smiled, understanding the signal that this alliance wasn't us giving up. I was negotiating terms that the wolf warriors within both of us needed.

"She's right," Anika said, motioning for Lydia to back off. "We wouldn't take the risk if there was another way. And it's not just Calla we're risking. I'm sending in our people too."

I watched the Arrow, assessing her expression. Her face was set, resolved, her eyes alight with the fire of impending battle. It was true. The Searchers were risking their lives by heading back to Vail. And they were doing it to pull Guardians—my packmates—out of danger. It was the last thing I'd expected. I found it both thrilling and unnerving.

"Damn straight," Lydia said, her own eyes bright as Anika's. "Wouldn't miss it for the world."

Gazing at the two women, I was suddenly relieved that I'd be going into the fight with them, not against them.

"And unless we walk into the best scenario possible, which is unlikely," Anika continued, "the rescue won't happen tonight. This mission's focus will be first contact. We need to go now because it's Saturday."

"Saturday?" Shay repeated.

"The weekend day patrols are made up of Calla's packmates." Anika cast a sidelong glance at me. "Am I right?"

"Yeah." I nodded, though I was more than a little unsettled that she knew it. *How did they find out about our patrol routes?*

"To make this alliance happen, we need to start by gaining the young wolves' trust, with the intention that a wave of revolt would spread through the Guardians from that initial point of contact. Calla's presence will secure that trust, hopefully with a first step today."

I almost smiled but stopped myself. For now I only wanted the Searchers to see me as serious in the face of battle . . . and dangerous.

"It would be some pairing of Mason, Fey, and my brother," I said. "They rotate through Saturday patrols."

"Here's hoping it's Mason and Ansel." Relief flickered over Shay's face. "That's probably the best pair you could hope to meet."

"But . . ." My own flash of joy at the thought of seeing Ansel and Mason wavered. "When I left Ren, he said that my packmates were being held for questioning. Do you think they're back on patrol?"

"Did any of them know about Shay's true identity?" Anika asked. "Or that he was going to be sacrificed at the ceremony?"

"No," I said. "They knew nothing." Guilt wedged its way into my chest, sharp as a knife between the ribs. How much danger had I put them in?

I thought of Bryn, of the last time I'd seen her.

"You ready for this?" Bryn asked. She offered me a bright smile, but I could hear an edge of fear in her voice.

"I'm not sure that's the right question," I said. I glanced at the ring again. This is where I belong. I've always known my path. Now I have to walk it.

"Just know that I'll be right behind you." Bryn took my arm. "None of the pack will let anything bad happen."

"You're not allowed to participate," I said, letting her lead me out, down the steps and into the forest.

"You think they'll be able to stop us if you're in trouble?" She elbowed me, making a smile pull at my lips.

"I love you, Cal." She kissed my cheek and headed for the ring of torches.

My blood was singing. I wanted to shift forms and howl, calling to the pack I'd left behind. *I love you too, Bryn. I'm coming for you.*

"Their ignorance works in our favor," Anika was saying. "Once the Keepers have determined that you and Shay were alone in the plot, they'll most likely try to return things to normal. They'll want to convince the Guardians that nothing is amiss—it would hurt them to suggest that they'd in any way lost control."

I nodded, swallowing the thickness that clogged my throat. "But Ren . . . they'll know he lied." My packmates hadn't known what I'd done or who Shay was. Ren had. Did that mean we'd be too late to save him?

"We don't have a clear picture of what's been happening among the Keepers and Guardians since we hit Rowan Estate," Anika continued. "We're hoping to get a better sense of that before we execute the next phase of the plan. Even if you don't meet the wolves you're hoping to, we'll still benefit from clearing up the confusion that's ensued in the past week. The scouting team will rendezvous with one of our contacts at a drop point tonight."

"You have contacts in Vail?" Shay asked. "You mean spies?"

"We do," Anika said.

"Where?" I asked, racking my brain for how there could be Searchers in Vail that we hadn't identified. It didn't seem possible.

"Right now there are only two," she said. "One in the school and one in the city."

"In the school?" I gasped. "That's impossible!" I ran through the faces and scents of my classmates, teachers, and the staff of the Mountain School. None fit into this scenario.

Anika laughed. "Not so."

"If there were Searchers in the school, I would have known. The Keepers would have known."

"Well, if we were stupid enough to use our own people as spies, we would have lost this war before it started."

The speaker was new, his voice muffled. I turned to see a strange figure in the doorway. His face was obscured by the mismatched stack of books and tightly rolled papers that swayed precariously in his grasp.

"A little help," he said. Adne, giggling, hurried forward and caught the scrolls that slid off the top of his pile.

"Hey, Adne." The new arrival grinned. Now that I could see his face, I was even more confused. He was a young man, no older than Shay. Thick black glasses only made the sharp lines of his face more striking. But his most noticeable feature was the mass of hair atop his head. Swirls of ebony and vivid cobalt battled each other like a roiling sea that formed peaks and waves just above his eyebrows.

He stumbled into the room, propelled forward by the weight of his armload, spilling the mass across the tabletop.

"Thank you for coming on such short notice, Silas," Anika said. "She's just woken up."

"I figured it was something like that." He turned and gave me an assessing look. Not only did he have crazy hair, but he was dressed in torn jeans, combat boots, and a Ramones T-shirt. If I'd been confused about the Searchers before, with his arrival I was utterly stumped.

Connor, followed by a still skittish-looking Monroe, came through the door, took one look at Silas, and turned back around.

"Catch you guys later," he said, waving good-bye.

"Stay," Anika said.

"Aw, man," he moaned. "Really?"

"Connor." She didn't veil the threatening note in her voice.

"I'm staying, I'm staying." But he was staring at Silas like the newly arrived punk look-alike had just crawled out of a Dumpster.

"Nice to see you too." The look Silas was giving Connor wasn't any friendlier.

"Calla, Shay," Anika said, ignoring their game of Let's Burn Holes in Each Other's Skulls with Angry Stares. "This is Silas. The Haldis Scribe."

I stared at his rumpled T-shirt and mad hair. "He's a Searcher too?" He didn't look like one.

Anika twisted her mouth and I thought she was trying not to

laugh. "As a Scribe, Silas can take a bit more liberty with his wardrobe. It's unlikely he'd be involved in a field action."

"What's a Scribe?" Shay asked.

"A paper pusher," Connor muttered.

"This coming from a quasi-illiterate," Silas snarked. "What an insult. How will I recover?"

"Would you two lay off?" Adne said, turning to Shay. "Scribes manage our intelligence and archives."

"That's hardly an adequate—" Silas began, puffing up his chest.

"It's adequate enough," Anika cut him off. "Just say hello, Silas."

"Fine, Miss Manners. Just trying to keep my reputation intact," Silas said, deflated.

Their exchange bewildered me, and not just because Silas was so odd. Anika held the reins of this bunch—that was clear enough. But she didn't seem to mind their constant jibing. Guardians had to submit to their masters. The sorts of comments the Searchers were always throwing around would garner severe punishment. But Silas, Connor . . . all of them treated Anika like she was a friend.

My muddle of thoughts was interrupted by the penetrating way Silas was staring at me. He cocked his head back and forth, as if trying to get the right angle on a strange new specimen that showed up on his lab table. "You're the alpha, huh? Pretty. That's interesting. I thought you'd be all haggish or something. We mostly hear horror stories about Guardians. You know, sin against nature all that."

Sin against nature? What the hell is he talking about? I blinked at him, utterly unable to respond.

Silas's eyes rolled to the side and looked Shay up and down. "Hmmm. And you must be the Scion."

He walked in a slow circle around Shay, pausing to eye the back of his neck, and smiled. "And there's the mark. Hey, hey. Things are looking up after all. Man, I've been waiting a long time hoping to meet you. I had my doubts that we'd get there. Grant says you like

Hobbes. That's fantastic. Too bad about the curse; sounded like your classmates were just about to embark on an interesting discussion when he got hexed. Oh, well."

"Grant?" Shay sputtered. "What the hell are you talking about?"

"Grant Selby," Silas said. "He's one of our agents."

"Wait," I said, blinking at him. "Our teacher? Our philosophy teacher is one of your spies?"

"He is." Silas smiled. "Good cover, huh?"

Anika crossed the room, sorting through the mess of papers Silas had dropped onto the table. "We obviously can't get near the Keepers without being detected. So we've taken to recruiting humans to be our eyes among them. Not many, obviously; we don't want to risk any more lives than we have to. Mostly they are people who stumbled across our world by accident, caught in the crossfire, that sort of thing. The ones who have a genuine interest in the war's outcome usually offer to help. The most able are sent right into it. Spies."

"And you have them teach us?" I asked. It seemed crazy. Dangerous and crazy. Who would sign up for a mission like that? Mr. Selby was either very brave or had a serious death wish.

"That school is the easiest place to track Keeper investments because it offers the juncture of human, Guardian, and Keeper lives," Silas said. "And they employ only human teachers. We've been able to keep at least one and sometimes two agents on its staff for the past few years. They've significantly improved our intelligence operations."

"He always has to bring that up," Connor whispered to Adne in a voice loud enough for all of us to hear. "It's not like he's the only person who's had an original idea in this outfit."

I nodded, ignoring Connor's snide remark, but then frowned. "If Mr. Selby knows about our world, why did he talk about Hobbes in class? Do you know what happened to him?"

Our teacher had discussed *The War of All Against All*—a topic raised by Shay but strictly forbidden by the school's proprietors, the

Keepers—and he'd paid for it. I remembered the way he'd flailed at the front of the classroom, spittle running down his face. Magical torture disguised as a seizure.

Anika grimaced, but Connor started laughing. "Yes, and it happened because he's a sentimental fool. Nearly got himself caught there."

He batted his eyelashes at Shay. "He was just so taken with the fact that the Scion wanted to talk about Hobbes. Thought it was a sign from on high or something."

Shay scowled.

"It probably is," Silas said. "If you'd crack a book, you'd appreciate the connection. But then again, you'd have to learn to read first . . ."

"You knew something like that was bound to happen when we let him recruit an agent." Connor ignored the Scribe, speaking to Anika. "Silas has all the wrong priorities."

"Grant has done exceptional work," Silas sneered.

"That slipup almost blew his cover," Connor said. "It was stupid, and he should have known better."

"Better than that troglodyte you brought on board," Silas said, shuffling through a mound of papers. "I wouldn't set foot in that dunghill he operates. Then again, you probably already have all the diseases you could catch in the Rundown."

"It's Burnout, moron," Connor said. "And it's as good a cover as the school. The wolves are there all the time."

"Burnout?" I gaped. "Tom Shaw is an operative?" I thought of the gruff manager of our favorite dive bar. A place we found refuge from the Keepers' scrutiny—and were never carded. Tom was Nev's friend, the drummer in their band. Was all of that just for show so he could glean information from us when we hung out at the bar?

"He is." Monroe glanced wearily between Connor and Silas.

"Hardly the keen observer that Grant has been for us," Silas sniffed.

"Tom's got better connections." Connor had pulled out his dagger and thumbed the edge of the blade while throwing menacing looks at Silas. "He'll be a linchpin in this alliance. Grant hasn't gotten his hands dirty the way Tom has. That school is a cushy place to cool your heels."

If you aren't being tailed by a succubus. Grant wasn't the only one who'd been punished at the Mountain School. I squirmed at the memory of Nurse Flynn's fingernails digging into my cheeks when she walked in on Ren and me. Then I blushed when I remembered what we'd been doing. I glanced guiltily at Shay, but he wasn't looking at me.

"I like Mr. Selby," Shay protested. "He was a great teacher."

"Of course you like him." Adne threw a stern glance at Connor. "He's a brave man and brilliant to boot. Connor just has no appreciation for intellect."

"You know you don't have to defend Silas just 'cause you're both overachievers," he said. "My point is, intellect won't save your hide at the end of the day."

"That's not necessarily true," Shay countered, looking ready to have a serious debate. But Connor shook his head.

"I call 'em like I see 'em, kid. I'm not going to argue with you."

"You just like free drinks." Silas began scribbling furiously in what looked like some sort of logbook.

"God, you aren't filing another complaint against me, are you?" Connor pointed the dagger at Silas.

"Actions unbecoming, threatening language . . ." Silas didn't look up.

"I'll just ignore it, Silas." Anika folded her arms across her chest. "You submit at least ten of those a week."

"Twenty."

I was getting impatient with all this bickering. "How do you get information from them? How do they avoid detection?" We'd been talking about a fight. Was that ever going to happen? My teeth were sharp in my mouth and I was working hard not to growl every time I spoke.

"We keep two post office boxes in Vail, under aliases of course, but we give them each a key," Anika replied, happy for the opportunity to interrupt. "That's how we communicate. We change the name and box every few months and distribute the new keys. Vail has a lot of ski bums and seasonal workers who move in and out; it keeps interest in the rotating names low."

I nodded, increasingly on edge. The Searchers had been watching us the whole time, and we hadn't even known it. They were unpredictable, but that seemed to make them more effective than I'd first thought. My pride in the effectiveness of Guardian patrols was being eroded with each revelation.

"You'll rendezvous with Grant tonight," Silas said, pulling a crumpled piece of paper out of his jeans pocket. "I just got confirmation."

Anika reached for the note. "Silas, we've talked about keeping correspondence neat."

"I was in a hurry." He shrugged.

"I wouldn't touch that if I were you," Connor said. "You don't know where it's been."

"Shut up, you louse," Silas snapped.

"Louse?" Connor laughed. "How deep did you have to dig for that one?"

"Quiet, both of you." Monroe spoke for the first time since rejoining our group. The calm, forceful demeanor that usually emanated from the Guide had returned. "Anika, my team is set. Can we execute today, like we'd hoped?"

I held my breath, waiting for the response. If she didn't say yes, I'd be damned if I didn't find my own way back to Vail.

"Yes," she replied. "Who's the team?"

I smiled, running my tongue over my sharp teeth. Shay looked at me. I could tell he was worried, but he nodded. He knew as well as I did how much this fight mattered.

"Lydia, Connor, Ethan, and Calla," he said, startling me. As much as I was eager for battle, it felt strange to be counted among the Searchers. Plus there was one name that still left me uneasy.

"Ethan?" I asked, remembering the raging eyes and maniacal screams of the Searcher not half an hour ago.

"He must adjust to this alliance as quickly as possible," Monroe said. "There isn't time to coddle him."

"I agree," Anika said. "Who else?"

"Isaac and Tess will help us stage the mission from the outpost." He paused, glancing at Adne. "Jerome will weave."

Adne sputtered, but Anika spoke first. "No. Jerome has been reassigned to a teaching post. He's an excellent Weaver and he's earned his place in the Academy. Adne is the Haldis Weaver effective immediately."

Adne closed her mouth, looking smug.

"I thought with the nature of this—" Monroe began.

"No discussion," Anika broke in. "Adne weaves. I trust that won't be a problem."

"No," Monroe said, though he folded his arms across his chest, clearly unhappy.

I frowned as I watched the exchange. *What's up with them?* Whatever the source of Monroe and Adne's bickering was, I didn't want it interfering with this mission. Luckily, neither did Anika.

"Good," she said. "There's no time to waste. Ethan's already there?"

"Yep," Connor said. "Should have cooled off by now. Tess works magic with the ravaged soul. Plus I think she gave him cookies."

He winked at Lydia. "That whole Betty Crocker thing is how she snagged you, isn't it?"

"I'm a sucker for oatmeal chocolate chip." Lydia shrugged.

"Maybe Ethan hasn't eaten them all yet." Connor laughed.

"You're about to find out." Anika smiled. "Adne, open a door."

FIVE

"WAIT." SHAY'S HAND WAS gripping my arm,

holding me back even though I hadn't yet started to go anywhere. "You're leaving now?"

"We only have a window of hours before an elder Nightshade patrol is out on the mountain, if indeed the younger wolves are still taking patrol routes—which we are betting on for the time being," Anika said. "Speed is essential if we hope to make contact. We've got the time zone working in our favor, but that's about it."

"Time zone?" I asked. "What do you mean?"

"It's an hour earlier in Vail." Lydia was examining the blade of one of her daggers.

"We're in a different time zone?" I gaped. "Where are we?"

"At the Roving Academy." Adne had come to stand in the center of our small group. "The heart and soul of all things Searcher."

"The Roving Academy?" I asked. I'd never heard of such a place. The information I'd been given about the Searchers made it sound like they squatted in hovels around the globe, trying to muster enough force for guerrilla assaults.

"The Academy is our greatest asset." Anika smiled. "It stores our knowledge and supplies us with food, crafts, and education. Most Searchers live here, except for those on assignment."

"It's called the Roving Academy because it moves out of necessity," Monroe added. "We don't stay in any location for more than six months to avoid detection. If the Keepers ever brought the war to us, it could mean the end of our resistance."

I hadn't seen much of this Academy, but I'd seen enough to know it was huge.

"How can you move a building?"

"Yeah." Shay turned in a slow circle, gazing at the high ceiling of the room. "I've been wondering about that too."

Adne winked at him. "If you're still interested in three months, I'll give you a front-row seat."

"Never mind." I scowled. "Where are we now?"

"Iowa," Anika said.

I frowned. "Why would you put it in Iowa?"

"Exactly." Connor gave me a mockingly solemn nod.

Adne sighed. "It moves all over the world. Now it's in Iowa. Next up is Italy."

A globe was spinning in my mind's eye. How had I gotten here?

"We don't have time for lessons right now." Anika gestured to Adne. "That comes later."

"Good point. Adne, just open the door," Connor said. "I've never been good at anticipation; it makes me blotch."

"That might improve your looks," Silas muttered. He picked up a folded set of papers from the pile. How he'd identified them amid the clutter was a complete mystery.

"Here's the next dispatch for Grant." He sent the stack sailing toward Connor like a Frisbee. "Try not to lose it."

Connor snatched the letter out of the air. "Thanks."

"What's going on?" I looked at Shay, making no sense of the strange conversation.

"Ariadne is a portal weaver," Monroe said. "It's the most important assignment a Searcher can take on."

The most important assignment. I eyed Adne and could have sworn she wasn't any older than Ansel. "She's leading our mission?"

"Not leading," Monroe said. "Just weaving."

"Isn't she a little . . . young?" I had no idea what weaving was, but if it was vital to our mission, I wanted someone with a little experience in charge of it.

"Like I said before." Connor patted Adne on the head. "Our little honey exceeds expectations."

"Just let me work," Adne muttered, jerking away from Connor's hand.

I started toward Adne, wanting to make sure she was actually as exceptional as everyone claimed.

Shay took my arm, pulling me back several steps. "I think it's better seen than explained."

Adne took the slender metal spikes from her belt.

"What are those?" I asked, tensing in case they were weapons after all.

She arched an eyebrow at me, taking in my defensive stance. "Skeans—the Weavers' tools. You'll see what they do."

She drew a breath as she closed her eyes. Then she began to move. The skeans slashed the air; each swift stroke left a blazing trail of light in its wake, and a bell-like note hung around us. Adne's body moved rapidly in a mad dance. She dipped to the floor and flung her limbs toward the ceiling, guiding the skeans in motions that resembled a crazed form of rhythmic gymnastics. The gleaming threads that bloomed from her skeans began to layer upon each other. The sounds that filled the ear created a rippling chorus of chiming notes. Her arms wove through the air as though the skeans were dipping in and out of a giant invisible loom. The intricate pattern of light blazed brighter until I had to pull my eyes away from the glare. Waves of sound poured through the room until I thought I might drown in an ocean of music and light.

All at once it stopped.

"Look," Shay whispered.

I turned back to Adne. She stood, breathless, in front of a giant shimmering rectangle. It hung in the air, a tapestry of light suspended and glowing. My breath caught in my throat as I moved closer. The undulating rectangle held an image: the inside of a warehouse. Stacks of crates filled the dimly lit room.

"Is that where we're going?" I murmured.

Adne nodded, still trying to catch her breath.

"Nice weaving." Connor patted her on the shoulder.

"No problem." She smiled, wiping sweat from her brow.

"So what do we do now?" I stared at the gleaming scene.

"It's a door," Adne said. "You walk through it."

I eyed the tall portal of light. "Does it hurt?"

"It kind of tickles," Connor said, mocking solemnity.

Adne whacked him with the flat side of one of her skeans.

"Ouch!" Connor rubbed his arm.

"It's fine, Cal," Shay said. "This is how I got to the Academy. I know it looks crazy, but it's safe."

"Crazy?" Adne protested.

"Crazy beautiful." Connor grinned at her. "I'll go first."

"Please," I said, not wanting to admit how much the shimmering doorway made all my hairs stand on end.

Connor strode confidently into the light-filled image. His body blurred for a moment and then there he was, standing among the crates. He paused, stretching his arms and yawning, and then suddenly dropped his pants and mooned us.

"Oh God, Connor!" Adne groaned. "Get through there and bite him, Shay."

"I'm not coming, remember?" Shay objected, but he laughed. "Even if I was, I wouldn't bite his ass."

"Maybe Calla will." Adne grinned.

"Not likely," I muttered, though on a second glance I had to admit that Connor's ass wasn't that bad to look at.

"Enough," Anika said, briefly embracing Lydia. "Be well."

"Of course," Lydia said, rushing into the portal in time to smack Connor's bare skin with the flat of her dagger before he could stumble out of the way.

Adne burst into laughter.

"Go ahead, Calla," Monroe said. "Adne will be right behind you."

"Wait." Shay held on to me. "What are we doing while they're gone? Just sitting on our hands until it's over?"

"No." Monroe came to his side, gently drawing him away from me. "We have a task of our own to accomplish."

"We do?" Shay's brow furrowed.

"We're dropping in on some of the Academy instructors," he said. "And you're going to convince them that it will be just fine when they have a pack of young wolves joining their classes."

So that's what an alliance meant. We wouldn't just be fighting with them. We'd be training with them, learning about their world. As much as that idea was strange, it was also exciting.

Adne began to tap her foot. "Come on, Lily. We try to open and close the doors quickly. This isn't window shopping."

The nickname jarred me enough to flash fangs at her. It was more than a little satisfying when she took a step back.

I glanced at Shay, who offered me a thin smile. "Good luck."

Returning the smile as best I could, I closed my eyes and stepped into the gleaming haze.

Connor wasn't completely wrong about the sensations that flowed over me once I touched the door of light, though moving through the portal didn't exactly tickle. For a moment my skin tingled, like I was caught in a space full of static electricity. In the next moment, stale musty air filled my lungs and Connor was laughing. Fortunately his pants were on again.

"You with us, Calla?" Lydia asked. "Trip's over. This is where you get off."

Connor coughed. "I could help you with that."

I shook off my bewilderment, glaring at him.

"Do you ever get tired of hearing your own jokes?" Lydia shoved him toward the door.

"Do you really need to ask?" He grinned, batting his eyelashes at her.

She tried to give him a stern look, but laughter bubbled up from her throat. "You're a disaster, boy, but I love you for it."

"Of course you do."

"Stop preening, Connor." Adne had emerged from the portal. I turned around. I could still see the flickering image of the room we'd left in the tall rectangle behind her. "Everyone's first time through a portal is intimidating."

"Not a bad way to travel, though," Connor said, rubbing his arms as if they were still tingling. "Is it, wolf girl?"

"No, it's not." My eyes fixed on the shimmering doorway. "But—"

"But what?" Adne's hands were on her hips. "You don't approve of my weaving?"

"It's not that," I said, still examining the portal. "But don't they make you nervous?"

Adne sighed, slashing her skeans across the portal in a giant *X*. The door vanished. "Look, Lily. This whole exercise was to show you that it's perfectly safe. I don't know what more I can do other than let you walk back and forth through the door all night."

"That isn't what I meant," I said. "Aren't you worried the Keepers will just open one of these to find you? It's perfect for a surprise attack. I mean, that's what we're using it for, aren't we?"

"Oh." Adne nodded. "I see."

"See what?" I asked. "You should be worried. That's a pretty big flaw."

"Yes, it would be," Adne continued, smiling wickedly. "If that were a problem, but it's not."

"Why not?" I was irritated by the smug expression on her face.

"Because our Weavers are so special," Connor said, sliding his arms around Adne's waist and kissing her on the cheek before she whirled around and shoved him away.

"You are such a jerk," she said, but she couldn't hide her laughter.

"I was trying to give you a compliment," Connor said, feigning an injured expression and not quite dodging quickly enough when she grabbed for him.

"Would someone please tell me why this isn't a problem?" I asked, put off by their easy banter when I was still so tense.

"Keepers can't create portals," Adne said simply, slipping out of her impromptu wrestling match with Connor to face me again.

"Why not?" I asked, frowning.

"It's one of the few benefits we have for not breaking the natural magic rules like they do," she said.

"I'm still not following," I said.

"Remember that whole sin against nature issue Silas brought up earlier?" Connor grinned at me.

"I do, not that it made any sense." I folded my arms across my chest. "And I'm surprised you're bringing it up now."

He held his hands up in surrender. "Only out of necessity. I think you're gorgeous, wolfie—no mutant features in sight as far as I can tell. Then again, you do have all your clothes on."

"Shut it, Connor." Lydia groaned.

"Yes, ma'am. Okay—so the Keepers broke some big rules on the way to all that power they have, creating Guardians included," Connor said, pushing his hands through his messy chestnut hair. "The truth of it is portals work on natural principles. And if you go around offending the earth all the time, like the Keepers do, you can't ask it for favors."

"Huh?" I couldn't make sense of what he'd just said.

"Everything in this world is connected—including all the places on the globe," Adne said. "Weavers use Old Magic to pull together the threads of that connection, linking one site to another. That's how we travel."

"But the Keepers—" I began.

"Can't pull the threads to begin with," Connor finished for me. "They have to travel the old-fashioned way. Or the new technology way, I guess. But no portals. They cannot weave. The earth won't allow it."

I still wasn't sure I understood, but our conversation was interrupted by the door on the other side of the room swinging open. Dropping to the ground, I shifted, ready to attack the man who had a crossbow aimed at us. Connor stepped in front of me before I could strike.

"Isaac, put that down! What did we ever do to you?"

The man with the crossbow grunted. "Oh, good. We were wondering when you'd get here. Why did you open a door in the storage room?"

"Because if it were Ethan with that crossbow, he'd have already shot her." Adne pointed to me. "I was being cautious."

"Not a bad idea," Isaac said. "Though all he could do right now is spew cookies at the wolf. He's been stuffing his face ever since he got here."

"Calla, you should try not to shift so much here," Lydia said, moving to embrace Isaac. "Where's my best girl?"

I shifted back into human form, swallowing a retort that hovered on my tongue. What did they expect? I didn't have a very good history with Searchers and crossbows.

"She's in the kitchen with Ethan," Isaac replied.

"How is Ethan?" Adne asked. "Aside from being filled with cookies."

Isaac looked at me. "He's coming around."

"That'll do," Connor said, taking my hand and pulling me to the door. "Isaac, meet Calla. She's the alpha who'll be leading our fabulous new Guardian revolt."

I'm doing what? The ramifications of this new plan came crashing down onto me like a rock slide.

"Is that all?" Isaac grinned. "Nice to meet you, rabble-rouser."

I shook his hand, giving Connor an unfriendly sidelong glance.

He slapped me on the shoulder. "Just making sure your reputation precedes you."

"Thanks."

We followed Isaac, whose wealth of long, minuscule braids swung from a ponytail at the nape of his neck as he sauntered into a large room that was empty except for the mats on the floor and weapons hanging from the walls.

Seeing my eyes wander, Lydia smiled at me. "Training room."

Isaac led us through another door, where we were greeted by a roaring fire, the smell of fresh coffee, and two faces. One smiling, the other scowling.

"Hey, beautiful." Lydia opened her arms to a woman who looked about the same age—thirty-five give or take a couple of years—and whose chin-length crop of springing curls was reminiscent of Bryn's, except for their blue-black hue.

"It's my lucky day," the woman said, kissing her.

"Can it be my lucky day too?" Connor asked, eyeing the lip-locked pair.

"Don't hit on my girlfriend, Connor." Lydia laughed, pulling the other woman into a fierce hug.

"I wasn't hitting on her," Connor objected. "I gave her a compliment. You think I'd poach your territory? You forget that I patrol with you. I don't want to be at the wrong end of your daggers."

"Smart man," Lydia said, then turned the other woman to face me. "Tess, this is Calla. She's the slumbering wolf we've been hoping would stir."

"And stir she has." Tess came to me immediately, offering both her hands. "It's an honor to meet you."

Again that word . . . honor. It threw me.

"Thanks." I took both her hands; they were soft and warm. When she smiled, it lit up her pale blue eyes, full of sincere kindness. I liked her instantly.

"Do we have time for a cup of coffee?" Isaac asked, holding up a pot. "Or are we jumping straight to blood and guts?"

I stared at him, startled by the questions that pitted coffee against gore.

"You won't be jumping anywhere," Lydia said, pulling Tess back into an embrace. "Reapers are to hold down the fort. Just Strikers and the wolf out on this run."

"And me," Adne said.

"I heard you're the new Weaver, Ariadne." Isaac was pouring himself a cup of coffee. "Welcome aboard."

"Adne," she replied. "It's just Adne."

"Still rebelling against your father, Ariadne?" Tess asked as she leaned against Lydia. "We've talked about that."

"You've talked about that," Adne said, pushing past them to grab a seat at the kitchen table next to Ethan, who was staring at his coffee and a plate full of cookie crumbs. "And would you two get a room? You know not everyone here has stumbled across true love and yet you two rub our noses in it every chance you get."

"Watch it," Lydia said. "We don't get that many chances and you know it. We're lucky to share an hour in the same time zone on most days."

"Besides, you're sixteen, Ariadne." Tess fixed her with a stern gaze. "You haven't had time to stumble across love yet."

"Sure she has." Connor slid into the chair on the other side of Adne, throwing his arm around her shoulders. "She just doesn't appreciate it yet."

Adne groaned and dropped her forehead onto the table. "I'll marry the first person who gets me a cup of coffee, I don't care who it is."

"Throw me a mug, Isaac!" Connor half rose.

"Oh, please," Adne mumbled onto the tabletop.

"Are you kidding?" Connor said. "A cup of coffee instead of a ring? That's the kind of proposal I'm ready for."

I traced the cool metal band circling my finger. When I caught Adne watching me, I hid my hands under the table.

"And all you can afford," Isaac added.

"Well, that too." Connor laughed.

"I still don't have any coffee," Adne said. "Even with my generous offer."

"Don't give up that easily, sweetheart." Isaac smiled, bringing Adne a steaming mug. "Coffee, Calla?"

"Uh, I—" I hesitated, still not understanding this bizarre chatter in the face of impending battle. "Shouldn't we focus on the attack? Anika said we only have a brief window for this to work."

The room went silent. I held my breath, clearly having said the wrong thing.

Tess took pity on me. "Sweetie, there's always time for a cup of coffee." She took my arm, settling me in the chair next to Connor.

"Time for anything good when you're staring death in the face," Connor added.

"Amen," Ethan muttered from the corner.

I gazed at their thin, bleak smiles and my confusion evaporated. I thought about their lives. About what they had to face. Keepers. Guardians. Wraiths. The stuff of nightmares.

Survival. That's what this was about. The Searchers were warriors, like Guardians. They looked at every fight like it could be their last. All of this—from oddly timed coffee to Connor's inappropriate jokes—fortified their defenses. Only this wasn't body armor. It was a mental bulwark. A way to save their spirits from despair.

As strange as it was, I could get on board with this strategy. Especially if it involved coffee, though I wondered if the crankiness of not getting any might give me the winning edge in a fight.

"What is this place?" I asked, trying to piece together the storage area, the training room, and now the kitchen.

"We have outposts adjacent to the major Keeper settlements across the globe. They have two main purposes: to keep us connected to our contacts in the human world and to use as staging areas for strikes against Keeper targets."

"It's home sweet Purgatory." Isaac sighed.

"It may be Purgatory." Lydia laughed. "But the coffee is damn good."

"Purgatory?" I frowned, then smiled when Isaac handed me a mug full of swirling liquid, black as tar.

"You know, it's the place you get stuck between heaven and hell," Connor said. "Heaven being the Academy and hell . . ."

"Is Vail." Ethan pushed his chair back and went to the far side of the room, apparently no longer able to tolerate my presence.

Tess shook her head at him, but he ignored her, drinking his coffee in solitary silence.

I decided that giving Ethan a wide berth was probably my best bet. Whether he trusted or liked me didn't matter. I hadn't come here to make friends. I was here to save my pack.

I turned back to Connor. "So where are we exactly?"

When I asked the question, I had to hide my own shudder; if we were close to the Keepers, how safe could we be?

Lydia answered as she and Tess joined us at the table. "We're in a warehouse in Denver. Weavers open doors from here to our strike sites. Strikers come and go according to their assignments."

"And we Reapers sojourn alone," Isaac said, looking mournful.

Tess clucked her tongue. "Are you saying I'm not good company?"

"Not if it means you'll stop cooking for me." Isaac flashed a grin at her.

"He's got you cooking for him now?" Lydia asked. "You're much too nice."

"Don't ruin my arrangement, woman!" Isaac protested. "Plus I do the dishes."

"He does," Tess said.

I took a sip of my coffee, trying to keep up. "What are Reapers?"

"There aren't many Searchers left in the world." Lydia's voice had a hard edge. "Most stay at the Academy teaching or training; they only head out for missions on an as-needed basis. But those who are still fighting the good fight day-to-day live in outposts like this one. Our teams always have the same distribution of members: groups of ten, specific assignments for each member. The Reapers gather supplies and run valuable goods through the black market, maintaining our cash flow in contemporary world currencies."

"Black market?" I frowned, a little nervous.

"Don't worry, Calla, we don't deal in nasties, like human organs."

Tess giggled, shaking her head. When I laughed uneasily, she hurried on. "It's mostly art and antiquities. Stuff we know how to find that other people wouldn't have access to."

"She's trying to tell you that Reapers are smugglers," Connor said. "But nice ones."

"Connor, you know we trained long and hard for this work," Isaac said.

"Longer than you," Tess added.

"How long?" I asked.

"Standard training for Searchers is two years of general skills and another year of specialization for assignment," she said. "Reapers do an additional two years."

"To learn how to smuggle?"

"Look what you've done now, Connor." Tess shook her head. "No, that's not how it works. Reapers know art history, language, and classics backwards and forwards. That's in addition to their combat training. Reaper work is almost more dangerous than the Strikers' duties."

I cleared my throat nervously. "And the Strikers are?"

"The Strikers are your counterparts," Lydia said. "They're trained to be the first line of offense against the Keepers. They execute hits against designated enemy targets. But that mostly means they kill Guardians."

"Great," I said, feeling my canines sharpen at her words. "And Weavers open doors. And Monroe, he's your—"

I tried to remember what they'd called him.

"Guide," Tess offered. "He's our Guide."

Ethan came forward, slamming his empty cup on the table. "Now that preschool is over, can we get moving? Anika had a point. We only have a few hours of daylight left."

"Ethan!" Tess was on her feet.

"Easy, girl." Connor stood up too. "He's right. We need to head out."

Lydia looked at me. "I'm sure you still have lots of questions. I'm sorry we can't answer them all right now."

"Don't worry about it." I rose from my chair, muscles humming. The caffeine buzz and the thought of getting into the forest had me itching to run.

It was time for this alpha to find her pack.

SIX

THE DOOR ADNE OPENED this time revealed a landscape I'd known my whole life. The snow-covered slope sparkled under the afternoon sun, cut at intervals by the shadows of towering pines.

"That's the eastern face," I murmured. The need to run, to track my packmates and bring them to safety was overwhelming. I ground my teeth as I fought for control.

"Yes," Adne said. "Will this work? We have the rendezvous point set nearby. Grant's on a snowshoeing trail about a half mile away; it's in the park reserve that runs up against the edge of your patrol routes, but he shouldn't draw the wolves' attack . . . hopefully."

"I hate winter," Ethan grumbled, lacing up his boots.

"I can't wait to make a snow angel," Connor replied as he strapped on a pair of snowshoes.

"Sometimes I really don't like you," Ethan said, reaching for gloves, but I could tell he was trying not to smile.

Lydia laughed and continued to put on her own winter gear. "Calla, Ethan and I are going with you to track down your packmates. Connor is heading in the other direction to meet up with Grant."

I nodded, though I silently wished it were Connor coming with us rather than Ethan. It didn't help that Lydia took point as we headed into the portal with Ethan bringing up the rear. I worried that having my open back in range of his crossbow might prove a little too tempting.

"I'll be waiting," Adne said, closing the door. She leaned against the tree. "Don't take too long. I think even my twenty layers might not hold up at this elevation. It's freezing."

Her comment pulled me back from thoughts of running wild through the snowdrifts. "Why don't you just wait inside?"

The Searchers stared at me. I stared back, not understanding why they were frowning. When a door was open, you could see the other side of a portal. It was blurry, but not that blurry.

Ethan grumbled something under his breath. Adne glanced at him before offering me a quick smile.

"Sorry," she said. "We forget you don't know all the rules. Portals are never left open."

"Never." Ethan stamped the snow. "And Weavers never join an actual strike—they stay at the outer edge of any mission zone."

Adne scowled, but Connor shook his head. "You know why it's necessary, peaches."

"Shut up."

Lydia placed her hand on Adne's shoulder. "Weavers are the most powerful and valuable instruments among the Searchers. We try to keep their risk minimal."

"But that's my point," I said, frustrated by how much I still didn't know about my supposed allies. "If she's on the other side, she can just close the portal at the first sign of danger."

"No matter how careful a Weaver is, we still make mistakes." Adne's eyes were like knives. "Something could get through."

"I thought you said Keepers can't do portals," I said.

"Keepers can't create portals," Adne said. "They can still go through them. So can their beasties. Guardians, wraiths, whatever."

"And if the Keepers ever got their hands on a Weaver," Lydia said, "if they forced a captive to open doors, we'd never see them coming. That's why portals stay closed and Weavers can't be Strikers. They work outside the danger zone . . . as much outside it as we can manage, at least."

Adne looked like she'd bitten into a lemon.

"That's why if anything comes that isn't us, you get back to Purgatory," Connor said to her.

"I know the protocol," she said. "Graduated, remember?"

"How could I forget?" Connor smiled, blowing her a kiss before tramping off through the snow.

"Okay, Calla," Lydia said. "You're obviously the best tracker. Lead the way."

I grinned, shifting forms and bounding through the snow. The crisp winter air poured into my nostrils. I longed to howl. A rabbit dashed from beneath scrub brush and my mouth began to water.

"Calla!" Lydia shouted.

I skidded to a halt, snow rising around me like a veil of white mist. *Oops.*

The thrill of running on the mountain had made me forget I wasn't with other wolves. Humans were slow. I wheeled and ran back to Lydia and Ethan, shifting forms when I reached them.

"Sorry."

"You can scout ahead, but don't lose us," Lydia said.

Ethan adjusted the crossbow on his back. "If we think you've gone too far, I'll shoot you in the tail."

Lydia glared at him.

"Kidding, I was kidding," he replied, but the grin he flashed me wasn't friendly.

Back in wolf form, I managed to range ahead of the Searchers but kept them in my sight. The fresh snowfall wasn't helping us. It smothered scents, muting new traces, erasing older scents.

The door Adne had opened was southwest of Haldis Cavern. I

headed toward the perimeter that I would have expected Guardian patrols to be running at this point in the afternoon. Adjusting to my new allies wasn't easy. Our inability to communicate was tedious at best, terribly frustrating at worst. Whenever I wanted to speak to them, I had to run back, change form, and then head out again. It only made me more desperate to get my packmates back. I tried to remember what it was like making this trek with Shay when he'd still been human. I'd been patient with his climb, and the Searchers were proving more than able to move quickly over the snowy terrain. Though it wasn't an ideal partnership, I knew it could work. I kept that thought in focus as I plunged through snowdrifts.

Pawing through snowdrifts to reach frozen earth, lifting my muzzle to test the air, I did everything I could to locate evidence of my packmates' trail. But I couldn't find anything. No tracks, no scents. Nothing. *Where are they?*

My hope was dropping as low as the sun on the horizon when Lydia called to me again.

"Anything?" She was looking at the looming shadows that spread like spills of ink along the snow.

"No," I said, kicking the snow. "This stuff is burying the scents. I haven't picked up any trails other than game."

"Wouldn't your packmates have broken fresh trail up here during their patrol?" Ethan asked.

I frowned. He'd pinpointed the very thing that had nagged me as we'd progressed over the perimeter. Even if the route had changed, I should have seen some sign of Guardians crossing this part of the mountain. We were too close to Haldis Cavern for the patrols to miss it completely. Except . . . except . . . we'd stolen the object hidden in the cave and the Keepers knew it. Our school had reeked of their fear, their tension after Shay had found the strange cylinder, claiming it for his own. Haldis no longer needed protection. There would be no more patrols. And the only reason wolves would be ranging the sacred perimeter was to wait for . . .

"Oh no," I said, smacking my gloved palm against my forehead. My blood felt icy.

"What?" Lydia asked.

I didn't want to tell them. I felt like such an idiot. How could I have forgotten something so important? My cheeks burned because I knew why. I'd been so caught up in the possibility of finding Mason or Ansel, even a grumpy Fey, of reuniting with my pack that I'd fallen into the expectations I'd always had as an alpha. This was where we ran patrols. This site had been the focus of my whole life. It hadn't even occurred to me to consider other options.

But why hadn't Shay said anything when we were making this plan? He knew Haldis was missing. He had it in his possession.

"Calla." Lydia spoke again. "What is it?"

As I grasped for an explanation and an apology, something caught my eye. It was a figure about one hundred yards away, coming at us fast.

"Heads up," Ethan said, aiming his crossbow.

"Wait." Lydia put her hand on his arm. The figure was on two legs and it was looking at us, waving its arms frantically. "It's Connor."

He was moving impressively fast for someone in snowshoes—the Searchers must have trained rigorously for winter combat.

"Come on," Ethan said, heading in Connor's direction.

When we reached him, he bent over, resting his hands on his thighs, gasping for breath.

"He's dead," Connor said between gasps. "Grant's dead. His throat was torn out."

Having been raised to create violence, I'd never thought death would unnerve me. But the image of awkward and kind Mr. Selby, lying in a pool of blood and mangled flesh, made me shudder.

"Damn." Ethan bowed his head.

Lydia closed her eyes. "That's a shame. And it means we need to get out of here. If the wolves are still hunting, they won't have any trouble tracking us . . . or sniffing out Adne."

Connor nodded but looked at me. "Did you find your packmates?"

"No," I said, still thrown by the news of Mr. Selby's sudden demise. "And I just realized that—"

The howl swallowed my words. The second and third howls raised the hair on the back of my neck.

"That's not my pack," I whispered.

"They know we're here," Ethan said. "Let's move."

"Stay close," Lydia said to me, taking up the lead once more.

We started back, but Lydia took us on a zigzagging path unlike the straight line we'd traversed on our way out. She broke new trail, heading in Adne's direction while avoiding the path we'd created on our trek out. In wolf form I doubled back, retracing our steps, constantly testing the air, listening for any sign of the wolves that had howled, trying to discern whether they were tracking us. But the approach of dusk brought an unsettling silence with it, and I remembered how snow swallowed sound as well as scent. A gust of wind lifted the top layer of snow, washing our faces in icy crystals, blowing in the direction the howls had come from.

Not good. We were upwind of the Guardians. They'd be able to smell us, but I wouldn't catch their scent until they were almost on us.

The howls rose again, much closer.

"I don't think we're getting out of here without a fight," Ethan said.

"Just keep running." Lydia's breath came out in white puffs.

We were closing in on the place we'd left Adne when a shadow dropped down from a tree branch above us.

Lydia wheeled, dagger in her hand.

"It's me!" Adne held up her arms.

"What were you doing up in a tree?" Ethan asked, peering into the branches.

"Hiding." Adne brushed snow off her legs. "I heard the howls and thought I'd better play it safe."

"Good call," Connor said, clearly relieved to see her unharmed.

"What happened?" she asked.

"They killed Grant," Connor said.

Adne paled. "Oh no."

My ears flicked up, drawn to new sounds in the woods behind us. The scrape of paws on ice. I didn't want to change forms, so I barked at the Searchers. It was enough.

Ethan readied his crossbow. "Adne, open a door."

I stalked forward, scanning the forest. A flicker of movement appeared. A russet wolf slipped between the trees. My heart leapt. It was a Nightshade. Sasha—Fey's mother and one of my mother's patrol mates. I dashed toward her.

"Calla, no!" Lydia called, but I kept running.

I barked again, this time calling to Sasha. Her form flashed between two tree trunks and I sent a thought chasing after her.

Sasha! Sasha, wait!

The red wolf wheeled, heading toward me. She was running at full speed, not slowing at all as she drew closer, snarling.

Welcome home, Calla.

My mind reeled as her body crashed into mine and we rolled through the snow. I twisted away, jumping to the side as her jaws snapped at my shoulder.

Stop! What are you doing?

She didn't answer but lunged at me again, her eyes filled with bloodlust.

My instincts kicked in and I struck back, snarling. My teeth sank into her chest, but the taste of pack blood in my mouth shook me to the core. Nothing about this fight felt natural. I was attacking one of my own, the mother of my packmate. It went against everything I'd ever known.

I tried to reach her again.

Please, Sasha. I'm here to help you.

I barely escaped her next strike.

Foolish girl.

The cold truth settled under my fur. Sasha was trying to kill me and if I wanted to survive, I would have to kill her. I was desperate to find another way out of this disaster.

This time when Sasha lunged, I rolled to the side, pivoting in the snow and clamping my jaws onto her hamstring. She squealed when my teeth cut through her tendons. I tore at the muscle and she yelped again, twisting and snapping futilely at me. Satisfied that she wouldn't be able to give chase, I released her leg and dashed back toward the Searchers. I could see the shimmering portal through the trees. But I heard the shouts of battle as well. I pushed harder, picking up speed.

"Calla!" Adne waved. I made a beeline for her. She was only ten feet away when something hard and heavy slammed into me. I rolled over and over, breath forced out of my lungs. On unsteady limbs I struggled to my feet and turned to face my attacker.

The huge wolf's fur was mottled gray and brown. He stared at me, snarling.

I thought my heart had stopped as my eyes locked with those of Emile Laroche.

The Bane alpha had been hunting us.

Fear paralyzed me as events crystallized in my mind. Sasha had been hunting with Emile. With Emile. It didn't make any sense. Sasha was my mother's hunting partner. She was a Nightshade. Nightshade wolves answered only to their own alphas, my parents: Stephen and Naomi Tor. Nightshades and Banes despised each other and avoided contact as much as they could. The packs had only ever cooperated by direct order from the Keepers.

But now Emile Laroche, the Bane alpha, was leading Nightshades. I bristled, snarling at him even as I fought my own disbelief. Everything about the reality laid stark before my eyes was wrong, unnatural. Why would Sasha follow Emile? Why had she attacked me? Where were my mother and father? Where was my pack?

Spittle dripped from the Bane's jaws as he stalked forward.

Come to beg forgiveness?

My limbs were shaking.

His muscles rippled when he shook his ruff.

I think you may find it's too late.

I growled. If Emile wanted a fight, I'd give him one, even though the idea felt hopeless—Emile had made his reputation among Guardians as a killer. He was an immense, powerful beast and had many more years of fighting at his back than I did.

I'm not sorry for anything.

I braced myself against the ground, waiting for his lunge. Even if I couldn't beat Emile, I could still make him hurt. A lot.

He crouched down, his growl almost like a throaty laugh. *That's exactly what your father said.*

My father?

I was still feeling the shock of his words when he yelped, twisting his head to wrench the dagger from his side. He rolled along the snow, leaving a trail of crimson in his wake as a second dagger sailed past him.

"Calla! Get to Adne!" Lydia shouted. She was running at Emile with two more daggers in her hands.

I scrambled up, dashing toward the portal.

"Go! Go!" Connor screamed even as he tackled another elder Bane, a few feet from our escape route. Guardian and Searcher tumbled through the snow, leaving a cloud of sparkling white dust in their wake. I caught the flashes of Connor's dagger in the sunlight with each slash at the wolf. The Bane's fangs snapped, searching for flesh but missing as Connor twisted and writhed, keeping himself beyond the reach of its jaws. As I ran past him, he parried the Guardian's gnashing teeth with the flat edge of one blade, deftly running it through with another. He kicked the wolf's limp body off his sword and followed on my heels.

Out of the corner of my eye I saw Ethan covering Lydia's attack with a suppressing fire of bolts from where he stood alongside the portal. I shifted forms, gasping for breath but needing to ask what came next.

"Come on!" An arm reached through the glimmering doorway and Adne jerked me into the warmth of Purgatory's training room while Connor shoved me forward, both of us tumbling out of the snowy forest.

"Lydia, we're clear!" Ethan shouted. "Get back here!" He had taken two steps toward her when four more wolves emerged from the forest, tearing toward the Bane alpha.

"Lydia!" Ethan shrieked, firing off more bolts.

She took her eyes off Emile and saw the approaching Guardians. Hurling two more daggers at the new assailants, she managed to take one down, slow another. But as she whirled and tore through the snow toward the portal, Emile sprang at her, sailing through the air.

The full force of his leap brought her down, flattening her against the snow. The three remaining wolves reached him as his jaws locked around her neck.

"No!" Connor shouted, pushing past me toward the other side

of the door. But Ethan was there, blocking his path. Ethan shook his head, then looked at Adne.

Connor swore but didn't argue.

"She's gone, Adne," Ethan said, not turning to see Emile tearing Lydia's body apart. "Close the door."

SEVEN

TESS LAY IN A CRUMPLED heap on the floor

while Connor spoke softly to her.

"We'd better take her with us," Ethan said to Isaac. "They can send another Reaper out for the time being. I'll keep working point until Anika's sorted this out."

Isaac nodded.

As Adne wove a door to the Academy, I sat at the table, trying to make sense of what had just happened. Lydia was dead. I'd barely known her, but the way she'd died haunted me. Nausea rolled through my gut, making me shudder. I buried my face in my hands.

I couldn't shake the thought that I'd brought this grief down on my new allies. Tess was sobbing, and each cry was like a razor slicing my skin. I'd run to Sasha. I'd assumed any Nightshade would be an ally. I couldn't have been more wrong. My poor judgment had cost Lydia's life.

Someone touched my shoulder. I lifted my head to see Adne gazing at me.

"Door's open," she said.

I followed her to the shining portal. Tess cried into Isaac's shoulder when he hugged her, murmuring good-byes, before Connor put his arm around her waist and led her through Adne's door.

When I passed Ethan on my way to the door, I reached out,

grabbing the sleeve of his coat. I might have been wiser to pick someone else, but words wanted to climb out of my throat.

"I'm sorry," I whispered.

He shook my hand off, but his gaze was more sad than angry.
"Don't be. This is who we are."

I could see that truth at work. With the exception of Tess, the
Searchers shouldered their grief and moved on in a way that was
brutal and beautiful.

"Send an update when you can," Ethan said.

"We will," Adne said, and gestured for me to pass her.

Anika was waiting for us. The Arrow's eyes were fixed on Tess,
who was struggling against her tears.

"Lydia?" Anika asked. Tess broke down again and Anika bowed
her head.

"And our operative," Connor added.

"Tess, you should retire to your quarters in the Haldis wing,"
Anika said.

Tess nodded. When she was gone, Anika approached Connor.
"What happened?"

"Can't be sure." Connor rubbed the back of his neck. "When I
reached the drop point, Grant was dead. He'd bled out at least an
hour before. His body was already frozen."

Anika frowned, turning her eyes on me. "And the pack?"

I shook my head, wondering if I should tell them about Haldis
and my theory that the patrol routes had been shifted. About the
horrible miscalculation I'd somehow overlooked. In light of what had
just happened, I decided against it.

"The wolves we encountered attacked us without hesitation,"
Connor said.

Working past the dryness in my throat, I said, "Something's
changed."

"What?" Connor looked at me sharply.

"One of the wolves that attacked us was a Nightshade," I continued. "Not one of my own pack, but an elder. And she was being led by the Banes."

"Are you sure?" Anika's eyes had narrowed.

"I am," I said, forcing my own voice to remain steady. "The wolf that killed Lydia was Emile Laroche."

"What did you just say?" Monroe was standing in the doorway, Shay at his side.

Adne was already crossing the room. She put her head on Monroe's chest.

"We lost Lydia," Connor said, watching as Monroe put his arms around his daughter. It was the first time I'd seen them behave like parent and child.

"And it was Emile?" Monroe asked, running his hand over Adne's hair. "The Bane alpha?"

"Yes," I said.

The group of Searchers near Anika had closed in around her in a tight circle, hurried words in low tones passing between them.

Shay started toward me and I walked to meet him. I didn't hesitate when he stretched his arms out. My head was spinning. Things had happened in Vail. Things I couldn't understand. I leaned into him, letting his scent pour over me, steadying me.

"Are you okay?" he whispered.

"I'm not hurt." I kept my voice low. "But things happened."

His arms tightened around me. "What things?"

"Not here," I murmured.

He kissed the crown of my hair.

Monroe looked at us, face grim. "We'll need to discuss this with Silas."

Anika nodded. "He should be in his study."

Adne had already pulled out of her father's embrace, wiping away tear tracks from her cheeks. "I'll come with you."

"You should get some rest."

"No." Any vulnerability had vanished, replaced by her usual rebellious expression.

"Then I'll come too," Connor said. He was watching Adne. I saw questions flickering through his eyes, anxious.

I wondered why he was being so protective. Adne struck me as nothing less than ferocious, and she was holding up remarkably well considering . . . *oh*. Connor's scrutiny suddenly made sense.

That had been Adne's first mission as the new Weaver, her first time out with the Haldis team, and they'd lost two people. Was she really taking it in stride like the other Searchers, or was it just for show until she was alone?

"This way," Monroe said, though he frowned at Adne before leading us from the room.

Rather than turning down the hall, he pushed through the glass doors. The air in the courtyard was frigid, but Monroe didn't show any reaction as he strode on the walkway. I glanced down at the barren earth. I could see twisting paths and empty fountains far below us. No one spoke as we walked. Our breath filled the air with tiny white clouds. The courtyard was massive. We'd walked half a mile by the time Monroe opened the doors on the opposite side of the Academy.

While the architecture of the hallway we entered mirrored that of the Haldis wing, its design was startlingly different. Haldis—from the walls to the dark woods of the tactical room—was filled with warm, rich ochres, crimsons, mahoganies.

The space we'd entered glittered as though it had been carved of ice. Frosty blue, lavender, silver, and gleaming white washed over the walls. The colors swirled and rippled, accompanied by a quiet rustling like the softness of a steady breeze.

"Where are we?" I asked. The constant shifting of colors on the walls made it seem like the building around us was moving.

"This is the Tordis wing." Monroe glanced over his shoulder. I realized he was still walking and I'd fallen behind the group. As stunning as this space was, the Searchers—and even Shay—must have seen it before. They didn't seem to notice its beauty, or if they did, they weren't moved enough to comment.

"How many wings are there?"

"Four," Monroe said as I caught up to him. "Haldis, Tordis, Pyralis, Eydis."

"Earth, air, fire, and water," Adne murmured.

"The four elements." Shay was sneaking glances at the walls as well. Maybe he hadn't seen it before. "Tordis is air."

Monroe nodded. "Each element has specific characteristics. We need the qualities of all four to survive, but each Searcher specializes when they enter the Academy."

"What's Haldis?"

"The earth makes warriors," Connor said, pinching Adne's cheek. "We're grittier."

"You wish." Adne punched his arm. "Besides, Pyralis makes Strikers too. Haldis is known for its Reapers ... and Guides."

She glanced at Monroe, who inclined his head slightly.

"What about you?" I asked her. "You aren't trained by Haldis? But you work with them?"

"Like I said." Monroe stopped in front of a narrow, intricately carved pine door. "We need all four elements to survive. Weavers train with each division—creating doors requires the use of all the elements in concert."

"Wow," Shay said, raising an eyebrow at Adne.

"It's not as impressive as it sounds." She threw a dark look at her father.

"Sure it is." Connor ruffled her hair and she stuck her tongue out at him.

"But most of us remain in a single division." Monroe knocked on the door. "Tordis—air—is the element of intellect. Scribes train here and live here."

The door swung open, revealing Silas. His arms were full of scrolls.

"What?" He scowled at Monroe. "I'm in the middle of something."

"We lost Grant."

The scrolls tumbled to the floor as Silas's face went white. "No."

"I'm sorry." Monroe pushed past him, gesturing for us to follow. Silas was still frozen in the doorway when I stepped past him.

"Uh . . ." Shay was staring at our surroundings. "This is a study?"

It was a good question. The room we'd entered looked like all the dictionaries on the planet had come here to die grisly deaths. The floor was carpeted by paper. Towers of books swayed precariously like monuments about to collapse.

"Don't touch anything." Silas, apparently recovered from his shock, shoved me aside and picked his way back to a desk—or what I could guess was a desk buried beneath more paper and maps—like someone treading through a minefield.

Connor strode straight across the room, kicking books and piles of notes out of his way.

"Damn it, Connor!" Silas shouted. "Now I won't be able to find what I need."

"Not my problem," Connor said, dropping into a chair after he'd tipped more books off its seat. "Like I give a rat's ass about your wunderkind special privileges. Just 'cause Anika babies you doesn't mean I'm going to."

Monroe walked across the room with a little more care, followed by Adne and Shay. I decided to take the path Connor had already cleared.

"Any other chairs, Silas?" Adne asked.

"This is my office," Silas sneered. "Not Tordis's archives. I don't usually have company."

"You can sit on my lap." Connor winked at Adne, slapping his thighs.

"What a gentleman," she muttered, leaning against Silas's desk.

"We'll be fine standing," Monroe said.

"Are you going to tell me how we lost an operative?" Silas was shuffling through mounds of scrolls. When he located a pen and a blank piece of paper, he began scribbling.

"We're not sure," Monroe said, glancing at me.

I stared at him for a moment, then realized that he wanted me to take the lead. *Well, that's who I am, isn't it?* I stood a little taller, surprised but pleased that Monroe acknowledged my place as alpha.

"Something's wrong with the Guardian packs," I said. "I'm not sure what's happened, but the patrols I knew aren't in play anymore."

Silas pursed his lips, then nodded for me to continue.

"Emile Laroche was leading Nightshade wolves," I said, my shoulders tightening at the memory of fighting Sasha. "I still can't imagine how that's possible."

When I spoke Emile's name, Monroe's jaw clenched.

"The Bane alpha was patrolling with Nightshades?" Silas didn't look up as he wrote.

"Not patrolling," I said, feeling cold as I spoke. "Hunting. They were hunting us."

The pen slipped from Silas's fingers. His eyes were wide when they met mine. "You think they knew our team was coming?"

"If they didn't know, they weren't surprised," I said. "I think they were waiting for us to show."

"They might have gotten information from Grant before they killed him." Silas sighed.

"I don't think so," Connor said. "I found him. Looked like he'd been ambushed, killed instantly."

Silas frowned. "They must be getting it from their own sources, then."

"You mean spies here?" Shay asked. "You think you have a mole?"

"Of course not." Silas snorted. "Our people aren't turncoats. I mean hers."

He pointed at me. The air went out of my lungs. It took less than a second for me to shift and leap onto his desk, snarling. My fangs snapped inches from his face. Silas yelped, tipping his chair over backward, and rolled across the floor.

"Calla!" Monroe shouted.

I shifted back, still crouched on the desk.

"What do you mean mine?" I glared at Silas, who was brandishing a letter opener at me.

"You do know she's not a werewolf, right?" Shay smirked at the Scribe. "That silver thing's not gonna be worth much."

"Monroe!" Silas's eyes bulged as I perched on the edge of the desk, ready to spring.

"Calla, please," Monroe said.

I didn't look at him. "Just tell me what you meant, Silas."

He swallowed hard. "I only meant that your packmates are the most likely source of information about you and Shay. They're probably being interrogated."

My limbs trembled and I almost lost my balance.

They're being held for questioning.

"But—but they don't know anything," I stammered. "Only Shay and I knew . . . Oh God."

"What?" Connor leaned forward. I could feel the blood draining from my face.

"Ren," I whispered. "Ren knew."

"How much did he know?" Monroe's voice cracked.

"I told him about Corrine—that the Keepers had executed her," I said, struggling with the fog of memories from that night. "I told him Shay was the Scion."

"Shit," Connor said. "There goes our alliance."

"Why?" Shay asked.

Silas was slowly rising, eyeing me all the while. "Because they'll have those young wolves under lock and key until they're sure where their loyalties lie. We won't be able to get to them."

Monroe's hands were covering his face. He swore and swung a fist, sending a tower of books crashing to the floor.

"I'm sorry," Adne said to her father.

He didn't answer.

Connor stood up, carried the chair to Monroe, and set it down in front of him. Monroe nodded gratefully, sat down, and rested his elbows on his knees, lost in thought.

"Since that option is out," Connor said, "what now?"

I slid off the desk, ignoring the way Silas cringed when I walked past him.

"I don't want to give up on my pack," I said. "We can't just leave them."

I'd known Ren was at risk, but the thought of Bryn and Ansel being interrogated was even worse. They hadn't known anything. Whatever had happened to them fell at my feet alone. My secrets alone put them in danger.

"We won't," Monroe said, staring ahead. "But we're looking at a rescue mission now. Not an alliance. At least not right away."

"And we need more information before we can even think about a rescue," Silas said, backing against a bookcase when I glared at him.

"He's right, Calla," Adne said. "We can't go into Vail blind. It might just be Ren they're questioning, but it might be all your packmates."

I looked at Shay. He nodded reluctantly.

"Then what?!" I snapped. "We just wait?"

"No," Monroe said. "Waiting isn't an option."

"It's time to go nuclear." Connor smiled at Silas. "Right?"

"That is the worst metaphor I've ever heard." Silas went back to his desk, whimpering as he lifted papers I'd shredded.

"What are you talking about?" Shay frowned.

"Haven't you figured it out, kid?" Connor cast a sidelong glance at him. "We're talking about you."

"Me?" Shay blinked.

Monroe looked up. His eyes were bloodshot. "Silas, it's time."

"Time for what?" I asked. My mind was still on my pack. On Ansel and Bryn. My chest was burning as I tried to fight off images of all the things that could have happened to them. That could still be happening.

"For Shay to learn who he is," Monroe said.

"I know who I am," Shay said.

"Wanna bet?" Connor laughed. "You're in for a surprise ... or a hundred. I'll give you two-to-one odds."

"Leave him alone," Adne said.

"Do you want the story or a plan?" Silas asked.

"A plan," I snapped. "What can Shay do that will help my pack?"

"He can't do much yet," Silas answered. "First we have to gather the pieces."

"Pieces?" Shay frowned at the Scribe. "What pieces?"

"The pieces of the cross," Silas replied in a congenial tone, as if that explained everything.

"The pieces of the cross?" Shay's brow creased further.

One eyebrow arched and Silas leaned forward, an almost accusing question jabbed at Shay. "How much of *The War of All Against All* did you read, exactly?"

I came to his rescue. "Look, Professor, we were running for our lives as soon as we realized the Scion was going to be laid on a sacrificial altar at Samhain. And I understand if we hadn't gotten here, you lot would be stuck trying to save him and probably failing. Watch yourself." I bared sharpened canines at him.

A shocked ripple moved through the room. Connor snorted, laughing as Silas reached for the letter opener again.

Monroe held up a hand. "She's right, Silas, not everyone has the luxury of devoting their lives to study as you do. We're fortunate that they are here, and chastising them for not managing to gather the full story before they fled is useless."

Silas shuddered like he had to force himself not to be sick, but after a moment he looked sullenly at Shay. "Sorry."

Shay offered a weak smile. "We only read bits."

"Okay, then." Silas took a deep breath, like he was trying to break a record for underwater swimming. "Each of the sacred sites has a piece of the cross. You need to bear the cross like the prophecy says. It's the only way we can win." After the words were out, he let out the rest of his breath explosively and ground his teeth.

"Writing SparkNotes would be a bad career choice for you, Silas," Connor muttered. "No appreciation of abridgment at all."

"Or sanity," Adne murmured, and smiled at Shay, who laughed but tried not to meet Silas's injured glance.

"Abridging is blasphemy," Silas said.

I leaned forward hesitantly, not wanting another chastising remark. "I don't get it. Shay already bears the cross. He has the tattoo."

Connor laughed. "Man, I wish you'd taken that bet."

Shay and I exchanged a confused glance.

Silas looked like a goose ready to lay a golden egg.

Shay frowned at him. "Well?"

"The tattoo is just a marker of who you are, a signal for those who sought you. It's not the cross." The gleam in the Scribe's eye was almost too bright to look at it, particularly because it was so smug.

"Then what is the cross?" I asked quietly.

Monroe didn't look at me; his brown eyes focused on Shay. A sober, almost regretful sigh emerged from his throat.

"It's a weapon."

EIGHT

"A WEAPON?" SHAY'S question emerged hushed, but not fearful.

"Technically it's two weapons," Silas said brightly. "But they're meant to be used in concert. As a single force."

"Two weapons?" I asked.

"Yes," Monroe said, his voice still quiet. "Two swords."

"Swords?" Shay frowned.

"The Elemental Cross," Silas said. "One sword of earth and air, the other of fire and water. If you look closely at the mark, you'll see that each bar of the cross has one pointed end. They're sword points."

"Swords," Shay said again. He sounded frustrated and a little disappointed.

"What is it?" I asked.

He grimaced, looking at his hands.

"Shay?" Monroe leaned forward, brow furrowed.

"It's just . . . so predictable," Shay mumbled. "I never really saw myself fighting with swords. Particularly now that I'm a wolf."

A warm current rushed through my veins at his last words, and I had to look away from his face to slow the sudden lurching of my heart. *Maybe he does understand what it means to be a Guardian. If that* was true, he could help lead my pack, which in my mind was worth more than any weapon.

"These aren't just any swords," Monroe said. "You're the only one who can wield them."

The only one? That was impressive. I looked at Shay; his expression was curious but wary. He laced his fingers together, frowning again.

I laughed, suddenly putting together his frustration and regret. "I'm sure it will be fine, Shay, but maybe not as exciting as a whip . . . or ice picks."

"Ice picks?" Connor perked up.

Shay nodded but kept his eyes lowered.

"I bet you're wishing you'd read more of those ninja comics now, huh?" I couldn't stop my laughter.

Adne glanced back and forth from me to Shay. "What are you talking about?"

"Shay's childhood aspirations," I said, grinning. "And his favorite training manuals."

"Swords just seem so . . . *ordinary*." He shook his head.

"If you're looking for graphic inspiration, *Path of the Assassin* or *Shaman Warrior* would be the best," Silas offered. "Lots of sword fighting and dual wielding, which you'll need to master. I could lend you my collections."

Shay brightened a bit and smiled at the Scribe.

"We'll continue the training you began at the Academy this week," Monroe said. "It won't be a problem. Connor can take care of it."

"I can help." Adne shot a dark look at Monroe. He frowned.

"She's right," Connor said. "I know she's not a Striker, Monroe. But Adne's got some serious combat skills."

He winked at Adne. "I'm sure we'll all be lined up to see your first match against the Scion."

Adne grinned at him. "See, Monroe?"

"Very well." He sighed. "Adne will help with the training."

"We still have to get all four pieces of the cross before that's even an issue," Silas added.

Despite my anger, my thoughts were churning. Pieces of the cross. Shay had said there were four maps in the Keepers' text. Was Haldis one of the pieces? And what kind of a piece was it? It didn't look like any kind of weapon I'd seen . . . unless. The Elemental Cross was two swords. The cylinder we'd found in the cavern obviously wasn't a blade, but I knew what it could be. Particularly since Shay was *the only one who could wield the swords*. And he was the only one who could touch Haldis. It had to be.

"No," I said quietly. "We only have to get three of the pieces."

The room fell silent, all eyes wide and on me.

"Excuse me?" Silas said at last.

"Shay and I went to Haldis Cavern," I said. "He has the piece that was hidden there."

Shay blanched. "Uh, I haven't told them about Haldis yet, Cal."

"I know." I let my gaze tell him exactly what I thought of *that* decision. "It's a hilt. Isn't it? A sword hilt?"

"Yes . . . it is." Monroe turned to face Shay. "What haven't you told us about Haldis?"

Shay reached for his inside jacket pocket. "Sorry. It's just that I didn't know if we could trust you. But I guess that's a moot point now." He withdrew the shimmering ochre cylinder.

The silence in the room had grown so thick it felt as though I could reach out and gather it in my arms.

"When did you retrieve Haldis?" Monroe finally murmured. His eyes were locked on the strange object.

"Calla and I went to check out the cavern in October," Shay said, rolling the cylinder back and forth in his palms. The more I looked at it, noting the way his fingers curled perfectly around its shape, the more convinced I was that I understood.

"That's when Shay used the ice picks," I said. "The Keepers had a giant spider guarding Haldis. He killed it."

"With ice picks?" Connor's eyes widened.

Shay shuddered. "It was horrible."

"I don't know," I said, a smile pulling at my lips as I recalled the fight. "You nailed that beast without too much trouble."

"With ice picks?" Connor said again, gazing at Shay as if truly seeing him for the first time.

"Yeah," Shay said, but he looked a little ill. He gripped the shimmering cylinder more tightly.

Silas snorted and leaned over to dig through a leather satchel half buried under papers on the desk. When he stood up, he had donned a pair of thick leather gloves. He reached out toward the gleaming object.

I started to open my mouth but then clamped my lips together and watched. His fingers brushed the smooth surface and he yelped and stumbled back, shaking his hand. The rest of the Searchers stared at Silas.

"That's odd," he said, reaching for Haldis again.

"I wouldn't if I were you," I said quietly. "The pain gets worse every time."

All eyes in the room focused on me. I stood my ground, returning each gaze with a challenging stare.

"You knew it would hurt me?" Silas's voice bubbled with outrage.

"I didn't know," I said. "Well, at least not for sure. I thought maybe it was just Guardians who couldn't touch it. But it seems that only Shay is allowed."

Silas's eyes bulged. "Even with enchanted gloves?"

This guy was nuts. "You thought gloves would let you touch Haldis?"

"Well, I had this theory. . . ." He scratched his head.

Monroe groaned, dropping his face into his hands.

"Silas, you didn't say it was a theory. You swore it would work. We told Anika it would work!"

"Moron." Connor snorted. He inched closer to Shay, examining Haldis while keeping a safe distance.

"What's wrong?" Shay asked, frowning at their defeated expressions.

"Silas devised our most recent Striker attacks." Adne smiled thinly. "Searcher strike teams have been trying to get to the sites in the hopes that we could pull the pieces of the cross ourselves and keep them safe until the Scion appeared."

"But none of you can touch them," I said. My confidence in the Searchers crumbled a bit. Could they really help my pack if they made mistakes like this?

"We didn't know that." Connor glared at Silas. "And dozens of Strikers were lost in attempts to even get close to the sites."

I had to look away, all too aware that we'd made the same kind of mistake today. *I can't blame them. We're all doing the best we can.*

Silas just looked slightly put off. "I was certain it would work."

"Why were you focused on the pieces?" I asked. "What's so special about these swords?"

"The Elemental Cross is the only force in the world that can banish wraiths." Monroe's voice was deadly quiet. "When the Scion wields the swords, he can expel them from the earth, defeat the minions of the Netherworld. Even Bosque Mar himself. Nothing else can."

Shay stared at Monroe, the boy's face suddenly chalk white.

"I can fight the wraiths?"

"Yes," Monroe said, placing his hand on Shay's shoulder. "You can and you will. In time."

Silas, apparently recovered from his moment of humiliation,

spoke up. "We must retrieve the Elemental Cross. It's the only thing that will give us victory over the Keepers."

I nodded, trying to imagine the type of power it would take to defeat Bosque and his horde.

"Why did you keep this from us?" Monroe turned on Shay, eyes flashing with anger.

Shay looked around at their dejected faces and sighed.

"I'm sorry," he said. "But I wasn't convinced you were the good guys. I wasn't going to trust you until Calla did."

I bit my lip, grateful for his words but regretting what it cost the Searchers.

"Fine," Monroe said gruffly, folding his arms across his chest. "Let's move on. At least we know the Keepers can't take the weapon from him once he has it."

"It's good that you have Haldis, Shay," Adne said. "That will save us a trip."

Shay smiled. "I suppose it will." He turned his eyes on Silas. "So who was the lady?"

"The lady?" Silas raised an eyebrow.

"The woman who was in the cavern; she sang, and then all the lights went out and Haldis was in my hand."

"Ah." Silas smiled. "That was Cian."

"Who?" Shay looked at him blankly.

"Warrior, prophetess," Silas replied. "The only reason we're here today."

"She was the first Searcher," Monroe added. "And your great-aunt several times over. The Scion's bloodline begins with the fore-bearers of Eira and Cian."

"Who was Eira?" I asked.

Monroe's face clouded and he looked at Shay. "Your very great grandmother. She was Cian's sister and the first Keeper."

"Her sister?" Shay's eyes widened. "How is that possible?"

Silas cleared his throat.

"Oh, just get it over with." Connor groaned. He unceremoniously dropped to the floor and stretched out, arranging a stack of papers into a pillow.

"It's really not that long of a story," Silas muttered.

Connor didn't open his eyes.

"And it's a good story," Silas pleaded.

"Good?" At that Connor's eyelids snapped up. "It's a bloody disaster is what it is."

"I mean it's *exciting*," Silas amended.

"Yeah, our lives are ruined and you call it a literary triumph."

"Just let him tell the story, Connor," Adne said curtly, and gestured to Silas. "Once upon a time . . ."

Silas beamed. "The spirit world wasn't hidden from human beings. Societies across the globe mixed with the forces of the earth and those of the Nether. That mixing is what most people would call 'magic,' but it's much more than that."

"How so?" Shay asked.

"Connecting to the elemental powers of the earth is natural. Something that comes along with life as a being on this planet. Everything is part of the same system, the same energies. The ability to tap into those forces varies from person to person, but the latent ability is there for everyone."

"So what's the problem, then?" Shay frowned. "If magic is just a part of people."

"Not just people," Silas corrected. "Animals, plants, earth, sky, stone. Everything."

"Elemental forces aren't the problem, Shay," Monroe said quietly. "But the earth's magic isn't the only kind that touches this world."

"You mean the Nether?" I asked. Cold fingers crept up my spine. "Where wraiths and succubi come from?"

Monroe nodded.

"Not bad, she-wolf." Silas smirked. "The Nether exists as a sort of oppositional force to the earth. Never truly part of this world but always alongside it. Like trains on parallel tracks."

"Or its evil twin." Adne laughed, but there was no joy in the sound.

"Too true." Silas nodded. "When more human beings were actively tapping into the spirit world, some thought it prudent to try to harness the forces of the Nether for their own gains."

"Why isn't any of this recorded?" Shay asked. "Even though people always knew about Nether."

"I'm sorry," Silas snapped. "I thought you were supposed to be educated. Haven't you read any history books?"

"Of course I have," Shay said.

"Well, if you'd been paying attention, you would have noticed people up until the mid-nineteenth century talking about witches, demons, and monsters nonstop."

"I thought that was just superstition." Shay's brow knit.

"Enter the scientific revolution and the modern age." Silas smiled. "Let's all give the Keepers a big round of applause."

Shay and I exchanged a confused glance.

"You're getting ahead of yourself, Silas," Monroe murmured.

"Of course, my apologies," the Scribe said quickly. "The idea of superstition is a modern invention. Its use of course is to explain away frightening beings that have always been very real and difficult to control. As you've just demonstrated, superstition was a very useful device and has had tremendous success in rewriting history."

Shay was incredulous. "You've got to be kidding."

"He's not," Adne said coldly.

"So what really happened?" I asked, still struggling against the wall of lies that had surrounded my life until now.

"As I said before, use of elemental power is all well and good, but dabblers in the Nether realm created problems for themselves and their neighbors. Creatures of the Nether don't mix well with humans."

"What do you mean?" Shay asked.

"You've seen it," I said. "We're their food. Wraiths, succubi, and incubi. They feed on the worst parts of this life. Thrive on our suffering."

Adne's face was ashen, but she jerked away when Monroe came around the table and tried to take her hand.

"Oh," Shay mumbled. "Right. Sorry."

Silas waved his hand dismissively. "Not a problem. But back in the day, some humans of noble character took it upon themselves to reign in the presence of the Nether. They curtailed the practice of irresponsible people who didn't realize they were playing with fire, and they fought off the actual Nether beings that manifested on the earth."

"But you can't fight off wraiths," I objected.

"Wraiths are new," Monroe said. "Well, relatively new, as in five hundred years or so."

"That's new?" I gaped.

"Historically speaking," Silas answered. "Wraiths came with the Keepers. Prior to their appearance, magicians could only raise succubi and incubi—they have more human traits and thus can cross over without requiring much power on the part of the summoner."

"How did the Keepers appear?" I asked impatiently.

"I'm getting to that," Silas replied, unfazed by my tone. "The warriors who elected themselves sentinels of the bridge between the earth and the Nether were successful. Vigilant, patient, and ferocious, they kept the forces of the Nether at bay and the destruction that its inhabitants could wreak in this world in check. But then a knight emerged in the fifteenth century who was beautiful, charismatic, and seemingly invincible in combat. She envisioned a new purpose for her peers. Eira."

Shay's voice was barely more than a breath of air. "What did she do?"

"She was ambitious," Silas said. "She claimed that the warriors could do more, not just protect the world, but rid the earth of the Nether once and for all. Close the doors between our world and the other."

"That sounds like a good idea," I said.

"It is," Silas replied. "But the road to hell is paved with good intentions."

"Almost literally in this case," Connor muttered. He'd thrown his arm over his eyes, but I could see muscles in his jaw and neck tighten.

Silas spared him a disdainful glance. "Eira decided she would lead the knights in this new mission. But in order to close the doors between the worlds, she needed to know how they had been opened. She sought knowledge of the Nether realm and it changed her."

"Changed her how?" Some of the color had returned to Shay's face.

"She found the source, the origin of the Nether's path into earth. A being more powerful than any humankind had encountered in their brief touches of the dark realm. This creature sent its emissaries into our world to draw power and carry it back to him, making him ever stronger and widening the doors and allowing more of his creations to infiltrate the earth."

I shuddered, feeling as though I were being pulled into a tunnel, blindfolded and not wanting to see where I was once the cloth was removed.

"Eira was strong, but her ambition proved stronger. More than anything else, the creature hoped that eventually he would open a path broad enough so that he could himself come into our world and make it his dominion. Lord of not one but two realms, both Nether and earth. He promised Eira a place at his side if she would aid him."

"And she did." Monroe stared at his hands, which were trembling.

"She wasn't alone," Silas said. "Too many of the warriors had tired of keeping the Nether at bay and sacrificing their own lives in exchange. The hunger for power among Eira's peers proved too great. She had no trouble assembling a mass of loyal followers."

"The Keepers," Shay said.

"The name they gave themselves," Silas said. "Keepers of a power too great for most humans. They considered themselves set apart, elite. Elected by fate to reign over the earth by harnessing the power of the Nether."

"But it's a lie," Connor spat.

"Is it?" I murmured. "The Keepers do reign over the earth; they reap all the benefit of using their power."

"They do," Monroe replied, eyes distant and broken. "But the power doesn't belong to them, and they live in fear of losing it. At the end of the day they are slaves to that same creature that seduced Eira. Our histories name him the Harbinger. You know him as Bosque Mar."

NINE

SHAY HAD FALLEN SILENT as we left the room. I didn't know whether I should talk to him, touch him. How would I feel if I'd just found out my only living "relative" was actually some sort of demon lord?

My skin crawled. We'd learned too many truths, turned over rocks that I wished still hid the ugliness beneath them. I'd known my masters were cruel, but now I had to face their real nature: the Keepers didn't just use the forces of the Nether, they'd willingly bound themselves to its darkness. That shadowy world bore creatures that brought only suffering, and its horrors were the very source of the Keepers' power. A power I'd spent my life fighting to protect.

I walked forward, forcing my stubborn body onward. I wanted to curl in on myself, close my eyes, and dream the truth away. I wished Bryn were here to talk about it—I was sure she'd find some way to tease me. Her jokes had always countered my doubts. Her bright laughter eased my tension when I had to make tough calls as an alpha. The image of her smiling face sent guilt spiraling through me. Where was she now? Had the Keepers hurt her?

"You should get some rest," Connor said. "I'll take you back to your rooms."

"I know the way," Shay said, wrapping his fingers around my upper arm. "We don't need an escort."

"Hush, boy," Connor said. "You're still our guest here. Show a little respect."

"Boy?" Shay bristled; his grip on my arm verged on painful. "You're only three years older than I am."

Connor squared his shoulders, his hand resting on his sword hilt. "I'm betting I've seen a lot more than you could stomach. Scion or not."

I could see where this was going. "Stop it, both of you." We were all exhausted and on edge.

"She's right," Adne said. "We've had a rough enough time as it is. We don't need you bloodying each other up as the grand finale to a sucky day."

"Ain't that the truth." Connor's hand hadn't left his sword hilt.

I tried to quell my own irritation by examining the crystal veins that rippled through the walls. Even in the halls, now lit only by the gentle flicker of sconces at regular intervals, the patterns gave off a subtle gleam. As we walked, the colors of Tordis, like icy spiderwebs covering the walls, became rose and pale yellow. The intricate weave of multi-hued lights began to twitch and shudder. Soon scarlet and blazing orange were jumping along the walls around us as if we'd walked into a furnace.

The colors weren't the only thing that had changed. The air around us warmed, but rather than comforting me, it made me uneasy. I sneezed, shaking my head to ward off a new, strange odor at the same moment that Shay's nose wrinkled.

"What *is* that?" he asked.

The invisible concoction assaulting my nostrils had familiar components—black pepper, sage, clove, and cedar—but the combination of scents was overwhelming. My eyes burned and watered. The warmth pouring over my skin began to itch—an unpleasant sensation like tiny gnats were biting me. Shay growled, scratching at his arms.

"Oh." Connor cast a sidelong glance at us. "We probably should have cut back through the courtyard."

Shay began to cough and glared accusingly at Connor.

"Don't worry," Adne said. "We're almost past it."

"Past what?" I cupped my hands over my nose and mouth, but I was coughing too, as if I'd inhaled smoke.

"This is Pyralis, and we're passing their Apothecary," Adne said, gesturing to a set of double doors that resembled those of Haldis Tactical, only the triangles carved into the Apothecary's doors were plain, with their tips pointing upward.

"Sorry," Connor muttered. "I didn't realize it would affect you."

"Why isn't it bothering you two?" I asked, taking shallow breaths though since we'd passed the doors, the acrid scents had begun to fade.

"The Apothecary creates our enchantments—the compounds we use to make our weapons more effective against . . ." Adne winced when she looked at me.

"Guardians."

I ran my tongue along sharpening canines.

Enchanted bolts; hope you're enjoying the ride. It was a good thing Ethan had stayed at Purgatory. Had he been walking alongside me, when memories of the Searchers' venom snaking through my veins made my chest throb, I wouldn't have been able to resist ripping a chunk out of his arm.

"Yeah," Connor added. "You should steer clear of Pyralis. It's never going to be a pleasant place for you to visit."

"Thanks for the tip," Shay muttered, releasing the collar of his shirt, which he'd pulled up like a tent over his nose.

I knew we'd reached Haldis when the fiery shades ceased flickering in the walls and became the gently waving dark hues found only deep in the soil. The burning fumes of Pyralis had vanished. I took deep breaths, enjoying the way the clear air soothed my stinging chest. The itchiness subsided, though both Shay and I had red scratches running up and down our arms as souvenirs from our brief trip past the Apothecary.

"So each of the wings reflects its elemental source?" I asked. "Earth, air, fire, and water?"

Having seen the other three wings, I wondered what the water section of the Academy was like.

"Yep," Adne said.

"Pretty, isn't it?" Connor asked. "Nice place to call home."

"Thank you." Adne grinned at him over her shoulder.

"Huh?" I frowned.

Connor laughed. "The Weavers pull the threads through the building. But Adne just decided to take all the credit."

The tension in my shoulders eased a bit at the sound of his laughter; I knew that Connor was returning to himself. The instant effect of his teasing made it obvious how much his fatalistic humor could be an asset to his allies. Even if it was often irritating.

"Threads?" Shay asked.

"It's the key to how we move the Academy," she said, rubbing her temples. "But honestly, my head is just pounding. Can I awe you with my mad skills another time?"

She'd come to a stop in front of a door. "This is you, Calla."

Connor spared me a sly smile. "I'm right down the hall if you have nightmares, she-wolf. Bed's big enough to share as long as you don't bite . . . hard."

I grabbed Shay before he could lunge at Connor.

"You really need to lighten up," Connor growled, shaking his head at Shay's balled fists.

"God, Connor," Adne groaned. "Headache, remember? Could you put the commentary on hold for tonight?"

"Sorry."

I was stunned. He'd never apologized for his jokes before. Connor went to her, pushing wisps of hair away from her eyes. "You should get some sleep."

"It's not late enough to go to bed." I thought I saw her shudder. "Even if it was, I don't know if I'll be able to sleep tonight."

"We can talk, then," he said. All evidence of his puckish humor had vanished.

She looked up at him, silent for several heartbeats, and then nodded.

"You can find your room, Shay?" Connor asked, not taking his eyes off Adne.

"I'm pretty sure I already said that," Shay said. "Like ten minutes ago."

"Uh-huh." Connor put his arm around Adne's shoulders, leading her farther down the hall.

I watched them walk away, puzzling over the roller-coaster ride of their interactions.

The sound of Shay clearing his throat pulled my thoughts away from Connor and Adne's strange relationship.

"Where's your room?" I asked.

He shoved his hands in his pockets, glancing down the hall but not meeting my gaze. "It's just next door, but I thought maybe . . ."

My pulse jumped and then my cheeks flamed as Connor's comment replayed in my head.

"You want to come in?" I asked.

He smiled, raising hopeful eyes to meet mine.

I took his hand, knowing he could feel my heartbeat racing through my veins the moment our fingers touched. My bedroom was dark, but I could make out the bed, a writing desk, and a few upholstered chairs. The room looked like a cross between a dormitory and a luxury hotel. Not bad.

But where should I go? I'd stumbled into unfamiliar territory. Shay and I were alone and we didn't have to hide. In this place there was no one to catch us. We were safe . . . in theory. My limbs were trembling, full of desire and the freedom of possibility.

Do I lead him to the bed? Is that too fast? Should I be coy? Man, I suck at this.

Shay stepped behind me. His arms encircled my waist and he drew me back against the curve of his body.

The warmth that filled me when his kiss moved along my neck sent silken tendrils through my limbs. I leaned back against him, relief flooding me. My body eased, each muscle relaxing. We were alone, no longer under the scrutiny of the Searchers—who despite their welcome still left me uneasy. Even if I wasn't completely comfortable with this new arrangement, at least I was still alive. Shay was still alive. I breathed in the realization that we were safe, for now.

I closed my eyes as his hands moved slowly over my body. Even through his clothes I could feel the warmth of his skin. It was incredibly soothing.

"So what do you think?" he asked. "About the Searchers? They're the good guys from what I can tell."

"Looks like." I shifted slightly in his arms. "It's weird—but they kind of remind me of Guardians."

"That makes sense to me. You're both warriors. And you make sacrifices because of the war." He pulled back the collar of my shirt, and his lips touched the top of my shoulder.

"Sacrifices." I shivered at the light brush of his mouth on my skin, suddenly thinking of Lydia. Of Mr. Selby. What did they think they'd given their lives for? There was still so much I didn't know about the Searchers.

"They're incredible fighters," I said, my mind flashing back to the eastern slope. "Even if they aren't wolves."

"Sometimes being human has advantages," Shay said.

"Like when?"

"Like if we were both wolves right now, I'd only be able to lick you."

I laughed, trying to turn to face him, but he held me still.

He kissed the underside of my jaw. "See, much better than licking." The sudden speed of my heart and flood of heat through my veins told me it was much, much better.

His lips brushed my ear once again while his hands slid over my hips, molding me against him. "I'm sure we could come up with other things that would be better too."

I turned before he could stop me, tilting my face toward his, eager for his lips to meet mine. When they did, it was like a flaming arrow scorched its path into the core of my body. He kept the kiss light, teasing. The gentle strokes of his mouth on mine made me ache, hungry for more of him. I twisted my fingers in the soft curls of his hair, pulling him into a deeper kiss. I took his lower lip between my teeth, and I heard a rumbling growl of pleasure in his chest. One of his hands pressed against the small of my back while the other slipped beneath my shirt, caressing, exploring.

"I missed you," he whispered, kissing me again. "So much."

"Me too," I said, almost gasping as his lips moved along my jaw. My skin came alive under his fingers, every touch an electric crackle through my veins.

He laughed, and I managed to catch my breath long enough to ask, "This is funny to you?"

"No," he murmured against my lips. "It's just that this outfit is much easier to deal with than that chastity contraption you had on the last time we were kissing."

I shivered as his fingers emphasized his observation.

"You mean my wedding dress?" I tried to focus on getting

coherent words out. "These are more comfortable, but it's a little weird to be wearing my enemies' clothes."

"They aren't your enemies anymore. And it's a good look for you." He smiled against my mouth. "I especially like those tight leather pants." His hands moved again and my legs threatened to give out.

"Do you want to pick up where we left off in my room?" he asked. "I mean, where we left off *before* we had to run for our lives?"

My heart fluttered, but another voice echoed in my mind. A voice from when we'd been running for our lives.

Do you love him? Ren's words swirled around me, filling my ears. I had to close my eyes against the sound of it, struggling against the storm of feelings that assaulted me.

This is only about love.

His rich voice sounded so close, so real. My eyes snapped open and I almost expected to see the alpha standing there: espresso dark hair, sparkling charcoal eyes, teasing smile, lips parted to greet me.

Hey, Lily.

But only tall leaded windows stared back at me from the room's outer wall.

With some reluctance I pulled out of Shay's embrace. *Why does this keep happening?* I couldn't escape memories of Ren. They were only getting stronger.

"I don't think we should." My voice was hoarse and my limbs still trembled, but I didn't know if it was from the lingering effects of Shay's touch or the unexpected vision of Ren that intruded on us.

He sighed as he watched me move away from him.

"What's wrong?"

I didn't want to tell him, so I grabbed for the other thought that nagged me. "The fight today was hard. Lydia died so I could make it back. She died for me. It's hard to believe that the Searchers don't hate me."

"I think Ethan hates you," Shay offered with a grimace.

"The feeling is mutual." I smiled ruefully. "I meant the rest of them. Monroe's reserved but never angry. Connor's actually pretty great."

"I see." Shay gritted his teeth.

"Not like *that*," I muttered. "Just funny and nice. You know, like Adne."

I let an edge accompany her name. Two could play the jealousy card.

He either didn't notice or ignored it. "Yeah, she *is* great. I spent the whole week with her."

"Doing what?" I asked, catching a growl before it left my throat.

"Aw, you're cute when you're jealous." He stroked my cheek, snatching his fingers away when I playfully snapped at them. "You know I only have eyes for you."

"Right." I laughed, but a snarl still lingered in the sound.

"Seriously." The warmth in his voice drew my eyes to his. When he leaned forward and kissed the tip of my nose, I melted, knowing he meant it.

"Adne just showed me around," he said. "We did some training. They're really big on that here—the training."

"What kind of training?" I ran my fingers over his shoulder, along his arm, lingering on his taut muscles.

"Combat," he replied, his jaw tightening. I felt his biceps flex under my hand.

"Oh," I said. "What's it like?"

He laughed sharply. "I know how to fight better, I guess."

"You were already pretty good before," I offered.

"You should see me now, baby." He grinned.

"Don't ever call me that again," I said. "Or you'll need those combat skills."

"Right," he said, holding up his hands in mock surrender. "No belittling pet names. I've sort of been learning about the Academy and how Searchers are trained, but as far as the future or what I'm supposed to do, I'm still blind and dumb."

"Shay . . . why didn't you show them Haldis until today?" Something about that secret bothered me, but I couldn't quite pin down what.

"I didn't want to give them anything until I knew I could trust them. Until you came back," he said, sending a spike of warmth beneath my skin that curled low in my body. "I think I do now."

"So you and the Searchers have been giving each other the silent treatment?"

"Pretty much." He laughed. "I wanted to be sure they meant it about the alliance with Guardians, that they weren't going to hurt you once you woke up."

"Thanks for that," I said, but it was still surprising that he'd deceived them. "Shay, you knew that we were going to try to find my pack. Why didn't you stop us?"

"You wanted to go," he protested, but I knew he was dodging me.

"All I could think about was getting to them," I said. "It didn't even occur to me that the patrols would have stopped . . . not until we couldn't find them."

Shay didn't manage to hide the twitch of a smile.

"You knew," I snarled. "You knew we wouldn't find them."

"I didn't know," he said. "I guessed."

"Why didn't you say anything?" My surprise became anger. Two people were dead. "My alpha instincts took over when I was hunting for Ansel and the others. I couldn't think about anything else. You should have."

"I wanted you to be safe," he said, his shoulders tensing. "I thought you could prove your worth to the Searchers without actually running into trouble."

"We ran into plenty of trouble," I snarled, furious that he'd thought he could protect me and that he'd tried to do so by lying. "People died. Good people."

"I know," he said quickly, and I could see he was becoming as angry as I was. "And I'm sorry for that. Calla, I didn't say anything because I thought there wouldn't be wolves near Haldis. How could I have known they'd be waiting for you?"

Because it's what we do best. I bit my tongue, not wanting to lash out at him anymore. Tears burned in my eyes and weariness settled deep in my bones, making them ache. I walked to the bed and sat down. It wasn't just the Searchers' losses that tore at me. My own disappointment pressed down on my chest, a painful, heavy weight. I'd barreled into that mission because I'd hoped so much to reunite with my pack. Now I didn't know what would happen, how we'd ever find them.

I slid down on the mattress, resting my head among pillows. A few lonely tears slipped along my cheeks as I closed my eyes. The bed caved beneath Shay's weight when he stretched out beside me. His lips touched the back of my neck, but I wasn't with him in the room anymore. I was back in Vail, with my pack. Facing Emile today hadn't just shown me what I was up against—it had reminded me of what I'd lost. I despised the Bane alpha, but I didn't hate his son.

Come to beg forgiveness? I think you may find it's too late.

Running had granted me freedom, but Ren was still in Vail. And he'd lied to help us escape. How had Emile reacted to that betrayal? What kind of forgiveness would the Keepers offer Ren, if any? Was he even alive?

Shay's fingers slid over my hip, drawing me back against him.

"Stop, Shay. Don't." My voice quaked as I rolled away from him. "I just . . . I can't."

I wanted him, but the flood of emotions pouring into me made me restless, uneasy.

He slid his arm around my waist. "Why not?"

It took me a moment to speak. "You know why."

A low growl slithered from his throat. "He's not here, you know. Your union, the alpha stuff, all of that—it's over. You don't have to keep acting like he has some kind of hold on you. I just wish you would—"

Shay didn't know how wrong he was. Ren was here; somehow he was still with me, haunting my every move. Union or no, as alphas we'd had a fierce bond. It had always been there since the first day I'd met him and our union had been announced. That connection, that loyalty still tied me to Vail, and to him. The only thing that had made me question whether Ren and I were meant to be together was this boy who now lay beside me. And I wasn't sure I knew what that meant.

Shay was silent, but I could feel his angry eyes boring into the back of my head.

"I don't get it," he said. "You're free now, Cal. You want this."

He was right. I did want this, but my own desires weren't the only thing that compelled me.

"No, I'm not. Not really." I sighed, flipping over to look at him. "I'm sorry, but until I know that my pack is safe, I don't want to make any more choices that make me feel like I've abandoned them."

As soon as the words were out, I knew how true they were. It wasn't just Ren haunting me; it was the choices I'd made.

His mouth cut into a thin, sharp line. "Loving me is betraying your pack? Even after everything that's happened, you'd still consider becoming Ren's mate for their sakes?"

"I—I don't know." And I realized that I really didn't know what I was going to do. I tried to make my voice coaxing. "With everything that's going on, don't you think it's better if we keep things neutral? We have more important stuff to deal with than you, me, and Ren. Right?"

Even as I spoke, my fingers found Ren's ring, tracing the shape of the band.

Shay's pale green eyes hardened into agates. "More important stuff?"

"Like saving the world? This war we're supposed to win for the Searchers? I'd call that important." I'd tried to laugh along with the words but failed miserably.

Shay wasn't laughing either. "Completely. Separate. Issues."

"I know." I couldn't hold his gaze any longer. "It's just. Okay—you're not going to like this."

"Doesn't matter," he said. "I just want you to tell me the truth."

What if I don't know the truth? What if my feelings slip through my fingers like water every time I try to grab hold of them?

"It's not over," I barely managed to whisper.

"What's not over?"

"Me and Ren."

"How can you say that?" he asked. "And why do you keep fidgeting?"

My heart froze when his eyes settled on my hand. "What is that?"

"Nothing." I tried to shove my hand beneath a pillow, but he grabbed it and stared at the gleaming metal and deep blue sapphire.

"Calla." He spoke slowly. "What is this?"

I cleared my throat, trying to stay calm despite my pounding heart. "It's a ring."

"A ring." When he touched the braided white gold band, I snatched my hand away.

"He gave this to you." I felt his entire body tense against mine and I heard him snarl. "Didn't he?"

I nodded. For a moment I thought he would shift forms and bite me.

"When?" he asked, his eyes still hard.

"The night of the union."

"Take it off."

"What?" I pulled a pillow in front of me like a shield.

"Take it off," he said again. "Why would you still wear a ring he gave you?"

"I don't—" I choked out the words. "If I took it off, I might lose it."

"So?"

I didn't answer, dropping my gaze.

"So when you say it's not over between you and Ren, do you mean you're still engaged to him? Is that why you're wearing his ring?" He sounded calm, but I knew he wasn't. I could smell the torrent of emotions rolling off him. His anger swirled between us thick as wood smoke, and beneath that something else. My chest cramped when I recognized the subtle, bittersweet scent of grief—dust and wilting roses.

"That's not what I mean . . . but I can't be with you. Not like this." My voice was shaking. "When he's back there and God knows what is happening to him. To all of them. Shay, we *left them behind.* How can we think about anything else? I can't. I just can't."

"But that doesn't mean—"

"No."

"Screw this." He rolled off the bed. "Go to sleep, Calla. I won't bother you any more tonight."

My stomach knotted as he walked away. I fought the desire to run after him and instead rolled onto my back, staring at the twinkling stars I could see through the glass ceiling and hoping that at some point sheer exhaustion would drive me to sleep.

I ran from Vail and that may have changed everything, but I still don't know where I belong.

TEN

MY FANGS CLOSED ON *his throat, crushing his wind-pipe. Hot, coppery blood poured into my mouth, down my throat. His heart slowed. Long, horrible pauses punctuated its beats. His eyes met mine, his lips curved into a smile, and I heard his voice in my mind.*

Welcome, Calla.

I scrambled back and shifted into human form, suddenly cold, sickened. Dead Stuart kept smiling despite the gaping hole in his neck. A light touch brushed my shoulder. I whirled and faced a woman. She wore a smile like the dead man's, beneficent, welcoming. Her dark auburn hair tumbled in waves down her back and her charcoal irises were shot through with silver. They sparkled with delight as she gazed at me. Her full lips parted.

"Calla." She murmured my name as if intoning a prayer, fervent and hopeful. Her dark eyes flickered down, and I followed her gaze. A child, barely more than an infant, lay slumbering in her arms. The child's peaceful face drew me forward a step. As I peered down, the child's eyes fluttered open. Night sky full of twinkling stars. Eyes like his mother's.

Ren.

He gazed at me. An exuberant cascading laugh escaped from his lips and he clapped in recognition and celebration. A warmth like home flared to life within my chest. I looked at Corrine Laroche and the smile died. The shadow loomed behind her, a gathering storm cloud of destruction. My mouth opened, ready to cry out a warning, but my breath wouldn't come. Translucent ink bands poured over her neck and shoulders. The snaking black vines wrapped around her arms. She began to scream and Ren tumbled from her grasp. He cried out in fear. I lunged forward to catch him, but another pair of sinewy arms snatched the child from the air. Corrine shrieked as the wraith took her, her body bound in undulating black ropes that pulsed and twisted along with the throes of her agony.

I dropped to my knees in horror. A snicker pulled my gaze from the tortured woman. Emile Laroche glowered at his mate, his watercolor blue eyes full of scorn. He glanced at the bawling child in his arms. His shoulders twitched and he shook his head; his dirty blond hair fell forward, brushing against his chin, shadowing his features, transforming his pointed face into a mask of devilish cruelty. Ren screamed and Emile's mouth slashed thin, a knife point of revulsion. He gripped the child more tightly. With a final disdainful glance at Corrine's convulsing form, he turned his back on her and strode away. Ren's shrieks of fear rang in my ears; the baby's cry united with his mother's screams in a ghastly chorus.

I couldn't move. My eyes were locked on Corrine's torment. A figure loomed beside me; my face turned. Ren stared at the wraith-bound woman. He was no longer a child but a young man, my intended mate. The boy's charcoal eyes that had sparkled like a galaxy were now flat and hollow. His dark hair was plastered by sweat to his forehead and neck. A mosaic of purple, yellow, green, and black bruises covered his torso. Crimson welts and burn scars created a grotesque pattern on his arms and back. His eyes moved slowly over his mother. He frowned as though the scene of horror that played out before him made no sense. He shook his head and sighed.

"Oh God, Ren." I reached for him, but my hand passed through his body.

He continued to stare at the screaming woman. His gaze didn't turn to me, but his lips moved slightly.

"Where are you, Lily?" His wrist jerked. Something caught the light, flashed blue: my ring, looped over the tip of his finger, swinging like a pendulum marking time he didn't have.

Slashes appeared on his shoulders, skin opened, blood poured down, washing his body in a crimson flood. Red liquid ribbons slid around his arms, wrists, fingers. He dropped to his knees, head bowed. Corrine and I screamed together.

I gasped for breath as my eyelids snapped open. The nightmare swirled at the edges of my mind. The screams had become howls echoing in my ears. I struggled not to thrash on the bed, trying to slow my heartbeat. A hollow sadness slowly overtook the fear that dragged me from sleep.

My heart slowed. The world returned. I was still weary and guessed I'd slept little more than an hour. Only half awake, my fingers clutched at the ring Ren had given me the night of our union. Even in the darkness of my room it gleamed, catching the faintest starlight that trickled through the glass ceiling. I rolled onto my side, closing my eyes, but the moment I did, I could see Ren bleeding again. Sleep wasn't an option—at least not for a while.

I slipped from my room, not having a sense of where I'd go. The only thought driving me from my bed was that wandering the halls of the Academy would distract me from the horror of that dream. I glanced at the next door down the hall. Part of me wanted to go to Shay, to apologize and seek comfort in his arms. But I was still too unsettled by this place, by the fight with Emile. Too many things about that battle shook me to the core, filling me with doubt. Not only Lydia's death but my own choices. I hadn't killed Sasha. I hadn't wanted to. Would I be worth anything to the Searchers in battle?

As I walked, I twisted the ring on my finger, remembering the way it had gleamed in my dream. What did it mean that I'd accepted this sign of Ren's devotion but still left him at the altar? Did that make me a traitor or just a coward?

My somber thoughts were interrupted when my nose twitched. A familiar, alluring scent led me to a staircase and down. I took another deep breath, letting the rich, heavy aroma pull me forward. Two flights down I walked into a long, broad room filled with tables. A few lamps glowed, gently illuminating the space.

I quickly found the source of that delicious scent. Several glass French coffee presses rested atop one of the tables. Steam curled from coffee cups the Searchers sipped while sitting and talking quietly with one another. Monroe poured coffee into Tess's cup. She wasn't crying now, but her face was tight with grief. Adne was with them, a guitar in her lap. Connor was there too, looking a bit haggard. I was surprised to see Silas sitting next to Monroe.

The mood of the room made it clear the Searchers had gathered to mourn their dead. As much as the coffee's scent enticed me, I didn't want to interrupt them. I had started to turn when I heard my name.

I looked over my shoulder. Monroe was beckoning. I approached the table hesitantly.

"Do you need something?" the Guide asked.

"No," I said, uncomfortable now that all their eyes were on me. "I wasn't sleeping well and I smelled the coffee."

"From upstairs?" Connor asked.

I nodded, shifting on my feet.

"Neat trick." He smiled, taking a flask from his belt and adding its contents to his coffee. Whiskey, I guessed, from the sharp, peat-like scent of the amber liquid.

"I didn't mean to disturb you," I said.

"You aren't." Tess gestured for me to sit, pouring a fresh cup of coffee and pushing it in front of the empty chair beside her. "Please join us."

"We're just sharing stories," Adne said. She idly strummed the guitar strings. "About Lydia and Grant."

"You could offer a story if you'd like," Monroe said. "It's how we honor the dead and keep them with us."

"Me?" I frowned, though I took the seat and wrapped my hands around the warm coffee cup.

"You saw Grant more than we did." Silas had a notebook open in front of him, but he looked up from his writing. "You must have a story you could share."

I thought about Mr. Selby. What could I say? He'd been a good teacher. But somehow *"Big Ideas was my favorite class"* only sounded lame.

"I'm sorry," I said quietly. "I really don't think I can."

"No worries," Connor said, taking a swig of his spiked coffee. "I don't think I can take any more tales of woe tonight."

"Don't be a boor." Silas had put pen back to page. "Show some respect."

"Lydia was a fighter," Connor said. "She'd think we were fools to mope over her."

"Connor," Monroe chided, looking at Tess. But she shook her head.

"He's right." Tess smiled. "We're all terribly disappointing to her right now, I'd guess."

"You could never disappoint her." Adne reached out and touched Tess's cheek.

Tess's eyes glistened, but she kept smiling.

Adne smiled too, but she wasn't looking at Tess. "Hey, sleepyhead, ever hear of a comb?"

I turned to see Shay hastily running his fingers through his hair, though it didn't do much to fix the mess of soft curls. He'd pulled on jeans and a T-shirt, but other than that, it was clear he'd just rolled out of bed.

"Sorry," he said. "I had some bad dreams and couldn't get back to sleep. Then I smelled coffee...."

"Like peas in a pod," Connor said.

I glanced at Shay, wondering if he was still angry. He dropped into the chair between me and Adne. When he offered a sheepish smile, I knew he was sorry we'd fought. So was I. I leaned in and kissed him on the cheek.

"I couldn't sleep either."

He put his arm around my shoulders.

Silas was eyeing us.

"What?" I asked, not caring for his scrutiny.

"I've been weighing competing theories about the Scion," he said. "I can't decide if it's more likely that your turning him enhanced his skills or sapped them."

"What skills?" Shay asked.

"You have innate power," Silas continued. "Because of your heritage."

"My heritage?" Shay was frowning. "You mean all that knights and demons stuff you were talking about before?"

"I mean your father, of course." Silas tilted his head, squinting at Shay's face before he turned back to his notebook, scribbling furiously.

I sat up. "Are you taking notes on him?"

"Of course." Silas didn't raise his head.

"Knock it off!" I slapped the pen out of his hand.

Silas gaped at me.

"You know." Connor grinned at me. "I think I kind of love you."

"I was merely recording my observations." Silas went after his pen. "This is a once-in-a-lifetime opportunity."

"I'm not an opportunity," Shay sputtered. "I'm a person."

"You're the Scion," Silas countered. "It's imperative that we have a full grasp of your potential before we make our next move. Anika has put me in charge of gauging your ability to carry out the necessary tasks."

Monroe sighed. "I don't think she meant for you to notate all your interactions with Shay, Silas."

"Yeah." Connor slugged back more coffee and refilled his cup. "Why are you always such a freak?"

"You're a knuckle dragger." Silas sat down, glaring at Connor. "I like me more."

"I still don't understand what you mean about my heritage," Shay said, pouring his own cup of coffee. "I don't even remember my father. He died when I was three."

Silas looked at him, brow furrowed.

"I've been toted around the world by Bosque Mar for the past sixteen years," Shay said. "You called him the Harbinger earlier today. He's obviously not my uncle. What's the big deal about my father?"

The room abruptly seemed colder, and even Silas blanched as Shay spoke the Keeper's name.

"Yes, that's true. Bosque Mar is not your uncle," Monroe said. "But your father was one of the Keepers."

Shay's face grew pale. "Thanks for reminding me."

"That's not what matters, Shay," Monroe said. "What matters is you're the Scion."

"Does that mean I'm not human?" The cup in Shay's hand began to shake as he looked at me, eyes pleading.

"You are human . . . or at least you were until I turned you." I rushed to reassure him, and then I glared at Monroe. "I can tell the difference between mortals and our kind. Shay isn't a Keeper."

"You're suddenly an expert on Scion lore?" Silas spat.

"Gently, Silas," Monroe said quietly. "The Keepers would have needed Shay to remain ignorant of his heritage." He focused on me. "And they would have kept such knowledge from the Guardians as well. And, Calla, it's important that you understand that the Keepers themselves are human. Just as we are."

The breath caught in my lungs and a sickening twist coiled through me.

"So they were lying," Shay said. "They aren't some mystical Old Ones."

"Lying is what they do best," Tess said.

I managed to choke out a question. "But how can they be human? They don't smell human, and neither do you, for that matter. And what about all their powers?"

"It's the use of magic you can sense, Calla, the lingering scent of that power. Searchers and Keepers are tapped into something outside themselves, but we are all still human. There was a time when humans were closer to the earth and its inherent powers," Monroe said. "Those with the strongest connection to elemental magics and the ability to wield them were set apart from their communities. They were healers, wise men and women."

"But they can't be human," I protested. "They're immortal."

"No, they aren't," Monroe said. "They wanted you to believe they are because of the way they will use their powers and we won't, as Tess just said."

"What do you mean?" Shay asked.

"Reverence for the earth, the natural power inherent in creation, and its cycles," Connor replied with a mocking smile.

"Searchers believe that mortality is a good thing rather than something to avoid." Silas ignored Connor, diving into a lecture. "We grow old and die. Death is a part of the natural cycle. Keepers use their power to extend their lives to preternatural lengths. Mixing with the Nether changes the essence of who they are, but they still started out as human and remain human at the core. They extend the life span of their Guardians as well. That's why there are rarely new packs. Only when it's deemed necessary are they asked to bear offspring. Our records show that there hadn't been new wolf pups affiliated with Haldis until about two generations ago. Then the Keepers seemed to take a new interest in establishing stronger family ties between their packs again."

Shay glanced at me; a fresh look of horror had overtaken his face, and I nodded to confirm Silas's words.

"But the Keepers have children," he protested. "I mean, there were Keeper children at our school. And Logan inherited your pack."

Silas smirked. "The Keepers are incredibly vain, and they guard their powers jealously. Too many Keepers would inevitably lead to struggles within their own ranks, which they won't risk. Only the most powerful among them are allowed to have children to continue their legacy in this world. Some of them reside in Vail, as you've seen. The rest are scattered across the globe, concentrated near the sites of power. And we have Searcher outposts to track their activities in those same locations. But their numbers, though greater than ours, still don't rival the human population. So the Keepers have taken to using humans as pawns in their own game of life. Politics, global markets, all of it."

"But how did they get the advantage?" My mind was reeling from the deluge of new information. Lies, all lies.

"Yeah," Shay said. "I get that they use their power to be quasi-immortal now, but didn't you have even numbers at the beginning?"

"More or less." Silas scowled, looking put out that his speech hadn't rendered us silent and awestruck at his erudition.

"This would be the part where they gained their advantage over us." Connor leaned back in his chair, shoulders slumping.

"I don't understand," Shay said.

"Maybe it would be better to start with who Shay is and let the history fall into place," Monroe said.

"But—" Silas began.

"Keep it simple," Monroe said. "Start with Shay's lineage."

"Fine." Silas sighed. "The Scion is the descendant of the first Keeper, Eira, and the son of the traitor. That's how the Searchers identified him. That and the mark."

"The traitor?" Shay looked even more confused. I was completely bewildered by the conversation. None of the Searchers appeared surprised; apparently this was old news to them.

"Yes, yes." Silas drummed his fingers on the table. "The portent of the Scion was that a Keeper, a powerful descendant of Eira herself, would abandon his kind, turn against them, and his heir would cause their downfall. The child of that Keeper is the Scion."

When Shay continued to frown at him, Silas flipped through the pages of his notebook, turning it to face Shay. "It's right here."

"That's in Latin," Shay said.

"Don't you read Latin?" Silas asked, incredulous.

"Not without a dictionary," Shay snapped.

"Silas, most of us don't read Latin as ably as you can," Monroe chided.

"Can we move along?" Connor had put his head in his hands.

"Wait," I said, throwing him an apologetic smile. "I'm telling you, even if the Keepers are magic-laced humans or whatever, there wasn't any of that on Shay. He didn't have their scent. I know Keepers, but I never identified Shay as one of them."

"Yes," Monroe said. "I know that. But that's because Shay's mother was human."

"His father betrayed the Keepers for love," Adne said.

"Why?" Shay still looked dumbfounded. "Why did he leave the Keepers?"

"Oh, come on, Adne, that's so cliché," Silas said. Adne glared at him, and he just stared back at her.

"It's cliché because love matters, Silas," Tess snapped, eyes misting over. "It's one of the few things on earth that actually makes people take risks."

I met Shay's eyes, feeling heat rise in my cheeks.

"Right." Silas sounded bored. "Anyway. He left because Keepers, loving their power as they do, have forbidden permanent unions between their kind and humans. Tristan eloped with Sarah and attempted to hide out with her. Birds and bees . . . baby." He pointed at Shay.

"So how did you find him?" I asked. "If he was hiding, then how did the Searchers even know that the traitor from the prophecy existed?"

"We didn't have to find him," Monroe said. "He sought us out."

"He did?" Shay's eyes widened.

"Yes," Monroe said. "He wanted protection for his wife and child. He knew who he was; he knew we would give it. Unfortunately it wasn't enough."

"The Keepers found them?" I asked.

He nodded. "On the Aran Islands. We thought we'd isolated them, kept the location in absolute secrecy, but we failed. They took the family, killed Tristan and Sarah, and Bosque Mar kept Shay under his guard. Until now."

Shay stared blankly ahead; his hands were still trembling.

"I don't understand why he's not a Keeper," I said. "Doesn't it matter who his father was?"

"It matters for the prophecy," Silas replied. "But in terms of his essence, his being, it's the mother that matters. It's always the mother that matters."

"Huh?" I frowned.

Tess smiled. "Because the power of creation rests in women."

"Gloat all you want, Tess. At least I get to keep my figure." Connor patted his flat stomach.

"Battle of the sexes aside," Silas said, "Tess is right. The mother's essence always seems to dominate, determines the nature of the child. That's why you only perceived him as human—in all respects he was. His father's use of the Nether's power didn't pass on to him. The only sign of his mixed ancestry is the mark."

"What do you mean, the mother's essence always dominates?" I asked. "Has this happened before?"

"With the Keepers, no," Silas replied. "None but Tristan ever dared repudiate the Keepers' taboo on reproduction outside their own ranks. The reason we know about the pattern is because of the era of the Harrowing."

"But that was just a war," I countered. What could it have to do with children?

"Alliances form for many reasons," Monroe said quietly. He turned his face away from the rest of us, his eyes suddenly distant.

Silas nodded. "In the years leading up to the Guardians' revolt, the ties between Searchers and the wolf soldiers grew very strong— in many respects. The records tell us that children from resulting partnerships always reflected the mother's line. If the father was a Guardian, the child was a Searcher, if the father was a Searcher, the child remained a wolf."

My eyes widened. "Searchers and Guardians had children?"

"A very long time ago," Monroe replied; his jaw tightened and he continued to look away. "The Keepers did their best to wipe out all those offspring, to sever the ties forever."

My hands were trembling. "But Guardian females can't just have children—"

I stopped, feeling heat rushing up my neck into my cheeks. I hadn't meant to say that. The words had just blurted out. So many secrets about my life had been spilled, but this was one I'd wanted to keep stashed away.

When I spoke, it brought Shay out of his own far-off thoughts. "What?" He looked at me sharply.

I stared at the table.

No. No. I don't want to talk about this. It was too private. And too horrible.

Monroe cleared his throat. "Part of the Keepers' attempts to exert more control over the Guardian packs was through the regulation of partnerships and births among their soldiers. Something they started doing after the Harrowing. They use their power to stop and start the reproductive cycles in Guardian females, so they only become pregnant when the designated mate and the right time are established by their masters."

"Oh my God," Shay murmured.

I was finding it hard to breathe. *What will he think of me now?*

"It's not your fault, honey." Tess slid her arm around me. Her scent was all comfort—apple blossoms and honey. I let myself lean into her, grateful for her constant kindness. "They're real bastards."

Silas spoke. "But the Harrowing was the advent of that practice; the Keepers hadn't been so careful about such things before the revolt."

"Your mother was human, Shay," Monroe said with a brief, sympathetic glance in my direction. "Your human essence was that with which you were born and the one that Calla perceived."

"So my father's betrayal of the Keepers signaled that I was the Scion," Shay said.

I was relieved we seemed to be moving on in the conversation and decided to continue to push it forward.

"And the mark. But he can't see it." I gestured to Shay. "When I told him about the cross tattoo, he had no idea it was there."

"There's a ward on the symbol to keep it hidden," Silas explained. "It's not just a birthmark, not a tattoo. It's a mystical emblem."

"So humans are blind to the tattoo?" I asked.

Silas rolled his eyes, his hand flipping briefly before his face as though brushing away an irritating gnat. "It's a subtler enchantment than that. They're good at that, the Keepers: manipulation, subtlety.

It's their art, really. The tattoo only suggests to those who might take note of it that it should be ignored. We use a similar tactic to keep people from stumbling across the Academy. Humans will always look away, dismiss it. Just enough so that no one would walk up to Shay and ask who his tat artist was."

He glanced at Shay, eyes misty with a rather wry sort of reverence. "They'd think you didn't scrub your neck well enough after a nasty rugby match or the like. You know: muddied up, that sort of thing."

"But I could see it," I said.

"You're not human," Silas said. "You're—"

I cut him off. "An abomination. Right. How could I forget."

He pushed his chair back as I bared my fangs.

Shay grimaced and gingerly fingered the back of his neck. "Great. So I'm the Chosen One, but I have no skill at personal hygiene."

Silas's face illuminated with a startling grin. "Exactly."

Adne chortled and laid a devastating gaze on Shay. "Help me, Obi-Wan, you're my only hope . . . but could you manage a bath first?" She fluttered her eyelashes at him. "I'd wash your back for you anytime."

Shay's pale face went crimson and I threw Adne a reproving glance. But she was looking at Connor, who simply added more whiskey to his coffee.

Silas's grin didn't fade. He leaned back in his seat, studying Shay. "But now that your wolf girlfriend here turned you and all, you should be able to see it. Guardians wouldn't be affected by the spell."

"I'm not his girlfriend," I snapped, and then winced as Shay flushed even more deeply. The Searchers all stared at me, surprise written on their faces.

"Well, I'm not," I finished lamely, feeling cold and slippery as marble. I couldn't look at Shay again. It was harsh, but I'd spoken the truth. I loved him, but I didn't know what I was to Shay. Everything in our lives was constantly changing. I couldn't find stable ground to stand on.

Shay put his head in his hands. "I thought knowing the truth would make this easier. But it hasn't. I can't believe the only family I've known is some sort of Nether creature."

"Not just any Nether creature. He's more powerful than any other enemy we've faced, and you're the key to securing his reign," Monroe said. "The Harbinger couldn't trust your protection to his minions alone. As you can see, they failed in their duty. I'm sure some have suffered terribly because of your escape."

At the word "suffered," I began shivering and found I couldn't stop. *What is happening to my pack?* Shay put his hand on mine, glancing at Monroe.

"It's happened before, hasn't it?" Shay asked. "We read about the last time Guardians tried to rebel."

"You mean the Harrowing?" Silas asked. "That was a momentous period in our history. The closest we came to victory. Though it ended rather badly."

"No." I straightened, looking directly at Monroe because I knew he had the answers to the questions that were burning through me. "That wasn't the most recent revolt."

Monroe drew back. "No."

"Drop it, Lily." Adne had locked an accusing gaze on me. "That isn't your business."

I flashed my fangs at her. "Could you not call me that?"

"Not when it always gets that reaction from you. It's nice to know you are somewhat human. That austere wolf thing creeps me out, you know."

I stared at her. *I've known this girl for less than a day and she can read me like a book. How is that possible?*

"Adne's right." Connor leaned toward me. I could smell the whiskey on his breath. "Leave this alone."

"I will not," I said. "What happened to the Banes? How did Corrine Laroche die?"

"I said leave it." Connor slammed his fist down on the table.

"Back off," Shay snarled at him.

"Monroe?" Tess murmured, glancing anxiously at Connor.

"It's fine," Monroe said quietly. "They should know."

Connor shook his head, emptying the rest of his flask into his coffee cup. "So much for no more sad stories."

ELEVEN

MONROE LEANED BACK IN his chair. "I first came to Purgatory when I was twenty years old to serve as a Striker. I was a brash young man, all spitfire and ambition and no sense to speak of. I thought quite highly of myself."

He chuckled, running a hand through his dark hair. "I didn't appreciate the rules set by our Guide at the time. He was a meticulous man named Davis. I was impatient with his insistence that young Strikers always patrol in pairs. That we spend as much time gathering information about the Keepers as planning and executing attacks."

He folded his arms over his chest, his face lost in memories. "One day, when I was supposed to be training, I headed off on my own. Trekked up near Haldis, convinced I could take out a Guardian or two solo. I was a fool. If circumstances had been anything other than what they were, I would have been dead."

"What were the circumstances?" Shay asked.

"I encountered a lone Guardian. She was on me faster than I would have imagined possible; I didn't even have time to draw a weapon. I had completely underestimated the skill of my adversaries. She knocked me down, and I thought she would kill me." His voice tightened and he swallowed. "But then it wasn't a wolf over me anymore. It was a young woman." He glanced at me and smiled. "Barely older than you, Calla."

I nodded, my heart pounding. "Why did she shift into human form?"

Monroe's jaw clenched. "She asked me to kill her."

"What?" Shay gasped.

I heard a muffled sob and glanced over to see that Tess had begun to cry again. Adne wrapped her arm around Tess's shoulders.

"I was stunned," Monroe continued. "She could barely speak through her tears. She clung to me, sobbing."

Torrid emotion rippled through Monroe's eyes, and I suddenly found it difficult to breathe.

He shifted restlessly in his chair. "She was mated to a cruel man for whom she had no love, tormented by constant fear of a master even more wicked than her husband, terrified for the well-being of packmates for whom she did care deeply but whose lives were as unpredictable and devoid of free will as her own." He paused and drew a slow breath before he spoke again. "But all these things, she said she'd been able to bear. Until that moment."

"What changed?" Shay whispered. He glanced at me and saw my contorted face. His fingers slipped between my own and I gripped his hand.

"Her master had ordered her to bear a child." Monroe closed his eyes. "And she couldn't face the idea that she would bring another life into this world who would be forced to contend with the same pains that plunged her into despair every day."

"What did you do?" I asked in a whisper.

"I offered to help her." Monroe's eyes opened; they roiled with violent emotion. "I told her about the Harrowing. The true history that undermined all the lies she'd been told from her birth. A time when Searchers and Guardians united to fight back against the Keepers. I was desperate to convince her that there was another way. Something besides death to give her hope. I had never encountered pain like that. I wanted nothing more than to save her."

Shay and I sat in silence, fascinated by his tale. Connor was staring into his cup, while Adne had begun to stroke Tess's hair. Silas didn't seem to be paying attention at all, his energy redirected to his notebook, occasionally pausing to peer at Shay.

Monroe smiled sadly. "We began to meet in secret. I brought her as much information as I could about how the alliances of the past had formed."

I felt a caress on my hand. I glanced at Shay and he smiled gently at me. Monroe watched the exchange and his eyebrows rose. "Sounds familiar?"

Shay nodded.

Monroe's smile became a grimace and he spoke again. "Davis had been furious with me for disobeying his directive, but he jumped at the chance to have Guardians on our side. It looked like our best chance to overturn control of Haldis. Corrine was able to gather support among several of her packmates. Our plan was to bring them out first, gather a significant force of several Searcher teams, and then make a combined assault against the Keepers in Vail."

"But something went wrong?" Shay frowned.

Monroe nodded. He cleared his throat, but his voice remained thick. "Corrine became pregnant. She'd hoped to avoid it somehow"—he winced—"but such things can be difficult to control."

He was quiet for a moment; he folded his hands on the table. "She was afraid to run while she was pregnant, and she didn't want to take extra risks with the newborn child, so she asked for the plan to be put on hold. To wait until the child had grown, until her son was a year old and wouldn't be so vulnerable when we made our escape. I agreed." He paused; I saw his hands trembling.

I forced my question out, despite my growing fear. "What happened?"

"In the intervening period, the plot was discovered." Monroe's knuckles whitened as his hands locked together fiercely. "Instead of the escape, the team of Searchers encountered an ambush at the Bane compound. We lost more than half our number."

"And Corrine? And her allies?" Shay's voice was stern.

Monroe replied in a flat tone. "They had already been handed over to wraiths. All dead before we even arrived."

I had to close my eyes as Monroe breathed life into the scenes from my nightmare. My organs felt brittle, ready to shatter.

"But they let Ren live?" I whispered. "They didn't kill her child."

"It's been hard to put the pieces together, but from what I understand, Corrine's mate was loyal to her master, never a conspirator against the Keepers. And the child remained in his care. After all, the young alpha for the new pack was still needed. And as you've already said, he knew nothing about how his mother truly died."

Shay squeezed my hand again and I realized that tears were coursing down my cheeks. I swiftly brushed them away. He looked at Monroe. "Do you have any idea how she was betrayed?"

Monroe's jaw set; he stared at his hands.

"I think that's all, folks," Connor muttered. "Are you satisfied?"

Shay's head snapped around. "Would you just—"

"No, Shay." I put my hand on his arm. "Thank you, Monroe."

Monroe rose, giving us his back. "I'll bid you good night."

"Me too," Tess said. She followed Monroe back to the staircase.

"Way to clear a room," Connor mumbled, staring into his empty coffee cup.

"Leave it, Connor," Adne said, and stood up. "Let's just find another way to pass the time."

He grinned at her. "I have a few ideas."

"Mine are better and in the realm of possibility." Adne sat on the table, put her feet on the bench, and rested the guitar on her knees. She strummed the chords and tilted her head.

"Requests?"

"Ladies' choice," Connor said.

She began to sing, her voice rich and low.

"Rage, rage against the dying of the light," she sang.

Shay perked up. "Dylan Thomas?"

She paused, shrugging. "Yeah. It's kind of our mantra here. I made up a melody to go along with the poem."

"How long have you been playing?" Shay watched her fingers move along the frets, clearly fascinated.

"Since I was four," Adne said. "My mother taught me."

"She's a natural, but that's no surprise. Adne's good at everything. Child genius and all." Connor pushed a strand of Adne's mahogany hair off her forehead. His brown eyes gleamed in the firelight as his fingers lingered on her skin.

A nagging suspicion crept through me. Something lay just beneath the surface of Connor and Adne's constant bickering. I was sure of it.

So many hidden stories linking all of them together. These two have secrets of their own.

"I can tell," Shay murmured, his eyes fixed on Adne's swiftly moving fingers. "Could you teach me?"

Adne's strumming paused. "To play?"

Shay nodded.

She smiled at him, patting the bench next to her. "Of course."

Shay moved to her side and she placed the guitar on his thighs. I swallowed hard when she moved to sit behind him on the table, leaning over him so she could guide his hands on the guitar.

Despite my suspicions about Connor and Adne, I wondered if their story was in the past—and Adne had her eye on a future with Shay. I didn't doubt Shay's feelings for me, but jealousy still nipped at me anytime I saw him and Adne together. Even if he wasn't interested in her, they were becoming fast friends. And that made my chest ache. I missed my friends. Especially Bryn. Even if she had to pry information from me about my feelings, her constant concern, her presence had sustained me. Every alpha needed that support.

I forced my eyes off Adne and Shay. The thought of turning into a wolf and pinning Adne to the floor was becoming more and more appealing.

"I think I'm gonna call it a night." Connor yawned loudly, though he had fixed a hard gaze on the impromptu music lesson. "Adne, can I escort you to your room?"

"What?" Adne barely glanced at him. "I suddenly need an escort? Did we have a time warp to the nineteenth century that I missed?"

Connor glared at Shay and then kicked the floor with the heel of his boot. He looked vulnerable, something I'd never seen in the ever-joking Searcher before.

"No, I—" he mumbled. "Night, then."

"Night." Adne's attention was back on the guitar.

Connor looked back at Shay and Adne once more, hesitating. The expression on his face was strange, caught somewhere between anger and sadness.

"I think I'll go to bed too," I said. *Before I tear her fingers off.*

"I'll walk you to your room. I'll even sing you a lullaby . . . and maybe you could show me what makes you howl," Connor said, a smile sliding across his mouth.

"Hey!" Shay snapped out of his trance to glare at the Searcher.

"Down, boy." Connor laughed.

"Come on, Shay," Adne chided, pulling his hands into place on the guitar. "Pay attention. Put your fingers here and here. That's a G chord."

Shay flushed, wrenching his neck to look at Adne. "Sorry. Uh . . . okay, G chord."

"Don't worry; you'll get the hang of it." She rested her chin on his shoulder.

I followed Connor out of the dining hall, a burning knot occupying the place my stomach used to be.

"You hanging in there, kiddo?" He glanced at me as we climbed the stairs. "Pretty big changes happening in your life."

I rolled my shoulders back, not certain how to take his question. "Why do you care?" I regretted my harsh tone, but I was still bristling from watching Adne wrap herself around Shay at the table. Plus hanging out with Connor was like riding a roller coaster: I didn't know whether he'd be making inappropriate comments or asking thoughtful questions. The Searchers were giving me emotional whiplash.

"You know you will have to trust us . . . eventually," he said.

I flashed my teeth at him rather than giving him a true smile. "Eventually."

"Fair enough," he said, pausing at the door to my room. "Sweet dreams, alpha."

"Thanks," I said, and pushed the door open.

I didn't bother turning on the light; instead I collapsed on the bed and stared at the dark sky above, my mind too frantic for sleep to be a real possibility. Nonetheless, I still felt sapped, weary. But the ache was deeper than that.

I'm lonely.

Until that moment I hadn't realized that in truth, I'd never been alone. I'd always had the pack, no matter what challenges life had thrown my way. In their absence I felt lost, utterly without purpose. I'd run from Vail to save Shay but also to save my friends. Now that choice seemed less like a solution and more like an ephemeral hope that moved further and further away from materializing.

What am I doing here?

I rolled over on the bed, burying my face in a pillow, and closed my eyes. The room was a little cold, but I didn't bother to pull the thick down comforter over me. The uncomfortable chill that crept along my limbs further fed my disconsolate spirit. My body tensed, but I didn't stir when I heard the door open and then quietly click shut once more. I caught the scent of sun-warmed grasses and clover. Shay's gentle footfalls crossed the room and then paused.

"I know you're awake, Calla."

I sighed, flipping over to face him.

"What happened to your guitar lesson?" I sounded catty, and it only made me angrier that Adne had so easily gotten under my skin.

"I wanted to make sure you were okay." He crawled across the bed.

I leaned away, rolling onto my back.

"You left Adne all alone? I think she was looking forward to teaching you." *I think she was looking forward to more than that.*

"She had to go back to Denver," he said. "Silas showed up with a report for her to take back to the outpost. But now that I'm here, it sounds like you'd rather I left *you* all alone."

I couldn't decide if he sounded irritated or amused, so I didn't answer. I let my eyes wander back to the starry sky. Then the tiny, winking lights were replaced by shadow as Shay moved close to me. My breath caught when instead of stretching out beside me, he positioned his body over mine. His weight pressed me down into the mattress.

"Shay." I was startled, but unafraid. "What are you doing?" My hands moved up to his chest and kept his torso suspended just above me.

His fingers circled my wrists, holding me down, preventing me from pushing him off.

"No more hiding behind your fear, Calla. No more running away," he said. "You can try to tear both of my hands off if you really want to. But I am going to kiss you now."

I swallowed as I took in the bright, confident gleam in his eye. He had no fear of me. Even through the light clasp of his fingers, I could feel the depth of his strength; it was surprising and enticing. He no longer approached me with the trepidation he'd had as a human; now he was a Guardian. And not only that, but the Scion: he would bear the Elemental Cross. A weapon the likes of which the world had never seen. He was a true warrior. My equal. Perhaps more. My lips curved in a smile when I realized that Shay's vulnerability, which had first provoked me to save his life, had ebbed away and was replaced by iron strength that matched his fierce, unrepentant will. He no longer needed me to be his protector, but he still wanted me. The expression etched on his face was hungry, full of the need to know that I wanted him too. And I did.

I'm free now. I love him. There isn't any reason to stop.

He released my wrists, waiting, watching me. I didn't push him away but let my hands rest against the hard muscles of his chest. He bent toward me and I slid my arms around his neck, my fingers twining in the soft curls of his hair. Then his lips were on mine, parting them gently.

Shay's kiss held the promise of that freedom I'd longed for. Sweet and tender like the first green shoots that push up to find the spring sun. I closed my eyes and let pure sensation wash over me. Honey and clover. Soft, warm rain filling my mouth, pouring over my body. He was brilliant sunlight that drove away winter's chill.

His body pressed harder into mine, and I wrapped my legs around him. A low sound somewhere between a groan and a growl slipped from his throat. His kisses lingered, exploring my mouth, each caress drawing more desire from deep inside me. My hands moved along his back, feeling the strength in his shoulders, wanting to know more of him. He slid his hands beneath my shirt, stroking the bare skin of my stomach, and began to move up slowly. My blood was on fire.

I pulled my shirt up over my shoulders and tossed it away. I felt every inch of Shay's body suddenly tighten as his eyes took me in. I slipped my own hands under his shirt, my fingers moving not up but down, finding the buttons of his jeans, toying with them, wanting to go further but not certain I should. He leaned down, kissing me hard. I moved against him, needing to be closer to him, hating the remaining clothing that separated us. My fingers undid the first button of his jeans and slipped down to the next. My breath came in gasps at the scorching trail his hands made as they slid over my skin.

"Calla," he murmured against my lips. "You have no idea how long I've wanted to do this."

Something about his words made me falter, like I'd tripped in the darkness and was suddenly falling, falling. And then it wasn't Shay above me, but Ren. His dark eyes gleamed in the dim light of the room, his hands slipping over my skin. *Just let me kiss you, Calla. You don't know how long I've wanted to.*

It was as though an icy wind swept through the room. The fire licking my skin was smothered, replaced by hollow cold. I shuddered and my stomach lurched. I began to shake my head.

"What's wrong?" Shay's hands paused.

"Stop." My fists came up to his chest, and this time I pushed him away hard enough that he backed off, startled. I closed my eyes, grabbing my shirt off the floor, no longer able to look at him. "I can't."

My entire body shook so violently I could barely pull my shirt back on. The dark chasm that resided in my chest roared to life, sucking my brief calm into its yawning oblivion. I hated myself for pulling away from him, knowing I wanted Shay, loved him. *Why can't I let go of the past? What is wrong with me?*

Alarm filled his voice. "What happened? You've gone white." He tried to pull me into his arms, but I scrambled from the bed.

"I'm sorry," I mumbled, unable to further vocalize the sudden conflict of impulses that tore through me. I clasped my hands against my chest. Unbidden but instinctively my fingers traced the surface of Ren's ring.

Ren's voice filled my ears. *Tell me you'll come back for the pack. For me.*

It felt like the room was spinning. I'd left him behind. He'd risked everything for me, and this was how I was repaying him. By giving myself to someone else when I was promised to him. *What am I doing here? With people who have always been my enemies? I belong with my pack.* The fire in my veins turned to ice as I realized I wasn't free. I wouldn't be free until my pack was safe. A part of me was a prisoner to the fear that I'd sentenced them to a terrible fate.

"Calla, what is it?" Shay stepped toward me, but both our heads snapped around at the sudden banging on the door. In the next moment, it flew open and Adne burst in.

"Calla!" Her eyes were wild. "We have to go back to Denver now!"

"What's wrong, Adne?" Shay rushed to her side. "An attack? The Keepers?"

"No." She stared at him for a moment as if shocked to find him in my room. She shook off her surprise, turning back to me. "Ethan took down a Guardian out on patrol."

"A Guardian?" My heart began to pound as I saw the terrified sparks in her gaze.

Her voice trembled. "He says he's your brother."

INFERNO

PART II

Abandon hope, all ye who enter here.

Dante, *Inferno*

TWELVE

"WHAT?" MY QUESTION emerged as a hoarse whisper.

"Her brother?" Shay gaped. "You mean Ansel?"

"I didn't get a name," Adne said. "Why are you still standing there? Come on!"

I snapped out of my shock and bolted for the door. Adne was already running down the hall. I could hear Shay's feet pounding just behind me.

Ethan took down a Guardian. *Took down?* The electric adrenaline that pulled me after Adne transformed into a numbing dread. Fear's icy tendrils turned into sharp spikes of terror when I caught sight of the glimmering open door.

I stopped, not recognizing the man who stood alongside it. "Good, you've found them," he said. "Everyone else has gone through."

"That's just Jerome, Calla. Go on." Adne pushed me into the portal.

I stumbled forward, landing on my hands and knees in Purgatory's training room.

"What were you thinking?!" Monroe roared. "He's a child!"

I was afraid of what possibly could have made Monroe so angry.

"He was running at me, Monroe. Screaming like a banshee, I swear,"

Ethan yelled, his voice choked and full of strain. "He yelled, 'I'm a Guardian, I'm a Guardian,' over and over. What was I supposed to do?"

Isaac, Connor, and Silas were staring at something on the floor in front of them, their faces ashen. That was when I saw the blood pooling at their feet.

Monroe tore his raging eyes from Ethan at the sound of our approach. His anger gave way to fear when he saw me.

"Calla—" He stepped over the rivulets of blood that moved out from the circle of Searchers and grabbed my arm.

I wrenched away from him and shoved aside Connor, who had stepped behind Monroe in a second attempt to shield whoever was on the floor from my view.

Ansel wasn't moving. His clothes were dark with blood. I screamed and covered my mouth with my hands. Crossbow bolts protruded from his chest.

"Ansel! Ansel!!"

"I didn't know who it was . . . ," Ethan began, and stared at me with wild eyes. "He just threw himself at me. I thought he would claw my eyes out."

I lunged at Ethan, but Connor's arms wrapped around me from behind.

"Whoa, girl," he said, trying to keep his voice even, but I could hear his anxiety. "Let's not do anything hasty."

"I will kill you," I growled, struggling against Connor.

"Oh God." Shay was beside me, staring at Ansel. He looked at me. "Can you help him?"

The red wave of rage had pushed all rational thought from my mind. I closed my eyes, trying to draw breath.

"If his heart is still beating," I murmured. "Maybe."

"Okay, then let's do that. I'll help you. You have to focus, Cal. Save Ansel." Shay touched my arm. He looked at Connor. "Let her go."

Connor glanced at Monroe, who had positioned himself between me and Ethan. Monroe gave a slight nod. Connor eased his grip on me, and Shay took both of my hands, pulling me to Ansel's side. I knelt in the blood and put my hands on Ansel's chest. I could hear his breath, wet and ragged. His pulse was there, but it was weak and slowing.

I choked on a sob. "Oh God, Ansel."

"I'm sorry." Ethan was staring at us, his face a mixture of grief and horror. "I didn't know he was your brother."

I glared at him, rage making every beat of my heart deafening.

"Stop talking, Ethan," Monroe said, and moved to block my view of the Searcher.

"Calla." Shay's voice brought me back to the task at hand. "Ansel needs help now. What can I do?"

I shook my head, trying to focus. "He needs blood, and the arrows have to come out."

Shay nodded.

"When I tell you, pull the shafts as quickly as you can."

"All right."

He moved to the other side of Ansel's limp form and grasped a crossbow bolt. I raised my forearm to my lips and bit down. I slid my hand underneath Ansel's head and tilted it up. I wedged my fingers between his lips, parting them. Then I leaned down and murmured in his ear as I pressed my bleeding arm against his mouth.

"Listen, baby brother. Please listen." I was sobbing as I spoke. "I need you to hear me. You have to drink, Ansel. Please drink."

My blood poured into his mouth. Down his throat. I closed my eyes and pressed my forehead against his temple. The Searchers stared at us, silent and frozen in place. A mixture of horror and curiosity played across their faces.

Ansel didn't move. My blood was filling his mouth; it began to trickle out one corner of his lips.

"Calla?" Shay's voice was edged with fear.

"Please, Ansel," I whispered again. "Drink. I love you. Don't do this. Drink."

Ansel's body jerked, a sharp shuddering movement. His jaw opened and he swallowed. His muscles convulsed and his head pulled away from my arm.

"Adne, Connor, get over here," I shouted. "He's going to fight. I need you to hold him still."

They both came to my side and pinned his shoulders to the floor. He jerked again, and they had no trouble holding him still. Even through my fear I frowned. His struggling was weak. Something was wrong. I put my bleeding arm back against his mouth.

"Come on, An," I said. "You need this. Keep drinking. Don't fight it."

He swallowed again and then began to drink steadily.

"Keep him down," I said, glancing at Adne and Connor.

They grimaced and nodded.

"Shay, start pulling the arrows."

"Okay." Shay sucked in a quick breath. "Here goes nothing." He jerked the first shaft out of Ansel's chest.

Ansel's eyes didn't open, but he bucked up and snarled, spewing blood from his mouth. Adne grunted, but Connor just kept steady pressure against Ansel's body.

"Hold him down!" I shouted, and pushed my arm back against his mouth.

My anxiety grew by the minute. Ansel was barely putting up a fight. *What if my blood came too late to save him?*

"Again, Shay," I said, pushing back the sickening fear that crawled up my throat. "We have to get the arrows out as quickly as possible."

Shay nodded and pulled out two more arrows. "That's all of them," he announced, tossing the crossbow bolts aside.

I kept my arm pressed to Ansel's mouth. He stopped flailing and drank deeply, more steadily. I braced myself against the floor with my other hand. He was taking a lot of blood.

"Calla—" Shay moved to my side and put his arm around my waist.

"I'll be okay," I said.

Ansel stopped drinking. I hesitantly pulled my arm from his mouth and clamped my hand over the puncture wound. His eyes fluttered open.

"Calla?"

I sobbed, pulling him against me.

Monroe expelled a shuddering sigh. "Thank God."

"No wonder Strikers have such a hard time killing them," Silas quipped. "Did you see how fast that was? I'll talk to the Academy about some new enchantments to counter that."

"Not now, Silas," Connor said through gritted teeth.

"It's really you," Ansel said, blinking at me, his voice still a bit unsteady. "I can't believe I found you."

"Ansel." I buried my face in his matted hair. "Oh God, Ansel."

His eyes remained slightly unfocused as they slid over the circled Searchers, finally resting on Ethan, who took a step back.

"He shot me." Ansel sounded oddly amused. "That's the one who shot me."

"Don't worry—" I began. "It's all going to be okay. He didn't know who you were, but you're safe now."

Ansel looked at me again. I didn't recognize the empty smile that cut across his mouth.

"You should have let him kill me."

THIRTEEN

MY FINGERS DUG INTO his shoulders as I stared at him, unable to speak, not believing what I'd just heard. I could barely recognize my brother's scent beneath the other vile odors that covered him. Filth, blood, and the sharp tang of fear.

Shay crouched beside us. "Ansel, hey. Take a breath. Everything is cool."

The knot of sickness tightened when Ansel began to laugh. I'd never heard a sound so chilling. Harsh and devoid of joy.

"Is it, Shay?" he asked, smiling that horrible smile again. "Is everything cool?"

"Ansel, what's wrong?" I pushed back the hair that was caked on his forehead.

He swatted my hand away, trying to pull himself out of my arms. "Knock it off. Just let go."

My grip on him only tightened. I couldn't make anything of his strange behavior. He pushed at me, but I didn't move an inch.

Shay's eyes widened as he watched Ansel stop fighting. He stood up, face paling. "Oh no."

I glanced at him. "What?"

Shay shook his head, his gaze resting on Ansel. "I don't even know if it's possible, but I think—"

"You think, chosen boy?" Ansel looked up at Shay with a shudder. "You know. Of course you know." The smile vanished, replaced by a blank, defeated expression.

"What are you talking about?" I whispered.

"I—" He lifted his eyes to mine. For a moment rage flared within his gray irises, making them flash like a thundercloud full of lightning, but then the light was gone, replaced by a vast fog, thick and hopeless.

Monroe took a cautious step toward us. Ansel didn't react. He stared ahead, looking at nothing in particular. Monroe knelt beside him, frowning.

"Is he hurt?"

"I don't know," I said, keeping my eyes on Ansel. "Baby brother, please. Talk to me."

"They took it." Ansel's whisper was so low I could barely hear him.

"Took what?" I asked.

"Calla." Shay's voice had a warning note. "Maybe we should let him rest. Let him be."

"Me," Ansel continued, not meeting my eyes. "Everything. It's gone. I'm dead."

"They can't touch you here." Monroe spoke gently. "Your sister is right. You're no longer in danger."

"It doesn't matter," Ansel said.

My patience snapped. "What is wrong with you?"

I shoved him away and he tumbled along the floor like a rag doll. *Oh God. What just happened?*

He lay still for a moment and then his shoulders began to shake as he beat the floor with his fists, sobbing.

Connor gaped at my brother. "Can all Guardians just toss each other around? Or was that because you're an alpha?"

"No!" I fought the terrible realization that spilled over me.

I crawled to Ansel's side, gingerly turning him over.

"Ansel?" I reached out, but he scrambled back.

"Don't touch me."

"Why can't you fight me?" I thought I already knew the answer, but my instincts screamed out against it.

He glared at me, fists held tight against his sides. "I told you. They took it."

"You have to explain, An. I don't understand." But I did understand; I just couldn't believe it.

Shay's voice came from right behind me. "He's not a Guardian anymore."

I turned to look at him. His face was still pale and a little green.

"That isn't possible." *No, no, no.*

"It is," Monroe said quietly, keeping a respectful distance as he watched my brother begin to rock with grief.

"No, it isn't!" I shrieked, not wanting to believe what I was seeing before my eyes.

"Guardians can be made," Monroe continued. "And unmade."

"No!" I was on my feet, standing before my brother as though he were under attack. "It can't be!"

"Monroe's right." Silas smoothed the front of his shirt. "Guardians are aberrations of nature. The Keepers know how to manipulate their creations as they see fit."

I snarled at him.

He gazed at me, unfazed. "It's true."

"Shut up, Silas." Connor cuffed him on the back of the head.

"Ow!" Silas cried, rubbing his skull. "What? I'm just pointing out—"

"Leave it," Monroe barked.

"Why?" Shay crouched beside Ansel, watching him intently. "Why would they do this to you?"

Ansel scowled, glaring at Shay. "An example. They needed an example."

My mouth went dry. "An example for whom?" I croaked.

Ansel turned his gaze on me and I fell back onto the heels of my hands. How could my own brother look at me like that?

"For your pack," he hissed. "Or did you forget about us since you have all these new friends?"

"Easy," Shay said, putting himself between me and Ansel. "Calla isn't the one to blame. She did what she did to save my life. If you're going to blame someone, blame me."

Ansel smiled at him, empty and cold. "Congratulations, man. You're the wolf that I'm not. She made you for herself and left us behind."

"That's not how it happened. Ansel, they were going to kill him!" My eyes burned, tears spilling down my cheeks.

"Better him than us," he said, staring at the floor again. "The whole pack will be dead soon enough."

"No," I whispered. They wouldn't, would they? Kill the young wolves? All of them? My mind reeled, screaming against the possibility. The Keepers had executed Guardians for revolts in the past. Had I sealed that fate for my packmates when I ran?

Monroe was suddenly beside us, resting his hands on Ansel's shoulders.

"Listen carefully. We can help you and your friends, but you must tell me the truth. Were you followed?"

Ansel's eyes rolled up and he spat in Monroe's face.

Adne gasped, but Monroe held up his hand.

"I understand you're in pain," he said quietly, but without anger. "But I need you to trust me. We aren't your enemies. Your sister is safe here. You will be too."

I could hardly breathe. Tears still ran down my face, dripping from my jaw onto my collarbone. What had I done? Faces swirled before my closed eyes. Bryn. Mason. Ren.

I felt a hand on mine. "Calla," Shay murmured. "It's not your—"

"Don't." I jerked my fingers away from his. "It *is* my fault."

Ansel drew a long shuddering breath. "They threw me out of a van downtown. They just said I'd find my sister if I was lucky."

"Ethan?" Monroe was on his feet.

"He was alone," Ethan said. "No trackers. No Guardians."

"He's probably just a warning," Connor said. "It's the sort of thing they like to do."

Adne shuddered and Connor put his arm around her shoulders.

"You're likely right," Monroe said.

Adne stepped forward. "We should get him cleaned up. I can find some clothes."

"I just want to be left alone," Ansel muttered, but the rage was gone from his voice.

I crawled to his side.

"Let them help, An. They really can help us."

"I shouldn't have said those things to you." He shivered, finally looking at me, eyes glassy and brimming with grief. "I'm glad you're not dead."

I laughed through my own tears. "Thanks."

"Why did you leave us?"

"I couldn't let Shay die. I just couldn't," I choked. "I didn't want to leave you. I'm so sorry."

He leaned his head against my shoulder, shivering when I put my arm around him. "So am I."

FOURTEEN

WE GATHERED AT Purgatory's kitchen table. Silas and Adne set steaming mugs of tea before us. No longer caked in blood and grime, wearing clothes that Adne had scrounged up, Ansel looked himself again. Almost. His face remained a shadow of the one I remembered, and he shivered even under the blanket wrapped around his shoulders. My brother had always glowed with optimism, a smile constantly twitching at the corners of his lips. Now his features were drawn. His eyes, half hidden by the fall of his sand brown hair, were distant and dull.

I sat across from him, watching his every move, wondering what he was thinking, if he was in pain. I'd tried to sit closer to him, but he'd shifted his chair farther away. It was as though he couldn't tolerate my presence.

He wasn't a wolf any longer. I understood the weight of that loss. Wolves were who we'd always been. To live without that part of myself would be . . . impossible. I would be lost in the world. *But why won't he be near me? I know it isn't his fault. Is he ashamed? Is he afraid of me?*

Ansel had been thrown not to the wolves, but from them. Abandoned like refuse in the street, no longer useful to his masters.

We sat quietly, waiting for him to answer the question Monroe had just asked.

He didn't move, fingers clasping the mug in front of him.

Monroe cleared his throat. "I know it's difficult, but you need to tell us what happened after Calla and Shay left Vail."

Ansel pushed his mug away, hiding his shaking hands beneath the table.

"We were waiting for her in the clearing."

I closed my eyes, suddenly back in the forest. I heard the drums, Sabine and Nev singing. I remembered catching Shay's scent, finding him bound and blindfolded. My heart began to pound in my chest, matching the memory of the fierce drumbeats.

"But she never came." Ansel's voice pierced the fog of images and I opened my eyes to find him staring at me.

"She found me," Shay said. "I'd been kidnapped. They had me tied up, waiting to be sacrificed in that ceremony."

"Interesting," Silas murmured.

"That's not interesting," Connor snapped. "It's sick."

"What are you even doing here?" I bared my fangs at Silas. "Aren't you just a paper pusher?"

"That's my girl." Connor smiled.

"Scribes coordinate all intelligence from the outposts," Silas said, puffing his chest. "We lost a key operative today; this boy might be able to tell us how that happened."

He raised an eyebrow at Ansel, but Ansel just stared blankly at the tabletop.

Silas cleared his throat, looking to Shay. "Tell us about the sacrifice. Was there any ritual preparation involved?"

"Ritual preparation?" Shay asked. "Uh . . . no. I was knocked out. If there was anything that happened before I ended up in the woods, I don't know what it was."

Connor glanced at Shay. "You okay, kid?"

"I'm fine," Shay replied, though he looked a little pale.

"Can we hold questions till he's finished?" Monroe said, gesturing for Ansel to continue.

The group fell silent.

"None of us knew what was going to happen," Ansel said, pausing for a moment. "Well—at least none of my pack did. We just thought it would be Ren and Calla together. We knew there would be a kill, but we thought it would be—"

He stopped, glancing around the room.

"Oh, how sweet." Connor laughed darkly.

"What?" Adne asked.

Ethan grimaced. He rose, pacing beside the hearth. "One of us. They thought it would be one of us to kill."

Isaac coughed up some of his tea. Adne handed him a dish towel.

An uncomfortable silence filled the room.

"That's the past," Monroe said finally. "Leave it."

Ansel looked at Monroe and after getting a nod, he continued.

"We'd been waiting so long that Efron ordered some of the elder Banes into the forest. They started howling almost immediately. We all ran. Wolves and Keepers. Then I saw her."

"Flynn," Shay and I said together.

Ansel nodded. "I couldn't stop staring. I didn't know why she'd be in the forest in the first place and now she was dead, obviously killed by one of us."

He paused, looking at me. "Did you know she was a succubus?"

"Not until she attacked us," I whispered, remembering her wings, the fire that spewed from her throat.

"That was when everything went crazy," Ansel continued. "Efron and Lumine were screaming orders. I tried to stay with Bryn, but elder Banes grabbed us. I didn't know what was happening. They threw me into a car and then we were downtown."

"Downtown?" I asked, frowning.

"At Eden," he said. "But not in the club. Underneath it. Efron has some sort of . . . prison there. That's where they took us."

"Well, that's helpful," Silas murmured.

"What?" Shay asked.

"We didn't know where the Keepers' detention facility was," Monroe said. "Keep talking, Ansel."

"I didn't know why we were being treated like the enemy." His words were tumbling out now. "They put me and Mason in a cell together. And I think Fey and Bryn too—I didn't see them, but I could hear them yelling."

I began to tremble. Shay twined his fingers through mine, and I didn't pull away.

"Nothing happened for a while." Ansel's voice was so quiet that we all leaned forward, straining to hear him. "They put shackles on us and we couldn't change forms. But that was all at first."

Shay glared at Monroe. "You guys have a swap meet or something?"

Monroe didn't answer.

"What?" I frowned, looking at Shay.

"They had those on you when we first arrived at the Academy," he said.

"If she came to while we were moving her, she would have attacked without knowing what she was doing," Connor said. "We didn't have a choice."

Shay opened his mouth to respond.

"Don't, Shay," I said quickly. "It's fine."

"And then they brought Ren down." Ansel didn't seem to have noticed any of our exchange. He was lost in the past, or worse, trapped by it.

At the sound of Ren's name I jerked my hand free of Shay's. Ren. Ren had tried to help us. He lied to the Keepers for us. What had it cost him?

Suddenly I could hear his voice. *This is only about love.* I felt his breath against my skin, his lips on mine. The fierceness of his embrace before I left him.

"And that's when it started." Ansel jerked in his seat, shoulders trembling violently.

"When what started?" Monroe urged gently.

"The punishments," Ansel whispered. "The wraiths came."

"Adne, you should leave now," Monroe said, keeping his eyes on Ansel's shaking form.

"No," she said, despite her own trembling hands.

"It would be better if you didn't hear this," Monroe said. "I'll fill you in when we're through."

"No," she repeated.

"Why wouldn't she stay?" Shay asked.

Monroe's jaw clenched. He didn't answer Shay, instead keeping his gaze locked on Adne.

Adne swallowed hard but straightened to her full height. "Wraiths killed my mother."

"You should go," Monroe said quietly. "Please."

"It's okay, Monroe," Connor said, moving to Adne's side and taking her hands in his own. "She's strong."

Monroe frowned, but didn't argue further.

Ansel was still talking, shaking. "First they came into our cells with Lumine and Efron. They'd take us, one at a time. Making the others watch. Sometimes it was Emile and the elder Banes. We'd be chained up in human form and they'd attack, teeth and claws tearing at us. Enough to make you bleed but not kill you. Other times the Keepers would come and summon wraiths. Wraiths were worse than Guardians. Much worse. It's like they swallow you whole and you're trapped inside; you feel your flesh coming apart. It's like being eaten alive slowly . . . so slowly. For a while you just scream. Then you pass out. When you wake up, they're gone. But a couple of hours later they came back and it happened all over again. I could hear Bryn and Fey screaming sometimes."

I dropped my head, fighting images of Bryn wrapped in writhing black bands of shadow. Adne swayed on her feet. Connor slipped his arm around her waist, steadying her.

"Did they ask you anything?" Monroe asked. "What did they want from you?"

"They wanted to know where Calla was," Ansel said. "And they kept asking about the Scion. I didn't know what they meant."

"They meant Shay," I said. "Shay is the Scion."

Ansel's smile was grim. "I know that now. I know they want him dead. Some things fell into place as they kept asking us questions."

"What about Renier?" Monroe asked. His hands rested on the table, balled in tight fists.

"They brought us out of the cells into a large room. Everything was new, bright like a hospital. Except this room. It was dark, and old. I felt like we went from a prison into a castle's dungeon. And everyone was there."

"Everyone?" I asked.

"All the Guardians. Over a hundred of us and all the Keepers with their wraiths. They were all looking at a pile of raised stones. Like a stage, or an altar."

An altar.

No, no. Not Ren. Please, not Ren.

"Was Renier on the altar?" Monroe's voice shook. I looked at him, surprised that his fear was the same as mine.

"No. He was beside the altar with Emile and my father," Ansel said, and then turned his gaze on me. "My mother was on the altar."

I was on my feet, though my quaking muscles barely held me up. "What?!"

The flat smile returned to Ansel's face. "Surprised?"

"How can you ask me that?" I shrieked. "Mom had nothing to do with this."

"But she's the alpha female," Ansel said. The calm of his voice terrified me almost as much as his words. "She was supposed to teach you your place."

My place. Everything I'd hated about my destiny. The other reason I'd run. It was almost as bad as the threat of losing Shay.

"And she failed," Ansel whispered. "That's what Lumine said. She failed to perform her duty."

I sank down onto the bench, not flinching when Shay drew me into his arms. "What did they do to her?"

"They let Emile kill her while Dad stood there."

My limbs turned to jelly. I would have fallen off the bench without Shay holding me up.

Monroe glanced at Adne, who went very pale. "They murdered your mother?" she whispered.

Connor pulled her closer, murmuring into her ear. Tears dripped onto her cheeks, but she didn't make any sound.

"They said it was both of their punishments as alphas. She died because you ran away. Dad lost his mate."

I choked out a sob, my eyes were burning, and my tears blurred Ansel's face.

My mother. They killed my mother because of me. What kind of monster am I?

"But they let the Nightshade alpha live?" Silas asked. He was taking notes and I wanted to gnaw his fingers off. Slowly.

"There isn't a Nightshade alpha anymore," Ansel said.

"What do you mean?" Shay pulled me tight against him. I felt numb, unable to move.

"The rest of the punishment," Ansel said. "The Keepers disbanded the Nightshade pack. Emile is the only alpha now. He's been given both packs. Efron and Lumine told us that would be the new order. The Banes had proved more loyal and they would reign over the Nightshades until the Nightshades demonstrated their loyalty."

"But how could they do that?" Ethan asked.

"They're supposed to bring him back." Ansel pointed at Shay. "That's the new directive. The Guardians have been ordered to find him and return him to the Keepers. Whoever succeeds will gain their favor. If it's a Nightshade, that wolf will become the new alpha and lead a pack of their own."

"But that's impossible," I said. "Alphas can't be promoted, they're born. As long as our father is alive, he's the Nightshade alpha whether the Keepers acknowledge him or not."

"Tell that to the Keepers." Ansel glared at me.

"That could work in our favor," Ethan murmured. He caught Connor's eye and Connor nodded.

"How?" I asked. "How could that help us? We're going to be hunted down."

"It could—" Connor began, but Monroe interrupted.

"Wait," he said. "Ansel, what of Renier Laroche?"

Ansel sighed, low and long. "They called him a traitor, like Calla. They made him kneel before the altar."

Somehow I found my voice, a hoarse whisper. "Did they kill him?"

Ansel shook his head and something inside me that I thought was dying came to life again.

"What happened?" Monroe asked, his clenched fists relaxing slightly.

"They said that his betrayal was Calla's fault. That women can't be trusted. That females were born to seduce and deceive. That Calla tricked Ren. That he was only trying to save the mate he believed loved him."

The mate he believed loved him. I'd fallen in love with someone else, but Ren was still a part of me. We shared something I couldn't name. Was that love too? Guilt pierced me like a thousand needles in my skin. I forced myself to straighten, wiggling away from Shay's arms.

Silas nodded. "Mmmm, yes. The burden of Eve. That's a nice touch."

"Silas, I swear I will break your jaw if you say anything else," Connor said, tightening his grip on Adne's shoulders.

"There's nothing wrong with understanding the choices of your opponent," Silas said loftily. "If we don't examine them, we won't anticipate their next move."

"Let it go, Connor," Monroe said. "Silas, now is not the time."

Silas grumbled under his breath while Connor continued to glare at him.

"They set a wraith on him." Ansel shuddered. "Longer than I've ever seen. When it was over, I couldn't believe he was still conscious. They said he could choose his fate. That he still controlled his destiny."

"What was his answer?" Monroe asked.

"After the wraith he couldn't speak. I was surprised he'd even survived it. It had him for so much longer. . . ." He curled in on himself, making a soft retching sound.

Cold crept over me, like frost forming in my bones. My limbs were shuddering, out of my control.

My mother is dead. Ren tortured. And it's all my fault.

"They took him away." Ansel wiped spittle away from his mouth. He tried to take a sip of tea, but the cup shook too violently in his grasp. "I don't know where. But if he doesn't give the answer they want to hear, I'm sure they'll kill him."

Monroe made a quiet sound of grief. His eyes moved to the flames in the hearth, his mind going to a place far from this room.

"And then they brought me to the altar," Ansel said.

I extended my hands across the table, hoping he'd take them. He glanced at my upturned palms and then looked away. I pulled my empty hands back, feeling hollow inside.

"Lumine said the children of Naomi Tor couldn't be trusted," Ansel said. "She put her hands on my chest. I thought I was being torn in two. I heard myself howling, saw my wolf form floating in front of me, and then it was on fire. Burning, burning. The fur smoking. I could smell it, feel it, being burned alive. And then the wolf was ash. Lumine waved her hands and the ash blew away. And I knew. I could feel that the wolf was gone. I was nothing."

"Being alive isn't nothing." Monroe had come up behind him. He put his hand on Ansel's shoulder. Ansel shuddered but didn't pull away. "We're only human and we think life is worth living."

"I'm not human," Ansel said. "I'm a Guardian. I was a Guardian. I don't know what I am now."

"I could turn you back," I said suddenly. "You can be a Guardian again."

"No. I've been unmade." Ansel's face twisted with rage. "That's what Lumine said. She told them all. I can only be re-created through the Old Magics. An alpha cannot turn me. I'm cursed."

"We'll help you," Monroe said. "We can teach you other ways to fight. You don't have to be a wolf to be strong."

"This war would have ended a long time ago if only the wolves were strong," Ethan muttered.

"I don't want to fight any other way! I want to be a wolf again." Ansel turned to Monroe, a fever burning in his eyes. "Can you do that? I know you have magic."

Monroe was silent.

"You said you wanted to help me." Ansel was frantic. "That's what I need. Calla, make them help me."

"We don't make Guardians," Monroe said finally. "We don't alter nature."

"What are you talking about?" I asked. "Ansel's nature is the wolf. What's unnatural is what they did to him."

"That may be the case," Monroe said. "But frankly, we don't have the means to undo it. We won't destroy another creature to make him whole again."

"What you do mean, destroy another creature?" Shay asked.

"We'd have to take the essence of another wolf—killing the animal in the process—to give your brother what he wants."

My skin crawled. "I don't understand."

Silas looked up from his notes. "Guardians were created by years of experimentation with the laws of the natural world. The Keepers have always been fond of bending nature to their will. Guardians were one of the first demonstrations of the power they'd gained by allying with the Nether realm. They took animals and people, trying for years to blend the two and create the ultimate warriors. There were many, many failures. Mangled bodies, mutilated creatures not fit for this world or any other. And then there were Guardians. But the creation, the creatures, they are abominations against nature itself. The very reason Searchers fight against the Keepers."

I stared at him. "Did you just call me an abomination?"

Silas looked me up and down. "Yes. Yes, I did."

"That's enough, Silas," Monroe said.

My skin felt like insects crawled over me, stinging, biting, leaving my flesh raw. "Is that really how Guardians were first made?"

I thought of the story I'd been told as a child. The first Keeper—a noble warrior, injured, dying, saved only by the help of a lone wolf. The reward of being elevated. The bond of service and love that couldn't be broken.

"It is. Did they have a pretty tale to offer you about your origin?" Silas quipped, obviously wanting to say more, but he was silenced by a glare from Monroe.

"More lies," Shay whispered. He stared at his own hands. I wondered if he regretted being turned now that he'd heard this truth—that my kind had been born not as a reward for loyalty, but as a violent twisting of the natural order. One of the first acts of so many horrors for which the Keepers were known.

"Calla, you have to do something," Ansel whispered. "Even if you can't help me. Before they sent me away, Lumine said they would unmake the rest of our pack, one by one, as an example. You can't let that happen. They're your pack."

I couldn't speak. My tongue felt as thick as wet cotton in my mouth and it was choking me. What could I do? All the choices I'd made had destroyed my world. My mother was dead, my brother a bruised husk of the boy he'd once been. And for what? Shay and I were safe, but had we done any good? Were the Keepers any less of a threat? My head ached. I put my hands to my temples, trying to sort through the chaos of doubt.

"We won't let it happen."

I raised my face at Monroe's words. His face was grim. His jaw set.

"We're going to save your pack."

FIFTEEN

I DIDN'T THINK I COULD get any colder, but as Monroe's words settled around us, I could have sworn the temperature in the room dropped.

It was Shay who cleared his throat, speaking slowly. "What do you mean, we're going to save her pack?"

Monroe didn't answer.

Shay wouldn't look at me. "I hate to say it, but Ren obviously knew the risk he was taking when he made those choices, which means he understands the bigger picture. He was willing to make that sacrifice."

"Sacrifice?" I hated how often that word was cropping up in my life. My mother had been sacrificed. My brother seemed to think he'd be better off if he'd been killed as well. I couldn't bear the thought that Ren would soon number among the casualties that I'd created by saving Shay.

"No." I glared at them. "Ren is not a sacrifice. We are going to Vail to get him."

Ansel was nodding even as he continued rocking back and forth where he sat. Shay refused to meet my eyes.

"Going to Vail to do what?" Shay asked. "Get killed? Look how well your last trip went!"

"Shay," Monroe said. "We can't leave the young wolves to the Keepers. It would be cruel. We could still bring a few of them back—salvage this alliance. It just won't happen as quickly as we'd hoped."

"I'm not trying to be cruel," Shay said. "You're the ones who keep telling us this is a war. Wars make casualties."

Monroe kept his eyes on Ansel. "They are children. It's different."

"Children?" Shay's laugh was harsh. "We're talking about the other alpha. I know Calla's young, but I wouldn't call her a child. Renier Laroche is no different. He knew what he was doing. It's over."

"How can you say that?" I glared at Shay. "The only reason he might die is because he was trying to save us!"

"I'm being honest," he replied coolly. "If we go to Vail, it will be a bloodbath. You can't take that risk. I won't let you."

"Won't let me! Who the hell do you think you are?" Blood roared in my veins; my teeth were so sharp they pierced the surface of my tongue as I shouted.

I whirled to face Monroe. "We cannot leave him!"

Monroe grasped my hand. "We will not leave him, Calla. You have my word."

"How can you say that?" Shay was shouting now. "What could possibly justify a suicide mission like this one?!"

"He loves Calla," Monroe said quietly. "He already risked his life to save her. He won't betray her. He'll die for her."

Guilt ripped through my belly like a knife. Shay swore under his breath.

"You can't know that," he said, fists clenched at his sides. "He's a Guardian. I've seen what they can do. I've read their history. They've followed the Keepers without question for centuries. Ren is one of them."

Monroe turned on Shay, his jaw tightening. "He is not just a Guardian. He's Corrine's son. She changed her mind. So will he."

"Corrine is dead," Shay hissed. "Forget your love story, old man."

A solid crack sounded when Monroe's fist met Shay's jaw and sent him hurtling across the floor. Adne gasped and crouched next to Shay where he'd fallen. Ethan came to Monroe's side, lips thin and eyes mysterious.

"Come on, Dad," Adne murmured. She must have been upset because I'd never heard her call Monroe anything other than his name. "Please be reasonable. Shay's just afraid for Calla. He loves her too."

Make that really upset. That was the first time she'd ever acknowledged Shay's feelings for me. It might have been reassuring, but I was too angry with Shay for her words to affect me. Even if it was because he loved me, he had no right to stop me from helping my pack.

"We're clearly past reason," Shay grumbled, and rubbed his jaw as Adne helped him to his feet.

"I'm sorry." Monroe shook his head slowly, staring at his still-clenched fist.

Connor glanced at my stunned expression once and scrambled to stand between me and Monroe, and Adne and Shay.

"Look," he said. "The last thing we need is to fall apart. We're all on the same side."

"You could have fooled me," Shay muttered.

"Cool it, Chosen One." Connor smiled wryly. "If you're serious about changing things, about making the world better, we have to help the Guardians. Their lives are hell; we have to get them out of there. And Monroe's right. Even getting a few out could be the first steps toward an alliance. We have to start somewhere."

Monroe nodded.

"Ethan," Shay said. "Help me out here."

"I know you're the Scion and all, kid," Ethan murmured. "But I think Monroe and the wolf girl are right. We should go in, and soon."

"You're the last person I expected to sign on to People for the Ethical Treatment of Guardians." Connor laughed.

Ethan smiled at Connor before glancing at Ansel, who was still hunched over, pitiful, clenching and unclenching his fists. "I think I may have misjudged them."

"And how do you propose we help them without losing everything?" Shay asked, rubbing his bruised jaw.

My heart skipped a beat when all the Searchers looked at me. But it was Adne who spoke.

"Me."

"What?" Monroe broke out of his mournful reverie to glance at her, his eyes sharp and alarmed.

"Stealth extraction just before dawn. That still gives us a few hours to prepare. Take a small team. I'll open an inside door."

"No." Monroe's face paled.

"Every Weaver has to successfully create an inside door in order to take up a post," she said. "I passed all the exams. You have my papers. I can do it."

"What's this?" Shay frowned.

Ethan smiled at Adne. "Clever girl."

"No," Monroe said again, taking a step toward his daughter. "Inside doors are for emergencies only. They aren't meant to be used by a strike team."

"What's an inside door?" I asked.

Adne faced me, eyes bright. "That's what we call a portal that is opened in a place that the Weaver hasn't seen. You have to create the door based on your own mental image of the site you've targeted with only sketchy information to go on."

She turned back to Monroe. "In this case it offers the perfect element of surprise, which we need."

"It's against protocol," Monroe said. "I won't allow it."

"The protocol is moronic," Adne said. "I can get a team in and out. It's the only way."

She glared at Monroe. "It would have saved Stuart and Kyle."

Monroe's jaw twitched, but he didn't speak.

Connor put his hand on Adne's shoulder. "That's a big risk, kiddo. You sure about this?"

She nodded, but Monroe shook his head. "I forbid any further discussion on this matter. It's out of the question. Protecting the Weaver is a team's first priority."

Adne's laugh was haughty. "You were willing to throw everything away five seconds ago. This isn't about protocol, it's about me. Give it up, Monroe. I'm offering you the only feasible strategy and you know it."

Monroe stared at her, his eyes tight.

Her voice dropped low. "Please, I can do this. Let me help them."

Ethan looked at Monroe. "She's right. It's the only way this might work. It will probably still be a total disaster."

"It would have to be a very small team," Connor said, his eyes on Adne.

"How small?" Shay frowned at him. "I mean not counting those of us here now."

"You're not going," Connor said curtly. "You're the Scion. If you die, we all die."

Monroe expelled a long breath. "The Scion won't go. Adne, you can open a door near Eden, but not inside."

"But that might not be enough," she countered.

"An inside door in the club would be suicide. The risk that we'd lose and both Weaver and portal would be compromised is far too great," he said. "And we just learned about the location of this detention site. You'd be going in blind. I won't risk it. Across the street from wherever he's being held or in an alley. We'll strike from there, make the extraction, and get out again."

"Who's going?" Shay asked. He didn't look happy, but the outrage had fled his eyes.

"Only volunteers," Monroe said. "This isn't coming from the Arrow. It's personal. We won't be going back to the Academy; the strike will happen one hour before dawn. Whoever is coming, you should get some rest or whatever else you need to do before we reassemble then."

Ethan cleared his throat. "I'll go."

I couldn't stop my snort of disbelief.

He offered me a cold smile. "I may not like you, wolf, but I'm sorry I almost killed your brother. And those bastards killed mine. I'd like a crack at them . . . and to piss them off by snatching their prisoners."

Monroe frowned at him, but Ethan shrugged. "Like you said, Monroe. This is personal."

"All right, Ethan. You'll go and I'll go."

"Two?" Shay gaped at him. "You're only taking two?"

"No." Monroe smiled at him and then looked at me. "We'll be taking an alpha Guardian with us. That should be all the muscle we need for a stealth extraction."

"Don't take Calla," Shay said. "They'll want to kill her. It's too dangerous."

I jumped up, flashing my fangs at him. "Do you even remember who I am? I don't need you to protect me!"

When he met my gaze, my outrage dissolved. His eyes were full of fear . . . and love. "I know."

"We need her to help us find her pack," Monroe said. "She has to go."

Shay's shoulders slumped, but he nodded.

"I'll go too," Connor said suddenly. "If it's gonna be the last party, I'm sure as hell not missing it."

"It's settled, then," Monroe said. "Silas?"

"What?" The Scribe had been poring over his notes.

"Can I trust you not to report to Anika . . . at least not yet?" Monroe asked.

He started writing again but nodded. "I'll make you a deal. Find out how they got Grant and I won't run back to the Arrow. The report I can make right now is sparse at best."

"Thank you," Monroe said. "Ethan, let's talk about logistics. Isaac, could you fix this boy something to eat? Connor—"

"Already on it," Connor said, heading toward the door. He glanced over his shoulder at Adne, Shay, and me. "Come on, guys, I won't be able to carry all of them myself."

I glanced at Ansel, but he'd returned to staring at his hands and shuddering. Better to leave him alone right now. I wanted to help him, but if I was heading into a fight, I needed focus. Looking at Ansel tied knots in my gut. All I could see was his brokenness and a vision of my mother's body bleeding on an altar. I swallowed bile and rose to follow Connor. Adne was already leaving the kitchen.

"Carry all of what?" Shay stood up.

"Weapons." Connor grinned and strode through the door.

SIXTEEN

"WEAPONS?" SHAY REPEATED, watching Connor's jaunty gait as he strode across the training room.

"Oh, just go after him." Adne groaned. "Boys and their toys. You'd think he'd grow up."

"What are you talking about?" I asked, falling in step beside her. "Doesn't he already have his swords?"

"Only two," Adne said.

"Two isn't enough?" Shay muttered under his breath as we followed Connor.

At the opposite end of the room was a narrow door. Connor unlocked it and we followed him inside. Darkness swallowed us fully since the room had no windows. I frowned, shaking my head, which had filled with a strange humming.

"Ow!" Connor shouted. "God dammit. I think Silas left his training manuals on the floor again. Now where is the stupid light . . . ?"

"Here," Adne called, and in the next moment dingy light from the bare bulb washed through the room.

I gasped and Shay whistled. All four walls of the room, floor to ceiling, were covered with weapons: wickedly curving swords, ranging in length from a foot to the height of a full-sized man; daggers with hooked and jagged blades; single- and double-headed axes; maces and clubs; quarterstaffs and pole arms. All the weapons gleamed, even in the poor light.

The room pulsed with Old Magic; it poured off the enchanted weapons filling the room, making the air around us vibrate with power. My amazement gave way to a sickening twist low in my belly. Gazing at the weapons reminded me that Searchers spent their lives perfecting ways to kill Guardians. And this was how they did it. As if on cue, my shoulder throbbed. The muscles seemed to remember the damage done by these weapons.

"Look at this," Connor said, kicking several sprawling texts out of his way. "If Silas loves his books so much, why does he leave them lying around?"

"Silas trains here?" I was still staring at the weapons, but the thought of the Scribe using any of them was bizarre. "I thought Scribes didn't do combat."

"They don't, but all Searchers learn how to fight. Every one of us does a rotation at an outpost," Connor muttered. "Even Scribes. Including the useless ones."

"He's not useless, just forgetful." Adne crossed the room to climb a ladder that gave access to the topmost weapons hanging on the wall. "What do you want?"

"Get the French gladius," Connor said. "And bring down a couple kataras too."

"You're so predictable," Adne said, pulling weapons from their hooks. One appeared to be a standard short sword, but the pair of stunted blades she grabbed next were unfamiliar to me.

"I know what I like." Connor grinned, catching the sword she dropped into his hands.

"How many blades do you carry?" Shay asked as Connor took the next two broad-bladed punch daggers from Adne.

"Depends," Connor replied. "I think six is ideal. Maybe seven."

"Ethan and Connor think their manhood is equal to the amount of steel they have tucked beneath their clothing." Adne snickered. "I think they're trying to make up for something."

"Hey, now!" Connor said.

"They once had a competition to see who could carry the most at once," Adne said.

"Who won?" I asked.

"I did," Connor said. "Twenty-two."

"Really?" Shay's eyebrows shot up. He began eyeing the various shapes and sizes of weapons on the wall.

"Great." Adne rolled her eyes. "Looks like you've got a new challenger."

Connor shook his head. "I wouldn't recommend it, Shay. Once you get past fifteen, things start to poke in nasty ways anytime you move."

"I'll keep that in mind." Shay grinned.

"Besides." Ethan was leaning on the door frame. "Connor cheated. Poniards are not real blades."

"One through the eye or jammed under the throat kills just fine," Connor said.

"Still, that's a girly knife and you know it."

"I know you aren't dissing girls," Adne said, glaring at him. "Because that could prove hazardous to your health."

"Of course not," Ethan said. "Just dissing Connor."

"You're just pissed 'cause you lost." Connor held the sword blade up to the light. "This needs sharpening."

"You should take better care of your weapons," Ethan said, ignoring the gesture Connor made and speaking to Adne. "So is this tonight's green room?"

"Seems like that's what it's turning into," Adne said. "You need more bolts? And target practice to take the edge off while we wait?"

"You know it." He grinned.

While Adne gathered more blades and Ethan rummaged through storage crates, Shay sidled up next to me and shoved his hands in his pockets.

"I'm sorry about what I said back there."

I ground my teeth, fighting anger but not wanting to snap at him.

"I just don't want to lose you."

I nodded but didn't look at him. Even if it was out of love, I resented his words. I hadn't deserved them. Neither had Ren. My chest was tight, thinking of Shay and the Bane alpha. I wondered if they'd ever be able to fight together.

Shay was looking at me out of the corner of his eye. He shook his head and sighed.

"Are you okay?" I asked, swallowing the last of my anger.

"Yeah," he mumbled. "Just thinking."

He looked at me and sighed again. "So he's going to come back."

"Who is?" I asked, watching steel glint as Connor brandished weapons.

"Ren," Shay said, and with that name hanging in the air between us, he had my full attention. "I mean, if this works. He'll be here. With us."

I looked away.

Ren.

Ren would be here. I couldn't ignore the rush of heat through my veins at the thought that he would be safe. And that he would be close to me.

"What does that mean?" Shay pressed.

"I don't know," I said truthfully, moving forward to inspect the deadly wall ornaments.

He grabbed my hand. "Calla, hang on."

When I turned to face Shay, his eyes were bright as spring leaves sparkling with dew.

"I don't want to talk about this, Shay," I murmured. "I have more important things to think about. Like not dying."

"You don't have to talk," he said. "Just listen."

Both of his hands came up, cupping my face. "I don't care that Ren will be here. Okay, that's a lie. Just the thought of him being around you makes me crazy. I can't think straight and all I feel is the wolf inside me. That's why I said . . ."

A growl rose in his throat and I could see the wolf flash in his eyes, predatory and defensive. "It doesn't matter. I swear I want to help the pack. And I don't want anything bad to happen to Ren either . . . well, most of the time. All I care about is you and me. Things have been different between us since we've been alone. At least, I'd like to believe they have been."

I didn't want to look at him. My heart seemed to be throwing itself against my rib cage, like it was trying to escape this conversation.

"You aren't in Vail," he continued. "The rules have changed. I'm going to fight to be the one at your side."

Had they? I didn't know whose rules applied anymore or where my place in any of this was.

"Shay—" I tried to pull back, but his hand slipped around my waist and he held me in place.

"Tell me that isn't what you want and I'll walk away," he said, leaning in so his lips brushed my cheek.

My throat closed. I wanted to tell him that I loved him. I did. In a way I hadn't believed was possible before he'd been in my life. He deserved to know that. He should have some reassurance that his feelings were fully returned. But I didn't trust myself anymore. Not after Ansel's story. I'd brought torture and death to the people I loved. My mother had been killed. My pack was still in danger, my brother mutilated and hating himself. All of that was my fault. How could I answer? When I made choices for myself, they destroyed everyone I loved. What did I really have to offer Shay when all I brought with me was carnage?

"What are you two whispering about?" Adne called from her perch. "Here, catch!"

She pitched a sword at Shay. I flinched, but he stepped forward, easily catching its hilt.

"What is this for?" he asked. "I'm not even going."

"How else are we going to pass the time before Monroe sends us out?"

"I know I'm not sleeping," Connor said. "Don't feel like a tussle, Shay? Just 'cause you're getting left behind doesn't mean you can't take a few swings for fun."

"I guess." I caught sight of sharp fangs when Shay snarled at Connor.

"Want one, Calla?" Adne gestured to the wall of arms.

"No, thanks," I said, eyeing the myriad of gleaming axes, swords, and dozens of other weapons I couldn't name. "I'll go with natural assets."

"Those you've got—in abundance." Connor wiggled his eyebrows at me.

When I smiled, showing sharp teeth, he stopped grinning.

Ethan laughed, smiling at me for the first time. "Good girl."

Next to me, Shay swung and dipped the sword, trying it out.

"What do you think?" Adne asked, descending from the ladder and walking toward him.

"I'm not sure," he said wistfully. "I wish I knew what the Elemental Cross was like. It would be nice to practice with something similar."

"There's nothing similar," Connor said, hurling daggers at a practice dummy. Every blade landed squarely in the target's chest. My stomach flipped over. *Where will those blades lodge when we attack Eden? In the hearts of wolves I used to know? That I once fought beside?*

"I guess." Shay eyed the wall. "But none of these will be as good. I just wonder if practicing with them will be all that useful."

"Stop insulting our weapons, Chosen One," Connor said, whirling two swords rapidly before him. I took a couple steps back from the deadly flurry of blade strokes that Connor produced so casually. "They aren't so bad."

"I'm sure they aren't." Shay laughed. "I only meant . . ." He spread his hands helplessly. "Never mind."

"I know what you meant." Connor grinned. "And practice won't hurt you, even if it's not with your holy of holies Elemental Cross. If one-on-one is boring you, maybe you're ready to try your hand against two of us at once?"

Shay looked at him and then at Adne. "I guess."

"Don't taunt him, Connor." Adne shook her head. "Ignore him, Shay. You don't have to try fighting both of us. That's crazy."

"I'm sorry," Connor said. "Do your enemies usually stand in line waiting their turn?"

"Connor." Adne put her hands on her hips.

"No," Shay said, frowning. "He's right. Let's try it."

"Are you sure?" Adne asked, though a smile crept over her mouth.

"Yeah," Shay said, suddenly grinning. "Toss me another sword."

"Let him try out the tsurugi," Connor said. "Its hilt kind of looks like the Haldis."

"Got it." Adne went back to the wall, reaching for a slender, slightly curving sword.

"And what will my lady be using?" Connor asked. The casual way he twirled the swords in front of him demonstrated the fatal control he held over the weapons.

"Let's see how he takes to qi jie bian," Adne said. "That's something different."

"The chain whip?" Connor asked. "Not a bad idea."

"He's pretty good with whips." I shivered, flashing back to the night of the union. The dark forest and Flynn's wicked smile. The way she screamed when I tore her hand off, how Shay had snatched the shadow whip from her severed limb's grasp, in the next moment turning her own weapon against her.

"Is there anything you're not good at?" Adne's smile was blinding. I laced my fingers behind my back so I wouldn't choke her.

"Golf," Shay said with a grim smile. "I have no patience for it."

The air hissed as he swept it with his blades.

Adne rolled her head back and forth, stretching her neck as she moved toward him. In each hand she held a wood-handled whip made of seven metal links. The end of each whip was tipped by a sharpened dart. They were frightening, appearing almost alive as they twisted through the air, guided by Adne's graceful strokes.

"Those are whips?" Shay asked, gazing at the snaking metal Adne swirled easily before her body. The weapons didn't look like any whip I'd laid eyes on.

"They are indeed," she said, flicking her wrist. The silver links shot out, and before I could blink, the dart was impaled in the throat of a nearby practice dummy.

"Whoa," Shay said, taking a step back.

"Not bad," Adne said, jerking the whip free.

"And what are those?" I asked, watching as Connor strapped the short blades to his belt.

"Get close with those big teeth of yours and I'll show you."

Ethan snorted, raising his crossbow. "I'll never understand why you like kataras."

He fired four successive bolts into a dummy with startling speed.

Shay walked to the target. "How do you shoot that fast? I always thought crossbows were slow. Powerful, but slow."

"You're thinking of European crossbows," Ethan said, coming to

Shay's side and jerking the bolts out of the dummy. "This bow is based on the Chinese design. Built for speed, not force. It has a magazine that loads a new bolt after each shot."

I clasped my fingers over my chest, remembering too well how quickly Ethan's bolts had lodged in my chest. He glanced at me, nodding. "If you can't hit Guardians fast and often, you're dead."

Connor was eyeing Ethan's bow disdainfully. "I'd get bored as hell using that thing."

"Brute force isn't the only way to fight," Ethan replied.

"You're just afraid of getting your hands dirty." Connor pulled one of the kataras from his belt. His fingers wrapped around the handle, which ran horizontal to the short, wide blade.

"Bloody," Adne said, gazing at the weapon. "The word you're looking for is 'bloody.'"

Connor cast a sidelong glance at her, drawing the other katara. In the blink of an eye his body blurred. He leapt through the air, twisting around the dummy, landing on the balls of his feet in a crouch behind the target.

Shay whistled, staring at the lacework of deep gashes Connor had left on the practice target in the few seconds he'd been near it.

I coughed. "Ninja."

Shay looked my way, sparing me a thin smile.

"Show-off." Ethan laughed. "Couldn't you tell it was already dead?" He held up the bolts he'd just pulled free of the dummy.

"You two aren't the ones who are supposed to be showing off," Adne said.

"What's this?" Ethan asked.

"Shay needs practice." Adne swirled the whip so that it coiled and uncoiled like a metallic serpent.

Shay scratched the back of his neck, looking a bit uneasy. "Maybe we shouldn't."

"Aw, come on," Connor said. "I'm sure you'll be fine. And I'm dying to blow off steam before we do this crazy business in a few hours."

"It's a thought." Shay rolled his shoulders back. "I'm kinda edgy too."

Ethan laughed. "Don't worry. I'll be the referee and make sure these two don't play dirty."

"You're no fun at all," Connor said, swapping the kataras for his usual swords.

"Are we ready?" Adne asked.

"Always." Connor grinned.

Shay nodded, eyeing the two Searchers who'd slowly begun to circle him. I could see the veins in his throat pop up, beginning to throb as they neared him. Adne's whips reached him first, flying low, striking at his ankles. Shay dodged the blow as easily as if he were skipping rope. But as he landed again, Connor came at him, his sword blades no longer moving in a casual dance but whirling with such speed I could barely see where one blade ended and the other began.

I started to move forward, my instincts screaming to throw myself between the gleaming steel and Shay. My body tried to follow the call for blood. I felt like I was suffocating, pushing down the weight of the wolf that was desperate to claw its way out of the human prison that held it back. But I couldn't interfere. Shay needed this. It was time for the Scion to fight on his own. I just hadn't anticipated how hard it would be for me to let him go. Backing against a wall to put more distance between myself and the fight, I jumped forward when the spikes of a hanging mace pressed against the skin of my back.

Shay's eyes locked on Connor. Their swords met, the clang of blade on blade bouncing off the walls and ceiling. As the two young men focused on each other, Adne stalked Shay from behind. The whips flew toward his unprotected back. I gasped as Shay suddenly forced Connor's blades down while launching his own body into the air, flipping over Adne and landing just behind her. Connor shouted, crashing to the floor as he barely escaped catching the sharp points of Adne's whips on his chest. Shay grabbed Adne around the waist, drawing her back and resting the blade of one sword against her throat.

"Yield?"

Her face was frozen in a mask of shock. She swallowed, nodding carefully so as not to press her neck against the sword.

"Holy shit." Connor was laughing as he rolled back onto his feet. "I get it now. The Scion is chosen because he has eyes in the back of his head. If you just shave that mop off, we'll see them, right?"

Adne was breathing hard as Shay lowered his sword, smiling when she craned her neck to gaze at him.

"How did you do that?" she asked.

The same question was ringing in my own mind. I'd never seen anything like what Shay had just done. I was stunned. My hand pressed into my chest as I tried to catch my breath, fingertips vibrating with my racing heartbeat.

He shrugged. "I'm not sure. I just knew you were coming. I could feel you behind me."

Ethan remained silent, but he and Connor exchanged a glance.

"Okay," Connor said, raising his swords. "First round to you. Two out of three?"

"Adne?" Shay asked.

"You won't pull that move on me twice," she said, playfully shoving him back to free herself.

"Let's see." Shay grinned.

I couldn't take any more. Watching the ferocity of the fight, listening to the easy banter between them, all of it made me feel like an outsider. Neither needed nor wanted. Their strength, fluidity, and laughter were all barbs digging into me. It was as though none of what had been revealed in the kitchen mattered. My mother was dead, my pack forsaken, and they'd already moved on. I would grieve alone.

As sadness dragged my mood into a tar pit of self-pity, I thought of Ansel. How much worse must all of this be for him? Guilt grabbed hold of me, reminding me that I wasn't the only one who'd lost a loved one. Naomi, our mother, had been ripped away from us, but that wasn't all Ansel had lost. His wolf had been taken from him and *destroyed*. I could grieve, but I was still whole. Still a Guardian. There would be no return for him.

No one noticed when I turned away, sidling toward the door, as Connor hurled himself at Shay, startling him into dropping one sword.

"Hey!"

"You think you get a warning after that last match?" Connor barked. "Adne, take him down!"

"With pleasure." She laughed, entering the fray.

Shay ducked, rolling along the floor to avoid Adne's swift kick. "Not happening!"

The ringing of steel on steel trailed after me as I slipped from the room.

SEVENTEEN

A SPEAR OF YELLOW light cut through the hallway from a room at the top of a stairwell I'd discovered when trailing Ansel's scent, the door open just a crack. I quietly pushed the door back, peering inside.

"You're killing me, kiddo." Isaac rubbed his temples as he faced my brother. "What else can I say?"

I knocked on the door frame. Isaac turned and Ansel glanced up, only to duck his head low again the moment he saw me.

"You the relief team?" Isaac asked, coming to the door.

I nodded, watching Ansel sit on the edge of the bed and stare at his shoes.

"Glad you're here." When Isaac approached me, he lowered his voice. "Tess is way better at this stuff than me. She always handles our houseguests."

"I didn't know there were bedrooms in the outpost," I said, looking around the small, spartan room.

"When strike teams come in, they sometimes need multiple days to stage a mission," Isaac said. "These are the quarters they use when they aren't staying at the Academy. Plus the Reapers live here."

"Right," I said, before asking, "How is he?"

"He's says he's not in pain," Isaac said. "But the kid is clearly distraught. I couldn't get him to eat. I warmed up a stew for him. It's on the nightstand. Maybe you'll have better luck."

"Thanks for staying with him," I said.

"No problem," Isaac said. "If you're okay here, I should get back downstairs."

"That's fine," I said, already walking past him.

I sat next to Ansel on the bed. He didn't say anything. He was staring at his hands, which were cupped around something I couldn't see.

"So you won't eat?" I said, gesturing to the untouched bowl of stew.

"I'll eat when I'm hungry," he mumbled.

"I've been eating their food," I said, trying to lighten my tone. "I swear it's not poisoned."

He didn't laugh, but his hands opened as he shoved whatever he'd been holding into his pocket. It looked like a crumpled slip of paper.

"What's that?" I frowned.

"Nothing." He crossed his arms over his chest. "What do you want?"

"You've been through a lot," I said, giving up light conversation. "You need to make sure you're taking care of yourself."

When I reached out to touch his shoulder, he jerked away.

"Don't touch me."

"Why not?" I asked carefully. "I'm so happy to see you, An. I've missed you."

He laughed, but it was that awful tinny sound again. "Have you? I wouldn't have guessed."

I didn't know what could relieve the painful gnawing in my gut spurred by the hollow sound of his words. "I had to leave."

He didn't respond.

"I had to. They were going to kill him."

"They killed Mom," he whispered.

"I know," I said, choking on the words. "But the ceremony, An. They were going to make me kill Shay."

"How many times are you going to tell me that?" Ansel asked softly. "It doesn't make what happened to us right. You don't know what they did. You weren't there."

He was dragging his fingernails over his wrists. I leaned closer and saw the raw red tracks he'd made. I grabbed his hand, jerking it away.

"Stop that!"

He laughed again. "Why should I?"

"I might not have been there, but I can see how much they hurt you."

He shuddered, clutching at his stomach as though he were about to be ill. "It's like I can still feel them tearing it out of me. I can't stop remembering how they took it."

His voice dropped to a whisper. "I can't live like this."

"Ansel, your life isn't over. You're still you—and I love you." I gripped his hand in mine. "Please don't hurt yourself."

I couldn't say that it didn't matter that he'd been unmade. It would have been a lie. I knew what losing the wolf meant.

"We'll find a way to make it better."

"The only people who could make me whole again are the Searchers," he said. "And they've already said they won't. And the Keepers . . ."

"What they did to you is horrible, but you can't give up. Please. You have to be strong for me. For Bryn."

He scowled. "Even if Bryn isn't dead, she'd be better off without me."

"That's not true."

"She deserves someone who can be with her. If she were with me, she couldn't be her true self. She needs a Guardian."

"No, she doesn't," I said.

"How do you know that?"

"It hasn't always been that way," I said quietly.

"What are you talking about, Calla?" He looked at me, angry in a way I'd never seen before. *He feels like he's lost everything that matters.*

"Because I found out that Searchers and Guardians have fallen in love before." I squeezed his hand gently. "You don't have to be a wolf to be worthy of love."

He stared at me, disbelieving.

"It's true. A long time ago," I said. "We were allies ... and sometimes more."

"A long time ago." I watched his eyes go flat, saw him giving up again.

"But I also know because I loved Shay." My voice began to shake. "Even before I turned him."

Ansel gazed at me. For a moment the dull cast of his face changed and I was looking at my brother again. "I knew it." He almost smiled.

"I know you did."

"I guess that's worth something." He sighed. "I did tell you I'd run away for Bryn. Maybe this is all my fault." The corner of his mouth began to curve up. Then he frowned at me. "Did you ever love Ren? I thought you might. I mean, you guys obviously had a connection of some sort. Was it only because you're both alphas?"

I shivered as raw, frightening emotions scampered down my spine. "I—"

Images danced in my mind, memories of Ren's laugh, his face, his touch. I'd only admitted my love for Shay when I thought I would lose him. Now Ren was the one in danger. Was my need to save him about love too?

And then it was as if he were there, whispering to me. *This is only about love.* I could almost feel his breath on my skin.

When I didn't answer, Ansel shook his head. "Never mind."

He crawled across the bed, lying down. "So do you trust them?" he asked.

"The Searchers?"

"Yeah."

"I think so," I said. *Not as much as I'd like.*

"What will you do next?" he asked. "If you reunite with the pack tomorrow, what then?"

"Then we help Shay," I said, still slightly lost in thoughts about Ren.

"Help him do what?"

"Save the world."

"Is that all?" Ansel laughed, and this time it sounded real.

"Yeah." I smiled. "That's all."

We both fell quiet for several minutes.

In the silence of the room my heartbeat was deafening. "Ansel, I think we should try."

"Try what?"

"Turning you," I said. "The Keepers always lie. They could be lying about this too."

I watched the muscles of his throat work as he swallowed. "Do you really think so?"

I didn't know what I thought, but I hoped with every ounce of my being that they had lied about this.

"They always lie," I whispered.

He turned his head to look at me. "Okay." His body was trembling.

When I shifted into my wolf form, he winced. I couldn't imagine how hard it was to watch my transformation, so effortless, so natural, when that power had been robbed from him.

Ansel scooted up on the bed, watching me. I slowly lowered my muzzle to his forearm, ears flicking. I glanced up at him and he nodded. I bit him, fast and deep. He drew a quick breath. I caught the acrid scent of his fear.

I shifted back, reaching out to lift his chin so his eyes met mine.

"*Bellator silvae servi.* Warrior of the forest, I, the alpha, call on thee to serve in this time of need."

All I could hear was the sound of our breathing, shallow and fearful, as I waited. I closed my eyes, hoping for the surge of power to move from me to Ansel, linking alpha and packmate. Squeezing my eyes tight, I spoke again; this time my voice shook.

"*Bellator silvae servi.* Warrior of the forest, I, the alpha, call on thee to serve in this time of need."

Nothing. No magic twined in the space between us.

When I opened my eyes, Ansel was shaking his head. His own eyes were closed. A tear slid down his cheek.

"*Bellator silv—*"

"Stop," Ansel croaked, his reddened eyes meeting mine. "Don't."

I didn't know what to say. They'd really done it. Ansel's wolf was gone, and I couldn't bring it back. In that moment I hated the Keepers more than I ever had.

"Let me give you blood." I choked on the words and realized that I was crying too. "You're still bleeding."

"No." Ansel pulled off his shirt, tying it around the puncture wound in his arm. "I don't want it."

"Ansel—" I reached for him.

"I don't want it!!" The fury in his gaze paralyzed me.

He slid down on the bed. His face had emptied of emotion, but his blank expression was more frightening than his anger.

"You should go," he said, staring up at the ceiling. "You'll need to sleep before tomorrow."

"I won't leave you."

He reached into his pocket, pulling out the crumpled paper.

"Ansel, what is that?" I asked, trying to get a better look.

"Leave me alone." His eyes rested on the dirty scrap for a moment before he gripped it in a tight fist, pressing it against his chest. "It's from Bryn, okay? I managed to hang on to it while the Keepers had us separated."

"Oh." She must have written him a poem. My heart pinched and my eyes were burning. Did she have anything of him with her? My brother and my best friend, whose love I'd wanted to hide from the Keepers. Maybe it would have been better if they had run away together. Could that have led to anything worse than what was happening now?

Ansel rolled over, facing away from me. "Just go."

I stayed at the edge of the bed, knees tucked up under my chin. When his long, steady breaths assured me he'd fallen asleep, I stretched out, careful not to touch him, resting my head on a pillow, still watching my brother sleep.

After a while he started to make sounds, soft mewling like a young animal in pain. It went on and on as he quaked and trembled next to me, stirring but never waking. I finally drifted to sleep, still listening to the soft cries manifested by whatever nightmares clawed at Ansel's mind.

EIGHTEEN

"CALLA," SHAY WHISPERED, gently shaking my shoulder.

The sound of his voice drew me from dreams haunted by cries of anguish and slithering shadows that threatened to engulf me.

For a moment I couldn't remember where I was. I only heard the warmth of Shay's voice and caught the subtle allure of his scent. I started to lean forward, aching for his closeness.

He looked puzzled when my fingers traced the line of his jaw. "They asked me to wake you. It's time."

The sweetness of the moment was driven away by the sudden cold slap of knowing where I was and what I was about to do. I blinked sleep away, sitting up quickly and then regretting it when Ansel stirred. He didn't wake fully but continued to mutter, restless in sleep as he had been all night. My mood plummeted even further when I remembered that I'd tried to help him, but couldn't.

"Come on," Shay said. "The others are waiting downstairs."

We left the room quietly.

"How is he?" Shay asked as we descended the stairs.

"I tried to turn him." I had to lean on the railing as grief knocked against me.

"You did?" Shay asked. "From the expression on your face, I'm guessing it didn't work."

I nodded. He slid his arm around my shoulders, brushing his lips against my temple.

"It's good you tried, Cal. I'm sorry."

"Me too."

"Is he going to be okay?"

"I don't know," I said, glancing back at the dark hallway. "He just seems . . . broken."

"Yeah," Shay said with a shudder. "I've only been able to change for a little while, but it's such a part of me. I can't imagine losing it."

I nodded, watching him. Was it true? Did Shay really have such a strong connection to his inner wolf? Or was he just trying to sympathize with Ansel?

"I should be going with you," he said.

"No," I said. "The Searchers are right. You're too much to risk."

He dropped his arm from my shoulders, shoving his hands in his pockets. "You still don't think I can fight."

"I know you can fight," I said. "I've seen you fight more than once. You're a warrior. That's not the issue."

"I could help," he said, glancing sidelong at me. "I know I could."

"How well you can fight doesn't matter this time." I shook my head. "We'll still be facing wraiths. Until you have the Cross, you can't fight them."

"Neither can any of you," he growled, and I saw his sharp canines catch the light.

"I know." A heavy weight lay on my chest like a boulder.

A suicide mission.

We were risking so much, and I didn't even know if the rest of the pack was still alive. If Ren was still alive. What if we'd already lost all of them?

I could hear the Searchers milling around in the empty foyer. As we reached the bottom of the stairs, Shay grasped my upper arms, turning me. Before I knew what was happening, his lips were on mine. I leaned into him, opening my mouth, welcoming the kiss. His hands slid down my arms, fingers digging into my skin. I could taste his fear and wondered if I should pull away, knowing he drank in my own anxieties with each caress. I began to tremble, both from the fire that lit my veins as the kiss deepened and the sudden awareness that if things in Vail went badly, I might not kiss Shay again. Ever.

He broke off the kiss, resting his forehead against mine. "Maybe you shouldn't go. Ansel needs you. Let Monroe take the Searchers in. They can pull off the rescue without you."

"I have to," I said, pushing him back. "I'm the only one who can convince the pack that the Searchers can be trusted."

"If anything happens to you—"

"Here they are." Adne appeared in the stairwell, clucking her tongue. "No time for long good-byes. Haven't you heard? Romance is dead. We're on the clock."

"Sorry." I slipped out of Shay's embrace, fearful that if I stayed close to him any longer, I'd give in to my fear, abandoning any hope that I could save my packmates.

You're still their alpha, Cal. The pack needs you. You know who you are.

I clung to that idea as I strode across the empty space, finding Ethan and Connor awaiting me.

Connor nodded as I approached. "Isaac will keep an eye on your brother while we're gone."

"I will too." Shay had come up behind me.

"Thanks," I said, unable to look at him, worrying I'd have an attack of cowardice sprouting from my own selfish desire to stay near him.

What have I become? Had giving in to my love for Shay made me weak? I felt like I had no strength, nothing that reflected the person I'd always thought I was. Steel resolve, independence—those traits

I'd valued seemed to have drained away over the last week. I desperately wanted to find myself again. I had to prove to Ansel and my pack that I hadn't abandoned them. If I didn't do this, I wouldn't be able to live with myself.

Monroe came striding in from the kitchen. "What's the situation?"

"All present and accounted for," Connor said, sheathing a dagger in his boot.

Monroe nodded. "The door Adne will open is in a dead end alley adjacent to Efron's club. We'll break in through the side entrance and make our way to the prison."

"What will Adne do once you're inside?" Shay asked. "Are you leaving her at the portal alone?"

Monroe nodded.

"What if she's attacked?" Shay frowned. "Let me go with her. I'll stay at the portal, just in case."

"Not an option. Under no circumstances are you to join this fight, Shay." Monroe's jaw tightened, but he smiled grimly at his daughter. "And if the portal is hit, she can defend herself."

Adne started, eyes widening. "Thank you."

"I think I'm gonna cry," Connor said, burying his face in Ethan's shoulder.

"Oh, shove off," Ethan growled, and readjusted the crossbow slung across his body. "We're all probably going to die in an hour. Maybe less."

"All the more reason to treasure every moment." Connor pretended to wipe tears from his face.

"Adne, could I speak to you alone for a moment?" Monroe asked.

"No, no way." She shook her head. "I'm not going to let you give me some sappy father-daughter speech because we might die. Just let me do my job."

"That's not—" Monroe began, but Adne turned her back on him.

"Connor." Monroe watched Adne draw the skeans from her belt. He jerked his head away from our small group. "There's something we need to discuss."

Connor frowned but followed Monroe to a darkened corner in the space.

"Ah, yes." Ethan grinned. "To the woodshed with you."

Adne glanced over her shoulder at Shay. "You're not going to try to jump through this door after I open it, are you? I'm wondering if I should make you take an oath."

"You'd better not," Ethan said. "We've been over this. I'm not risking my neck unless I know you're safe here. In fact, why don't you just go to bed?"

"I'll go upstairs to watch Ansel after you leave," Shay said, but I heard the faint rumble of a growl behind his words. "I'm not going to pretend that this isn't happening."

"Suit yourself." Ethan shrugged. "If I were you, I'd sleep in."

"He's just the gentleman you're not," Adne said, throwing her arms around Shay and brushing her lips over his cheek. "Thank you for caring, Shay. We'll be fine."

Suddenly I was the one who wanted to growl.

"You're damn right I'm no gentleman," Ethan said. "If you grabbed me like that, I wouldn't let you get away with just a kiss on the cheek."

Shay scowled, rubbing his neck as a rosy blush washed over his skin while Adne giggled over his reaction.

My eyes settled on Connor and Monroe and stayed there. I couldn't make sense of what was happening, but both men were agitated. Monroe's lips moved rapidly, and he had something in his hands. What were those? Envelopes? Connor paced back and forth beside Monroe, raking his hands through his hair and shaking his head. I peered at them, wondering what had transpired.

Finally, Monroe grabbed Connor's shoulders, pressing the papers against the younger man's chest. I saw Connor slump, as if he'd given a long sigh, defeated. He took the envelopes from Monroe's hands and slipped them into his jacket pocket. Monroe squeezed Connor's shoulder once before coming back toward us. I averted my gaze, still puzzled by what I'd just witnessed.

"She's nearly there," Ethan said as Monroe approached. I turned back to Adne, who leapt and spun in the ecstasy of weaving. Though I'd seen her open doors before, I was still astonished at the blazing patterns of light that swirled before her.

I started at a sudden presence beside me. Connor stood nearby, silently watching Adne weave. All traces of his mirth had vanished; his face was now pale, drawn with strain. I glanced at Monroe, again wondering what had taken place between the two men.

Blood roared in my ears as the other side of the shimmering portal came into focus. A dark alley edged by snowdrifts. In the distance I could just make out a streetlight casting a dull gleam on the shuttered businesses of downtown Vail.

Home.

NINETEEN

IT WAS COLD ON THE other side of the portal. Fresh winter air nipped at my skin. I took a deep breath, letting the icy wind pour down my throat. The resulting visceral shudder reached into my very bones, making me feel alive. I ached to run, to howl, to hunt. I watched my breath curl like smoke in front of my eyes.

I glanced behind me and saw Shay's hazy image pacing before the open doorway. I wished I could reach out and reassure him in some way. When Monroe had given the order, I'd leapt through the portal without a backward glance, not wanting to show any doubts about our mission. Now I regretted not giving him something: a smile at least, or another kiss. I only felt worse when I realized Adne had been the last person to kiss him. She stood beside the portal, swords drawn and face serene as Connor and Ethan scouted the alley.

"Aren't you worried someone will see the light?" I asked, gesturing to the shimmering portal.

"There aren't any windows in this part of the alley," Adne replied. "That's why we chose it."

Her words left me only a bit reassured. At least the door wasn't as bright as it was during the weaving, but it was still noticeable, like the twinkling of Christmas lights. It was close enough to the holiday that I hoped we'd be lucky and anyone who saw it would assume that's what it was.

"We're clear," Ethan said, reappearing from the dark alley. "No obstacles or patrol between here and the side door."

Connor didn't speak, his eyes scanning the shadows.

"Good," Monroe said. "Let's move."

Ethan took point with Monroe, and I shifted into wolf form, padding along the alley on silent paws while Connor brought up the rear. My heartbeat thrummed in my veins, so deafening to my sensitive wolf ears that I could hardly believe it wasn't audible to the Searchers. None of them spoke or even looked at me. Each of the men's faces was set as they stalked silently along the narrow corridor.

When we reached the side door, Monroe raised his arm.

"Alarm?"

"No," Ethan said. "Just the lock."

"On it." Connor pulled something metal from his pocket and moved to the door.

Ethan took up his position guarding our flank.

There was a click and a groan when the door swung open. Monroe and Connor were through the entrance instantly, dropping low, waiting for an attack.

None came.

They exchanged a glance but gestured for us to follow. Ethan closed the door behind us.

We slipped down the hallway. My gut twisted, remembering the walk along this hall to Efron's office. Was the Bane master here now? I lifted my muzzle, testing the air. The club reeked of stale sweat peppered by the lingering, sickly-sweet scent of succubus breath. I pawed at my nose, wishing I could rid myself of the noxious mixture.

As far as I could tell, there were no new scents, nor any movement, in the club. The pounding bass and blur of colorful lights had been replaced by silence and gloom. No dancers, no succubus go-go girls, no Guardians. The only sound was the muffled beat of the Searchers' footfalls as we crept forward through the shadows. I didn't find our apparent solitude reassuring. There was too much silence, too much stillness for a place like Eden that fed off the pulse of blood and lust.

"Here are the stairs," Connor whispered. He stood at the top of a wrought-iron spiral staircase. I leaned over the railing, watching the tight coil of metal drop down into a bottomless pit of darkness.

"No lights?" Ethan asked.

"Not yet," Connor said, beginning his descent.

The stairs led down, and down, and down. The sharply turning circle of steps made me dizzy. The darkness enveloped us, making it seem as though I'd closed my eyes and started spinning.

Even with my ability to peer through the darkness, the descent set me on edge. I was grateful when a fluorescent light appeared, growing brighter as we moved down the stairs, washing our surroundings in a greenish gray. The spiral staircase pulled us further into the club's depths. I felt like we'd been walking forever. How far into the earth had we traveled?

"This must be it," Connor said, at last stepping free of the iron staircase into a square room that had probably been painted white but with time had succumbed to the dingy shade of cobwebs. He'd taken another step when a dark shape lunged from the shadows behind the staircase, knocking him down and sending his sword flying into the corner.

Behind me Ethan swore, throwing himself over the railing and dropping to the floor while I pushed past Monroe to lunge at the wolf. Ethan fired bolts into the Guardian who had Connor pinned to the concrete as I sank my teeth into its unguarded flank. The wolf snarled and thrashed its head about as the bolts lodged in its shoulders. Baring its teeth, the wolf snapped at me, but I easily dodged, crouching to make a second lunge.

With the Guardian's attention diverted, Connor pulled a katara from his belt, thrusting the short blade into the wolf's belly and twisting. The Guardian yelped before its whine became a gurgle. It slumped across Connor, unmoving. Connor shoved the wolf's corpse off him. Ethan held his crossbow at the ready, scanning the room.

"Only one?" Monroe asked, coming toward us with his swords drawn.

"For now," Ethan said, lowering his weapon.

"Lucky us." Connor wiped blood off his hands. I went to his side, peering at the wolf that lay dead near him. It was an elder Bane, but not a stranger. This one I knew: Sabine's father. They'd just killed Sabine's father.

I shifted forms, shaking my head.

"You okay?" Connor asked.

"Something isn't right," I said, eyes flicking through the small room, uneasy to be human when danger was so near. "That wolf shouldn't be here."

"What do you mean?" Monroe asked. "I'd be surprised if a Guardian wasn't posted here. In fact I *am* surprised we've encountered only one."

"No," I said, struggling against the way my gut had begun to pitch back and forth. "It's this wolf. I know him . . . knew him. He doesn't work security for Efron; he's a mountain patrol Guardian. Like the wolves in my pack."

"Couldn't they have shuffled positions?" Ethan asked.

"That doesn't happen," I said. "Not with the mountain packs."

"I'd wager a lot might have changed since your disappearing act," Connor muttered.

"Maybe." I felt unsteady as I stared at the dead wolf. *He shouldn't be here. I know he shouldn't.*

"We'll be alert, Calla," Monroe said, guiding me away from the body. "But we need to keep moving; it took us longer to get down here than I'd anticipated. We can't lose any time. I'm sorry it was someone you knew."

Behind the spiraling stairs was a single door. Connor tried the knob, then pulled out his lock-picking tool. He carefully opened the door, revealing a narrow hall lit by the same buzzing fluorescents. There were six doors in the hall, one at each end and two on each side. The side doors were harsh metallic rectangles cut by a narrow slot at eye level.

"What now?" Ethan asked.

"We start opening doors," Monroe said. "We can each pick locks; everyone try a door."

"No, wait." I grabbed Monroe's arm. "Just follow me."

I shifted forms, keeping my muzzle low, sniffing along the hall. When I reached the far door on the right side of the hall, I whimpered, scratching the metal surface.

"This one?" Monroe asked.

I whimpered again, desperate to get through the door. Every beat of my heart throbbed in my neck as Monroe picked the lock. I couldn't breathe as the door swung open.

Two young men sat, leaning against opposite walls of the cell. Chains bound their wrists to the walls, keeping them apart, their movements limited. They remained still, eyes closed. Remnants of clothing hung from their bodies. Torn pants, shredded shirts. Both of their faces were a muddle of bruises and swollen flesh, green, purple, red. A sickening rainbow painted on their skin.

The light in their cell flickered constantly, making the room waver as I stared inside.

I yelped, dashing into the room.

Mason's eyelids flipped up at the sound of my cry. He slowly turned his head, squinting at me.

"No way."

Nev groaned, keeping his own eyes shut. "Just tell me when it's over."

"Calla?" Mason leaned toward me, wincing.

I licked his face, shifting into human form so I could speak. "Mason. It's me. I'm getting you out of here."

"Seriously?" Mason regarded me as if I might be a figment of his imagination.

"Calla?" Nev's eyes were open now.

"You mean she's real?" Mason reached up, chains scraping the concrete floor, and touched my face. "Oh my God."

"Can you walk?" Monroe had come to our side, crouching to address Mason.

"Who are you?" Mason frowned, his nose crinkling. "Hey! You're a Searcher. What the hell!"

"It's okay, Mason," I said, taking his hand. "They're on our side."

"Searchers? On our side?" Nev laughed. "Maybe she's not real."

"I'm real," I said quickly, feeling the press of time. "Please answer him. Can you walk?"

"I think so," Mason said, stretching his legs. "I haven't tried in a while. Are you going to tell us how you got here? And why the Searchers are helping you?"

"After we've put miles between us and Vail," Connor said. "Story time can wait."

"He's right—but later, I promise, this will make sense."

"As long as we're out of this hellhole, it doesn't have to make sense," Nev said, covering his eyes.

"I don't know that we'll be much good to you," Mason said. "I haven't been able to shift since they put us in here."

"It's the chains," I said, touching the iron at his wrist. "You'll be able to shift once they're off."

"Connor," Monroe said, gesturing to Nev. "Get him out of the restraints."

Monroe bent down to free Mason.

"I don't know if that's a good idea," Ethan said, glancing warily at the two chained Guardians.

"What are you going to do, shoot them?" I snapped. "Do you even remember why we're here?"

"Our rescuers want to kill us, huh?" Mason asked, noting that Ethan's crossbow was trained on his chest. "Nice."

"Well, it fits the way everything else has been going lately," Nev said. "I'd say I'm surprised, but I'd be lying."

"They aren't going to kill you." I glared at Ethan until he slowly lowered his weapon.

"What if—" he began.

"What if it's a trick?" I said. "Look at them. How are they going to fight like this? I'm worried we won't be able to get them out in one piece."

"That makes two of us," Connor said. "And here I was hoping for wolf reinforcements as we went along."

"If there's a fight, we'll fight," Nev growled as the chains dropped away from his arms. Then he was a wolf, snarling while he limped toward Mason.

"Oh, man." Ethan backed away, raising the crossbow.

"Knock it off!" I said. "They aren't your enemies."

The moment he was freed, Mason shifted too. The two wolves circled each other, sniffing, licking, nuzzling, and finding comfort through their contact. I watched, longing to join them but wanting to let them have their own moment of reunion.

"Whoa," Ethan murmured as Mason bared his teeth, sinking fangs into Nev's shoulder, lapping up the blood that poured out.

"It's okay," I said quietly. "They'll heal if they do this now. Then they can fight with us."

Nev took blood from Mason's chest; I could sense the power of their bond flowing through the room, replacing their wounds with strength.

"Glad that worked," Connor said, apparently sensing the tension in the room lift in the same way I did. "But we need to move."

Ethan was frowning. "Hang on."

"What?" Connor asked.

"The blood thing is going to be a problem." Ethan turned to me. "How the hell are you going to kill any of the others?"

My brow knit together. "What are you talking about?"

"If you wolves take bites out of each other, won't you just heal up anytime you swallow?"

I had to work hard not to punch him in the face.

"That's not how it works," Monroe said.

I glanced at him, startled, though given his connection to an attempted Guardian revolt, I probably shouldn't have been surprised that he'd already uncovered the secrets of pack healing.

With my hands on my hips, I glared at Ethan. "It's not just drinking Guardian blood that heals wounds. The blood has to be gifted; otherwise it's just blood."

"Gifted?" Ethan stared at me.

Mason had been watching the exchange. He shifted into human form.

"She's right," he said. "It can't be taken. The blood must be offered to invoke its healing power." The bruises on his face weren't gone, but they'd faded considerably.

"That's much, much better." He smiled, holding his arms out to me. I flung myself into his embrace.

"I'm glad you're safe," he said. "I pretty much thought you were dead."

"Gifted," Ethan murmured again, his expression fixed somewhere between puzzlement and wonder.

Nev remained a wolf, standing at Mason's side protectively, but when I smiled at him, he wagged his tail.

I pointed to the Searchers. "Connor and Ethan, meet Mason and Nev. Monroe is in charge. He's helped Guardians before."

Mason's eyebrows went up.

I shook my head. "Like I said, I'll explain later. Where are the others?"

"I don't know," he said. "They moved us around a lot. Kept separating us, rearranging us. We've always been in pairs."

He paused, swallowing. "They must've thought we'd break faster if we had to watch another packmate being taken by a wraith. Nev and I have been in the same room for a while now, but I haven't been able to keep clear track of the days. I don't know how long it's been since I saw any of the others."

"Do you think they're still alive?" Monroe asked.

"Yeah." Mason sighed. "The Keepers don't have quiet executions. If they killed another wolf for what happened, we'd have been dragged out to watch it."

He turned sad eyes on me. "Your mom, Calla. I . . . I'm sorry—"

"I know," I murmured, cutting him off as a lump rose in my throat. "Ansel told me. He found us."

"Is he okay?" Mason paled. "What they did to him . . ."

"He's in rough shape," I said. "But he's safe."

"You said they moved you around," Monroe interrupted. "Where?"

"There are four cell blocks down here," Mason said. "Each is set off of the Chamber."

"What's the Chamber?" Ethan asked.

"Where violence becomes a spectacle," Mason said, smiling grimly. "I've been writing a song about it in my head. You know, to pass the time. It's where they killed Naomi."

Mason took my hand when I cringed. "And where they punished Ansel . . . and Ren."

When he said Ren's name, his eyes met mine, full of questions. My blood ran hot, pulse racing with the need to find him.

"We need to check those other blocks," Monroe said, his voice tinged with the same urgency I felt. "Let's go."

Connor checked the last cell in that block, finding it empty. Mason and Nev were the only prisoners here.

"I guess it's door number five, then," Connor said, moving to the door at the opposite end of the hall from where we'd entered.

The wolf at Mason's side, his coat a mixture of copper and steel gray, began to snarl.

"What's the matter with your guard dog?" Ethan asked.

Monroe threw him a stern look.

"No offense intended," Ethan added quickly.

"That leads to the Chamber," Mason said, his hands beginning to shake.

"Is there another way to access the other cell blocks?" Monroe asked.

Mason shook his head.

"Open the door, Connor," Monroe said.

TWENTY

NO FLUORESCENT CEILING panels hummed in the Chamber. Instead tiny lights bobbed and hiccupped, circling the room, the multitude of oil lanterns signaling us like a somber warning. Bathed in that wavering, dusky yellow, the broad space yawned like a hungry maw. I felt as though a jackhammer was at work against my ribs.

"Did we go through a time portal or something?" Connor asked.

"Either that or this is the site of the world's most depressing Renaissance festival," Ethan said, stalking into the room, crossbow at the ready.

As I glanced around the space, I tried to swallow my stomach, which wanted to climb out of my throat. They were right. Unlike the sterile, modern cell blocks, this room had been constructed from flagstones, piled one atop the next, like mounds of slugs, a dark slimy gray that looked perpetually sodden. The dimly lit space was empty save a dais, a gothic mockery of a stage that jutted out from one wall. Words had been carved in the stone facing behind the platform.

Abandon hope, all ye who enter here.

Dante. I shuddered, thinking of the hellish images that lined the walls of Efron's office upstairs and how those scenes were probably re-created in this chamber. The room smelled of must, cobwebs, urine . . . and blood. So much blood. I faltered. The scent was over-whelming. Death poured into my lungs, making my stomach churn. Mason caught my arm, steadying me.

"I know," was all he said.

My eyes kept wandering to the dais, though I tried to tear them away. My mother had been killed there. Murdered by Emile Laroche while my father was made to watch. My brother had been mutilated. And Ren. What had they done to Ren? Tears burned trails along my face until Monroe rested his hand against my cheek, his thumb brushing away the stinging saltwater.

"Someday all of this will be torn down, stone by stone," he said. "That is why we fight."

I nodded, unable to speak.

"The cell blocks branch out from each side of the room," Mason said, pointing to the nearest door—a mirror image of the one we'd just passed through.

"Is it always empty?" Monroe asked, his question echoing through the cavernous Chamber, emphasizing his point.

"Not when I've been here," Mason said. "It's been packed with Guardians waiting for the Keepers' decrees."

"I don't like it," Ethan said.

"Neither do I," Monroe said, glancing at me. "Can you lead us to the others?"

I took a breath and almost retched. The remnants of torment had oozed into the floor. I felt like I was trying to track a scent amid a pile of decaying corpses. Nausea made me waver on my feet again.

"Not here," I said. "Maybe in the blocks, like the one we just left."

"We should do this as quickly as possible," Monroe said. "Connor, Ethan, and the wolves take point while I try the doors."

We moved to the south door first. Monroe picked the lock while Connor and Ethan kept their eyes on the room, scanning for signs of an ambush. Both Mason and Nev were in wolf form now, circling our group, testing the air, their ears flattened, fangs bared against the assault of violent scents that swirled around us.

Monroe opened the door and I followed him inside. Though still unpleasant, the scents inside the block didn't overwhelm. I took a few steps forward before shifting into human form.

"This one's empty," I said. "Next block."

"No luck?" Ethan asked when we returned to the Chamber.

Monroe shook his head.

"Where to next?" Connor rolled back his tight shoulders, eyes still traveling over each point of access to the Chamber.

"West block," Monroe said, moving across the room. I glanced around the room. The order Monroe had selected meant we'd search the north block last if we didn't find everyone in the next set of cells. The north block lay nearest to the dais—and I wanted to go nowhere near the stones that were stained with my mother's blood. Would her blood stand out amid the stains? Would I fall apart if I caught her scent spilled across those stones?

As I pulled my eyes off the dais, I thought I saw movement, as if the shadows near the ceiling had shuddered. I stopped, peering into the darkness.

"Calla?" Ethan paused by my side.

I waited, watching the spot where I thought I'd caught movement. Only shadows rested there. My racked nerves were making me see things.

"It's nothing," I said, hurrying after Monroe.

When we reached the south door, Nev whimpered, scratching at the space between the door frame and the floor.

"What's wrong?" Monroe asked.

Nev shifted forms. "I can smell Sabine. She's in there. Other wolves too."

Mason whined, turning in circles, head bent low.

"How many others?" Connor's grip on his swords tightened.

"I'm not sure," Nev said. "But it's not only Sabine on the other side."

"What about the rest of your pack?" I asked. "Is Ren inside?"

"If he is, the other wolves are covering his scent," Nev said. "I can't pick it up."

"But you can smell this Sabine?" Ethan frowned.

"She smells like jasmine—it's a distinct scent. Easy to pick out even in a crowd."

"Uh . . . okay," Ethan said, his eyes growing curious. "Jasmine?"

"Can we talk perfume later?" Connor snapped. "I'm guessing we have a fight waiting behind this door."

"We're ready," Nev said, shifting back into wolf form, hackles rising as he growled.

"I'm opening the door now," Monroe said. "Be ready for anything."

The lock clicked. The door opened. I shifted forms, hackles raised.

The hall was empty, identical to the others we'd already searched.

"Which door?" Monroe whispered, looking at Nev.

Nev stalked past the first two cells, muzzle tracking low, sniffing. Mason stayed on his heels, ears flat against his head.

He paused in front of the far door on the right and looked at Monroe, who nodded. Connor and Ethan had their weapons raised as Monroe turned the doorknob. He hesitated, glancing at the others.

Not locked, he mouthed.

The Searchers exchanged a grim look, setting their shoulders as Monroe swung the door open.

I heard the snarls before two elder Banes leapt from the cell. The first slammed into Connor, yelping when a dagger slid between its ribs. Two of Ethan's bolts lodged in the second wolf's chest. It hit the ground, yelping but still on its feet, and whirled to strike again. Mason launched himself at the wounded Bane. They rolled along the floor, a furious tangle of teeth and claws tearing at each other. Nev rushed to Mason's aid. Ethan ducked into the room.

"Go with him, Calla," Monroe said. "If your packmates are inside, they'll need you to convince them we're allies."

I nodded and slipped into the cell. Ethan was staring down at a third Bane, who was crouched in front of a limp figure along one wall. I saw the spill of dark hair, the curve of slender limbs barely covered by the shreds of a dress. Sabine. She wasn't moving. My blood ran cold. Was she dead?

"Calla?" I turned at the sound of my name and I thought my heart would burst. Bryn gazed at me, eyes wide with disbelief. She was chained to the wall just as Mason and Nev had been. Her face was thin, cheeks hollow, her own dress only slightly less tattered than Sabine's. My throat closed as I realized they were still in the gowns they'd been wearing the night of the union—or what was left of them.

I yelped, starting toward her, but stopped when I heard Ethan's low voice.

"If you know what's good for you, you'll step away from the girl," he said, taking aim at the Bane snarling in front of Sabine.

The wolf's ears flattened, keeping its eyes locked on Ethan. It bent over Sabine, its fangs close to her throat. I could hear the vicious pleasure in its low, steady growl.

She moaned softly, eyes fluttering open. The rush of relief that she was still alive was overrun by horror as the Bane lowered its muzzle, taking Sabine's neck in its jaws.

"Calla, you have to do something!" Bryn shouted, straining against her bonds. "Efron ordered the Banes to kill her if anyone attempted a rescue."

I wheeled, focusing on the other wolf.

Ethan was already moving. With a shout, he tossed his crossbow away, barreling into the startled wolf. Human and Guardian crashed to the ground. Ethan swore when the wolf's teeth sank into his shoulder. I lunged across the room. The wolf moved to strike again, its attention fully on Ethan. My jaws sank into the wolf's shoulder. Blood spurted and I heard a crunch as my teeth hit bone. The Guardian squealed, twisting to attack me. I rolled along the floor away from its snapping jaws. That split second of distraction was all Ethan needed. He drew his dagger, sliding beneath the wolf, and thrust the blade up into its throat. The wolf shuddered and went still. Its limp body dropped to the floor when Ethan kicked it off of his dagger.

Sabine's hand was at her throat and she was staring at Ethan. He went to her side, touching her arm gingerly.

"Are you hurt?" he asked, eyes moving over her body. He looked away, blushing when he realized how much flesh her torn dress revealed.

"No," she whispered, still watching him. "Who are you?"

"Ethan," he said, clearing his throat while trying to find a safe place for his eyes. "I'm here to help you."

She drew a sharp breath. "You're a Searcher."

He nodded, finally meeting her gaze. "But I'm on your side."

I almost choked, not because of the blood in my mouth, but because I'd never imagined those words could come from Ethan.

"I thought I was going to die." Tears slipped down her cheeks. "I was certain of it. He said I would never leave him and live."

"Who said?" Ethan slowly reached out, touching her cheek. I saw that his fingers were shaking.

It was Bryn who answered. "Efron."

"Efron Bane?" As if remembering himself, Ethan snatched back his hand and pivoted to face Bryn. "The Keeper."

She nodded. "He . . . likes to keep Sabine close. I think he took her choice personally."

"What do you mean, close?" Ethan frowned. Sabine met his eyes and something seemed to pass between them.

His fist closed. "God damn that bastard."

Sabine looked away, another tear sliding down her cheek.

I shifted forms, taking a step toward Sabine. "What choice?"

"He said I could swear a new oath of fealty," she whispered, more tears coursing over her skin. "Return to Emile's pack if I denounced you and your packmates."

A choice. The Keepers or me. I shuddered.

"I wouldn't," Sabine continued, grimacing before she brushed the moisture from her cheeks. "I don't know why you left, Calla, but what they did to Ansel . . . I knew they would do the same to Mason and Bryn. I couldn't be part of that."

"Efron came down hard on her," Bryn said. "The wraiths were here every day. And only for her. They came for me a lot less. Four, maybe five times. I got off easy."

"I wouldn't say that." Sabine offered her a weak smile. "Once is hard enough."

"I'm so sorry for what you've been through." I knelt beside Bryn.

She hugged me so tightly I couldn't breathe. "I'm just glad you're alive."

"I'm so sorry," I whispered again, horror crawling under my skin. I might have been a captive, but I had been safe, well treated, and far from the agony that my packmates had been subjected to day after day since I'd fled Vail.

"Don't," she said. "You didn't do it. They did."

"I know, but—"

She cut me off, choking out words. "Cal—I don't know what they did to Ansel after they hurt him. I think he might be . . ."

"No." I grabbed her shoulders, forcing her to meet my eyes. "I know what they did to him, Bryn. It's horrible, but he's not dead. He's safe. He found me and Shay."

"He is?" Her voice shook, eyes wide, desperate to believe me but not trusting my words.

"I swear you'll see him as soon as we get to Denver."

Connor burst into the cell, swords dripping blood. Mason and Nev were just behind him, their muzzles the same crimson as Connor's blades. "We under control in here?"

"Yeah," Ethan said. "Can you get her out of those?" He gestured to Bryn's chained wrists, turning his own attention to Sabine's shackled limbs. "I've got this."

Mason followed Connor to Bryn's side. He changed forms and bit his wrist, letting her take his blood while Connor freed her. Ethan made room for Nev, who knelt beside Sabine.

"You holding up okay?" Nev whispered, extending his arm toward her.

"Barely," she said, sinking her teeth into his flesh.

Ethan hovered over them, watching as Sabine's sallow complexion flushed with new life. I heard him expel a long breath when she raised her face and smiled.

"How do you feel now?" he murmured.

"I'll be fine," she said, sounding shy in a way I'd never witnessed from Sabine. She lifted her eyes to meet his. "You saved my life."

It was Ethan's turn to avert his gaze. "I—uh . . ." He rubbed the back of his neck, fumbling for words.

Free of the chains, Sabine leaned forward and wrapped her arms around Ethan's neck, pulling him into an embrace.

"Thank you," she said. "Thank you so much."

He stiffened in her arms, his tensed muscles finally easing when she didn't pull back. He let his cheek briefly rest against her hair.

"Jasmine," he murmured.

"What?" Sabine asked, looking up at him.

He cleared his throat. "You're welcome."

"Even a Searcher." Nev snickered. "Only you, Sabine. I swear."

"What are you talking about?" She glanced at Nev, frowning. Nev just grinned.

"Never mind," Ethan said quickly, clearing his throat while casting a cold glance at Nev. He freed himself from her arms, rising. Sabine smiled again, only for him, and Ethan looked a little dazed.

Nev chuckled, shaking his head.

"What's so funny?" Sabine asked as he helped her stand.

Monroe appeared in the doorway before Nev could answer. "Who did we find?"

"Two more," I said, gesturing to the girls. "Bryn and Sabine."

His face fell a little. "No sign of the rest?"

I shook my head, knowing we both shared the same creeping sense of despair. We hadn't found Ren. I wondered if we would.

"If they're healed, we need to move," Monroe said. "We still have others to look for."

"Can we afford another ambush?" Connor asked. "The Keepers obviously were expecting us; this first group might just be the beginning. The next fight we encounter could be much, much worse."

"We're finishing what we started," Monroe said. "And our numbers have doubled."

Connor opened his mouth to protest, but Monroe shook his head.

"We finish this," Monroe said. He turned his back before Connor could reply, already walking swiftly down the hall.

TWENTY-ONE

BRYN TOOK MY HAND, leaning into me as we left the cell.

"I've missed you so much, Cal," she said. "I didn't think I'd ever see you again."

"I missed you too," I said, though I didn't feel worthy of her affection. She'd been through so much while waiting for me to come back. They all had.

"I'd better stay on my toes," she said, returning my smile before she dropped to the ground—a bronze-furred wolf. She joined the other wolves, who trotted side by side, tightly bunched, nuzzling each other, tails wagging.

Ethan and Connor watched the young wolves reestablish the pack bonds. The Searchers' faces were puzzled. I guessed they were trying to make sense of the way their sworn enemies demonstrated affection, loyalty, even playfulness. Traits the Searchers associated with their own kind, but not with Guardians. Only Monroe seemed unsurprised by the wolves' behavior. He strode ahead, driven by a single purpose.

We crossed the room, heading for the north cell block. The dais loomed before us and the scent of blood, old and fresh, grew stronger. The sharp tang, layer upon layer of agony, flooded my senses in a blinding wave. I stumbled, gagging as we approached the raised stones. The violence witnessed by this place seemed to have leached into the floor and the walls. I dropped my head, wanting to cover my ears. I thought I could hear my mother screaming. Connor caught my elbow, steadying me.

"Hang in there," he murmured.

I nodded, trying not to look at the stains on the hideous stage.

Monroe unlocked the cell block door. He'd pushed it open only partway when something flickered in my peripheral vision. It was just like earlier, a furtive moment in the shadows.

"Wait." I grabbed Monroe's arm.

"What's wrong, Calla?" he asked, watching me.

My eyes tracked over the spot where I thought the movement had come from. Then I saw it.

A gargoyle.

It wasn't moving at all now. It looked just like a statue perched against the stone frieze that ringed the ceiling, but every nerve in my body screamed that it wasn't.

"Ethan." I pointed at the creature, whispering. "Shoot that. Right now."

"That's a statue." He frowned. "Creepy as hell, but I can't waste bolts."

"Just shoot it."

He looked at me for a moment and then took aim. The bolt flew true. Ethan swore when it didn't bounce off a carved monster but buried deep in flesh. The gargoyle screamed, stone coming to life.

"What the hell!" Connor jumped back as the creature dove from the ledge, flying at us.

I covered my ears, thinking that my eardrums would burst from its hideous screeching. Bryn snarled, leaping to meet the creature midair. Startled by her fearlessness, the gargoyle balked, screaming its outrage. Bryn's teeth tore through one of its wings and the creature dropped to the floor, gray milky blood oozing from its torn flesh. Sabine leapt onto its chest, pinning it to the dais. Bryn struck again, this time jerking her head fiercely when she took hold of its throat. I heard the crack of bone as the gargoyle's neck snapped.

"It's been watching us the whole time," I breathed.

"Are there others?" Connor asked, turning in a swift circle, keeping his eyes on the ceiling.

"No, but Calla's right. It must have been tracking our movements since we arrived," Monroe said. "I think we may have just triggered the alarm."

Each one of us went still, taking in the significance of Monroe's words. Our silence was met by a low, urgent sound in the distance, like faint drumming. The scrape of nails on wrought iron, footpads hitting the steps. Coming fast, the drumming became pounding as our enemies descended from the upper level of the club.

"They're coming for us," Monroe said, glancing toward the door that would take us out of the prison and back up the stairs.

"Do you know of another way out?" Connor asked, looking at the wolves. My packmates glanced at each other. Sabine whimpered before she shifted forms.

"None of us have seen another exit," she said. "That's the way we were brought in. I'm sorry."

Her eyes found Ethan as she apologized.

"We're trapped down here, then," he said, staring at Sabine as if he were weighing the possibilities of how he'd like to spend his last moments on earth.

"The rest of the pack has to be in this block," Monroe said. "If we can free them, we'll be able to put up a decent fight. Maybe get out of here."

"Not all of us," Connor said.

"We don't have any other choice," Monroe said.

"He's right." Ethan loaded new bolts into his crossbow. "Time for the last stand. Always knew it would come someday."

"No," Sabine said. "I'm not dying down here. I won't give Efron the satisfaction."

She dropped into wolf form and howled. The rest of my pack-mates raised their muzzles, joining her battle cry. From the levels above us I heard the answering howls of the approaching Guardians, singing out their own challenge.

The wolves' howling seemed to revive the despondent Searchers.

"I can jam that lock!" Connor was sprinting across the room. "If it really is the only way in, it might buy us some time."

"Good thinking," Monroe said. "Ethan, help Connor and the wolves. Try to keep them at bay. Calla, come with me."

I followed Monroe into the cell block, glancing back to see my packmates circling Connor and Ethan as they fiddled with the lock of the east prison door. I drew a slow breath and shivered. Beneath the harsh metallic odor of the cell block a whisper of wood smoke curled through the air.

"What is it?" Monroe asked.

"He's here," I whispered.

A howl from another part of the prison spilled into the cell block. The hairs on the back of my neck stood up. I'd recognized the cry— Mason was calling for help. Nev's answering howl sounded a moment later. Monroe looked at me. I heard the scrabbling of toenails on flagstones, followed by barks and snarls.

"Guardians," I said. "They've broken through."

"Find him. Let him know we're coming. I'll tell the others—make sure they keep the fight away from here—and I'll be back for you and the rest of your pack. I promise."

I nodded, swallowing my fear.

Monroe drew his swords and ran back into the Chamber.

The scent pulled me to the far door on the left. *Please be unlocked. Please.*

I turned the knob and the door swung open. This cell was larger than the others. Sparse, bright metal illuminated by buzzing fluorescent lights running along the ceiling. I caught his scent before my eyes found him. The warmth of sandalwood and rough edge of leather made my chest ache. Without thinking, I stumbled forward, running toward a figure crouched in the far corner of the room.

"Ren!" I wrapped my arms around his shoulders, pulling him against me.

"Calla," he murmured. His forehead rested against my throat, his hands pressed into the small of my back.

"Are you hurt?" I whispered, still holding him tight, bursting with relief that he was alive.

"No."

"Thank God." I pulled back slightly, catching my breath, barely able to hear my own words over the pounding of my heart. "We don't have much time. I can't explain right now. We have to get out of here."

Ren looked at me and suddenly I was dragged forward, crushed against him. His lips were on mine, feverish, burning into my skin. Memories rained down on me, drowning me in a flood of emotions.

Ren.

This was Ren as I'd known him for so long. My intended mate. The young Bane alpha. My rival and my friend. The one who would lead the pack by my side. A warrior like me. A wolf like me.

I kissed him back as tears burned in my eyes. The tide of the past carried me with it, and I pushed my body closer to his. I didn't know what to think or feel. All I knew was how good it was to be near him again. Pressing against him, I was haunted by the destiny that I'd anticipated but hadn't fulfilled. A time when I didn't know that lies were lies. When I thought I understood my place in the world. Some small part of me longed for that certainty, for the life I might have had before my world spun into chaos.

He pulled back, gazing at me. Lifting his hand, he traced the shape of my face. His other hand took mine. His fingers paused, lingering on the braided white gold band of my ring.

"With me," he murmured. "You belong with me."

The lump in my throat was painful, stopping me from speaking even if I could have found the words. How many promises had I made only to break? How much had I stolen from him by leaving?

He kissed me again, softly this time. His lips moved over my jawline, down my throat. He pulled me even closer, whispering in my ear.

"They said you'd come. I didn't believe it, but now you're here."

The whirlwind of emotions that lifted me stilled as his words brought me tumbling back into the present.

They said you'd come.

I lifted my face, looking at him more closely. He was here. Alive in the room. But unlike the others, he wasn't bruised. His face wasn't drawn from ordeals of pain and constant hunger. His clothes weren't torn or grime-covered. His scent was the one so familiar to me, warm and masculine but untainted by vomit, blood, or filth. I looked at his arms. He wasn't restrained. And he was alone.

Cold fear snaked over my skin.

"Ren?" I whispered. My heart was screaming out against the chilling facts that my mind was quickly wrapping around.

He leaned forward, kissing my earlobe.

"I missed you, Lily. So much," he murmured, taking my arms in a firm grasp. "I'm sorry."

Suddenly I was sailing through the air across the full length of the cell. My head slammed against the wall and for a moment I couldn't see anything. My body tipped over and I sank toward the floor. Fingers dug into my upper arms, lifting me up. I felt Ren's breath hot against my skin. His lips crushed mine again, but this time I tasted blood. I jerked my head away and gasped, fighting to regain balance and vision.

"Ren, stop. Please." My hands found his shoulders and I tried to push him away. "What are you doing?"

His gaze locked on me and I saw the tightness of his jaw, the strain in his eyes. Fury and sadness pooled in the darkness of his irises.

"I don't want this, I never wanted *this*," he said through clenched teeth. "I don't have a choice. You've given me no choice."

He slammed me against the wall again, forcing air from my lungs. For a moment he hesitated, staring at me, grief etching his features even as his grip on my arms tightened.

"It's the only way." He choked on the words as though desperate to believe them. "You're my mate. It's my duty to bring you back. To make you stay. They said I have to."

I stared at him. "Have to what?"

"Break you."

TWENTY-TWO

REN PINNED ME TO THE cold steel of the cell wall, his knee parting my thighs.

Shock drained the strength from my limbs. I couldn't find the will to change forms. *This can't be happening.*

"Oh God, Ren. No." I could barely whisper the words, staring at Ren. I no longer recognized the boy in front of me, madness and grief blazing his eyes, driving him to hurt me. Terror gripped me in a way it never had. I didn't want to believe this change was possible, but his fingers dug into my wrists, making me cry out. I tasted blood in my mouth. His teeth had torn my lips. *Does Ren belong to the Keepers now?*

My body shook; sickening waves crashed through my limbs. I was only upright because Ren still held me against the wall. The frenzy in his eyes terrified me, making me fully aware that his every choice was fueled by grief and pain.

"You don't have to do anything, Renier." A new voice came from the cell door, quiet but hard. "Let her go."

Ren's teeth were already bared as Monroe slowly moved toward us. He had a sword held low in each hand.

"You do have a choice." He continued to speak in low tones. "Leave this place, leave all of this behind. You can come with us."

"With you? Searchers?" Ren spat on the ground.

"We aren't what you think," Monroe said. "We came for you. Calla is here to help you. So am I."

I cast a pleading gaze at the alpha even as I twisted against his painfully tight grasp. "Please, Ren. It's true. Come with us."

"Your lies took everything from me." Ren's eyes were fixed on Monroe. "I'll kill you before I believe anything you say."

He glanced at me, his face contorted with outrage and sorrow that sent shivers racing over my skin.

"I hope it doesn't come to that," Monroe returned. "I'm not your enemy, but I can't force you to make the right choice. This doesn't have to be the end, but if you won't come with us, at least let the girl go. Don't make this worse."

"What could be worse than accepting the outstretched hand of a monster?" A man stepped from the shadows of the doorway.

My heart slammed around wildly when I recognized Emile Laroche, broad and bulky in contrast to his tall, streamlined son, his body all knotted muscle and coarse bristling hair. The Bane alpha looked straight at me. Though he remained in human form, he was flanked by three wolves: Dax, Fey, and Cosette. My heart splintered as their eyes locked on me and they growled in unison. I could pull their single, shared thought from their hateful stares.

Traitor.

I didn't want to see the truth that stood before me. Truth witnessed by the sharp flash of fangs and bristling fur, eyes full of hate as they stared at me.

A choice. They were given a choice. Just like Sabine.

Three of my packmates had turned on me. They belonged to Emile's pack now. They had chosen the Keepers over their friends.

Why?

Then I turned my gaze back on Ren. His fingers still dug into my arms. They'd given him a choice too. My gut clenched violently and

I thought I might be sick. I could see the pain behind his fury and knew Ren didn't want to hurt me, that he'd only chosen the Keepers because I'd left him behind. Because I'd betrayed someone who loved me. He'd lied for me and they had tortured him. He'd been broken and it was my fault. What other choice could he have made?

"Emile." Monroe's hoarse voice tore my eyes off of Ren. The Searcher's face became almost unrecognizable as he stared at Emile, eyes darkened by a hollow, endless rage.

Emile kept smiling. "You don't know how much I'd hoped to see you again, Monroe. Thank you for coming."

Monroe didn't speak, but his hands began to tremble.

Emile turned to Ren. When he spoke, his voice was cool and silky. "Renier, meet the man who killed your mother."

Ren's hands dropped from my arms; the color leached from his face.

I scrambled away, crouching against the side wall. My eyes flicked from Ren, to Monroe, to the door still blocked by Emile and the wolves. There was no way out.

Monroe drew a hissing breath. "You lying bastard."

The emptiness in his eyes brightened with the subtle gleam of tears.

Emile's laugh was like the snapping of bones. "Lies? Do you really believe Corrine would have died if not for you?"

With a sudden cry Monroe lunged at Emile.

But Ren was there, shifting forms in the air, and a dark gray wolf hunched snarling between his father and the Searcher, blocking Monroe's path of attack. Monroe faltered at the sight, losing his momentum. He pitched to the side, rolling out of the way as Ren snapped at him.

"I seem to have the upper hand, old friend." Emile grinned while Ren stalked toward Monroe, cornering him against the far wall of the cell.

"We'll see about that," Monroe said, keeping his eyes on Ren. The wolf's muscles were bunched, his snarls furious. I knew he would be on Monroe at any moment, craving the blood that he believed would avenge his mother's death.

"Ren, don't!" I shouted. "Monroe didn't kill your mother. He tried to save her!"

"Kill that bitch, Dax," Emile hissed, pointing at me. "Now."

Dax stalked toward me, snarling, revealing all his razor-sharp teeth. I'd never given much thought to how large Dax was when he wasn't in human form. I'd never thought I'd have to fight him. The best warrior of the young Banes. As I watched his muscles rippling beneath his fur, I realized he was the biggest wolf I'd ever seen. I shifted forms, hackles raised, and braced myself against the floor. He had the advantage of size and strength, but I had speed.

Even as I grasped for a way to defend myself, my mind was shrieking. *I don't want to kill Dax. How could I ever kill Dax?*

He was only a few feet away, a distance he could cover in a single leap. I snarled but reached out to him with my mind.

Don't do this.

You made your bed, Calla. Dax crouched, muscles coiling like springs, baring his fangs.

Even his teeth were huge.

A sharp growl pierced the room and Dax hesitated, turning in response to Ren's call. Their eyes met. Dax sounded a short, confused bark, looking from Ren to Emile.

Ren hadn't opened his mind to me—only Dax could hear him, but I was desperate to know what was passing between the two wolves.

"Don't interfere, boy." Emile glared at Ren.

Dax balked and I stepped another foot closer to the door, wondering if I could make a run for it. Even if I could, it would mean leaving Monroe behind. I froze in place, refusing to abandon him.

"I am your alpha," Emile said, showing Dax sharp canines. "Kill her. Kill her and take your place as my second."

Dax turned to face me, his eyes burning, full of bloodlust, and I knew he wouldn't hesitate again. I had to let go of whatever doubts still made me balk at the prospect of fighting a former packmate. Now. Or I was dead.

"Back off, fluffy!" Connor rushed through the door, throwing himself between Dax and me, brandishing his swords. "Sorry to break up the party, but it's time for us to say good-bye. Not that you haven't been wonderful hosts."

Dax darted forward. Connor feinted, slashing the wolf's shoulder. Dax lunged again, but Connor matched his speed, leaving two more gashes in Dax's side. The massive wolf gnashed his teeth, barking furiously while Connor circled him, keeping the blades flying between them at a dizzying speed.

Fey and Cosette started toward us, growling.

"No!" Emile shouted, pointing at Monroe. "Forget the girl. This man is who we want. Dax, fall back. Let the others leave. It doesn't matter. There's nowhere to run."

He turned his gaze back on Monroe. "We have more important business to take care of. Personal business."

Dax slowly backed away from us, still snarling. Fey and Cosette took up positions alongside Ren, barring any path of escape Monroe might have had.

"Connor," Monroe called in a steady voice as the four wolves closed in on him. "Take Calla and run."

Connor stared at Monroe, wild-eyed. "No."

"Now, Connor." Monroe didn't take his eyes off Ren. "That's an order."

"I will not." Connor's voice shook. "It's not worth it. It can't be."

"It is," Monroe said quietly. "You knew this was a possibility. Now get the girl out of here. And don't try to come back for me."

I was so startled I shifted back into human form. "No!"

Emile began to laugh. Ren still crouched between his father and the Searcher, his charcoal eyes blazing as he watched Monroe lower his swords.

"I won't hurt the boy," Monroe said. "You know that."

"I guessed it," Emile said, eyes flicking to the snarling young wolves. "Make sure he doesn't escape. It's time for Ren to avenge his mother."

"Ren, don't! He's lying. It's all lies!" I shrieked. "Come with us!"

"She's not one of us any longer," Emile hissed. "Think of how she's treated you, how she turned her back on all of us. Taste the air, boy. She stinks of the Searchers. She's a traitor and a whore."

He glared at me and I stumbled back at the livid fire in his eyes. "Don't worry, pretty girl. Your day is coming. Sooner than you think."

I jerked sideways when Connor grabbed my arm and tugged hard. He pulled me toward the unguarded door.

"We can't leave him!" I shouted.

"We have to." Connor stumbled into me as I fought to free myself but quickly regained his balance, locking his arms around me.

"Let me fight!" I struggled, desperate to go back but not wanting to hurt the Searcher who was dragging me away.

"No!" Connor's face was like stone. "You heard him. We're gone. And if you go wolf on me, I swear I'll knock you out!"

"Please." My eyes burned when I saw Ren's fangs gleam, and my breath stopped when Monroe dropped his swords.

"What is he doing?" I cried, dodging when Connor tried to grab me again.

"This is his fight now," he said through clenched teeth. "Not ours."

Ren jumped back as the swords clanged on the ground in front of him. Though his hackles were still raised, his growl died.

"Listen to me, Ren," Monroe said, crouching to meet Ren at eye level, not looking at the other two wolves bearing down on him with cruel slowness. "You still have a choice. Come with me and know who you really are. Leave all this behind."

Ren's short, sharp bark ended in a confused whimper. The other three wolves continued stalking toward the Searcher, undeterred by their enemy having abruptly laid down his arms.

Connor's arm swung around my neck, catching me in a painful headlock.

"We can't watch this," he snapped, slowly wrestling me out of the room.

"Ren, please!" I shouted. "Don't choose them! Choose me!"

Ren turned at the desperation in my voice, watching Connor pull me through the doorway. He shifted forms, staring bewildered at Monroe's outstretched hands, and took a step toward him.

"Who are you?"

Monroe's voice shook. "I'm—"

"Enough! You're a fool, boy," Emile snarled at Ren before smiling at Monroe. "Just like your father."

And then he was leaping through the air, shifting into wolf form—a thick bundle of fur, fangs, and claws. I saw him slam into Monroe, jaws locking around the unarmed man's throat, a moment before I was whipped around. Connor dragged me back down the hall at a breakneck pace.

I glanced over my shoulder, hoping to see Ren and Monroe emerge together, joining our escape. But all I heard were growls and snarls echoing in the empty space behind us.

TWENTY-THREE

WE'LL NEVER MAKE IT *back out. It was a trap.* I sobbed as I ran, broken by what I'd seen, by what I now knew. It had always been a trap. Guardians and Keepers would be swarming on the main floor of Eden now, blocking our escape. I ran on, still hand in hand with Connor though my steps felt heavier and heavier, like I was racing through wet cement.

Shouts reached my ears from the room ahead.

Connor flung open the door, shoving me into the Chamber. Any hope I'd been clinging to vanished at the scene we stumbled onto. Guardians pressed their way through the entrance to the eastern cell block two or three at a time. Ethan stood on the dais and fired bolts, laying a barrage of suppressing fire at them as quickly as he could, slowing their approach as they succumbed to the alchemists' compound swirling through their bloodstream. Wolves swayed on their feet, shook their muzzles, at last slumping onto the stone floor. Those hit by multiple bolts piled one atop the other in the doorway, creating a bottleneck that mercifully slowed the number that could get to us. My packmates were already in the fray, taking on those Guardians one-on-one who'd dodged Ethan's fire.

Connor swore, dragging me onto the stage.

"It's not looking good, friend," Ethan said through gritted teeth, aiming his bow once more. "I'm almost out of ammo."

"We'll be overwhelmed in less than five minutes," Connor said, scanning the room.

"Where's Monroe?" Ethan asked.

"We lost him," Connor said quietly. My veins went icy when he said it out loud.

"Well, that seals it." Ethan smiled grimly. "Any last words?"

"Calla," Connor said, "if we draw their attack, can you and the others get back to the stairs?"

I stared at the press of enemy wolves struggling over the pile of bodies blocking the corridor, snarling and jostling each other as they entered the Chamber.

"Even if I could, I think they have fifty or more Guardians backed all the way up to the first floor. We wouldn't make it out."

Connor shook his head, glancing back at the door to the northern cell block. I followed his gaze, wondering if Monroe was still alive, if there was any chance he might still emerge.

A deafening crack and a blinding flash flattened me against the floor; my ears rang as though lightning had struck the flagstones behind us. The room crackled with electricity and the air smelled of ozone. Ethan groaned beside me, flipping over and aiming his crossbow at whatever had thrown us down.

"I don't believe it," Connor murmured as Adne darted from the shimmering portal, stretching her hands to him.

"Believe it." She grinned, helping him up. Her smile faded as she saw the Guardians swarming into the Chamber.

"An inside door in Eden," Ethan gasped, staring at the portal. "You did it. You really did it."

"I'll happily receive your glowing reviews later," she said. "Right now we need to go."

"My pack," I said, scrambling to my feet.

"On it," Ethan said. He jumped from the stage, pushing his crossbow back and drawing swords. He cut his way through the mob, shouting.

"Show's over, kids! We just got our ticket out of here!"

Mason's ears flicked; he saw the sparkling gateway on the stage and gave a long, joyful howl. Nev turned, racing for the dais. Bryn released the throat of another wolf, dashing toward us. Sabine was pinned against the south wall, fighting three wolves at once.

"Hold on, Sabine!" Ethan yelled. "I'm on my way."

"Calla, keep the Guardians off Adne!" Connor ordered.

Connor followed in Ethan's wake, fighting off Guardians who attempted to pursue my retreating packmates. I shifted forms, tearing into any wolves who managed to get past him.

Ethan had reached Sabine, drawing two of the wolves off her with teasing sword strikes.

"Run!" he shouted as she took the third wolf down. "I'm right behind you."

She leapt past him, tearing for the dais. He ran one of the Guardians through, but the other locked its jaws around his arm. He swore, struggling to free himself. The wolf dug its fangs in deeper, unwilling to release. Ethan dropped the sword in his free hand and reached for a dagger. The wolf was still clinging to him when he plunged the sharp blade into its eye. The Guardian dropped to the floor, but blood gushed from the torn flesh of Ethan's arm as he stumbled back toward the dais.

"I've got you covered, man," Connor said, cutting down one wolf and slamming his fist into another's face as the two of them fell back.

"Here!" Adne shouted, waving to them. "Get through the door! I have to close it before they can follow."

Mason, Nev, and Bryn had already leapt through the light-filled door. Sabine waited beside me. She shifted forms when Ethan climbed onto the stage, wrapping her arm around his waist to help him through the portal.

"Go, Calla," Adne said, glancing around the room once more. "Connor, where's my father?"

"Go, Calla." Connor echoed her words, pushing me toward the shimmering gate.

I glanced over my shoulder as I passed into the light, watching as Connor pulled Adne against him, whispering in her ear. Her face crumpled and she slumped against him. Connor swung her body into his arms, carrying her through the portal and out of the fray.

My toenails crunched on gravel. I sucked in the cold predawn air. It tasted like freedom, but my relief was short-lived and bittersweet.

Behind me I could hear Adne sobbing and Connor murmuring. "You have to close the door, Adne. Please."

I heard the snarl and her scream at the same time. Pivoting toward the portal, I braced myself for a new fight. Two Guardians had leapt through the door. The first was on top of Adne, snapping at her face as she wriggled beneath it, while the second wolf squared off with Connor.

I scrambled toward Adne, catching blurred shapes racing past me out of the corner of my eye. As Connor raised his swords, Nev and Mason slammed into the wolf facing him. Fur and blood rained onto the ground as my packmates tore the enemy wolf apart.

I'd sunk my teeth into the flank of the other wolf, trying to pull it off Adne. The wolf had wrenched its snarling head around when it yelped and shuddered, all at once going limp. Adne grunted, pushing its body off, revealing the blood-covered skean with which she'd impaled the Guardian. Without hesitating, she rushed to the still open portal, ducking as another wolf leapt through it.

Adne slashed her skeans across the portal. The shimmering light that sparkled in the darkness winked out as I lunged at the new attacker. Our bodies slammed to the ground. We skidded across gravel, small stones scraping my skin even through the thick layer of fur. When we stopped sliding, the other wolf tried to scramble away, but I lunged forward, aiming for its neck but grabbing the upper part of its front leg in my jaws instead as it attempted to dodge. The wolf yelped, trying to shake me off, but I only bit down harder. The twang of Ethan's crossbow, followed by three brief thunks, reached my ears. The other wolf's bark became a whine and it slumped to the ground.

Snarls and shouts diminished, replaced by our panting and the Searchers' gasps for breath. Our heavy exhales formed tiny clouds in the cold air.

"Where are we?" Ethan finally asked.

He was half lying on the ground, propped up on one elbow, his mangled arm lying limp across his chest. Sabine crouched beside him, examining his shredded forearm. Bryn, Mason, and Nev were still in wolf form, huddling in a tight bunch slightly apart from the others.

Adne didn't answer Ethan; she had collapsed at Connor's feet. He put one hand on her head, stroking her hair, while he scanned our surroundings.

"Looks like we're on the roof of the building next to the club."

"The roof?" Ethan asked. "Is that right, Adne?"

She didn't respond.

"Adne," Ethan said again. "Where are we?"

"Leave her alone," Connor snarled.

"I'm not trying to be an ass," Ethan replied. "But we're not exactly out of harm's way yet. We need to get back to Denver."

Adne slowly uncurled her body, rising unsteadily. She stepped away when Connor reached for her.

"He's right, and yes, we're on the roof of a nearby building. I'll open a door home. Just give me a minute."

She stumbled away from us, wiping at her face.

I sat on the ground and shifted into human form, drawing my knees up to my chest. A part of me thought I should go to my pack-mates and make sure they were okay. Their first trip through a portal was probably a shock that only added to the stress of our escape. But I couldn't bring myself to join them; my mind was still reeling from what had happened in the northern cell block. I closed my eyes, body awash with not only grief, but a wave of confusion.

Just like your father.

What Emile had said didn't make any sense. The way he'd smiled at Monroe when he'd spoken the words made my skin crawl. Why would he have called himself a fool? For thinking he could ask Ren to hurt me when he still loved me?

My body ached with loss as I realized how likely it was that I would never see Ren again. And if I did, it would be as his enemy.

"Calla?" I opened my eyes to see Sabine kneeling in front of me. Now in human form, Bryn, Mason, and Nev stood just behind her.

"Yeah?" I said.

Sabine swallowed, her eyes glistening. "I was too busy fighting to see that you came back without the others. But now that we're here and they're not . . ."

A lead weight settled on my chest, making it difficult to breathe.

"They're dead, aren't they?" Sabine choked out the words.

I couldn't answer; my throat felt raw. I stared at her grief-filled face, not wanting to share a truth that would be more painful than what she believed had happened.

"All of them?" Bryn whispered, her own face crunching up in sorrow. "Even Ren?"

"No," I whispered.

Connor had quietly come up behind me. He laid a hand on my shoulder.

"You saw them?" Mason asked. "And they're still in there? Alive?"

Sabine's stricken expression became a scowl. "You let us leave them behind?"

Ethan rose unsteadily and joined our group, drawn by the rising tension. "What's wrong?"

Sabine was still glaring at me. "How could you?"

"Calla had no choice in the matter," Connor said.

"Of course she did," Sabine snapped.

Even Bryn's face fell, full of disappointment at my apparent cowardice.

I couldn't look at either of them anymore, so I stared at the ground, tears burning in my own eyes.

"We didn't leave them behind," Connor answered for me. "I was with Calla when she found the rest of your pack."

"Then why aren't they here?" Sabine's eyes narrowed.

"They stayed, Sabine," Neville said quietly, taking in Connor's somber gaze. "They stayed with the Keepers."

"No," Bryn said.

"That's impossible," Sabine hissed. "Cosette would never stay with them!"

"It's true," Connor said. "They attacked Calla."

"Why would they attack Calla?" Mason asked.

"Emile," I said. "They were taking orders from Emile."

"And Ren?" Bryn asked, voice quaking. "He stayed too?"

"Yes." *He stayed because of what I did to him.*

"Damn." Nev walked away, shaking his head. Mason followed him, sparing me a sad smile before he left.

Sabine was crying softly. "Oh, Cosette."

Ethan cleared his throat. "Look, if this Cosette stayed behind, it was only because she was afraid."

"More afraid of leaving than of what will happen to her with me gone?" She choked on the words. "I can't protect her from Efron now. She knows what he'll . . ."

"Better the devil you know," Connor said. "It happens."

She shook her head and sobbed.

"You were close?" Ethan asked quietly.

"I . . . I always thought of her like a sister," Sabine said. "I just don't understand."

"Calla." Bryn took my hand. "About Ren . . . are you—"

I held up my hand. "I can't, Bryn. Please."

Guilt. Shame. Regret. An avalanche of feelings crashed over me. I couldn't bear the thought of trying to explain what had happened.

"Okay." She stood up, frowning. "I'll leave you alone."

She went after Mason and Nev.

"Ethan, can you give us a minute?" Connor asked, crouching next to me.

"Sure," he said. He was already watching Sabine, who had risen, moving slowly away from us. But unlike Bryn, she didn't follow the other wolves, instead stumbling to the edge of the roof, alone. Ethan trailed after her, keeping a respectful distance.

Connor watched me intently. "Monroe told me you and Ren were close."

The thickness in my throat was painful, but I managed a nod. How could this get any worse? I didn't think I could bear any more questions about Ren and me.

"You heard what Emile said," Connor continued in a low voice. "Just before . . ." He couldn't finish, looking away from me. I watched him swallow grief.

"Yes," I said numbly, not knowing why it mattered.

Connor cleared his throat a couple of times before he could speak again. "I'm asking you not to say anything until I have time to talk to Adne."

Say anything about what? Ren was lost. So was Monroe. Half the pack had turned to the Keepers. Those we'd saved thought our losses were my fault. But what could I do to change that? After all, it was true.

"People know," he said quietly. "Or even if they don't know, they talk. It's not a secret that Monroe loved Corrine. But no one knew about the child."

The child.

I thought my heart would splinter into a thousand pieces as the truth seized me. Monroe's endless questions about Ren. The incredible risks he'd taken, all trying to save Ren. The way he'd laid down his weapons before the advancing wolf.

How Ren looked nothing like Emile, but he did look like Monroe. That was why the Guide had always seemed familiar when I spoke with him. Hair dark as coffee, the chiseled angles of his cheeks and jaw.

I won't hurt the boy. You know that.

Monroe was Ren's father. Corrine had asked him to kill her because she'd been ordered to have a child. And she'd fallen in love with Monroe while they'd spent months planning a revolt . . . a time in which her body had been unbound by the Keepers' enchantments.

"Oh my God," I whispered, feeling tears spill out of my eyes. "Ren."

Monroe's son—not Emile's—and yet a Guardian. *The mother's essence always seems to dominate, determines the nature of the child.*

"We can't do anything for him now," Connor said. "I wish it were otherwise. But Monroe wanted Adne to know the truth. Even if he didn't make it back. I'll tell her, but now isn't the time."

Though it was painful, I swallowed the thickness in my throat. "But . . . how? What about Adne's mother?"

"It was before my time." Connor kept his voice low. "But I've heard things. After the alliance, when the Searchers were ambushed and Corrine died, things were bad. Really bad. And nobody was in worse shape than Monroe. We're talkin' not-coming-back-from-the-brink worse. I think he was hitting the bottle hard. Reckless on missions. Looking to get himself killed."

"What changed?" I asked. It was too easy to imagine how much blame Monroe would have put on himself.

"There were so many losses that positions were shuffled all over the place after the Vail catastrophe," he said. "Diana—Adne's mother—was a new Striker assigned to Haldis. She befriended Monroe . . . was the only one who got through to him, saved him from himself. And eventually there was Adne."

"Did you know Diana?" I tried to envision a woman with Adne's mahogany tresses and bright amber eyes. In my mind's eye she was trading sword blows with Monroe and they were both laughing.

He shook his head. "I was her replacement," Connor said, shifting his gaze away from me to watch Adne. She stood at the edge of the roof, head bowed. "Whether Monroe ever told Diana about Ren, I guess we'll never know." Then his eyes were back on me. "Can you keep this secret?"

I nodded, overwhelmed by cataclysmic revelations that kept coming, each new secret throwing my world into chaos.

"Thank you," he murmured. I watched him rise, wondering how he would tell Adne she had a brother she'd never known and likely would never know except to kill him.

As Connor walked away, my attention was drawn to Ethan and Sabine's voices.

Ethan was leaning away from her outstretched arm. "I said no."

"Stop being a baby," Sabine said, and I saw blood dripping from her arm onto the ground.

"I'm not drinking your blood." He tried to scoot back but faltered, unable to put any weight on his mangled arm.

"Think about how much it will hurt to let that heal on its own," she said. "It will take forever. This will fix it instantly, plus you won't have any scars."

"I don't mind scars," he growled.

"I'm sure you don't, tough guy." She laughed. "But macho points aren't worth much if your arm is in a sling for the next month. You really think you can fight like that?"

"But I . . . ," Ethan sputtered.

"And I know you're still bleeding from that shoulder wound too," Sabine said. "Why won't you let me help you?"

"Just leave me alone," he said, sounding like a petulant child as he turned his face away.

"I will," she said. "After."

Sabine slipped behind him, wrapping one arm around his chest, pinning him against her body.

"Hey!" he shouted, eyes wide in alarm. His next words were lost as she pressed her bleeding forearm against his mouth.

He struggled to free himself, but Sabine was at full Guardian strength and had little trouble holding him still. She kept her arm welded against his lips, her blood trickling along his jaw. He flailed once more before he was forced to swallow. I watched something pass over his face—a mixture of fear and wonder.

The scene before me was too familiar, making me tremble. It was like watching a hazy reflection of the day I'd forced Shay to drink my blood. The same amazed expression had filled Shay's eyes. Ethan clasped Sabine's wrist, drawing her flesh further into his mouth instead of pushing it away. He closed his eyes and drank, shivering with ecstasy.

Connor, who'd been watching silently, uttered a sharp exclamation as the torn flesh of Ethan's arm began to mend itself before our eyes. Shredded muscle rebuilt like new, skin closed up, completely free of scars. Ethan's eyes remained closed. He was lost in the power of Sabine's blood flowing through him.

When the wound had healed, she gripped his shoulder, leveraging her arm from his grasp.

"Easy there, tiger," she murmured. "Or you'll make me faint."

Her voice brought Ethan back to the roof, the cold night, and five pairs of eyes locked on him.

He twisted away from Sabine, jumping to his feet, limbs shaking. "That . . ."

His face took on a haunted cast as he stared at her, backing away. The expression dissolved into a scowl. "I didn't want that."

"You're welcome," she said, shivering as a gust of icy wind rushed over her bare skin.

Ethan's eyes were still hard, but he shrugged off his leather duster and tossed it to her.

"I'm going to make sure there aren't any wraiths finding their way up the fire escapes."

Wraiths. Bryn whimpered. I glanced at her and saw that the pack, except Sabine, had reverted to wolf form. Nev and Mason pressed their muzzles against her, their own limbs trembling. I shuddered. It was too easy to imagine the torment that my packmates had been subjected to, the memories of fear and pain that would stay with them even though they were now free. I drew a slow breath, grasping for some way to ease my mind. We were lucky that only Guardians had ambushed us. We'd been able to fight them off.

Lucky . . .

"All clear," Ethan said, returning to our huddled group. "No one came after us. Is Adne ready to open the door now?"

"She is," Adne said, returning from her solitude. The tracks of tears still glistened on her face. "Are you sure no one is following us? They were outside before; that's how I ended up here."

"What happened?" Connor asked. "How did you get to us?"

"After you'd been gone about twenty minutes, there was a lot of activity on the street outside the club—cars pulling up; I heard shouting and movement," she said. "Dozens of Guardians went in through the side door. I worried I'd be spotted, so I closed the portal and opened a door to this roof. I waited until I realized you were in serious trouble."

"What made you open the door inside Eden?" Ethan asked.

"I watched the club from the edge of the roof," she said. "The Guardians kept coming. There were so many of them, and so much time had passed. I knew you'd be trapped. I decided I had to risk it."

"Thanks for that," Ethan said. "We'd all be kibbles and bits if you'd played it safe."

"Guardians don't eat people," I said, frowning. "We never eat people."

"You know what I meant." He grinned.

"I'm just glad I was paying attention when your brother described the prison," Adne said, offering me a thin smile. "Those were the details I used to weave the door."

"How do you do it?" Sabine asked, pulling Ethan's jacket tight around her body. "I've never seen anything like that."

"Adne can use magic to connect one place to another," I said, trying to make the explanation as simple as possible. "It's how they travel."

"Neat-o." Nev had shifted into human form. "And the Keepers don't just follow you?"

"The Keepers can't create the doors," I said quickly. "I'll explain that later." I didn't think now was the time to tell my packmates that the Searchers described our creation as a sin against nature. And I was distracted. Ethan's words buzzed in my ears. No one had come after us. Why? We were hidden, but not that well. It would only make sense for the Keepers to comb the streets, even the rooftops, hunting us.

Fighting back more than a brush of nerves, I raised my voice. "It doesn't make sense."

"What doesn't make sense?" Connor asked.

"Our escape," I said. "It was too easy."

"Too easy?" Adne hissed. "My father is dead!"

Sorrow spilled through me. I hung my head, thinking of Monroe, of Ren. Of how close a father had been to reclaiming his stolen son. I wondered if Bryn, Mason, Nev, and Sabine would carry the marks of torment like my brother. They seemed fine now, but would the adrenaline rush of freedom be sucked away by misery when they realized that nothing in their lives would ever be the same? Had we truly saved anyone? Regret drowned my unease, sending me into a spiral of despair.

Connor pressed his hand onto her shoulder. "Hang on, Adne. I don't think she means offense. What are you talking about, Calla?"

I shook my head, not wanting to dig myself into a deeper hole where I'd be suffocated by doubt and regret.

"No," Ethan said. "Tell us. You know the Keepers. What's bothering you about this?"

The strength in his voice pulled me out of self-pity. I tried to remember who I was, or at least who I'd once been. A leader. A warrior.

"It was a trap," I said.

"Obviously." Ethan nodded, his eyes narrowing while I spoke. "And a pretty good one."

"But not as good as it could have been," I said slowly.

"Keep going," he said.

"Wraiths," I said simply.

Connor left Adne's side and took a few steps toward me. "What about them?"

"Why weren't there any wraiths?" I struggled to keep confidence in my voice despite the new, sickening fear that snaked through my gut.

No one answered, but everyone's eyes were on me.

"Think about it," I said. "They knew we were coming, but we only fought Guardians. I didn't see any Keepers, and without Keepers there are no wraiths."

"What are you getting at?" Ethan asked.

"Where were the Keepers?" I replied. "Why weren't they part of the ambush?"

"Didn't want to get their hands dirty," Connor grumbled.

"No," Ethan said, a shadow of concern passing over his face. "She's got a point. Why wouldn't they use their most effective weapon if they wanted to make sure we didn't escape?"

"Maybe they were around but not in the building," Adne said, sweeping tears away with the back of her hand. "I've never opened an inside door before today. They could have been waiting for us to make a run for it once we left the club."

"Maybe," I said, but fear continued to swarm over my skin. "But then why aren't they down there looking for us?"

No one answered.

"Well, it's not going to do us any good to wait here and find out," Connor said. "Adne, open a door. Let's get back to Denver."

"Right," Adne said. "Just do the job. Like nothing's happened."

She turned away from him, sulking. Not a good sign. My unease grew by the second. We needed to get out of here and Adne's grief was slowing our escape. She might be gifted for her age, but she was still young and now it showed. Connor grabbed her shoulders, whirling her to face him. He took her chin in his palm, leaning close to her.

"You're not the only one who lost someone today, Adne," he murmured, resting his forehead against hers. "I loved your father too. So did Ethan."

I looked away, feeling uninvited into this intimate moment.

"But you're the only one who can get us out of here," I heard Connor say.

I cast a sidelong glance at them. Adne had pulled away from him and was drawing the skeans from her belt.

"I know," she said, and began to weave.

Bryn shifted forms and came to my side.

"That's amazing," she whispered, watching the door emerge from strands of light.

I nodded.

She took my hand. "I'm sorry I walked away from you, Calla. There's just so much that's happened."

"Don't apologize," I said. "It's all my fault."

"No, it's not," she said. I was surprised by the hard edge in her voice. "If the others stayed behind, they're fools. And it isn't your fault."

"But Ren . . ." When he'd kissed me, I'd felt how much he still wanted me, and from the way my blood had caught fire, I knew at least part of me still ached for him. The knowledge caught me by surprise, stealing my breath as I relived those horrible first minutes in the cell with Ren. I could still see the pain in his eyes when he'd thought he had no choice but to hurt me.

"No," Bryn said, her voice plowing through my flurry of thoughts. "Calla, I don't know why you left Vail, but I can guess. Ansel and I were guessing a long time ago. I don't blame you for following your heart."

"There's more than that," I said.

"I'm sure there is," she said. "But even if there wasn't, it wouldn't make leaving wrong. And you still wouldn't be to blame for Ren's choice. That's all it is. His choice."

I looked at her, stung by the love in her eyes. The forgiveness.

"Thank you," I whispered.

"What in life is worth a sacrifice, if not love?" She smiled sadly.

"You sound like Ansel."

"Like attracts like," she said, and I flinched.

"What?" she asked.

"Nothing," I said quickly, not wanting to tell her I'd heard that said before. That Ren had spoken those very words to me, and in remembering them, I now realized it was his way of telling me that we were meant for each other. The memory smoldered in my chest like lit coals, burning out much too slowly.

"I can't wait to see him." I realized Bryn had been in the middle of a sentence.

"I'm sorry?" I said, shaking myself free of the past.

"Ansel," she said. "He's there, right? In Denver?"

"Yes," I said. "But Bryn, he's—" I stopped myself. Maybe Ansel would change if Bryn were there to help him. I didn't want to make her any more afraid than she already was.

"He's waiting for you," I said, and she smiled.

When the door was finished, I gazed at it, puzzled. Something didn't look right. I couldn't see the room we'd come from. The image behind the portal was dark and hazy.

"Is that where we're going?" Mason asked, also wary of the darkness that lay before us.

"Yes," Adne said uneasily. "I'm not sure why it's dark."

"It's not important," Connor said. "Anyway, we don't have a choice; we have to go back. If something's wrong, we'll know when we get there."

"Very reassuring," I said. Bryn drew a quick, nervous breath and I squeezed her hand, sorry I'd said anything.

"But true," Connor replied. "Ethan, lead the way. Wolves, go right behind him and put on your game faces, just in case. Calla, Adne, and I will follow you and close the door as soon as we're all through."

"Game faces?" Bryn frowned.

"He wants you to change forms," I said.

"Happily," Nev said, and was a wolf in the next moment. Mason and Bryn both shifted. The three wolves circled one another, licking, nuzzling. Sabine was watching Ethan. She glanced at the other Guardians but didn't shift.

Connor smiled sadly at me. "Go on, that's where you belong."

My fangs were already sharpening when I returned his smile. "Just don't try to pet me."

Welcome back, Calla. Bryn licked my jaw. *We've missed you.*

Nev and Mason crowded in, pushing at me with their muzzles.

Are we okay? I asked.

You tell us, you're the alpha. Nev nipped at my shoulder. *I figure if this is our pack now, we'd better make the best of it.*

I wagged my tail. *Fair enough.*

Can we get out of here now? Mason pawed at the ground.

I glanced at Connor, who watched me, a mixture of awe and curiosity playing over his face.

Sabine gazed at us, but she kept her distance, remaining in human form.

Ethan raised an eyebrow, glancing from her to our pack, as though her choice to stay away from us surprised him.

"Looks like we're ready, Ethan," Connor said. "You want to lead the way? Now that you're a whole man again."

"Go to hell," Ethan growled, blushing when he cast a sidelong glance at Sabine.

She was still staring ahead, eyes distant, and she wrapped herself tighter in his jacket, shivering. I didn't think it was from the cold.

"Why don't you follow him, Sabine?" Connor said. "Stick close together."

She nodded, disappearing into the portal. My packmates rushed after her. I hesitated for a moment, watching them go, glancing back at the alley that led to Eden. That place had changed everything. It had taken my brother's soul, claimed Ren as its own, and become Monroe's grave.

Instead of following the pack, I returned to my human body and faced Connor. "What if—"

Connor shook his head. "No looking back."

I was surprised when he stepped forward, pulling me into an embrace.

"We all lost something today," he whispered, resting his chin against the crown of my hair.

Adne watched us silently; tears standing in her eyes reflected the subtle, wavering gleam of the open door.

I nodded, leaning into him for a moment before I shifted into wolf form and leapt into the portal's murky depths.

TWENTY-FOUR

A BLAST OF HEAT PUSHED me back, throwing me
toward the door from which I'd just emerged. For a moment I
thought something had gone wrong with the portal and I was trapped
between worlds, tumbling into oblivion, and would soon be burning
alive. I couldn't see. Thick smoke filled the air, stinging my eyes, filling my lungs. I shifted forms, wanting to call out to the Searchers, but
I dropped to my knees, coughing, grasping in front of me blindly.

"Calla!" A hand grabbed my arm, jerking me sideways. I could
just make out Ansel's face through the smoke.

"You have to get out of here," he hissed, drawing me farther from
the portal.

"What's happening?" I said, choking on the smoke. At last I could
recognize my surroundings. I was back in Purgatory's bare entrance.
Flames jumped along the walls, gutting the Searchers' hideout.

"There are two more by the staircase!" I recognized Ethan's
shout.

"Keep moving," Isaac yelled a second later. "Don't let them corner you!"

Ansel pulled me into a crouch on the floor as a dark shape slipped
in and out of the smoke plumes a few feet away from us. Fear slid
beneath my skin when I realized it was a wraith.

"Keep still," Ansel breathed into my ear.

My heart slammed against my ribs. Where was Shay?

I heard screaming but couldn't tell if the sound came from a man or woman.

Adne and Connor's silhouettes were illuminated against the light of the portal.

Connor flinched at the heat and began to cough. "What the hell?"

I saw the wraith turn, moving away from our hiding place but slithering toward them. Ansel tried to hold me back, but I pushed him away, lunging toward the confused pair.

"Run!" I shouted, slamming into them, knocking them away from the glowing door.

Adne scrambled from beneath me. "Oh my God. What's happened?"

"They found us," Connor said, drawing his swords. "The Keepers found us."

"Adne? Connor?" Ethan loomed out of the smoke, cradling an unconscious Sabine in his arms. Isaac had joined beside Ethan. Both of them brandished weapons, but their faces were bleak.

"Damn it." Connor peered into the smoke.

"What happened?" I asked, staring at Sabine's limp body.

"The building is coming down," Ethan said, thrusting his hand toward an immense pile of debris. "A whole section of the roof fell right as we came through the door. She was hit in the head. I lost the wolves trying to get out of the way. I don't know where they are. They may have been buried underneath."

"Incoming! Ethan, back up!" Connor held his swords low, but his eyes went flat and hopeless as the wraith approached. "Calla, stay behind me!"

"Adne, open a door!" Ethan screamed. "Get us out of here!"

The wraith was only a few feet away now.

There was still no sign of Shay or the rest of the pack. Were they buried under the rubble? Had they already been taken? Who led this attack? How had the Keepers found Purgatory?

"We aren't going to make it." Connor grimaced, placing himself between our huddled group and the wraith.

"Some of us are," Isaac murmured. He shoved Connor back and leapt onto the wraith.

"No!" Ethan shouted as inky shadows wrapped around Isaac while the rest of us stood frozen in horror.

Isaac made no sound. His body only crumpled in on itself as the Keepers' creature took him.

"Adne!" Connor moved between us and the horrible sight.

"It's open!" Adne shouted. I turned to see a new door shimmering behind her.

"Go!" Connor jerked his head and Ethan, with Sabine, bolted through the passage.

"You too." Connor took Adne's hand.

"I won't go until you do," she said.

"This isn't a discussion," Connor said. "If we aren't there in two minutes, you close the door. Understand?"

Her eyes brimmed, but she nodded and vanished into the doorway.

"Shay!" I screamed, desperately peering into the smoke for any sign of him or the others. "Ansel!"

"Through the door." Connor reached for me, but I darted away. "They came for *him*. They've probably already taken him. You have to go now!"

"I'm not leaving them!" I yelled, coughing as smoke tore at my lungs.

Several dark shapes appeared in the shifting gray clouds. Connor swore, looking from me to the door.

"I don't know how many more wraiths there are, but we can't wait to find out." He took my arm, drawing me back.

"Please," I sobbed. "I have to find them."

The silhouettes of four wolves materialized from the smoke—speeding toward us. My choked cry became a shriek of joy. Shay shifted forms and his arms were around me, pulling me tight against him. Then Bryn, Mason, and Nev stood beside him, their eyes wild and faces pale.

"Thank God you're okay," Shay whispered, pressing his face into my hair. "We've been running through the hideout like some crazy maze, dodging the wraiths."

"Where's Ansel?" Bryn was crying. "All the smoke, I couldn't track his scent. . . . I couldn't find him."

"I don't know where he is." My stomach knotted. Had I abandoned my own brother to wraiths?

"Get your asses through that portal!" Connor ripped Shay away from me, shoving him through the glimmering door. "We have to get it closed before the other wraiths find us."

"But—" Bryn began, eyes moving over the smoke, searching for any signs of Ansel.

Mason and Nev shifted forms again, sniffing the air and whining.

"That's it," Connor hissed, reaching for Bryn. "No more waiting."

"I knew you'd leave me behind." Silas's voice cut through the smoke. "Bastard."

He was slumped over Ansel's shoulders. My brother stumbled forward, supporting the Scribe's weight.

"Ansel!" I searched his body for signs of injury. "Are you okay?"

He nodded, not raising his eyes to mine.

"You hurt?" Connor asked Silas.

"Fell down the stairs when they showed up . . . I think I twisted my ankle. Lucky this one came along," Silas replied, nodding at Ansel.

"Get him to the other side," Connor said, turning away stiffly from the Scribe, but I saw relief wash over his face at Silas's appearance. "We're all leaving. Right now."

Ansel kept his eyes on the floor but nodded, dragging Silas into the shimmering portal. Bryn rushed after them. Shay kept his arms around me and we moved toward the door together with Mason and Nev at our heels. Behind us I heard a crash, followed by a thundering blast. An explosion threw us forward, ripping me from Shay's arms. I faded out of consciousness as I watched the bodies of my companions falling into the portal's light like shadows flickering against the sun.

TWENTY-FIVE

I WAS ON MY BACK, staring up at a dull gray sky. Bits of ash floated through the air, settling on my skin and melting.

Melting?

I took a deep breath, feeling icy cold pour into my lungs. Scattered flakes of snow continued to float down steadily. A rustling sound was all around me. The pressing heat of flames and suffocating smoke were gone. I rolled over, crouching, trying to make sense of where I was.

Slender, faded yellow columns reached for the sky in straight rows, stretching for what looked like a flat eternity, at last falling off into an infinite horizon.

What the hell? My hand brushed against a dried husk that lay on the frozen earth.

Corn. Cornstalks. I glanced at my feet; the earth below me was hard, caught in the grip of winter's chill, but even below the dusting of snow I could see the darkness of the rich soil. A field.

Nearby I heard someone gasping for breath. Adne rolled onto her side, grimacing.

"Welcome back to Iowa."

"Where are we?" I asked, shaking my head. My ears were still ringing.

"On the outer perimeter of the Academy grounds," Adne said.

Shay groaned, rubbing his stomach. "I think I almost got impaled by a cornstalk. Why aren't we inside the Academy?"

"I didn't want to risk us being followed," Adne said, standing up. "Don't worry, it's not far."

"Hey!" Connor's shout drew my attention.

Mason in wolf forms, snarled, while Bryn stood apart from them trying to hold on to Ansel, who kept moving away from her.

Nev was on his knees. His hands were locked in a choke hold, holding something against the ground—something that had Mason bristling, ready to attack. Not something—someone.

"What the hell?" Ethan turned and stared at him. He was still holding an unconscious Sabine.

"Calla, what's wrong with them?" Connor asked.

As I got closer, I could make out golden spikes of hair. *It can't be.*

I could hear words gurgling from within the windpipe Nev was slowly crushing.

"Pl . . . please," Logan choked. "I'm. . . . ungh . . . I'm . . . here . . . to . . . help . . . you. . . ."

"Nev, wait," I said, grabbing his forearm. "What is he saying?"

"I don't care." Nev scowled. Logan's skin was turning blue.

I stared at them, paralyzed by indecision, not blaming Nev for wanting to hurt the Keeper. Logan remained pinned to the earth, squirming futilely as air was cut off from his lungs. Nev's face twisted with rage, his grip on Logan's throat ever tightening.

"Who is that?" Connor was beside us.

"A Keeper," I said. "That's Efron Bane's son."

"What the hell is he doing here?" Connor blinked at Logan in disbelief. "And how did he get here?"

"I have no idea," I said.

Logan pushed futilely at Nev's arms. His eyes rolled up at Connor.

"Save . . . them . . . ," Logan's voice squeaked out. "Tristan . . . not . . . dead . . ."

"What?" Connor ducked forward, shoving Nev aside. Now it was Connor over Logan, keeping him down with one booted foot to the chest. Logan gasped and sputtered, reaching up to touch the dark bruises at his throat.

Connor shook him. "What did you just say?"

"Give me asylum." Logan coughed. "They'll kill me if you send me back."

"We'll take care of that for them," Nev snarled, still crouching nearby. "You don't have to go anywhere."

"Why would we ever give refuge to a Keeper?" I asked, staring at Logan. I didn't trust him for a moment. He and his father represented everything that had gone wrong in Vail. It was their fault Ren was . . .

The thought barreled me over. Ren. I'd lost him forever. Worse than that, my betrayal had turned him away from any life other than one that was dictated by the Keepers. Tears filled my eyes and I stumbled back. I wanted nothing more than to fall to my knees and claw Logan's eyes out, using his flesh to tear away the pain that knotted my gut.

Shay was at my side, putting his arms around me, his touch only making my guilt sting like salt in a wound.

"Don't," I said, pulling away.

Ethan gazed at Logan with flat eyes. "Kill him."

Connor nodded, drawing his sword.

Adne gasped when Logan began to laugh. "Such hypocrisy! I thought the Searchers were supposed to be noble. Foolish, of course, but noble all the same."

"For a dead man you sure jabber a lot," Connor said, lowering the blade to Logan's throat.

Logan tensed but kept smiling. "I only meant that if you hadn't harbored one of my kind, all of your hopes would be dashed already, wouldn't they?"

"What is he talking about?" Bryn asked. She was listening even as she hovered near my brother. Ansel kept sidling away from her, but she followed him, trying to hold him in spite of his reticence.

"My father," Shay said quietly. "He's talking about my father."

"I knew there was a reason you're the Chosen One," Logan said. "Remarkably observant."

"You aren't Tristan," Ethan snapped.

"But I can help you save him," Logan said.

"What?" Shay darted forward. "What do you mean?"

"What I've been trying to say since I stowed away with you," Logan replied. "Your parents are alive."

"You're lying." The sword Shay held began to shake in his grip.

"Not when my life depends on it," Logan said. "Tristan and Sarah Doran are alive. You can still save them."

"What the hell is he talking about?" Nev shouted, pacing next to Connor. "Kill that bastard. I can't stand the sight of him."

Mason stalked forward, hackles raised.

"No!" It was Shay who blocked his line of attack before turning back to Logan. "What do you mean, we can still save them? Where are they?"

Logan smiled slowly. "If you want to know, I need assurance that I won't be harmed."

"He's lying," Nev hissed. "Shut him up now. Cut his tongue out."

"Wait." The words wanted to stick in my throat, but I knew Shay was at least partly right about this. "If he knows something about Shay's parents, we at least have to find out what it is."

"How about if you don't tell us, I cut your tongue out?" Connor said, sheathing his sword after Ethan tossed him a dagger.

Logan's smile vanished. "Barbarian."

"I consider that a compliment," Connor said. "You gonna play ball?"

"Stop this!" Silas limped forward, looking a bit singed. "If he has information, we'll go through an official interrogation."

"I don't think I asked for your opinion," Connor said.

"It's protocol," Silas said. "Anika will be furious if you don't follow it. If this is indeed Efron Bane's son, he's not only a valuable informant. He could be a priceless hostage."

"Brainiac's got a point," Ethan said.

Adne sprang forward, one of her skeans raised. "I don't give a damn about protocol! My father and Isaac are dead because of the Keepers. I want his blood!"

Connor knocked her arm away at the last second, the slash of the skean's sharp point coming within inches of Logan's cheek.

"Let me go!" Adne shrieked, sobbing.

Logan was shaking, his eyes bulging as he watched Adne brandish her skeans. "I swear I have information you need. Plus if I wanted to harm you, wouldn't I have already summoned a wraith?"

No one answered him. I hated that anything Logan said made sense.

Connor lifted his foot and Logan propped himself up on his elbows, which inspired Connor to level the dagger with Logan's neck.

"If I give you something," Logan asked, "will you bring me to your Arrow?"

"Depends on how much we think it's worth," Connor muttered, his eyes fixed on Adne's struggle. "Your people have taken a lot from us today. And that's just today."

"I can tell you there's a traitor in your midst. I'll hand them to you as a sign of good faith." Logan's shaking gave way to a smirk that sent a chill skittering over my flesh.

"What traitor?" Connor asked, rolling the edge of the blade along Logan's throat.

"How do you think we found you?" Logan said. "We've been hunting you for years. Did you think we just got lucky today?"

"Someone led you to the Denver outpost," Connor said.

"Someone you trusted," Logan said. "Someone you brought back from the dead."

"No," Shay growled. "You're lying." He stepped in front of me, shielding me from something I did not yet know to be afraid of. What was he talking about?

Logan smiled at him. "You may have power, Scion. But not even you can protect her from this."

"You heartless bastard," Shay said. "Stop now or I'll—"

"Or you'll what?" Logan said. "Would you kill me to hide the truth? Are my words a crime when they'll protect your allies?"

"What are you talking about, Keeper?" Connor leaned down, pushing the dagger into his flesh. "I'm losing patience with you."

"Her brother," Logan choked against the blade's pressure. "Calla's brother. He made a deal with my father and Lumine."

"No," I whispered.

Mason snarled, pawing at the earth.

Logan's eyes were on me. "It's true. He betrayed you."

I searched frantically for Ansel, finding him cowering behind Bryn, who had shifted into wolf form and was already growling as if to protect him from impending attack. Mason ran to her, taking up a sentry-like position at her side.

Oh God.

"He's more of a threat to you than I am," Logan hissed.

Connor lifted the dagger's blade, looking up at me. "Calla?"

My throat had closed. I turned away from Connor, darting toward Ansel. Bryn bared her teeth at me, but I grabbed Ansel's shoulders, shaking him.

"Ansel, please. You have to tell them the truth. Tell them you didn't do this!!"

Logan had to be lying. He had to be.

The color had leached from Ansel's face; his eyes rolled up at me. Hollow.

"They said they would make me a wolf again."

Bryn whimpered. Mason barked, circling Ansel nervously while glancing at me.

I backed away, limbs trembling. I wished I could run—somehow escape this awful truth. But I had nowhere to go.

Connor shook his head. "We'd better sort this out with Anika."

"Agreed," Ethan said. His eyes met mine briefly as he readjusted Sabine's body in his arms, but I couldn't tell if he was angry or just full of regret.

A sharp whistle came from the dense maze of cornstalks around us, followed by several others. One by one, Strikers, armed to the teeth, emerged from the field around us, encircling our group.

My packmates stood back to back, growling and facing off against the Searchers.

"Wait!" I shouted, throwing myself between the wolves and the approaching warriors.

I was surprised when Ethan came to my side, still cradling Sabine against his chest.

"Stand down." Anika stepped out from among the warriors.

Nev, Bryn, and Mason backed off slowly, watching the Searchers, still bristling, waiting to see what would happen next. Ansel scrambled behind us, not speaking, hunched over as if he wanted to be as small and unremarkable as possible.

"Thank you," Anika said. She glanced at Ethan holding Sabine in his arms, then arched an eyebrow at him. His grip on the unconscious girl only tightened.

Anika's gaze kept moving. When it settled on Shay, seeing him unharmed, she seemed to relax slightly.

She turned to Connor, voice like a knife. "What is the meaning of an unscheduled drop? And with Guardians in tow? You're lucky we didn't you attack on sight."

Connor didn't flinch. "Couldn't be helped."

"I expect a full report." She clucked her tongue. "Where is Monroe?"

"Dead," Adne said. "And the Keepers hit Denver."

"How?" Anika gasped. "What happened?"

Connor looked at me, but he didn't answer her.

"The alpha's brother turned on her," Logan said, trying to sit up. Connor shoved him back down.

"Who are you?" Anika walked toward the pair.

"My name is Logan Bane," he said, glaring at Connor. "And I'm here to offer my help, if your muscle doesn't kill me first."

"Bane?" Anika said. "A Keeper?"

"Yes, I'm a Keeper," Logan said. "But I've abandoned my father and the rest of my kind. I don't belong there. I belong with you."

"Not likely," Connor growled.

"You'd be a fool to refuse my offer," Logan snapped. "I'm handing you the Scion's parents."

"Tristan and Sarah?" Anika knelt beside Logan. "For your sake, I hope you're telling the truth."

"I am."

"Don't listen to him." Adne pushed Connor away as he tried to grab her. "He's a Keeper. Anika, my father is dead!"

"Can we settle this later?" Silas limped to Anika's side. "I don't know how much time we have."

Anika took in his disheveled appearance, frowning. "What do you mean?"

"The Denver outpost is compromised," Silas said. "That's why we're uninvited guests. If they managed to get their hands on the intelligence that's housed there before the building burned down, they'll know where the Academy is."

The color slowly drained from Anika's face. "No."

"Yes," Silas said. "The Academy must be moved. Now."

TWENTY-SIX

THE SEARCHERS KEPT US moving at a quick pace.

Logan's hands were bound, his every move scrutinized by the four Strikers who escorted him to the Academy. I would have been relieved by their stern treatment of the Keeper if they hadn't treated Ansel the same way.

Though Logan walked with an undisguised smirk fixed on his mouth, my brother hung his head, stumbling between armed Strikers.

"We have to stop this," I whispered to Shay.

"I know," he said. "Once we're back at the Academy, I'll talk to Anika. I don't think they'll hurt him in the meantime."

I glowered at him. "He doesn't deserve this. You've seen how broken he is. He just didn't realize—"

"I know, Calla." Shay took my arm, his eyes telling me to lower my voice. "I know. I'm on your side, but we have to figure out what happened before we can convince them Ansel isn't a threat."

I jerked away from him, darting forward to where Connor walked beside Adne.

"Connor, can't you do something?" I hissed. "This isn't Ansel's fault."

"Not now," Connor said. "Even if I could do something, we don't have time to sort it out."

Adne's face was like stone.

"Adne," I began. "Please—"

"He's right." She didn't look at me. "We don't have time. We have to deal with that."

She pointed to the massive structure that towered above the cornfields. Outside, the Academy was even more impressive than it was within. The immense structure curved away from us, its marble surface gleaming as the winter sun split through the heavy cloud cover. Four slender spires stretched toward the sky, interrupting the smooth curve of the building at equal intervals. All four stories of the Academy were lined with windows, giving it the appearance of being filled with light.

I stared at the imposing structure, which loomed larger with every step we took. How could they possibly move it?

More Searchers were waiting for us as we entered the building. The bottom floor opened into the same structure of a hallway circling the central courtyard, but here the doors lining the walls were spaced at much wider intervals.

"The Haldis team?" a woman whom I recognized as one of the other Guides asked Anika.

She nodded, her face grim. "It's still unclear what happened. But we lost Monroe, and the Denver site was infiltrated. Declare an emergency relocation."

"You're not serious?" The other woman gasped.

"I am," Anika replied. "Go now."

"But the Eydis Links haven't finalized—"

"Now."

The Guide ran into the Academy.

Anika began barking orders. "Alert the Pyralis and Tordis wings! The move begins in fifteen minutes. Everyone to their designated posts!"

Searchers darted in multiple directions.

Anika turned to face the two sets of Strikers escorting Logan and Ansel. "Take them to the stockade. We'll deal with them later."

"No!" Several Strikers raised their weapons when I grabbed Anika's arm. She shook her head and they backed off.

"Calla, I understand that the boy is your brother, but until we know the truth of this matter, he must be treated with the utmost caution."

"Even if he told them about the hideout, I'm sure he was tricked," I said. "You don't know what they did to him."

She pulled her arm free. "I will know in time. But I can't address your concern now. I'm sorry."

She nodded to the Strikers and they led Ansel away.

"Ansel!" I began to follow them, but Shay held me back.

"Wait."

"They're treating him like a prisoner!" I shouted, writhing in his grasp. "This isn't his fault. He's been tortured. We need to help him!"

"We'll figure it out," he said. "I swear. We need Anika to know she can trust your pack. That has to come first, and then we can bring her around on Ansel."

For her own part, Anika had turned to Connor. "Can you explain to me what happened back there?"

"Not exactly," he muttered, pulling an envelope from inside his duster. "But Monroe asked me to give you this if he didn't make it back."

"He went into a mission with the idea that he wouldn't come back?" Anika snatched the envelope. "And how did you find the young Guardians? I was under the impression that we couldn't locate them."

Connor spoke without meeting the Arrow's penetrating gaze. "It was an urgent situation, Anika."

Anika's eyes had narrowed. "Are you telling me that Monroe led a strike into Vail without authorization?"

"Yes."

"And now he's dead?" She shook her head. "And we lost Denver."

"But we got the wolves," Ethan said, glancing at Sabine's unmoving form. "Some of them, at least."

"Let's hope that makes a difference." Before she turned away, I saw a tear slide down her cheek. "We needed Monroe."

"I know," Connor said, his own voice thick.

"The Guides will be waiting for me," she said. "We'll discuss this after the move. If we make it."

With that she strode away.

"If we make it?" I asked.

Connor didn't answer.

"Calla." I turned to see Ethan with Sabine still resting in his arms. "I'm worried she might have internal injuries. I need to take her to the Elixirs."

"The who?" Shay asked.

"Our healers," Adne said. "They're in the Eydis Sanctuary."

"She might need pack blood," I said, peering at Sabine. She wasn't bleeding or bruised, but sometimes the wounds you couldn't see were the most deadly kind.

Nev was hovering nearby. "I'll go with them. She can have my blood if she needs it."

"Okay."

Bryn and Mason approached cautiously. At last convinced I wouldn't chase after Ansel, Shay loosened his grasp and I pulled away from him. I knew he was being reasonable, but I hated feeling helpless about Ansel's situation.

"What now?" Mason asked.

"You come with us," Connor said.

The air was suddenly filled with a chorus of bell tones. The

Academy pulsed with energy, the sound growing ever louder. Though piercing, the crystalline chimes had a hypnotic melody—the walls reverberated with their music. I watched as the hall began to shudder with the sound. The maze of colors threading through the marble hallways undulated with each ringing note.

Adne bolted for the stairs. "I have to get to my post!"

"What's happening?" Bryn asked. She took my hand, trembling.

Connor led us after Adne, though unlike the Weaver, he didn't run. "The Weavers have to move the Academy."

"How is that possible?" Shay asked.

"It takes precise coordination." Connor glanced back at us. "Every Weaver has to pull the same threads to open a single door in unison."

"But how can you get the building through a door?" Shay frowned as we reached the second floor, heading to the next flight of stairs.

"The building doesn't go through the door," Connor said. "The Weavers move the door over the building."

"They—they what?" I stammered.

Connor didn't answer. He'd brought us back to the fourth floor. We found Adne standing halfway between the section of the hall that housed our bedrooms and the Haldis tactical center. With the skeans clasped in her fingers, she stood perfectly still, eyes closed, drawing slow, rhythmic breaths.

"Adne—" Shay started toward her.

"Shhh!" Connor threw an arm in front of him. "She needs to focus."

I glanced up and down the hall, noticing another woman standing twenty feet beyond Adne. When I looked in the opposite direction, I saw a young man standing about the same distance apart.

"Those are the other Weavers," Connor said, following my gaze. He looked at them and then at each of us. "You may want to sit down for this. It's a little intense if you haven't been through it before."

We all stared at him, but none of us sat.

"Suit yourselves." He shrugged, turning back to watch Adne.

A new sound echoed through the hall. Low, deep like the striking of an enormous bell. Its note reverberated through the Academy, settling into my bones. I shivered and Shay took my hand. I threaded my fingers through his. The bell sounded again and I saw Adne shudder just like I had. She didn't open her eyes. The bell rang once more. The echoes layered one on top of the others. The air was so thick with the deep tones I thought I could almost feel it pouring over my skin.

When the bell rang a fourth time, Adne began to move. She bent forward gracefully, almost in a bow. Farther along the hall I could see the other Weaver making an identical motion. Adne's head lifted, her arms twisting and curving as her body unfolded. New sounds trickled through the lingering sound of the bell. Tinkling and bright, notes rippled through the halls like the music of a wind chime. Along with this light music came color; the patterns in the walls were coming to life, their jewel tones glittering, casting rainbows along the floor and over our bodies.

Adne was moving faster now, leaping and twisting in the dance I'd come to associate with her portal weaving. On both sides of her the other Weavers swirled in perfect imitation of Adne's lithe body. She was breathing hard, sweating, but not once did she hesitate or break her rhythm. The ringing notes around us grew louder, piercing my sensitive ears so hard that I had to cover them with my hands. The rainbow patterns on the floors and walls began to spark, exploding in the air like fireworks. The dazzling colors grew ever brighter, blinding me. The floor beneath my feet felt like it was shifting. I dropped to my knees, still covering my ears. I curled over, burying my head against my thighs. I felt Shay's body wrap around mine, shielding me from the deafening cascade of sound and the bursts of light.

Fur brushed against me. I heard a whimper, then another as Bryn and Mason, now wolves, snuggled up against me, shoving their muzzles under my arms to rest their cold noses against my jaw. The sound was so loud it didn't even seem to matter that I was covering my ears. I thought I might scream.

And suddenly there was only silence.

I lifted my head, taking a slow breath. A strong, unfamiliar scent filled my nostrils: a mixture of salt and lush, green leaves and . . . fish? I took another breath; it was the same scent, but I couldn't recognize it. I thought I might also smell lemons.

"You all right?" Connor was looking down at us.

Shay stood up, rolling back his shoulders. "I guess."

"I told you," Connor said, grinning. "Intense."

"No joke." Adne stumbled toward us, moving unsteadily, as if she were drunk.

Connor caught her as she ungracefully fell into him.

"Nice job, kid." He brushed his lips across her forehead.

"Thanks," she mumbled. "I think I'll sleep for a week now."

Mason had shifted back into human form. He walked over to the tall windows of the outside wall. The light pouring into the hall was a gold-tinged red. I heard him gasp.

"Is that . . . the ocean?"

Bryn and I followed him to the windows. Staring out at the setting sun, I couldn't breathe. The Academy rested atop a steep terraced slope, stretching down for miles. The landscape was filled with carefully manicured rows of stunted trees with twisting branches, dark green leaves giving glimpses of sunny yellow. Lemons.

In the distance I could see a village that jutted out of the rugged terrain. Other villages speckled the coast, hanging on to cliffs as if they were suspended over the sea.

The sea. Waves lapped the shoreline. The sunset washed the

rippling surface with color, rendering it a deep violet with the occasional flash of rose. I stared at the water that stretched beyond the horizon, understanding why people once believed the ocean led to the edge of a finite world.

It wasn't until Shay put his arm around my shoulders that I noticed I was trembling.

"You've never seen it before, have you?" He gazed out the window.

I shook my head, still numb with the shock of the move and flustered by the way this new place seemed to reach inside me and squeeze my heart.

"Yeah, it's the ocean," Adne said. "Unless we landed in the wrong place."

The ocean. That was the scent I couldn't identify. I'd never smelled anything like it.

"Where are we?" Bryn went to the window.

"Cinque Terre," Connor answered.

She frowned. "Where?"

"Italy."

PARADISO

PART III

You shall leave everything you love most dearly:
this is the arrow that the bow of exile shoots first.

Dante, Paradiso

TWENTY-SEVEN

"ITALY?" MASON EXCLAIMED. His hands were pressed up against the glass. I knew how he felt. The barrier to the outside world made it hard to believe the paradise beyond these walls was real.

"Sorry." Connor grinned. "I know you're gonna miss the cornfields."

Adne rolled her neck back and forth, grimacing. "That was rough."

"You okay?" Connor asked, his smile vanishing.

"I'm fine," she said. "Tired but fine. They'll be expecting us to assemble in the main hall."

"I want to see Ansel," Bryn said suddenly. "Can we make sure he's okay?"

"He's fine," Connor said. "The move went perfectly. If we're here, he's here. It's an all-or-nothing kind of deal."

"But—"

"Look, kid," Connor said. "We need to let Anika cool off before we start asking her favors. Calla's little brother messed up big time. It's going to take a while before we can sort that out."

He and Adne exchanged a glance that made my teeth clench. Neither of them thought Ansel's predicament could be sorted out.

What is going to happen to my brother?

Bryn's shoulders slumped. Mason took her hand, looking at me. "He'll be okay."

I nodded, feeling less certain of that possibility by the minute.

"We'll get you something to eat," Adne said, frowning. "And then find you a place to stay. I'm sure you'd like to get cleaned up."

I traced her assessing gaze at Bryn and Mason. They did need cleaning up. Still wearing the wreckage of clothing from the night they'd been made prisoners, dried blood and grime caked their skin. A sharp pain gripped my stomach like I'd been sucker punched, their ragged appearance reminding me again of all they'd been through.

I kept silent as we fell in step behind Connor and Adne, who led us to the stairs. When we reached the first-floor landing, Adne gasped.

"Look!" I followed the line from where her finger was pointing. Mason and Bryn gasped too.

We'd paused just outside the glass doors leading into the courtyard. Beyond the invisible barrier, the broad central space was transforming before my eyes. The empty, slumbering earth had come alive with unfurling leaves and splashes of bright color from budding flowers. Fountains among the flower beds bubbled with water.

Connor whistled. "Man, the Links work fast. Nice."

"They always do," Adne replied. "But it always amazes me."

"What are the Links?" Mason asked, his brow knit like a vine curled around the marble staircase on the other side of the glass doors.

"One of the Academy specializations," Connor said. "Eydis and Haldis, mostly. They integrate the building into the local ecosystem."

"Like gardeners?" Bryn asked.

"Some of them do focus on the gardens," Connor replied, rubbing his belly. "Which is good news. Mediterranean climate means we'll be eating better fresh food. Too many root vegetables back where it's winter. What do you think? Olives and lemons are the specialty in this region, right? I thought I read that in the memo about this destination. But that was supposed to happen in the spring. Looks like stuff grows well enough now too."

"Wait a sec," Mason interrupted. "How is that possible? Those plants are growing at warp speed."

"Elemental magic," Adne said. "Eydis and Haldis—water and earth. The Links connect to the earth, the roots of plant life, and the natural aquifers. It's how we get our water supply and geothermal energy."

"Good to see they're working," Connor said. "I know they weren't as far along as is ideal for the relocation."

Mason was shaking his head, and I noticed his hands were shaking too. "That's just not possible. Who can do that?"

"We can," Connor said, turning away from the courtyard. "And as far as possible goes, who here can turn into a wolf?"

"He has a point," Shay said, smiling at me. "That's what got me to believe in all this stuff."

Mason nodded reluctantly, but he muttered under his breath as we descended to the bottom floor.

"I wish Monroe could have seen that." Adne sighed. She bowed her head and I heard a quiet sob.

"Just get through the assembly." Connor put his arm around her shoulders. "Then we'll have time to talk about your dad."

Unlike the near empty dining hall I'd entered the previous night, the Searchers' meeting space was now filled to capacity. Men and women milled around, shoulder to shoulder, the buzz of conversation swelling in my ears like a low roar.

"There's Tess." Connor moved into the crowd.

"Who's Tess?" Bryn leaned into me.

"She's part of their team," I said. "The Haldis team."

Bryn frowned. "The Haldis team?"

"I don't—" Words stuck to my tongue. Haldis, Eydis. The snippets of information I'd gleaned from my brief stay with the Searchers hadn't prepared me to answer her question. There was so much I didn't know yet about the Searchers, and now I'd thrown my pack, or what was left of it, into their world without any certainty of the future. What if I'd made the wrong decision? The buzz of voices was getting louder. My head started to throb.

When I didn't speak again, Bryn shrugged, turning to follow Mason to the table where Tess was sitting.

"Calla?" Shay was watching me.

"Go ahead," I said, pushing him after Bryn. "I'm right behind you."

As he threaded his way between Searchers, I slowly backed toward the hall and, reaching the stairs, I bolted.

I wasn't sure where I was running, but I knew that I needed to run. A week ago I'd been in Vail about to merge my life with Ren's, to take the first step on the path that had been set for me my whole life. My destiny. Did I even have a destiny anymore? Did it belong to the Searchers now?

A growl rolled through my belly at that thought. I wouldn't be caged by anyone. I'd served the Keepers unquestioningly, and look where it had led me. If the Searchers offered a way to fight my former masters, I would. They'd killed my mother and tortured the people I loved. I wanted them to pay. But I had to fight them on my own terms. I was making decisions for my whole pack now. I needed to be sure, and I wasn't sure of anything.

I was halfway across the globe, my former life ripped to shreds. What had seemed like the strong bonds of my new pack had disintegrated because of my choices. Fey, Dax, and Cosette—they'd all sought refuge with the Keepers, clung to that life despite all the pain it had brought us. I was certain that if Connor hadn't arrived, my fight with Dax would have been to the death. And my brother had become a shadow of himself, so much so that even he had been willing to betray me to recover what had been taken from him.

But Ansel wasn't the only one whose life had been twisted beyond recognition. Ren's future had been snatched away the night I'd run from our union. His pack was gone, his legacy handed back to Emile, who was more monster than man and wasn't even Ren's father. I stumbled, tripping over the truth that caught me unaware. Ren's future had been stolen long ago, when Emile and the Keepers killed his mother. My would-be mate's life had been built upon a foundation of lies, blood, and bones.

I clasped my hands, covering my eyes. Lies, blood, and bones. Had our lives been made of anything more? As my fingers pressed against my face, the cold metal of my ring snapped at my skin like a static shock. The ring Ren had given me. A promise of things to come.

I want you to know that I—

What? What had Ren wanted to say to me? What had stopped him? How much would he have shared with me?

The hall suddenly felt too narrow, like it was closing in on me. I had to get outside. I need to breathe open air. I ran faster, searching for any way out of the corridor. When I came to the next set of glass doors, I burst through them.

The salty richness of the ocean air poured over me. Bent over, resting my hands on my knees, I gulped it down like water. The vivid hues of the sunset had given way to the muted shades of twilight, lavender, and gray. Even in the shadows the braided, white gold band circling my finger glinted, catching any light and throwing it back at me. Mocking, hateful.

It reminds me of your hair.

Even now the rope of white blond hair hung over my shoulder, swinging as I stood up. The courtyard was massive, and what had been a near barren garden just yesterday now quivered with lush greens and filled the air with the crisp, mineral scent of fresh herbs.

I ran toward the nearest greenhouse, searching. Anything would do, as long as it was sharp. My breath was coming hard, ragged. I jerked the door open, stumbling past seedlings and potted plants. The scent of compost swirling through the humid air was sweet but a little sickening. I found what I wanted at the far end of the greenhouse, resting on the edge of a potting stand.

I grabbed the pruning shears with one hand and my thick braid in the other, just above where my neck met my shoulders. I didn't stop cutting until the twisted length came off in my hand. I stared at it, tossing it away like a live snake. My breath had slowed, and my head felt light, free. I set the pruning shears down and left the greenhouse.

It was raining when I stepped back into the courtyard, the softest of rainfalls. Bits of moisture touched my skin like the memory of raindrops, nothing close to a steady downpour, lighter even than mist. Warm night air slipped along my skin. I headed for the very center of the garden. The path led me to a wall of carefully trimmed hedges behind which I found a central square. Steps descended into a layer of flower beds lined by blossoming fruit trees. It was perfectly still, secluded from the rest of the world. At the heart of the square was a stone fountain of four carved figures. It was a strange group: a woman in armor like a knight, a man in a monk's robes, a child with scrolls in his hands, and a woman in a simple dress grasping a hewn tree branch. Water swirled in a pool at their feet, reflecting the silver hues of the clouds above.

I walked along the edge of the pool, trailing my fingers along the surface of the water. The sunken garden should have offered tranquility, but I couldn't sense anything beyond the storm in my mind. I raked my fingers through my shorn locks, startled when my hands came free just above my shoulders.

"Good hiding spot."

I whirled to find Shay coming up the garden path to where I stood near the central fountain. My jaw tightened. I became still as the four statues as I watched him approach.

"Quiet, secluded." His eyes flicked around the flower beds blanketed with shadows cast by tall hedges. "Creepy enough to keep most people away at night, but not too scary."

The corner of his mouth crinkled in a smile. "I give it an A minus, but only because the moon isn't out tonight."

He came a step closer.

"Thanks a lot." I kept a hard, warning edge in my voice. "How did you find me?"

He ran a hand through his hair, glancing at me sheepishly. "I followed your scent."

"Of course." I turned my back on him, moving away from the fountain, deeper in the shadows of the garden. "Go away."

"No." He darted in front me, blocking my path.

"I'm serious, Shay."

"So am I," he said. "I don't think you should be alone right now."

"That's really not up to you."

He reached out, pushing back the pale strands of hair that curled along my chin.

"No more braid?" He smiled, twirling my cropped locks in his fingers. "I like it. It's a good look for you."

I didn't answer and his smile disappeared.

"You don't have to do this alone," he said quietly.

"I am alone." My chest felt hollow.

"You know that isn't true."

I drew a sharp breath and fisted my hands. "Tell me what is true, then."

"You loved him." His eyes held mine.

"Yes." The word hung between us, naked in its truth. I couldn't find another breath to steady my trembling body.

He took another step toward me, and his words came out low but steady. "But not the way you love me."

I stumbled backward as if he'd struck me.

"Calla," he murmured, and reached for my arm. "You can't blame yourself. What you've done, how you feel, none of it makes Ren's choice your fault."

I twisted away from his outstretched hand.

"Stop," I said. "I don't want to talk about this. I can't."

"You're right," he said gently. "It's not the time to talk."

He moved so quickly his body blurred for a moment, and then I was in his arms. I gripped his shoulders, my nails digging deep into his skin, but he didn't let go. He only held me closer.

I snarled and struggled, but Shay kept me locked tight against him. I felt the steady beating of his heart next to mine. Moisture coursed over my face, the silky mist in the air mixing with my tears.

Shay kissed me gently, tracing the pattern of sorrow with his lips. I clung to him. Quiet, soothing murmurs passed from his lips as he continued to kiss me.

When the storm of grief subsided, I lifted my chin and my lips found his. He slowly pulled my lower lip between his teeth, and I threw myself into the kiss with such force that Shay lost his balance and fell, sending us tumbling down the garden path. We stopped rolling and I found myself beneath him. I'd barely caught my breath when I kissed him again, my fingers fumbling with the buttons of his shirt. I felt a growl rumble in his chest, and he shrugged the shirt from his shoulders. I twined my fingers in his hair, slightly damp from the subtle rainfall.

His lips moved down my neck. I could hear my own breath come in short, shallow pulls, almost gasps. The night air of the garden, sweet with budding roses but sharpened by the salt tang of the ocean, slipped between my parted lips.

Shay's mouth stroked the bare skin of my stomach, and for a moment I wondered what had happened to my shirt. And my leather pants.

His kiss moved further down the line of my body and I no longer cared where any of my clothes were.

Layers of silver clouds above us parted like gauze curtains lifted by the wind, and slender vines of moonlight curled around our bodies. Shay moved over me as the night sky opened up, his body silhouetted by pale light that shimmered in the garden. His lips brushed my cheek, his hips settled against mine. I could feel every pulse of his heart as we pressed together, skin to skin. I shivered as I felt something deep within me rising, opening, aching for something only he could give me. When he kissed me again, I thought I would break apart with need. He pulled back, watching me silently. A question waited for me in his eyes.

"Yes," I murmured.

I kissed him again and there were no more questions to be answered.

TWENTY-EIGHT

SNIP. SNIP.

Bryn's mouth twisted as she concentrated on the task at hand.

"Really, Cal, if you wanted a haircut, you should have just asked. You've made a complete mess of this."

I watched strands of my hair drift to the floor. It hadn't been easy to get here. I'd managed to disentangle myself from Shay's arms and slip unnoticed from his room, quietly making my way back to my own.

It wasn't that I was sorry for spending the night with him, but I didn't know what the morning would bring, and my head was already spinning with everything that had transpired in the last twenty-four hours. I needed some time alone before I'd be ready to talk to Shay about last night in the garden. And his room.

The memory sent flames licking through my belly and I shuddered.

"Calla, I swear I'm not going to hurt you," Bryn said through clenched teeth. "Can you please hold still?"

"Sorry."

Guilt had nipped at my heels with each step as I'd searched for my packmates, finding them at last exactly where I'd left them. My stomach rumbled as the scent of freshly baked bread and citrus rolled over me. The dining room was busy that morning, but not full to bursting as it had been when I'd fled from the previous night's assembly. Searchers moved in and out of the room, some grabbing croissants and popping grapes into their mouths as they went about their mornings, others lingering over steaming cups of coffee at various tables.

Nev, Bryn, Adne, Connor, Silas, Tess, and Sabine—who appeared to have fully recovered—were gathered at the same table where the Searchers had shared coffee two days ago. Ethan and Mason were conspicuously absent. I approached the table slowly. Someone else seemed to be missing too. My chest burned when I realized I'd been looking for Monroe.

I'd joined them at their table, ready to make up an excuse for my absence and answer all the questions they had about how I'd come to form an alliance with the Searchers.

But my appearance had stopped all conversation, leaving a heavy silence in its wake. Adne had furrowed her brow before shrugging, turning her attention back to her bowl of fresh fruit and cream. Silas kept tilting his head back and forth as if trying to figure out what exactly was different about me. Tess was kind enough to smile a greeting but not say anything. A grin kept sliding on and off Nev's mouth as though he wanted to laugh, but knew better.

It had taken less than five minutes of this for Bryn to stand up with a quick nod to Sabine. Both girls shuttled me out of the dining room and up to my bedroom. Bryn had been trying to amend the hack job I'd done on my locks ever since.

Sabine clicked her tongue, moving to stand in front of me so she could get a better angle on Bryn's work. "You're cutting all wrong. It's going to be uneven."

"Do you want to do this?" Bryn snapped.

"Yes." She grabbed for the scissors.

"Wait a sec." I straightened in the chair and Bryn had to jerk the scissors away to avoid impaling my neck. "Seriously, Sabine? You want to cut my hair?"

I frowned at her, not sure if I trusted her to give me a haircut that was flattering.

"It would be my pleasure, Calla. I always cut Cosette's hair." For a moment the skin around her eyes tightened, but in the next instant she smiled again.

"Oh, she had adorable hair." Bryn beamed. "You should let Sabine take over, Cal. I have no idea what I'm doing. I can style like a pro, but this cutting thing is out of my league."

I swallowed but nodded. If Sabine was going to be our ally, I had to let old animosities fall away.

Bryn handed Sabine the scissors with a relieved sigh.

There was the sound of a throat clearing behind us. We all turned toward the door.

"Uh, hey." Shay ruffled his hair, taking in the group of girls before him and looking like he might bolt.

"Hi, Shay," Bryn said, not quite hiding her giggle as she glanced back and forth between the two of us.

Sabine nodded at him but quickly turned her attention back to my hair.

"What's going on?" He took a couple of steps into the room, still indecisive about how safe it was to be there.

"We're trying to fix Calla's hair. She just hacked it off." Bryn curled a few strands around her fingers. "What did you use, exactly?"

"Pruning shears." I was staring at the floor. I shouldn't have left Shay this morning without talking to him first. Now everything felt awkward and I didn't know how to fix it.

"No wonder it looks so awful," Sabine muttered.

"I think it looks good," Shay protested, inching toward us.

Sabine barked a laugh. "You'd think she looked good if she had leprosy."

I blushed and Bryn giggled.

Shay smiled sheepishly, clearing his throat again. "Cal, I was hoping we could talk."

I bit my lip and kept my eyes off his face. "Sure, but I'm a little busy right now."

"Yeah, yeah, of course. Well, I'll be in my room."

"Okay."

He shoved his hands in his pockets, but at least he managed not to run from the room.

Bryn began to laugh. "I think we scared him."

"It's a tough room." Sabine didn't look up from her deft maneuvering of the scissors. "He's probably a little thrown."

I had to fight to keep still in the chair. "Thrown by what?"

"Being our new alpha. Ren's out, he's in. It's a lot to swallow. He's only been a wolf a few weeks; he's not used to it like the rest of us."

"What?!" Bryn and I exclaimed in unison.

"Calla, you can't jerk around like that; I'll either stab you or ruin your hair," Sabine said, unfazed.

I grabbed her wrist, but she continued to gaze calmly at me.

"What are you talking about, Sabine?" I said slowly.

The corners of her mouth turned up slightly, as if she were the only one aware of a hilarious, private joke. "You can't be serious, Calla. Don't you know?"

I frowned and glanced at Bryn, whose bewildered expression was giving way to one of astonishment.

Sabine's smile broadened. "See, Bryn knows."

Bryn nodded. "You're right—of course, you're right. I can't believe I didn't realize . . ."

She looked at me, guilt painting her cheeks rosy. "I just always thought it would be Ren."

"But . . . how?" I couldn't believe I had to throw that pleading question at Sabine.

"It's simple, really." Sabine shook my now limp fingers off her wrist and began shearing my locks once again. "We all know that alphas can't be, well, promoted for lack of a better word. Alphas are born. Shay's always been an alpha, but he wasn't a wolf. When you made him one, it put him in the running."

Sabine was right. Alphas couldn't be promoted. That was part of the reason the Keepers' solution to their Guardian troubles in Vail would be such a mess. But I couldn't make the connection to Shay's role in all of this.

Bryn smacked her palm against her forehead. "I'm an idiot."

"Well, I must be too," I snapped. "Because I'm still not following."

"You're not following because you are an alpha, Cal." She offered me a sympathetic smile. "Shay's always felt like an equal to you, right? He talks to you on your level, has never backed down if you challenged him?"

I chewed on my lower lip. "I guess I thought that was just a human thing. That he didn't know any better because he wasn't one of us."

"Nope," Sabine said. "It's an alpha thing."

Bryn threaded her fingers through mine. "Ren always saw Shay as a competitor. Even he must have known."

"And he was right," Sabine said, pulling strands of my hair between her fingers to measure their length. "You chose Shay."

"What?" This time the scissors did scratch my neck. "Ow!"

"Don't jerk like that." Sabine tilted my head. "No blood. I'm still cutting."

"I didn't choose Shay," I said, fingering the tender skin. "I was saving his life."

"I didn't mean the sacrifice," Sabine said. "I meant last night."

I managed not to skewer myself on the scissors, but I gripped the edges of the chair.

"Last night?" My whisper came out hoarse.

"Sabine." Bryn kicked her shin. "Don't."

"I'm not judging," Sabine said. "She's within her rights. Shay's an alpha. That means he's a contender. Plus I've seen his shoulders. I'd let Shay take me for a ride if he offered."

"Sabine!" Bryn shrieked, staring at me in horror.

But I was too shocked to be angry.

"How do you—" My cheeks were on fire.

"You smell like him." Sabine smirked. "That's the other thing. He smells good, doesn't he? What does he taste like?"

Bryn turned her back, but I was pretty sure it was to hide her grin because I could hear her laughing. "Stop, Sabine. Just stop."

"I took a shower!" I wanted to curl up into a ball and die.

Sabine chuckled. "It doesn't matter."

I cast a sidelong glance at Bryn. She was doing her best to twist her lips out of a silly smile.

"It's not like you smell bad, Cal," she said, trying to make me feel better. "And Sabine is right. Shay has a nice smell. You know, like a garden."

"Oh my God." I dropped my face into my hands.

"Well, I'm not going to be able to do anything with your hair if you stay like that," Sabine said, giggling.

"Fine." Squaring my shoulders, I sat up and took a deep breath. "Just finish it. And no more talking about last night."

"Really?"

I bared my teeth at how disappointed Bryn sounded.

"Calla, I'm trying to tell you, you probably did the right thing." Sabine moved to shape the layers near my face. "Ren made a mistake.

If he wanted you so much, he should have come here. He should have been here to fight for you."

I stared at my hands, embarrassed by the hot stinging in my eyes.

"Calla." Glancing up, I met Sabine's gaze in the mirror. "Don't blame yourself for Ren. We all know you cared about him. He made his choice. We all made our choices."

I stared at her and then at my own reflection. Pale blond hair framed my face in soft layers that tapered from my cheekbones, falling just short of my shoulders. My lip quivered.

"You made me look beautiful."

"I didn't do much." Sabine set the scissors aside and brushed stray hairs from my shoulders. "That's just who you are."

I opened my mouth, but words didn't emerge, only a choked sob.

"God, don't blubber, Calla. You're supposed to be an alpha," Sabine grumbled. But then she squeezed my shoulder and quietly left the room, letting Bryn wrap her arms around me while I continued to cry.

Bryn left my side, coming back with a tissue.

"So when did Sabine get a personality transplant?" I said. "I could have sworn she was just nice. Kind of."

"She is nice." Bryn smiled sadly. "When you're locked in a cell with someone for several days, you learn a lot about them. Sabine wasn't ever the bitch we thought she was. She was just angry. Really angry. The things she had to . . ."

She shuddered. "She has a lot to be angry about."

Bryn was right. Of all the young Guardians, Sabine's life had been the worst, but somehow I was the one crying. I blew my nose, then looked at her, still sniffling. "You must think I'm pathetic."

"Hardly," Bryn said. "We've all been through a lot. And if it had been me, I would have done the same thing."

"Thanks," I said. "But I don't know how you can say that. You don't know what happened."

"Connor filled us in," she said. "And Silas kept interrupting, trying to explain the history of all of it. He's really weird, huh?"

"Yeah, he is," I said. "What did Connor tell you?"

"Well, I guess he couldn't tell us how you felt," she said. "But it's easy enough to imagine. He told us who Shay is and why he's so important."

"Did he tell you about the alliance?" I asked, already nervous that any alliance between Guardians and Searchers was off the table.

She nodded. "It sounds like they can teach us some pretty amazing things."

"Like what?" This was new. I tossed the crumpled tissue into the trash bin.

"Combat, magic. Our real history." She crossed the room, shaking her head. "It's still hard to believe. All the lies."

"I know."

"For all their magic, I wish the Searchers could do something for Ansel." She was at the window, staring at the rolling surface of the ocean, now a gleaming turquoise under the bright morning sun.

"So do I."

"They're treating him well," she said, running her fingertips over the gauzy drapes. "He's not in a cell. It's just a small bedroom."

"You visited him?" Guilt bit into me much harder now. Why hadn't I visited him yet?

"Mason and I have been staying with him in shifts," she said. When she turned around, it was like a shadow passed over her face. "But he won't talk to me even when I'm there. Mason said it's the same for him."

"He won't?"

She shook her head.

"Maybe he just needs time," I offered, though my stomach was twisting itself into a knot.

"Maybe." She shivered. "Calla, I'm afraid we're going to lose him."

"I swear I won't let the Searchers hurt him," I said, a growl edging out with the words.

"No." She rubbed her arms. "It's not them I'm worried about."

The painful twisting in my belly wasn't a knot anymore. It was a knife.

"I barely recognize him," she whispered. "He's drawn so far inside himself. I don't think he wants to live. He's been scratching his arms so much that they bleed."

"We'll help him." I worked past the lump in my throat. "We'll help him get better."

She nodded, brushing tears from her cheeks.

"Wanna go see him now?" she asked. "It's time for me to switch with Mason anyway. He gets grumpy if he doesn't eat like every two hours."

"I think that's true of every teenage guy." I smiled, taking her hand. "Let's go see Ansel."

"So are you really not going to tell me anything about last night?" A wicked smiled flashed across her mouth.

"No." But I smiled too. My world had been spinning out of control. Having Bryn around made everything better.

We'd only made it a few steps out of the room before Bryn stopped, turning to face me.

"What's wrong?" I asked.

"Nothing," she said, taking my other hand in hers, squeezing my fingers tight. "It's just . . . Sabine's right."

"About what?" I tried to puzzle out the expression on Bryn's face; she didn't look upset, just curious.

"About Shay," she said. "He's our new alpha, and he needs to be part of the pack."

"Oh." I shifted my weight, uneasy. While I wasn't against the thought of Shay as my alpha mate, I was still getting used to the idea.

"You should go get him," she said. "Come together—the alpha pair. It will show Ansel that things are changing. That he . . . that we have a future."

I nodded. Would that help Ansel, knowing that the world that had hurt him so much was no longer the one that ruled us? He'd always believed that love came first. Maybe seeing Shay and me together, by choice, would bring him around.

"Okay." I nodded, drawing my fingers from hers. "I'll go find him."

"Great!" She threw her arms around me. I leaned into her, resting my cheek against her springy ringlets, remembering how much Bryn's scent reflected her personality—sweet and spicy like a mix of toffee and cinnamon. The kind of smell that made you feel at home anywhere.

She bounced down the hall and I went to Shay's room. I knocked on the door. No answer.

I knocked again. Maybe he'd fallen asleep.

"He's not in there."

I turned around to see Adne approaching.

"What do you mean?"

"Anika has him locked up with the Guides in Haldis tactical," she said, jerking her head in the direction of the meeting room. "They're strategizing the Tordis pickup."

"Why didn't they tell me?" I frowned.

"That's part of the discussion," she said. "With your brother's questionable status, some of the teams have expressed concern about bringing Guardians along for the retrieval."

I didn't know whether to be shocked, outraged, or both. "They're planning the mission without us?"

"They're weighing their options," she said, smiling briefly. "But that's a good thing for us."

"What do you mean for us?" I asked, wary of the sudden flash of her eyes.

"I need your help on another mission," she said, fingering the skeans at her waist. "Under the table."

"What mission?" The hairs on the back of my neck were standing up.

Adne's mouth cut into a hard line. "We're going to get my brother."

TWENTY-NINE

FOR A MOMENT I THOUGHT the floor had dropped out from under me and I was falling.

"Calla?" Adne grabbed my arms as I swayed on my feet, dizzy. "You okay?"

I shook my head, trying to clear away the buzzing heat that flooded my skull.

"Did you hear what I said?" she asked, guiding me along the hall.

I nodded. "Your brother?"

"Yes."

"You mean Ren?" It was hard to say his name. "You can't be serious. That would mean going back to Vail!"

She put her hand over my mouth. "Not here."

I had to bite the inside of my cheek to keep myself from asking more questions. Adne pulled me down the hall, past my room and a few others, finally unlocking a door and slipping inside.

While the layout of the room was identical to mine, it couldn't have looked more different. My bedroom had the blasé décor of most guest rooms, inoffensive but utterly devoid of character.

Adne's room was a riot of color: violet, black, and crimson on the walls, a crushed velvet throw spilling over the side of her bed. She trotted over to a radio, adding a blast of sound that made the bright walls swim before my eyes.

"Do you like the Raveonettes?" She turned up the volume.

I nodded, pulse pounding in rhythm with the ethereal voices that floated around me.

"Sorry." She flopped onto the bed. "I can't afford for anyone to hear us. Not that I don't usually play music this loud anyway."

"It's fine."

"Have a seat," she said, gesturing to the bed.

I was too edgy to sit, but I hovered at the edge of the bed, playing with the fringes of the throw. "So Connor told you."

She shook her head, leaning over to reach beneath the mound of pillows at the top of the bed. "My father told me."

She pulled out an envelope, drawing a letter from inside it. "Connor just delivered the news."

"Monroe wrote you a letter?" I stared at the folded pages in her hands. There were several. How much had he told her? What secrets of the past had he spilled onto those pages?

She laughed, blinking away tears. "Connor said my father knew I'd never let him corner me for a touchy-feely talk. I made a habit of avoiding those ever since Mom . . ."

Her eyes wandered to the bed stand. Following her gaze, I saw a framed picture of a woman. She had copper blond hair and bright amber eyes. Her arms were around a beanpole of a girl wearing a foolish grin: a much younger Adne.

Adne thumbed the edge of the pages. "Apparently she brought them together. Ren's mom, I mean. Corrine. After she died, my dad hit rock bottom. My mom was the one who got him through it. Then I came along."

I watched her, not knowing what to say. She rolled onto her back, pressing the letter against her chest.

"I'm the reason he didn't go after Ren," she said, staring at the ceiling. "He didn't want to risk leaving me and Mom. He thought he'd done enough damage to Corrine, but he never got over it. He wanted to get Ren back so much. It's all in here."

She rustled the pages.

"I'm sure he did," I said. "But I don't blame him for wanting to protect you. Ren didn't know anything about this. He still doesn't know the truth. He thinks Emile is his father."

"I know," she said. "That's why we have to go back."

"I don't know if he'll even want us to come for him," I said, remembering the way he'd thrown me across the room. "He might want to stay. Like the others."

"Do you really believe that?" she asked.

I didn't answer; I couldn't. The truth was I didn't know. I wanted to believe that Ren could be saved, but I'd seen how the Keepers could break Guardians. My own brother had almost killed us because he'd been manipulated by our old masters. Could Ren believe anything other than what they'd told him about his past?

My gut kept twisting and untwisting.

Adne's gaze pierced me. "We have to try."

I sucked in a quick breath. "Adne, how can we? We barely made it out."

She flipped over, sitting up and swinging her legs over the edge of the bed. "That's why it will work now. There's no way they'll expect us—and we're only trying to find Ren."

"But how—"

"We'll locate him. I'll open an inside door like last time. We'll grab him, come back. It will be over." The words tumbled out of her mouth. Her eyes were shining.

"Locate him . . . how?"

She cleared her throat, casting her eyes down. "Um. I noticed. Well. That ring you're wearing."

"My ring?" My hands went to my chest, the fingers of my un-adorned hand covering the others.

"You were promised to him, right?" She didn't look up. "Did he give that to you?"

"Yes, but . . ." I was about to explain that rings weren't part of a Guardian union. That Ren had given it to me on his own because he was . . . because he was what? Trying to tell me he loved me? Show-ing me he wanted our union to mean something more than follow-ing orders? It was as if my own thoughts threw me against a brick wall, leaving me breathless. I couldn't finish.

Adne didn't notice. "Then we can use it to find him."

I ignored the pounding of my own heart, trying to focus on what she was saying. "The ring can find him?"

"If he gave it to you, it will have a connection to him. I can use that to pinpoint his location."

"How is that possible?"

"The ring will hold a thread," she said, looking up at me with a thin smile. "We follow the thread through Vail until it reaches him. That's when I'll open the door."

"Does that really work?"

"It's how we found Shay."

"Oh." My palms had begun to sweat.

"I know it's a big risk, Calla," she said. "But from what I've seen—and to be honest, from how freaked out Shay gets about him—I know you care about Ren. You can't want to leave him there."

I managed to get out a cracking whisper. "I don't."

She stood up, twisting her fingers through her long mahogany tresses. "He's my brother, but I don't know him. This isn't about me. It's about my dad."

She took the last page of the letter, handing it to me.

Only two words had been inked on the ivory surface.

Save him.

My eyes were burning. I looked up at Adne, the page shaking in my hands.

"I have to do this, Calla," she said. "Will you help me?"

The trembling had moved up my arms and into my shoulders, but I nodded.

She blew out a long sigh, her muscles relaxing.

"Thank God."

"Who else?" I asked, stretching the page toward her. I couldn't look at it any longer, those lonely words staring up at me, tearing a hole in my own heart.

"No one else." She frowned. "It's just you and me."

"You think we can pull this off?" The odds weren't in our favor, even if we had help.

"No one else will let us get away with this," Adne said. "If we mention it to anyone, we'll have a chaperone 24/7."

I frowned. "Maybe some of my pack."

"No," Adne said. "We only have a little time to spare. We need to move now; we can't afford to have a recruiting session."

"What do you mean now?" The hairs on my neck were standing up.

"I mean today," she said. "Well, tonight, back in Vail."

"That's insane!" I couldn't stop myself from shouting.

"Things will be a mess back there and the Keepers are probably still focused on Denver." Her deadly calm voice made me gape at her. "We can slip in and out without notice, probably more easily than we could at any other time."

I opened my mouth and closed it again. Okay, that was logic. Crazy logic, but still.

"Can't we at least take Connor?" I asked. I'd feel better with another fighter along, and Connor already knew about Ren, plus he seemed to back Adne up on almost everything.

She shuddered. "No way. He's the last person I could ask to help us."

Fear made me lash out. "What the hell is up with you guys anyway?"

She took a couple steps back. "What do you mean?"

"Half the time you're fighting, but then I think you're secretly making out or something!"

She blushed, then went pale, finally turning her back on me. "There's nothing going on with Connor and me."

I pressed on. "That isn't the way he acts."

When she turned around, her eyes were hard. "Calla, you are coming in mid-scene here. You have to understand Connor and me to get what that's all about."

"How about reviewing the first act for me?" I asked.

She shrugged, walking to the stereo to flip through her CDs. "I was eleven when my mother died."

I straightened abruptly, unsure how to respond. I'd been goading her and now we were talking about dead mothers.

Adne continued, "Connor came to the Haldis team right after she died."

I came to stand beside her. "Adne, I'm sorry. You don't have to explain."

She ignored me, fiddling with the stereo, skipping several tracks on the album. "He was only sixteen. Not unusually young for a first assignment as a Striker, but he was by far the closest person to my age. He brought me through the worst of it. He never left me alone. Teased me constantly. I went through a terrible awkward phase the same time we lost my mom. All arms and legs and no ability to use them properly. Connor gave me a hard time, but I needed it. Kept me from thinking about my mother. He didn't give me a moment's peace."

She grimaced. "And a moment's peace would have killed me then."

I watched emotions run over her face like passing shadows. She closed her eyes, smiling.

"At night he would sneak into my room and tell me ridiculous stories about the Roving Academy until I fell asleep. It kept the shadows at bay. Being alone at night would have been unbearable. He was my best friend, all the way up until I started training here."

"Did you have to come back to Denver for your assignment?"

"No." She didn't look at me. "But I wanted to. The Academy trained me to be a Weaver. I never wanted to be anywhere but Denver. The Haldis team has always been my family. I belong with them."

She dropped her head, her dark hair veiling her face.

A moment later she laughed, wholly herself once more. "The first thing Connor said when I saw him after he'd been at the outpost for a few months was, 'I see you got breasts, congratulations. I hope you know how to use them.'"

"You're trying to tell me that's his way of just being friends?" I asked.

She arched an eyebrow at me. "Do you take his comments as a serious come-on?"

"I guess not," I said. She was right, sort of, but somehow the way Connor hit on other girls seemed different than what he said to Adne.

"Exactly. With Connor that sort of talk is just his MO." She smiled at me, but her words had a nervous edge. "Though Silas did make it worse."

"How's that?"

"I lost a bet with him and he made me kiss Connor." A slow flush climbed up her cheeks. "It definitely gave Connor more ammunition to use against me." She reflexively squared her shoulders, as though ready for a challenge.

I smiled at her aggressive posture. "Why would Silas make you kiss Connor?"

Her laugh darkened. "Because Silas is a brilliant intellectual but not that creative. He *hates* Connor and so couldn't imagine anything worse for himself than having to kiss Connor. So he made me do it."

"I see," I said, scrutinizing her face. "And you kissed Connor?"

"Yes."

"And?" I couldn't see her expression as she turned her back on me, searching for a particular track on the Raveonettes album. She remained silent as the song began, swaying to the music.

"And nothing." She held her palm out. "Connor's not coming. You gonna hand over that ring?"

I ground my teeth but pulled the ring off my finger, dropping it into her grasp. With its weight absent, my hand felt strangely bare. I clasped my fingers tight, trying to ignore the emptiness that made my bones ache.

Adne drew a single skean from her belt, resting its sharp point on the edge of the white gold band. She closed her eyes, drawing slow, long breaths. I stood perfectly still, not daring to take any breaths of my own. The air around her seemed to thicken, shimmering as if someone had flung gold dust over her.

Very slowly she began to draw the skean away from the ring. As her hand moved, a single, thin line pulled away with it. A tiny golden strand.

Her eyes fluttered open and she smiled slowly. "There it is."

The breath I'd been holding whooshed out of me.

She glanced at me. "It's okay, Calla. I know what I'm doing. A location thread weaves a window; we can't go through it, but we can see what's on the other side. Now we'll be able to find him."

I nodded, but my legs were shaking. "What if he's not alone?"

"That's the point," she said, handing the ring back to me. "The thread will lead us to him, and we'll have enough time to decide if he's in a place we can get to him or if we have to wait. Okay?"

"Okay." I was relieved she wasn't insisting that the two of us could take on an entire Guardian pack.

Adne began to move her arm in a slow circle, around and around. The golden thread grew longer, swirling into a slender spiral in front of her.

"You want to watch this?"

I sidled closer, peering over her shoulder. The spiral was shimmering, stretching into a slender cone. In the distance I could see the other end of the thread moving, lengthening. I began to see shapes flashing by the spiral, blurry and unfocused. It was as if we were soaring through the air at incredible speed, moving too quickly to make any sense of the terrain. I squinted into the spiral, which now pulsed with bursts of light, trying to glimpse anything familiar. I thought I made out a tree, then a steep rock face. The outline of buildings. All at once the spiral shuddered, the golden light clearing, giving us a view of a pine-covered mountain slope, wilderness interrupted by a swath of clear-cut forest.

"Do you recognize anything?" Adne asked.

I nodded, though my body felt like it was turning to stone.

"He's here," she said, peering into the spiral. "But I don't know if he's alone. Considering it's the middle of the night in Vail, anyone who's there would be sleeping."

"He's alone," I murmured.

"Are you sure?" She glanced at me, frowning. "If you are, I should open a door right away."

I couldn't take my eyes off the window Adne's thread had created, leading us to this place. To Ren.

"I'm sure."

Adne closed the door and turned to me.

"What is this place?"

Without the gleam of the portal, the sliver of moon hanging above us cast only a little light on the clearing. Half-built structures formed a semicircle around a paved cul-de-sac with a dry fountain at its center. Foundations had been poured, now only gaping holes in the ground, and wooden beams rose at different heights toward the night sky. Here was the legacy of the Haldis pack: skeletons of houses, carcasses of lives that might have been.

My throat felt like it had been stuffed with cotton. I had to clear it several times before I could speak.

"This was where my pack was supposed to live. We were going to move here after the union."

"Really?" She frowned, and then her eyes went wide. "Oh."

I bit my lip, nodding.

"Where do you think he is?" she asked, gazing at the silent construction site.

I pointed at a structure on the crest of a short rise, the only completed house on the lot.

"There."

"Are you sure?"

"That was supposed to be our house," I said, unable to look at her.

"Oh, man." She put her hand on my arm. "Calla, I . . . I didn't know."

"It's okay," I said, though I didn't feel as confident as I tried to sound. "No one else will be here. This place has been abandoned. The pack it was being built for no longer exists."

"Right," she said. "So how do you want to do this?"

I stared at her. "You don't have a plan?"

"My plan was to find my brother. I did. The end."

"But we have to convince him to come back!" I couldn't believe I was managing to whisper, considering my rising panic.

"That's why I brought you along," she said, gazing around the abandoned plots. "And was that the right call or what?"

I bared sharp canines at her, but I didn't argue, turning back to gaze at the house fifty yards away.

"If I were to suggest a plan," Adne said slowly, "I'd say you should go talk to him. Howl if you get in trouble. Or scream. Whatever works."

"Thanks," I said, sparing her a dark look.

"I'd be happy to go," she said, folding her arms over her chest. "But he doesn't know me. You're the one he cares about. You're the one who can bring him around if he thinks the Keepers are telling the truth. You are the only one, Calla."

"I know." The reality of this scene was settling into my bones, making them ache. This was the only chance I had to make up for leaving Ren behind. If I ever could.

Cold winter air covered my body like a cloak. Its chill slipped beneath my skin, restless, already battling the tiny spark of hope crackling in my veins. In the short time since I'd joined the Searchers, I learned the true cost of the Witches' War. Its casualties no longer strangers—Lydia, Corrine, Monroe, my mother, even Ansel—the weight of their deaths and my brother's loss were now chained to me like an anchor threatening to drown me in a dark ocean of fear and regret.

This place was as quiet as that kind of death. Choked with the skeletal remains of my former life, casting twisted, ghoulish shadows. They posed no real threat—only snatches of the past, painful memories that clung to me like cobwebs.

Hope was real. Burning brighter than the stars that hung above us in this empty winter night. Corrine and Monroe were gone. They'd sacrificed everything for their son. And he was here. It was too late for them, but Ren could still be saved. And I was the only one who could save him.

This is only about love.

He was out there. Alone. Waiting for me in a house where only the ghosts of our past were welcome.

Staring at the wreckage of the life we could have had, I knew it *wasn't* about love or Shay or the Searchers now. It was about sacrifice—and redemption, loss that could have new meaning.

Hope. A second chance. Ren could help us win this war. Together we could make the blood, the grief, the pain worth something. I knew I couldn't leave him behind again. Not now and not ever. Even if it meant I'd end up sacrificing myself as well.

ACKNOWLEDGMENTS

Three cheers for the Wolfsbane pack! Charlie Olsen, Richard Pine, Lyndsey Blessing, and the fabulous team at InkWell Management have been priceless navigators, always keeping this ship on course. Without the wit and wisdom of Michael Green, my sojourn in the world of publishing wouldn't be half as enjoyable. The insight and sharp eye of Jill Santopolo deftly shaped this book into beautiful form. Jill—thanks for sharing adventures in writing and trapeze with me! Penguin Young Readers Group have become like family: Don Weisberg, Jennifer Haller, Emily Romero, Erin Dempsey, Shanta Newlin, Jackie Engel, Linda McCarthy, Katrina Damkoehler, Amy Wu, Felicia Frazier, Scottie Bowditch, Courtney Wood, Anna Jarzab, Julia Johnson, and all the fantastic sales reps. Thank you for the work you do and for cheering me on.

So many labors of love made this book possible. Thanks, always, to my amazing critique partner Lisa Desrochers. One of the benefits of being a writer is gaining so many exceptional writing friends: Cynthia Leitich Smith, Becca Fitzpatrick, and Kiersten White—I'm so grateful for your kindness and enthusiasm. To my parents, Darrel and Patricia Robertson, for possibly being even more excited about my books than I am. For my brother, Garth, for never letting me give up. And for Will, who lit a fire inside me that will never go out.

The story continues in

Is true love worth the ultimate sacrifice?